FUR AND FANGS

Other Books by Rae D. Magdon

Lucky 7

Tengoku

Death Wears Yellow Garters

Amendyr Series
The Second Sister
Wolf's Eyes
The Witch's Daughter
The Mirror's Gaze

And with Michelle Magly

All The Pretty Things

Dark Horizons Series
Dark Horizons (Revised Edition)
Starless Nights

FUR AND FANGS

BY

RAE D. MAGDON

Desert Palm Press

Fur and Fangs
(Chapters 1 – 10)

By Rae D. Magdon

©2019 Rae D. Magdon

ISBN (trade): 9781948327190
ISBN (epub): 9781948327206
ISBN (pdf): 9781948327213

Desert Palm Press
1961 Main Street, Suite 220
Watsonville, California 95076
www.desertpalmpress.com

Editor: Lee Fitzsimmons
Cover Design: Gabriela Epstein

Printed in the United States of America
First Edition Marach 2019

DEDICATION

For my darling Mona

Chapter One - Riley

THE WORST THING ABOUT living in the middle of Manhattan is the smell. It's nothing like the woods down in Georgia, where it's warm and damp and aggressively green after the first spring rain. Something's always growing or scurrying in the dirt and hovering over it all is a sweet layer of smoke from someone's bonfire.

New York City is different. The only burning smells here are diesel fumes and cigarette smoke. Dampness lives down in the subway terminals, but it's sharp and metallic. The subways themselves are filled with the smell of a hundred different body washes and lotions, and the stir of scents can be strong enough to knock a dog off a gut-wagon.

Despite all that, riding the subway is one of my favorite parts of the day, because I get to indulge in one of my guiltiest pleasures: people-watching. That's the reason I moved to New York in the first place. It's one of the only cities in the world where humans, zombies, witches, vampires, faeries, and even werewolves like me can sit in an enclosed space together without incident. Or, at least, usually without incident. Last week a mummy punched through the safety glass and delayed the train fifteen minutes when a satyr stepped on his wrappings, but that's part of the weird beauty of this place. On the subway, you never know what you're gonna get.

Today, the cast of characters is pretty disappointing. There are a few humans, a succubus with her face buried in a magazine and her earbuds in for protection against unwanted conversation, and a centaur in the extra-wide seating section. I'm at the far end of the car, pressed against the back wall for a prime viewing spot, pretending to look at my phone.

The churning sound of the tunnel-wind fades, and the rattling sway of the car slows to a stop. After one last screech-and-hiss, the announcer calls out Broadway-Lafayette. The doors open, letting in even more unfamiliar smells.

I watch the new passengers file in. Most are gussied up in suits and ties, headed for the financial district like me, but there are a few shoppers as well, in addition to a group of nervous-looking human tourists. The impractical clothes and the crumpled maps and brochures sticking out of their pockets are a dead giveaway. One smiles when she sees me, but her eyes widen in surprise when I smile back.

In Georgia, smiling with teeth is normal, at least in the more integrated neighborhoods. It's just polite behavior. In New York, you're not supposed to smile at all—especially if it's to a tourist and your teeth happen to be pointed. The woman grabs her man's arm and scurries to the opposite end of the car.

I settle in my seat. Today isn't off to a great start. That is, until one more passenger slides on just before the doors close. Suddenly, I'm so distracted I manage to blank out the announcements. The woman couldn't be more than five foot four, but she seems to tower with every step. She's curvy, with dark skin, and unlike just about everyone else, she's not wearing some shade of black. Her dress is bright yellow, knitted, and it manages to highlight everything important with a neck that scoops clear to the Promised Land. She's got black leggings on underneath, ending with high-heeled purple boots—and such a pretty collision of colors I never did see. Chunky pink sunglasses are perched on her nose even though it's early morning in September, but somehow, they go with everything else.

I choke on my next breath. This woman sucked the wind right out of me. For once, I don't even bother pretending not to stare. She's left me so dumb I don't know whether to check my ass or scratch my watch.

The strange woman sees me. She tips her sunglasses down, peering at me over the tops of the bright pink lenses, and her hazel eyes drown me. They're like a cat's, and I'm so entranced that I almost don't notice the gleaming white fangs pricking her plump bottom lip. Then they're both gone, her eyes and her fangs, and I feel like I've just been run over by the subway instead of riding it.

She's a vampire. When my lungs decide to work again, my nose confirms it. I can pick up traces of flowers and heavy suntan lotion, which is definitely odd considering her skin tone, but underneath that is the unmistakable scent of copper. It's surprisingly delicious, and strangely reminds me of home, hunting under a full moon. My tongue wants to loll.

All too soon, the subway stops again. The announcer calls out Cortland Street, and I realize I've missed several stops while lost in my haze. I still can't figure out what to do with my hands as the vampire in the yellow dress leaves her seat and sways to the doors. It takes an effort of will not to stare at her backside, but I manage—barely, and only because the riot of tight black curls around her head bounces as she turns to look over her shoulder.

Our eyes meet once more over the tops of her sunglasses, and my frantically pumping heart stops for a split second. The glance seems to last longer than a month of Sundays. Then she's gone, disappearing between the silver doors. I crane my neck, trying to catch a glimpse of her, but I only see a flash of yellow as the train takes off again.

I lean back into my seat, grinning as the train rushes off toward the financial district. I'll say this for Manhattan: it's never boring.

***

By ten thirty, I'm itching to get out of my skin. It's still over an hour to lunch, but my memories of the subway, and the beautiful vampire, have me jonesing to drop to all fours and chase my tail for a while. It would probably be more productive than what I'm doing now, staring at a computer screen and pretending to read numbers. The work at Gragnar, Mrglsptz, & Smith pays okay, but the days here pass slower than molasses running uphill in winter. Just when I'm fixing to go crazy, there's a knock on the wall of my cubicle. A familiar face peeks in, and I smile when I see Colin Duncan. He's a selkie, one of the seal-folk, and looks it. His silver hair is short around his handsome face, and his piercing blue eyes are the color of the sea.

"What's got your tail in a twist, Riley? Looks like the dog isn't having her day."

I sigh. There's no harm in confessing, and Colin is one of my best friends. Besides, anything is better than pretending to work. "I got a question for ya, Colin. When you see someone pretty on the subway, what do y'all do up here?" Selkie gentlemen, as everyone knows, have a special way with the ladies, and Colin is no exception.

He steps the rest of the way into my cubicle, leaning a hip on my desk and folding his arms across his chest. He's already got his sleeves rolled up to his elbows, against dress code of course, and he looks like a man on a mission. "Depends. Was she making long eye contact with you or reading a book?"

"Long eye contact," I say, a little offended that he's even asking. "I'd never bother someone showing signs she didn't wanna talk."

He waves me off. "Did she seem interested?"

I swallow, remembering. If that look over her shoulder hadn't

3

screamed 'interested', I'd put on Colin's sealskin and dive in the fountain outside the building, the one with the statue of an ugly bronze troll in a suit.

"Yup."

"Then you should talk to her!" Colin grabs my shoulder, giving it a light but insistent shake. "Now, what kind of hottie was this? Faerie? Succubus? Maybe a witch?"

"Vampire," I rasp. My mouth has suddenly gone dry. "She was wearing this yellow dress..."

"Ooh. Vampire? Well, that's interesting..."

Before Colin can elaborate on why, there's a loud cough from somewhere near his waist. Both of us jump, but it's too late. Standing behind us is our boss, Mr. Mrglsptz. Like most demons, he's got long, pointed ears, twisted horns, and tomato-red skin.

"Duncan, what are you doing in Evans's work area?"

"Nothing, sir," Colin says, suddenly the picture of seriousness. "I was just about to leave, sir."

"Employee fraternization during work hours is strictly forbidden."

"Of course, sir."

"And your shirtsleeves are not being worn at an acceptable length."

Colin fixes his sleeves and scurries away—the traitor—leaving me alone with our boss.

Mrglsptz doesn't seem any happier for Colin's departure. His scaly lips are firmly set in a scowl and his brow is lowered over his red eyes. "I expected better of you, Evans. When I agreed to give you this job on Colin's recommendation, both of you assured me your friendship wouldn't interfere with work."

"Yes sir. I was just asking Colin a question, sir."

"Glad to hear it. Now, please get back to work."

He stomps off, arrowhead tail swishing behind him, leaving me alone with my computer and my thoughts. *Colin's advice was useless anyway. Ain't like I'm gonna see her again.* The thought leaves a hole in my stomach. Desperately, I check the clock. Still almost an hour until lunch. This is gonna be a long day.

***

I do see her again, the very next morning, on the very same train.

4

She gets on at the same stop, Broadway-Lafayette, and my heart flies into my mouth. I try to swallow it down, but it sticks stubbornly in my throat as she passes through the doors.

Today, she's wearing a bright pink dress that swishes around her knees and silver leggings that match the shining belt around her waist. Her lipstick is blue, of all possible colors, and I've never seen a louder outfit that still seems so put together. Her sunglasses are the same pink ones from yesterday, and once again, she tips them down to peer at me. It's a look that leaves me panting like a hound dog in June.

This time, she winks, actually *winks* at me before pushing her glasses back up the bridge of her nose and settling into her seat. She sets her purse on her lap and starts rummaging through it, leaning forward just enough for me to see the valley of her cleavage.

She must notice me staring, because when she finds what she's looking for—a pack of gum—she makes eye contact again as she straightens up. Like the coward I am, I look away. My eyes end up on her hands instead, which is a mistake. Her fingers are long and graceful, and her nails are the same powder blue as her lipstick. The packet she's opening says: *BluddBubble! Extra oxygen included!*

My stomach churns as she opens her mouth. Once more, I catch a glimpse of her fangs. They're longer than I expected, even longer than mine, and I suppress a shudder. They say vampires can make their victims *want* the bite, but I've never believed that particular stereotype...until now.

I sit there, totally entranced, watching her chew until the train comes to her stop. She rises, and once more, she gives me a long, lingering look before slipping out through the subway doors and disappearing into the station.

When she leaves, it's like all the warmth in the room leaves with her. All that's left is a flush on my cheeks and a throbbing ache between my legs. It's only then that I realize I didn't even try to talk to her.

***

On the morning of the third day, I'm determined to do something other than sit there. I'm not exactly Don Juan, but I did all right with the ladies before my move to the city. Then again, none of those ladies were as pretty as the vampire on my train. The bar I've set myself this time is low: a simple "Hello". No lines, no stupid rambling. Just hello. Nothing can possibly go wrong.

At least, that's what I tell myself as I board the train and sit in my usual spot. I run the possibilities over and over in my head, completely ignoring the other passengers for a change. Maybe she'll smile at me? Maybe she'll say hello back? Maybe, if I'm lucky, she'll even ask for my name?

Those questions keep my bubbling brain occupied until the vampire finally boards the train at Broadway-Lafayette. My eyes are drawn to her like magnets as she saunters into the car, wearing a blazing white dress with big black polka dots. Her gloves and boots are white to match, and her lipstick and nails are bubblegum pink.

I'm still adjusting to the vision of loveliness while she picks her seat, and I'm overjoyed when, after considering her options, she chooses one just a few spaces away. It's the closest she's ever been to me. The scent of suntan lotion, coconut, and a hint of sweet copper drown out everything else. I almost wipe my chin on my sleeve to make sure I'm not drooling.

A faint thought blunders around in my head, like a lost moth trying to get inside a lightbulb, but eventually I remember I'm supposed to say hello. I open my mouth, but no words tumble out—not a single one. All the while, she's watching me with those bright hazel cat's eyes, as if she knows I'm about to speak and she's just waiting.

The train hisses to a stop, and the announcer calls out Cortland Street. My heart pumps into overdrive. I watch with increasing desperation as the vampire adjusts her sunglasses, hitches her purse up on her shoulder, and gets up from her seat, heading toward the doors. I have to do something. This might be my only chance.

"Hi?"

Out of the corner of my eye, I see her stop. She turns, and her pointed, pearly-white smile lights up her entire face and mine. "Well hey there, baby."

She sits back down, not in her original seat, but in the one right next to me. I can almost feel the heat of her thigh against mine as she settles in. "I'm Isabeau," she says. Her voice is sweet and slow and syrupy, like dripping honey. "What's your name?"

Isabeau. A wide grin spreads across my face as my misfiring brain realizes she's told me her name. Eventually, when she continues looking at me, I remember she's asked me a question. "Riley?"

"You sure about that?" she teases, but it's lighthearted and not at all condescending.

I cough and try again. I should know how to hold a simple

6

conversation, even in front of someone this good looking. "Riley. Uh... I didn't hold y'all up, did I? I mean, you missed your stop."

Isabeau doesn't seem concerned about it. "Y'all?" she repeats. "You aren't from New York, are you?"

"Georgia. Just moved here a couple months ago."

"Well now... a transplant. I was born here, but I've got folks in New Awlins." Her accent is normal for these parts, not heavy Bronx, but standard mid-Atlantic—but when she says New Orleans, it dips into something vaguely southern.

"Hope I'm not stepping on any tails," she continues, "but I'm curious... what's a wolf all the way from Georgia doing in New York City? I imagine running in Central Park gets boring after a while."

"It ain't—it's not so bad," I lie. Full moon runs in the cordoned-off areas of the park *do* get tedious after a while, but there aren't many other choices unless you want to go all the way out of the boroughs. "You meet plenty of interesting folks."

"I'll bet," she laughs, and the sounds got my head ringing with silver bells.

It's an opening for conversation, and I take it. "One time, a sphinx forgot to leave her pedestal. She ended up treed with a whole pack baying after her."

Now that I'm saying it out loud, it sounds like the stupidest story in all creation, but Isabeau doesn't seem to mind. She's still looking right at me, smiling, and my stomach loops into slippery knots.

"And? What happened?"

"Scared 'em off," I mumble, modestly. "City wolves can't hunt proper anyway."

Isabeau laughs. "So, is this your usual method for impressing girls? By telling them about the time you rescued a cat from a tree?"

"Well..." I rub at the back of my neck, which is already starting to sweat, and has probably stained the back of my shirt. "Probably explains why I'm single, huh?" *Smooth, Riley. Real smooth.*

"Single in New York is nothing to be ashamed of," Isabeau purrs. Her tongue peeks out to touch the tips of her fangs. "In fact, it opens you up to all kinds of adventures."

My throat goes dry. She's leaning in, and my entire world is those plump pink lips, her sweet smell, and those big hazel eyes. Then the announcer calls out Fulton Street, and a sad weight settles on my shoulders.

Isabeau must notice the look of disappointment on my face, because her fingertips, with those bright pink nails, just brush the edge of my knee, so light it might have been an accident.

"See you tomorrow, Riley," she says, and then she stands and disappears through the doors before I do.

I'm all the way at Wall Street before I realize I've missed my own stop too.

***

"You know what you have to do now, right?" Colin asks me later that day. We're waiting in line at the deli next to our office, him nudging my arm excitedly, me with my hands in my pockets. "You have to ask her out! She gave you the biggest opening of all time."

"But ask her out where?" It's the same question I've been mulling over all morning. That 'see you tomorrow' has me certain I'm sniffing up the right tree but figuring out how I'm gonna do it is harder. In small towns, everybody knows everybody else's business, but Isabeau's a total stranger.

Colin gives me an exasperated look. "Does it matter? Ask her to your place for a nightcap."

As good as he is with women, I'm not so sure about that suggestion. "In the morning? Before work?"

"She's a vampire," he insists. "Her morning is your evening anyway."

My shoulders slump. Sealfolk might be able to get away with asking strangers up to their apartments without seeming sketchy, but werewolves? Not so much. We're not considered prime dating material by most other species, unless they like it rough and don't mind extra hair in unusual places. We've even got a name for those folks: tail-chasers. I've been a few human girls' sexual experiment before, and it's not an experience I want to repeat.

I've pondered whether Isabeau might be one of them, but I doubt it. First of all, she's a vampire, so I'm sure she's got her own dating problems to deal with. More importantly, with the way she talks, the way she looks, the way she smiles like I'm the only person in her universe in that moment, I just can't feel bad about myself.

Colin is still staring at me, like he's waiting for me to promise something, but we reach the front of the line and he has to stop pestering me. The faerie behind the counter giggles when she sees him, and Colin forgets about my problem for a moment as he leans closer to smile at her and tell her his order.

I don't mind. My thoughts are still on the train, with Isabeau in that polka dot dress. Just remembering sets the fine hairs on my skin to prickling, and my fingertips start to itch. That's the *other* reason people sometimes exclude us from their dating pool. We only turn into wolves under a full moon, but we do have a tendency to sprout claws and get a little fuzzier when we're emotional or turned on. It was the glowing eyes that did my first human girlfriend in, back when I was sixteen. She tried to play it off, but I knew what was going on. I'd always held onto the hope my prospects might be better in a big city like New York, but it hadn't worked out that way so far. Not until Isabeau had strutted onto my train.

"Excuse me?"

I blink. The faerie behind the counter and Colin are both waiting expectantly. "Huh?"

"Excuse me, may I take your order?" the faerie asks. Her pretty face looks annoyed now instead of flirtatious.

"Meat. Raw. Anything you got."

She gives me an odd look, but she starts shoveling something into a bag.

"You need to work on your game, Riley," Colin tells me, sighing and shaking his head.

I sigh too. "Don't I know it."

* * *

The next time I see Isabeau, she's wearing a lime green dress that sets off her skin, and her lips are a deeper, juicier pink than the day before. She sits right down beside me again, and my nose is in heaven. The smell of suntan lotion is starting to become an aphrodisiac.

"Hey, Riley," she says, and her voice has me floating on clouds. "Don't you look all dressed up?"

"Thanks." I had taken a bit more care with my appearance, and I was flattered she'd noticed. Gel never tames my hair for long, but I figured it only had to hold 'til Fulton Street—and 'til I figured out how to ask Isabeau on a date without seeming creepy. "So, um, where you headed?"

Isabeau tips her sunglasses down, and I'm drowning in hazel again.

"I haven't decided yet. What about you? Where do you go every morning?"

"Uh..." Working for a financial company isn't the most glamorous job, and I'm not sure how to dress it up without sounding like a jerk or giving the wrong impression.

"Let me guess," Isabeau says, leaning in closer until our knees brush. For once, she isn't wearing leggings, and I gulp, trying not to stare at her thighs. "You work in an office. A boring nine to five that makes you wear collared shirts."

"You got me pegged. Can't claim anything more interesting than that, I'm afraid."

"Me neither," Isabeau says. "At least, most people wouldn't find it interesting... but I love what I do."

"And what's that?" I'm eager to know more about her, hungry for any scrap of information.

"I'm a tutor," she says. "I only Turned recently, about twenty years ago, so I'm still connected to this day and age. But lots of other vampires, wizards, and other long-lived creatures were born centuries ago. They have no idea how to adjust to living in a world that moves so fast, or how to make a steady paycheck in a city like New York. I teach them basic things, like how to use a computer."

"Teaching centenarians all about the wonders of the internet. Now *that's* gotta be fun."

"One of the witches in my class figured out how to shop online the other day," Isabeau confides in me. "We ended up with seventeen boxes of newt eyes and frog toes delivered to my classroom. And yes, before you ask, we've had 'incidents' with porn."

I laugh along with her, but then the two of us drift off into silence, simply staring at each other. It isn't awkward—it's electric, and I inhale softly. I can't look away. Those hazel eyes have a hypnotic pull.

"Can I ask you a question, Riley?"

I decide to try teasing her a little. "You can ask me another one, sure."

She has the decency to laugh at my bad joke before saying, "So, why did you decide to say hello to me the other day?"

I decide to go with the truth. "Because I noticed you the day before. You have a beautiful smile. I wanted to see it again."

Isabeau seems surprised by that answer but pleased too. She smiles, and my stomach does a somersault. "Hmm. People don't usually compliment a vampire's smile."

I suddenly realize I might have done the exact same thing to Isabeau that I hate human girls doing to me. "Not because of the fangs," I tell her, trying desperately to recover. "You just looked so happy. People on the subway usually ai...aren't. You walked in with that yellow dress and that smile, and you were like this beam of sunlight. I couldn't help wanting to talk to you."

"A beam of sunlight?" she repeats, shaking her head in disbelief. "You really are something else, Riley."

"Shit." I pinch my forehead in embarrassment. "I didn't think about that one either."

"No, it's sweet. I love the sun, even if too much of it can kill me." She touches my arm with her fingertips, pulling my hand away. I can barely feel it through my sleeve, but it sends a jolt through me. "You get off work at five, right?"

I answer automatically. "Yup."

"So, I'll meet you then, if that's okay?"

In my haze, it takes me several seconds to realize what she means. The beautiful creature before me has just asked me out on a date. *Me. On a date.* At least, I think it's a date? It's definitely a something. Maybe I'm not so rusty after all.

"Absolutely," I say, still half convinced she's joking and going to take it back.

But she doesn't take it back. She just smirks as the train hisses to a halt and the doors open. "You'd better get off," she says.

True to form, my filthy mind jumps to the dirtiest interpretation of those words. My face is on fire as I scramble to reply. "So, I'll see you later?"

Isabeau winks. "For sure. Now you'd better run along, or you'll be late."

I stagger off the train more befuddled than the group of zombies next to me, my head swirling and my nose still full of suntan lotion and coconut.

***

My concentration is shot for the rest of the day. If it weren't for Colin keeping an eye out for Mr. Mrglsptz, I probably would have ended up with a spit-polished oxford shoe up my butt before he could even say the words 'You're fired'. All my projects remain unfinished as the minutes tick by, and the little work I do get done is full of mistakes.

By two in the afternoon, Colin's fed up with me too. He corners me in the unisex restroom next to the supply closet, and I almost burn my hands under the faucet.

"Calm down," he says, noting my look of surprise. "Mrglsptz is busy chewing out Aelwen, that banshee in accounting. But what the hell is going on with you?"

I bite my lip, and my eyes dart nervously toward the door—which he happens to be standing in front of, blocking my escape. There's nothing else for it. I'm awful at keeping secrets.

"Well, Isabeau said she'd meet me after work."

"Isabeau?" Colin's silvery eyebrows lift all the way to his hairline. "So that's the vampire hottie's name? Is she French or something?"

"Or something," I mumble.

Colin's grin only grows. "And she's meeting you after work? You dog, you."

I nod, weakly.

"This is awesome! You're finally getting laid. I thought I'd have to resort to desperate measures."

"Hey, I got plenty back home," I protest, but it's weak. Instead of excitement, my stomach churns with something much more unpleasant. It's not that I'm not attracted to Isabeau. My daydreams lately have featured peeling her out of every one of those colorful dresses. But when it comes to sex, my experiences haven't always been great in the past.

"You really think so?"

"No doubt about it," Colin says, but then he notices my shoulders sink. He folds an arm around them, giving me a gentle shake. "Hey, what's wrong? I thought you liked this girl?"

"I do. A *lot*. That's the problem."

Suddenly, Colin understands. "You worried about going feral?"

Coming from someone else's mouth, the term 'going feral' might have been offensive, but there's no malice in Colin's tone when he says it.

I sigh. "Yup. Kind of."

"So? She's a vampire. She knows what she's getting into, mixing it up with a werewolf, right? Besides, she's got super strength. I'm sure she can handle anything you dish out. Between the two of you, I bet you could destroy an apartment."

I hadn't thought of it that way. My previous relationships had been with human girls, ones who always seemed to realize they didn't want to bother being with someone so different after a few dates and a roll between the sheets they could whisper to their friends about later. Isabeau's different. At the very least, she isn't stepping into it blind. Besides, she's a bonafide city girl. She's probably seen weirder things than claws and glowing eyes.

"I guess she can't think I'm weird when she's got a fridge stocked with blood smoothies."

"Exactly." Colin lets me go, clapping me between the shoulders. "Now go get your girl, Tiger."

I look at him strangely.

"Uh, wolf?"

I give him a cheerful howl before stepping out the door... and right into the path of Mr. Mrglsptz.

"Evans, where have you been? Why are you howling in the bathroom?"

"Uh..." I glance back over my shoulder, but Colin has ducked into one of the stalls. I'm on my own.

"Never mind. Just get those reports done before five. I need them by the end of the day."

"Yes sir. I'm on it." I scurry past him and head back to my cubicle. Five o'clock can't come soon enough.

***

By the time five does roll around, my pulse is through the roof. I can barely keep my breathing steady, and my legs definitely aren't as I dart into the bathroom for one last peek in the mirror. Not too bad. My hair's getting shaggy at the fringes, but the extra gel has kept it somewhat presentable. I straighten my tie, smoothing it down beneath my sweater vest. Isabeau's hinted that she likes sharp-dressed gals, and while I can't quite claim that, I think I look decent.

As I stare at my reflection, my mind keeps galloping on ahead. What if Colin's right? What if Isabeau *does* have something sexual in mind? I could be walking into anything from a coffee date to a grand slam.

I close my eyes. *Either way, you'll be fine,* I tell myself. *This ain't your first rodeo.* But I'm not very convincing. It has been over a year since last time, and I care way more. I check my watch. I've only got a few minutes to hit the train station—and today of all days, I can't be late.

On my dash for the front door, I nearly bowl Colin over. He calls something after me, 'Good luck' or 'Go get her!', but I can't really tell which because my heart is pounding in my ears. Everything's white noise. I don't even wrinkle my nose at the smell of gasoline and rubber as I hurry down the sidewalk and into the subway station.

I catch sight of Isabeau immediately. She's waiting past the turnstiles, but instead of the lime green dress she'd worn that morning, she's wrapped in blood red with lipstick and nails to match. She's absolutely eye popping against the sea of black, white, and grey, and I can't tear my eyes away. Lucky for me, my feet carry me in her direction all on their own. I'm so focused that I run gut-first into the turnstile, and I end up fumbling for my card.

Isabeau swipes her own through, saving me further embarrassment. "Why the rush?"

I tug at my collar, desperate for a bit of cool breeze, but the entire world around me feels like it's burning. I do manage to make a decent recovery, though. "To make sure I didn't miss you, of course."

"You're right, that would have been a tragedy," Isabeau says. She takes my hand, and oh sweet Jesus why didn't I wipe it on my pants first to get off at least some of the sweat? If she notices that my fingers are dripping, she doesn't let on that she minds. I'm not even sure how much she can feel, because her hand is strangely cold, almost like touching a statue. It makes me wonder what the rest of her skin is like, if she has any trace of warmth. I want to find out.

"Where we headed to?" I ask.

In that same practiced, seductive motion, Isabeau slides the tops of her glasses down to look at me. "Nowhere special yet. I was thinking we'd keep it casual and grab some food from one of the carts by my place."

Her place? I grin. "I like the sound of that."

***

Our quick train ride is silent, but it doesn't feel that way, because our bodies sure do a lot of talking. Isabeau's cold hand stays in mine, and she brings them to rest on her thigh. I think I feel a hint of warmness there, but through her dress, I can't be sure.

We only make it to Fulton Street before Isabeau leaves her seat, pulling me along with her. The crowd of people parts for her, and she strides up the steps and out into the dying sunlight like a queen. The glare reflected from the skyscrapers doesn't seem to bother her, although I notice her sunglasses are firmly in place.

"So, what you said earlier, about the sun killing you..."

She seems to sense my question. "Special lotion. Lots of it. If you're lucky, I'll let you lotion me up tomorrow morning."

Tomorrow morning? Does that mean she's already decided I'm staying the night?

We end up stopping by a cart, one that has specialty hotdogs with all the fixings. I prefer my meat raw, but I'll eat it any way I can get it. Isabeau passes on the hotdogs, but a block down we find a gelato stand, and blood is one of the flavors.

"Is it hard to find food you can eat in the city?" I ask as we walk and munch.

"Not really," Isabeau says, licking her spoon clean. My heart lurches. I hadn't known it was possible to be jealous of a piece of plastic. "This is just artificial flavoring. To get the right nutrients, I have to go to the blood bank and pick up the real stuff. Human's expensive, so I only get it when I want to splurge."

"What else is there?"

"Animals—cow, mostly—and your various humanoids except for demons. Werewolf's on the menu too, actually," she drawls, giving me a sidelong look. "But that's even pricier, because of the extra iron."

I blush. It's hard not to think about what she's implying.

"Oh, don't worry," Isabeau says, noticing my wide eyes. "I don't bite unless I'm asked *really* nicely. And I've got a stocked fridge. I even keep regular food for guests."

I finish my hotdog and throw the container in a nearby trash can. Unsure what to do with my hands, I shove them in my pockets and I'm relieved to find an open pack of gum there. Thanking future Riley, I pop a piece in my mouth so I won't taste like onions if...when...something happens.

I almost drop the rest of the pack when Isabeau reaches out and brushes my arm with her fingertips. I gasp. It's like tiny electric shocks.

"Are you okay, Riley? You still seem a little nervous."

"Don't pay me no mind. I get this way around beautiful girls."

It must be a good recovery, because Isabeau smirks. "Do I still count as a girl even if I'm fifty-two?"

"Sure do."

Isabeau finishes her gelato and tosses it, sliding her hand into the crook of my elbow. "I'm still getting the hang of this whole vampire thing. You'd think twenty years would be enough time to adjust, but sometimes, it feels like it happened yesterday."

"How'd it happen? I mean, what made you decide?"

Isabeau sighs. "Love. You know the story. Young, beautiful ingénue dates a mysterious stranger...only we broke up two years later. It doesn't always work out like in the movies."

"Whoever dumped you was an idiot," I tell her, more vehemently than I'd intended.

"Don't I know it," Isabeau chuckles. "I don't regret it, though. I found a useful purpose, and my apartment's rent controlled. What about you?" She peers at me curiously. "Why hasn't someone snatched up a tasty morsel like you?"

"Well, there's the werewolf thing..."

"So? Plenty of werewolves get dates. You're on one right now."

My heart flutters at the confirmation that we are, indeed, on a date, although there's really no question. "Maybe I just don't put myself out there enough? I wasn't the most popular gal on the market back in Georgia. Went out with a few girls, but none of 'em stuck."

"You put yourself out there to me just fine on the train," Isabeau says. "And I think most of Georgia needs to get their eyes checked. Oh, here we are."

Isabeau stops in front of a brownstone. It's charming, crumbled only in the right way, with some well-placed strands of ivy. The vertical brass numbers at the foot of the stone steps read '1260'.

"You have your phone, baby?"

I dig it out of my pocket, and Isabeau poses against the post. I swear, the woman would look right at home in the centerfold of a fashion magazine.

"Take a picture and send it to somebody you trust. That way they'll know where you are and who you're with."

I'm touched. No one's ever tried to make *me*—the big, bad werewolf—feel safe and comfortable before. Usually, I'm the one struggling to make the girl I'm seeing feel safe from me. I zoom in just enough to get a full body shot. I'm sure Colin will appreciate it, anyway. "Say gelato."

"Gelato." Isabeau flashes her fangs, and I'm so dazzled I barely remember to snap the picture. My thumb fumbles as I open my most recent text message with Colin and send it along. He responds almost immediately: a string of emojis with lots of teardrops and 'ok' signs.

"I take it your friend approves." Isabeau sneaks up beside me again, close enough for our arms to touch. "You have no idea how much I love smartphones. Before them, doing my makeup was a real chore with the whole mirror thing. Now I can just prop an iPad up on a stand in the bathroom."

"I bet that helps." I tuck my phone away. "So, uh, should we...?"

Isabeau hooks her arm through mine and leads me up the steps. I've never felt her curves so close, and I almost choke on my tongue as the swell of her breast presses into my upper arm. Her apartment's on the first floor. She unlocks the door, and I'm hit with a wash of bright colors. There are royal blue drapes, green throw rugs, and decorations of all different shades. The wide shelf of books that takes up one wall is practically a rainbow. To top it all off, the main item of furniture is a huge yellow couch with fluffy pink throw pillows. Somehow, it all goes together, although I sure as hell can't figure out how.

Isabeau notices my shock. "I keep my black drapes and coffin in the bedroom," she teases, and I blush.

"No, I love it," I assure her. "It's just..."

"Surprising?" Isabeau removes her sunglasses, setting them on a small table beside the front door. Also, sitting on the edge is a giant bottle of lotion marked: 'Nightshade SPF 100, Extra UVB Protection Added, blocks 99.9% of harmful rays!' I'm guessing that's the source of the scent that always swims around her.

I look up from the bottle to see Isabeau staring at me. Without her sunglasses, her cheekbones and nose are even more beautiful. "It's you," I say. "Definitely you. You can't hope to turn a home into more than that."

"Riley..." Isabeau cups my cheek, gazing straight into my eyes and probably beyond them too. "I really want to kiss you. Would that be okay?"

Would that be okay? The real question is, how have I survived *without* kissing her for this long already? I nod and lean in.

Our lips touch. As it turns out, Isabeau's mouth is the only part of her body that's warm so far. Her hand might have been a block of ice, but her lips radiate heat. It's like she was storing up all the warmth she had just to kiss me with, and my mouth burns with it—or maybe that's just because my face is on fire.

Then there's the taste. The hint of copper I'm expecting is subtle, and the rest is lip gloss mixed with something uniquely her. It's a sweet, sticky flavor I can't get enough of. I want to drown in her, and my knees buckle beneath me. It's not my fault that was one hell of a first kiss.

Isabeau holds my elbow, and I stumble, embarrassed. Before I can stammer an excuse, her eyes slide suggestively toward the yellow couch. "Let's get somewhere comfortable. That is, if you want to."

She doesn't have to tell me twice. When she takes my fingers in her cool ones and leads me over to the couch, I trail obediently behind. Once she gets there, she turns and fists my sweater vest, pulling gently.

We collapse onto the couch, lips locked, hands roaming everywhere. Isabeau's body shifts constantly against mine, all soft curves and winding limbs and rolling hips. Even through our clothes, I can feel every inch of it. She's underneath me, but she still has total control of the kiss, and as her tongue sweeps across my teeth, I feel her fangs—not biting down, but scraping the edge of my bottom lip. It sends a thrill through me, part danger and part curiosity.

Isabeau pulls back a centimeter, gazing up into my eyes, and I can tell she's trying to gauge my reaction. I have no idea what to say, but I smile to let her know everything's okay. Kissing is easier than talking for me, and I'm getting more confident.

Our mouths meet again, longer and deeper. Isabeau runs her fingers through my tousled hair, curling her legs around mine to cradle my pelvis. Part of me still can't believe I'm doing this—making out with a vampire, a practical stranger, in an apartment that looks like Lisa Frank got drunk and threw paint all over it—but it feels unbelievably right, way better than making out with girls I've known for longer. I want more. So much more.

Isabeau moans when I slide my fingertips up along her thighs, and I take that as a sign of encouragement. I don't want to wander too high and ruin the moment, but her legs are so smooth. Even the subtle coolness doesn't bother me. It's a nice contrast to the furnace my body has become, and I'm entranced by the imprints my fingertips leave as they press into her soft skin.

"You're beautiful," I mutter without even realizing it.

Our string of kisses tapers off as Isabeau caresses my cheek. She seems to approve of the compliment, if the way she runs her tongue over her plump lips is any indication. "And you, Riley, are just *delicious*."

Those words unlock a fierce hunger within me, one that *hurts*. Suddenly, I'm kissing Isabeau again, without conscious thought. Our mouths clash, all tongues and teeth, and my nails dig deeper into her thigh. It's only when I feel a soft, breathy gasp against my lips that I realize how hard I'm squeezing.

"Sorry," I mumble, loosening my hold.

"What for?" Isabeau's skin might be cool, but her eyes are warm and soft. "I like it a little rough occasionally."

"You do?" My head is spinning.

"Of course. I like it all kinds of ways..." She begins toying with my shaggy hair, twisting it around her fingers. "I like it rough and fast. I like it slow and passionate. As long as it's with the woman I want, I'm happy. So just be you, Riley. Show me what you've got. That is, if you want to."

My heart swells. No one's ever said that to me before with such honesty and conviction. No one's ever checked in with me this often, either. I kiss Isabeau again and keep my hands right where they are on her soft, smooth thighs.

We spend a long time just kissing, but somehow, it doesn't feel like long enough. Isabeau's lips have me drunk, and even when we break apart to breathe, her eyes keep me dizzy. I feel like I'm being sucked down into a whirlpool, but I don't want to escape. I just want more of her lips, more of her tongue, even more of her fangs nibbling the corner of my mouth.

It isn't until Isabeau links the fingers of her left hand through my right and brings it up along her stomach that I remember there's still a lot of landscape left to explore. She guides me until I'm cupping her breast, and I feel a little more heat, as well as a faint heartbeat. It beats slow, maybe once every five seconds, but it's unmistakable.

Isabeau chuckles at my surprise. "Where do you think the blood I drink goes? I'm using it."

"Well, I didn't get vampire biology lessons in school."

"Nothing like hands-on learning," Isabeau purrs. She gives my hand another squeeze, and I suddenly remember where it is and what it's holding. Her breasts are large enough to fill my hands and then some, but they've still got some firmness. I give a tentative squeeze, and when Isabeau hums in approval, I take it as a sign to keep going.

Soon, I've got the straps of her dress pulled down, both of her breasts in my hands, and one thigh riding between her legs. Her nipples are long and thick, and she whimpers every time I tug them. She starts rubbing against my knee as I kiss down her neck, and she pushes lightly on the top of my head, asking without words.

The sounds she makes when I take one of the stiff peaks between my lips are an angel's chorus. Her skin tastes sweet, but I think it's got nothing to do with the lotion and everything to do with her. My nose twitches, and I realize her scent is changing. It's becoming thicker, muskier, and wetter—and as she rocks against my thigh, I realize why.

19

She's turned on. There's a damp spot in the middle of her panties that I can feel with her dress rucked up. I kiss and nip my way over to her other breast, and the smell gets even stronger. New York can be exhausting to a werewolf's nose, but this particular scent, Isabeau's scent, makes the extra sensitivity worth it.

But I don't just want to smell. I want to taste. I want to kiss my way down that cute, curvy stomach of hers in search of the faint but growing heat I can feel between her legs. I want to know for sure if the flavor in my nose will sit even better on my tongue. I start peeling her dress the rest of the way down, and she lifts her hips to help.

The sight of Isabeau's body, naked except for her underwear, is riveting. Her breasts sway a little with each ragged breath she takes, and even though she looks so soft and vulnerable all spread out beneath me, I can tell she's anything but.

"Take off your shirt," she asks, striking a note somewhere in between a plea and a demand.

I'm more interested in getting rid of her panties, but it's only fair. I sit back on my heels and strip off my sweater vest, then the shirt underneath. My binder comes next—a tip from Colin—and Isabeau's eyes widen as I strip it off. She licks her lips, and I sigh with relief. Judging from the look on her face, she likes what she sees. Hopefully that won't change when she sees the rest of me.

"Come back here," Isabeau says, opening her arms.

I'm powerless to resist. This time, her mouth finds my collarbone. She inhales deeply, burying her nose in the crook of my neck, and I shiver, wondering exactly what she smells.

She must feel me go stiff, because she plants a soft, wet kiss on my pulse point. "I don't bite unless invited, remember?" But when she kisses me again, she lets her fangs skate over the same sensitive spot. I'm not ready for her to bite me, not yet, but the idea has butterflies erupting in my belly.

"I want you to fuck me, Riley," she whispers into my throat. "Can you do that for me?"

A growl rumbles in my throat—pure mating instinct. Even if it's been a while, that's definitely something I remember how to do.

I run my hands up along Isabeau's legs and hook my thumbs in both sides of her underwear, finally tugging them down. The sight I'm graced with as she spreads her legs is more than worth the wait. She's shaved, except for a small strip of black hair pointing down to the prize. Her outer lips are dark, puffy, with the faintest ring of pink just inside

20

her entrance. Then there's her clit, swollen past its hood, just the right size to fit in my mouth. It's all shining and slippery and smooth, and I whine as the smell around me grows stronger.

I touch with my fingers first. She's not scalding-hot, but she's warm enough for me to feel it on my fingertips. When I graze along her entrance, she groans. When I touch her clit, her whole body twitches. Isabeau remains patient at first, letting me play for a while. Her eyes stay right on me, while mine flick between her face and what my hand is doing. When I first slip a finger inside her, it's almost by accident. She's so wet that I can't really help it, and her muscles pull me in effortlessly. But when she hums and shudders, clenching down around me, sealing me in, I push deeper—this time on purpose.

It doesn't take me long to find her spots. Isabeau is incredibly responsive. She tilts her hips to show me where to press and rocks them to show me how fast she wants me to move. Soon, I'm curling into her front wall with two fingers, and my lips are latched onto her nipple again.

"Riley," she gasps, tangling her fingers back in my hair. "Harder."

Hearing Isabeau say my name is heady praise and hearing her say 'harder' lights a flame in my stomach. I hook harder, and when she yelps, I know I've found the perfect angle.

"Yes, just like that...but harder..."

My brow furrows, and my eyes flit back up to her face. "You sure?" I rasp, releasing her breast with a soft pop. "I'm already going pretty hard. I don't wanna hurt you."

"You won't," she promises, and looking into her eyes, I believe her.

I remember what Colin said, about a vampire being able to take everything I can dish out. Every hair on my body tingles. The tips of my fingers and ears begin to itch. I run my tongue over my dry lips and notice my teeth are even sharper than usual. I'm teetering on the edge of going feral, and it takes an effort of will to push it back.

"Come on, Riley," Isabeau says, and the way her lips wrap around my name feels like a caress. "Give me all you've got." I close my eyes, praying she really means it.

When I open them again, I know they're glowing. I know because Isabeau's breath hitches, but instead of recoiling, she beams. "They're like lanterns," she murmurs, almost in awe. "You're gorgeous."

At first, I'm stunned Isabeau thinks they're pretty. "You...like it?" I ask, a little uncertain. No other girl has ever thought to pause and sincerely compliment me before when I'm in this state. It freaks them out and they ask to stop, or they keep going because they want to check 'fuck a werewolf' off their bucket list. I hadn't realized how much a simple positive statement could mean.

Isabeau kisses me again, soft, but a gesture of absolute certainty. "'Like' is an understatement," she pants when it's over. "I liked you before, and I really like you now."

We gaze into each other's eyes a while, then suddenly, I remember I'm still knuckles deep inside her. I start thrusting again, my forearm muscles flexing. Far be it from me to leave a lady disappointed. Isabeau rolls and arches beneath me, encouraging me to go faster and deeper. I plunge in and out of her, hooking against the special spot I've found on each thrust, but she can't seem to get enough. Her moans get higher and prettier and her lashes brush her cheeks as her eyelids flutter, half way between open and closed.

She reaches up to caress my cheek, and at first, I think she's about to draw me in for another kiss. She does, eventually, but not before playing with the new points of my ears. It tickles, and I end up laughing into her lips even as I pump my hand harder, going as rough as I can without digging my claws in.

Isabeau pulls my bottom lip between both of hers and sucks. Her fangs dig in, not deep enough to break the skin, but that isn't what sends a shockwave through me. It's the way her inner walls start rippling around me, pulsing quick and light. I can tell she's about to come, I can smell that she's about to come, and the knowledge that I'm the one helping her hit that high sends me over the moon.

I rub my thumb in circles, searching for the bud of her clit, and once I start massaging the shaft through its hood, Isabeau's muscles go wild. She clenches tight around me, then releases with a wail, covering my hand with more sticky heat as her hips jerk in time with her contractions.

It's magical, feeling her like this. My only regret is that I can't watch the pleasure passing over her face, because our mouths are still locked together. But I can smell her, and I can feel her pulsing around my fingers and into the pad of my thumb, and that's enough.

Or, it would have been, if my mouth hadn't started watering. I don't just want her coming around my fingers. I want her in my mouth, spilling all over my tongue. I break away from her lips and start kissing and nipping my way down her body as fast as I can. She hooks her knees over my shoulders and spreads her legs wide, and we smile at each other before I lower my head.

I'm right. Isabeau tastes even better than she smells. She's sweeter than strawberry pie and twice as sticky, but I don't mind the way she clings to my chin. At first, I'm all tongue and no technique, lapping up every drop I can get. Lucky for me, Isabeau doesn't mind. She squeals, and to my surprise, she comes again, tugging sharply at my hair. I growl as more wetness washes over my lips, desperate to catch it all.

It's only after I've licked her clean that I move back up to Isabeau's clit. She twitches as I suck it into my mouth, but with a few feather-light flicks, she's shaking and muttering. "Yes, Riley...Fuck, yes, just like that. Oh, your mouth..."

I'm determined to show her just what my mouth can do. I alternate between sucking and licking, flattening my tongue against her twitching opening before sliding back up to tease her clit. Isabeau's all sighs then, her calves tightening against my back, heels digging in. If I can make her come a third time, forget the moon. I'll fly clear out of the solar system and take her right along with me.

I feel the second it hits—the tension, the stillness. She goes rigid, and then melts, screaming my name to the ceiling. A salty-sweet river flows into my mouth, and the only thing I can compare it to is the fresh burst of blood that comes right after I bring down a deer. It's a comparison most humans would probably find terrifying, but I bet Isabeau would understand—not just because she's a vampire, but because she's been so damn nice to me, right from the beginning.

By the time Isabeau's quivering stops and she pulls me away, both of us are panting. She's not sweating even a little, but my skin's practically soaked, and the short, fuzzy patches of fur I've grown in a few places feel a bit matted.

"Your turn," Isabeau says, and in a flash, she reverses our positions, tossing me onto my back. She's has some superhuman strength and speed going on, because with the way she's holding my wrists in one hand and fishing into my pants with the other, I'm not sure I'd win in a wrestling competition. Those curves must be hiding some serious muscle underneath.

She doesn't waste time. Her fingers delve into the wiry hair between my legs until she finds my clit. Not that it's hard. It's already slick and swollen, and I howl when she hits it. I'm not quite sure how she tears my pants the rest of the way off without breaking contact, but I reckon they're in shreds somewhere on the floor. I don't care. After making her come, I need to also, and I'm way too turned on to be self-conscious anymore.

Isabeau's fingers roll and pinch and flick, experimenting, but I can't even tell what I like best. It all feels so good. I open my legs and lift my hips, offering myself up for whatever she wants to do to me. Her lips glide along my skin, starting near my shoulders and moving down to my breasts. She spends some time there, sucking my nipples to hard points, and leaves a cool trail of saliva behind when she finally starts kissing along my abdomen.

Her teeth skid along a sensitive patch of skin near my navel, and the tease sends more heavy pulses straight between my legs. I'm wet and hot and aching, and her fingers are the only thing bringing me any relief. That is, until she looks down into my eyes and whispers, "Inside?"

I nod, and she slides two of them inside me. There's no resistance. I'm more than ready for her. I'm a whimpering mess as she switches her position and begins kissing up along one of my thighs. I tremble as her breath washes over me, and I give her what I hope is a pleading look.

Her hazel eyes flash as she draws me into her mouth. It's wet, and her lips are sealed tight, and the sucking drives me absolutely insane. I can feel her fangs on either side of my clit, still not sinking, but *there*, and once more, the thought of her biting me crawls beneath my flushed skin until I'm breaking out in a fresh round of shudders.

I come like a freight train, roaring just as loud. With Isabeau's fingers thrusting inside me and her teeth teasing the shaft of my clit and her tongue swirling in circles around the tip, I'm a wreck. A few tears leak from my eyes, simply because all the different feelings are so much to handle, but my face hurts from smiling.

I give and give and give until I've got nothing left and Isabeau's face is dripping with me. She smiles too, fangs and all, and gives her fingers another nudge. I'd thought I was finished, but I start twitching again as she hits a place that sends stars shooting in front of my eyes.

"God," I groan, hoarsely, as I tumble over again, and Isabeau just laughs.

"Isabeau is fine. Or Izzy, if you want."

"Izzy..." It suits her, I think as I finally return to the couch, but Isabeau does too. Izzy is the cheerful yellow, and Isabeau is the sophisticated red. She's both of those things, and they go perfectly together.

We stare at each other, and I see the tenderness in her face, and even though it's too soon for me to call this floaty feeling love, I've definitely come down with a dangerous case of like. The moment's interrupted by a shrill buzzing noise. I wince, and Isabeau casts a glance toward my missing pants. As I suspected, they're ruined. Grunting, I sit up as best I can without dislodging her and reach for my phone, only just remembering to wipe my hand.

I see a text from Colin—several, actually—and most of them are thumbs up and heart emojis. This one, however, asks: "How'd it go? Are you ok?"

Isabeau smirks. "Tell your friend you're fine...and that you won't be coming home tonight."

I grin back. "Good thing we're both nocturnal, because if I'm invited to stay, I ain't planning on letting you get much sleep."

Rae D. Magdon

Chapter Two - Isabeau

I LOVE NEW YORK City. I was born here, and on the day my eternity ends, I'll probably die (again) here. The sights, the sounds, the smells— New York is alive and energetic, and I've always been the type of person who thrives on energy.

I love the glow of the lights at night, because I can look at them and see the beautiful colors without my sunglasses. I love the kiss of the wind on my face as it whips through the skyscraper tunnels, because it reminds me of flying even when I'm not. I love spotting another person dressed up in bright, bold patterns like the ones I wear and making eye contact, forming a brief connection. It feels like joy, like discovery, like inspiration. I'm convinced that places have auras just like people, and New York City's aura is a beautiful, bustling, constantly buzzing mess. At least, it's usually beautiful.

"Hey, baby," a voice calls from behind me. "Why don't you turn that fat ass around and walk by again?" Several chuckles follow and my shoulders tense.

I have three options. One, keep walking and pretend I didn't hear. Two, turn around and start shouting about how this creep's father should have raised him better. However, I decide to take option three. I glance over my shoulder.

A beefy white man in a stained wifebeater is standing on the bottom step of a stoop just off the sidewalk, lingering in the doorway with a small group of similarly disheveled 'friends'. His thinning hair is greasy, and his gut sticks out from beneath his shirt.

"What's with the frown, mama? Why don't you give me a smile?"

I shoot the catcaller my biggest, most brilliant grin.

His pale face goes ashen when he notices my fangs. He backs up, wide-eyed, almost bumping into his companions. They look as shocked as he does, and I can't keep from laughing. As soon as I run my tongue over my teeth, they scramble away like scared rabbits, crashing into other groups on the sidewalk.

I almost never take pride in frightening people, but catcallers are my weakness. I can't resist turning something disgusting into a story to laugh about later. Not to mention maybe they'll think twice before bothering some other girl without sharp teeth. I continue down the sidewalk, the spring back in my step.

One block away, I reach my office: a two-story building with brightly colored windows and very little parking space. It had been a brownstone once upon a time, but the front does a good enough job of pretending to be a business now.

I'm about to open the door when I hear a soft 'whoosh' from somewhere above my head. I turn in time to see a small figure swoop down and land on the steps behind me. It's a cupid, only three feet tall, with a rosy androgynous face, flowing golden hair, and a pair of fluffy white wings poking out of their back. They're holding a large bouquet of sunflowers mixed with white daisies that almost tips them over with its weight.

I gasp in delight—both because the flowers are beautiful, and because they match my dress. I've got on a soft white A-line with asymmetrical splashes of cheerful yellow across it. "How beautiful! Are those for me?"

"Are you Isabeau LaCour?" Despite the cupid's cheerful appearance—at least, what I can see of it behind the enormous bouquet—they're speaking in the dreariest monotone I've ever heard.

"That's me."

The cupid thrusts out the bouquet in a wobbly motion. "Here."

"Thank you." I take the flowers, curling a protective arm around them.

"Hmph. Sign here." They shove a handheld scanner at me next, and I balance the flowers on my hip as I sign the screen. No sooner have I finished scribbling than they're off, soaring back into the grey evening sky. Their abrupt departure doesn't dim the grin that's broken out across my face, though. Even without reading the card, I know who the flowers are from.

Riley. It's only been one day since she left my apartment with an adorable blush and a murmured promise to be in touch, but this isn't at all what I was expecting. I must admit, though, flowers are much sweeter than a text. She's obviously put some thought into this, and it's working. She certainly has my attention.

I brace the bouquet on my shoulder and open the door, only to bump into someone else. The pink foil around the flowers crinkles as we collide, and I step back, full of apologies. "Elyse? Oh, I'm so sorry, I didn't see you—"

"How could you, over that mess?"

I peer around the sunflowers to see Elyse's face. Her eyes are narrowed, but she's wearing a thin smirk, the only sort of smile I can usually get out of her. She's not the type of sorceress who does a lot of cackling. Her sense of humor runs much drier, and she looks very plain, as New Yorkers go: dark curly hair not so different from mine and a pair of bookish glasses. I've tried before to get her to wear brighter colors, with limited success. She looks about thirty, even though she's actually several decades older.

"It's not a mess," I say, sliding past Elyse and into the office. "They're a gift."

"Kind of a bummer of a gift." She takes the flowers from me and sets them on the edge of the nearest table. The front room has several, all in rows, with two computers stationed at each one. "I know you like bright, shiny things, but these are kind of rude."

I take my sunglasses off and clip them onto the front of my dress. Fluorescent lighting doesn't bother my eyes the way natural sunlight does. "How are flowers rude?"

"*Sun*flowers," Elyse clarifies, with extra emphasis. "For a vampire. Aside from the whole 'sun can kill you' thing if your skin care regimen slips, they starve all the other plants, hence the name. And you just so happen to be interested in a slightly different kind of lifeblood. So, I repeat, kind of rude."

I chuckle. Riley probably hadn't thought that part through. "I'm sure she picked them because of the color."

"She? Not a secret admirer, then." That catches Elyse's interest. She leans on the table next to the flowers, cupping one between her fingers. "I haven't heard you talk about a 'she' in the twenty years I've known you. Tell me more. A best friend needs to know."

It's true. I don't date seriously...for good reason. I've been burned before, and with an eternity to get over my last relationship, it's not like I'm pressed for time.

"And when my best friend needs to know, I'll tell her."

Elyse sighs and shakes her head. "There's no need to be rude just because your new admirer was. I'm looking out for you. Where did you meet this person? How old is she? What's her name? Her address? I'll put them in my phone—"

She reaches for her pocket, but I stop her. "It's really not that serious yet."

"Izzy…"

"Fine," I sigh, "I met her on the train, younger than me, Riley, and I don't know. She hasn't invited me."

"Congratulations," Elyse drawls. "You've managed to answer all my questions without really telling me anything useful. Come on, can you blame me for wanting to know more about this girl? Strangers on the train don't give out flowers…unless they're part of some cult, I guess. What is she, a nymph?"

"Werewolf, actually."

"Interesting. Werewolves picking sunflowers." Elyse heads toward our offices, which are side by side on the first floor. They had been bedrooms at one time or another, and Elyse still occasionally uses hers as such. There's a mezuzah on the doorframe since, as she claims, she 'practically lives there', and I know for a fact she stashes a pillow and breakfast bars under her desk.

I stay back and start turning on computers. Soon, the room is humming softly. There are twenty in all, mostly PCs with a few Macs off to one side for specialized use. Personally, I prefer the latter, although Elyse disagrees with me.

"So, this werewolf, this mysterious new 'she'—" Elyse's voice drifts toward me through her open office door, and I can hear her rattling around her desk for something. "Did she ask you out, or did you ask her?"

It's a simple question, but I flounder for an answer anyway. My face flushes with the slightest tinge of warmth. It's a surprising reaction, since I haven't eaten in a while, and I don't have much blood to waste on things like blushing.

"She spoke to me first."

"Ah, I see. But you went for it, didn't you? What am I saying? Of course, you did."

I smile, remembering. I've had strangers stare at me on trains before—sometimes with admiration, sometimes with fear—but none like Riley.

"She couldn't take her eyes off me. It was flattering for once."

"So, what made you pick her, anyway?" Elyse pokes her head back through the door, a spare power supply and a bundle of multicolored cords in her arms. "There are plenty of dogs in the pound. Why is this one so special?"

That's a really good question, one I'm not sure I have an answer to. It's true that I've had other opportunities. I've had a handful of one-night stands over the past twenty years...not many, but enough to know I have options.

"She told me she liked my smile," I say at last, shrugging helplessly. "No one had ever said that to me before, and it was just so genuine. It wasn't, like, a *line* or anything. I had enough of those with...I had enough of those before."

Elyse doesn't hound me about my hesitation. "And? Did you share heated stares? Scoot closer to each other between stops? Kiss over the turnstiles? Give me something!"

"And we had a nice time."

Nice doesn't begin to cover it. Nice doesn't explain how tender Riley's eyes were, how hungry her hands had been, or how warm and delicious she'd smelled when I tucked my nose into her throat.

"You schtupped her, didn't you?"

It's a statement, not a question. My eyes widen in surprise. "I...I didn't say..."

Elyse grins. "Your fangs, Izzy."

I prod them with my tongue. They've extended a few centimeters, and it takes an effort of will to draw them back. Sometimes, they have a mind of their own. I heave a sigh. "I'll get some juice."

"This conversation isn't over, Isabeau LaCour. Only temporarily delayed. More questions are coming. It's for your own good, you know."

I sigh. I can't really blame Elyse for being concerned about me. She's big on dating safety, and she's the reason I reminded Riley to text her friend the evening before.

On the way to my office, and the convenient mini-fridge within, I pass the flowers again. Though I've decided to leave them out in the open for all my students to enjoy, I notice on closer inspection that I've forgotten the card tucked into the bouquet. I open it and smile when I see a few lopsided lines of scratchy handwriting. Apparently, penmanship isn't one of Riley's talents.

Isabeau,

Thank you for a beautiful time last night. Hope you like the flowers. The color reminds me of you. I'll probably be too chicken to text you first, so I hope you'll text me.

Riley

I lower the card, but it's too late. Elyse has already read it over my shoulder.

"This Riley is smooth."

"'Smooth' isn't exactly the word I'd use," I chuckle. I can still recall Riley's desperate, croaked 'Hi' when I was about to get off the train for the third time.

Elyse isn't convinced. "She's expressing herself while giving you space to make the next move. Sounds pretty smooth to me."

A little of my good mood fades. I enjoyed thinking about Riley a lot more before the word 'smooth' was involved. My previous girlfriend, Natasha, was smooth, and that didn't exactly work out in my favor. I force a smile, try to shake the shadow off.

"But you just said she wasn't smooth—"

"I said she chose a weird gift. One doesn't preclude the other. And hey...it got your attention. That's rare."

"Which is why you're putting me through the wringer," I interrupt.

"Calm down. I'm not trying to ruin your meet-cute. I'm just trying to keep you from getting hurt again. You don't always have the best judgment."

I can't deny that. Elyse has known me long enough to become totally intimate with my flaws, including my previous poor taste in women.

"Class starts in a few minutes," I say, trying to end the conversation. If I don't stop her, Elyse will circle on and on. "I'll have to text her later."

"Correction: I'm going to make sure you text her later," Elyse says.

I give her a confused look. "I honestly can't tell whether you're excited for me or worried for me."

"Both, always. You know it's my mission to find you the perfect girlfriend."

I swallow. "Who said anything about a girlfriend? We had sex. She gave me flowers. That's all."

Elyse shrugs. "Those are potentially girlfriend or pre-girlfriend activities. Oh, crap." Her eyes have drifted over to the clock, and I breathe a sigh of relief. I'm saved by the minute hand. "Go get juiced up. You'll need the boost when our kids get here."

Our students are anything but kids. In fact, many of them are older than we are, despite our unnaturally long lifespans. But somehow, when Elyse says it, it's charming instead of awkward. "Fine," I say, hurrying off. I don't want to give her the chance to get started again, even if her meddling is good-natured.

"Just don't forget—this conversation is to be continued later! And you're going to text her!"

***

'Later' doesn't come as soon as I'd like. I spend the next several hours wandering from computer to computer, leaning over to help my students whenever they have questions about Elyse's instructions—and there are a *lot* of questions.

I've got a witch waving her mouse around like a wand, a cranky vampire muttering something about how things were simpler when Roosevelt (the first one, I suspect) was president, and a faerie typing some *very* inappropriate words into the Google search bar.

"You need to keep the mouse on the pad like this, Agatha, see?" I say to the witch, trying to deal with one problem at a time. "If you lift it up, it won't work."

"Why not?" Agatha protests. "I'm pointing where I want it to go."

"The sensor needs to stay in contact with a flat surface," I tell her as patiently as I can. "Just give it a try."

She huffs but puts the mouse back on the pad before she accidentally hits one of her neighbors. Next up is Eolande. She's got 'Leprechaun Gangbangs' pulled up in Google's image search, and I have to side-eye her in order to keep a straight face. I'm half-convinced she's doing this just to mess with me.

"I'm sorry," I say, ignoring the pictures that have popped up on the screen, "but you need to look for that material on your own time. This isn't an appropriate use of the learning center's computers."

Eolande sighs. "But this is so much easier than finding real Leprechauns! You type it in, and they just appear in the magic box..."

Now I know she's fucking with me. Eolande isn't nearly as bad with computers as she pretends.

"Let's reactivate your safe-search features. They shouldn't have been turned off to begin with."

I close out of the browser and fix Eolande's settings while she pouts.

Next up is Francis, the grumpy vampire. "Since you're so interested, why don't I show you how to search for information on President Roosevelt?"

"What do I need information about him for?" Francis grumbles. "I've lived through thirty-two presidents, girl. *I* was there. I remember what happened—"

"Of course, you do," I tell him, "but just in case..."

I type 'President Theodore Roosevelt' into the search bar and leave Francis to his own devices. Free for a brief moment, I glance at the clock on the wall. Still another half hour to go. I love my job, and I love helping people, but I have to admit, it can get a little tiring. When I look away, Elyse catches my eye. 'Text her,' she mouths, jerking her head toward the bathroom.

I smile. This is exactly why I love her. Before another student can ask me a question, I slip away from the computers and head for the bathroom.

Once I'm alone, I pull my phone out of my dress pocket. Dresses with pockets are hard to find, but so, so worth it. I'm a little disappointed to see that I don't have any missed texts, but I remember what Riley wrote on the card. Maybe it's like Elyse said and she's waiting for me to make the next move.

Twenty years on the market, and I still feel so clueless, like I've never done this before. Finding company has never been a problem for me. I've had several dalliances, for lack of a better term, since Natasha, but those were one-night stands. I enjoy the thrill of meeting people and falling in love for a couple of hours. It feels like magic, like destiny.

Something about Riley is different, though. No one else has looked at me the way she does. No one else has sent me flowers the morning after. No one else has sounded so sincere about wanting to see me again. I want to keep her around for a little while, assuming I haven't forgotten everything I know about dating in the past two decades.

During the night Riley spent in my apartment, I had felt so powerful, so in control of everything that was happening. Now, I feel the exact opposite, but it's kind of a nice change. I'm at the top of a rollercoaster, about to go hurtling down.

I pull up her name on my phone. Just because I have an eternity ahead of me doesn't mean I'm the type to waste time.

'Thank you for the flowers! They're beautiful.'

Dots appear at the bottom of the screen almost immediately. I wait impatiently.

Riley: *You liked them?* 😄 *I hope I picked a good color.*

'I loved them. They're perfect.'

Somehow, that doesn't seem like enough. I hesitate, then add: *'Perfect enough for a second date.'*

My stomach flutters nervously as Riley types back.

Riley: *Just name the time and place.*

I sigh with relief. Spending time with strangers was fun while it lasted, but maybe it's time for something different. I've got a whole lot to gain, and nothing to lose but a heart that's already been broken or maybe just dented a bit around the edges. I'll have to wait and find out.

And I already know exactly where I'm going to take her.

***

By the time sunrise hits and my shift ends, I'm still awake and full of energy. I set Riley's sunflowers in the window so they'll last as long as possible, but before I slip out the door, I pull one out of the vase. Using the screen of my phone—since the bathroom mirror doesn't show anything but my dress, my sunglasses, some eyeshadow and a lipstick print—I secure the stem behind my ear and tuck my hair over it.

"Going somewhere special?"

I turn to see Elyse staring at me. "Just breakfast," I tell her, pulling a small bottle out of my purse and slathering extra sunscreen on my bare forearms. The cat's out of the bag, but I want to try and keep Riley to myself for just a little while longer.

"Hmm." It's clear from Elyse's tone she doesn't believe me, but she doesn't push the issue. "Go ahead and lock up. I'm going to crash in my office for a while."

I move onto my face, painting a stripe across the bridge of my forehead and down along my nose. "Don't you want to go home and sleep?"

"Sleep is for the weak and coffee is the most powerful potion of all."

I sigh and recap the bottle. "If I find you asleep on your desk when I come back to work tonight..."

"You aren't coming back to work tonight," Elyse says, matter-of-factly. "It's Saturday. Take the evening off."

It's a surprising offer, and way too generous. "I'm not letting you do them on your own," I protest, but Elyse holds up her hand.

"We've only got two classes, and they're small ones. I can handle them solo." She gives me a knowing smirk. "Spend the evening with your new squeeze. After two decades, you deserve a date."

"You're meddling," I tell her, but she just clicks her tongue.

"Sometimes, meddling is a good deed."

Normally I'd argue harder, but Elyse has a point. It has been a while...and if I don't hurry, I'm going to be late. I don't have time to pout until she takes back her favor. "You're the best," I say, leaning in for a hug.

Elyse stays a little stiff, but she allows it. "Yeah, yeah. Now, go, and tell me all about it later." She slips out of my arms and pushes me toward the door. "And text me where she lives if she invites you over! I promise not to stalk her...offline, anyway. I will be Googling her address, just to be honest."

After waving goodbye, I practically skip out onto the sidewalk. It's a beautiful sunny day, and even though the morning glare makes my skin tingle and ache a bit, I'm happy for the clear weather. It's the perfect morning for a breakfast date, and I'll be sitting across from the perfect person.

***

"Crossbones?" Riley says, reading the sign above the wooden double doors.

While she studies the entrance to the restaurant, I continue studying her. I'm still lingering several seconds in the past, when I'd first spotted her waiting for me in front of the building. Her collar is a bit crooked, her hair a little messy, but on her, the slightly disheveled look is too cute. We'd hugged warmly for a few seconds, and I'd caught a whiff of something delicious near her throat—not any particular body spray or scent, but just her.

"It's got the best grits in the city," I declare. "At least, that's what my family says when they come up to visit."

"Really?" Riley's eyebrows lift skeptically, but her grin broadens. "That's quite a claim. I've had some mighty fine grits, and that's not even countin' the ones my daddy makes."

I take her hand, enjoying how warm her fingers are as they lace with mine. One benefit to having cold hands—I get to soak up all the heat when I hold someone else's. "Just trust me. But you have to promise me to get them cajun style."

Riley wrinkles her nose. "Shrimp? I'm usually more the red meat type..."

"It's good, I promise." I begin taking her toward the door. "If you want, we can split them."

"Fair enough."

The two of us head into the diner, which is packed at this time of day. There are all sorts of interesting people around, and I notice Riley staring wide-eyed at a two-headed cyclops laughing in one of the corners.

"Sorry," she says when she realizes I've caught her. "I... um, like to people watch."

Riley is saved from embarrassment by the arrival of the hostess, a succubus with an overly cheery smile. When she notices me, however, she breathes a sigh of relief and puts on a more neutral, and more pleasant face. I'm enough of a regular that she knows I never complain and tip well. "Two today," I tell her, and she leads us over to one of the nice tables by the window.

"So, people watching," I say to Riley once the hostess leaves. "Is that what you were doing on the subway the day we met?"

Riley laughs. "Yup. Well, sorta. After seeing you, I couldn't recall anyone else who was on that train if I tried."

Her accent is inconsistent, I notice. She drops her 'g's only occasionally, as if she's trying to downplay her drawl.

"Sweet talker." I lean forward, resting my elbow on the table and my chin in my hand. "I'll tell you a secret, though. I like to people watch, too. I don't think there's any harm, as long as you're looking for the positive."

"I'm still getting used to it," Riley confesses. "It's just so crowded."

"Compared to where?"

"Talbot. It's small, maybe 'bout five hundred people in the city proper." She shrugged. "Mostly just humans and wolves back home, and we never did mix too well. Not like here."

"New York isn't without its problems..." I trail off and murmur a 'thank you' as the waitress arrives with the grits and a glass of sheep's blood. "But at the very least, there's always someone else just as strange as you are."

Riley nods, but her eyes have locked onto the plate. She takes a big sniff, and I can practically see her tongue lolling. "These are for you," I say, pushing them her way.

"I can order my own," she protests, but she's already unwrapping her fork from her napkin.

"Vampires don't eat much food anyway." At her look of confusion, I explain. "We can if we want to, but mostly for the nostalgia. We can't taste much, and it goes right through us."

"Not blood, though?" Riley mumbles around a mouthful of cheese and shrimp. From the glaze in her eyes, I can tell it's an effort to concentrate on the conversation. Her mouth is in heaven.

My own mouth starts to water. I'm getting hungry, and I'm all too aware of the way her pulse is beating in her neck. The sheep's blood next to me isn't doing much to sate my thirst. "We don't need as much as you think, although the more we have, the easier it is to keep warm. Unfortunately, if you're single and want anything fancier than cow or sheep or pig, you have to pay extra."

Riley pauses in the middle of shoveling grits into her mouth. "Mmh, these grits are amazing...wait, single?"

"Well, yes. Most of us don't go around asking our friends for a snack, because of the side effects."

Riley's expression grows even more concerned. "Side effects?"

"Not those kinds of side effects. They're actually, ah, *pleasant*, if you know what I mean."

Riley's eyes grow very large, and from her blush, I can tell she knows exactly what I mean.

"Don't get me wrong," I say before she can make the usual leap. "I'm not here with you right now for a free meal. I just want to spend a little more time with you. No teeth necessary."

"I didn't think that at all," Riley says with a soft smile.

"You didn't?"

"Naw. You're way too nice."

I arch an eyebrow at her. "Nice? How do you know?"

"Wolf sense," Riley says, with complete sincerity.

I can't help it. I giggle. "Wolf sense?"

"Yup. Wolves can sense when someone's bein' dishonest." I must look skeptical, because she adds, "Swear!" much more insistently.

"I believe you," I say, still with a slight laugh. "So, is that what you do at your job? Use your wolf sense to figure out which bankers are on the up-and-up?"

"Duller than that, I'm afraid. I'm just a numbers gal, living in a cube. Took the first job I could find up here that would cover rent. Now, your job..." She looks at me with clear admiration. "That sounds interesting."

"I'd say it's rewarding more than interesting. Certain parts of the job are predictable. Like when you teach older people from different centuries how to use computers, there's always porn. *So* much porn."

"Can't blame 'em. If I was from the sixteenth century and learned I could see sex on a magic box..."

The atmosphere changes. We lock eyes, and Riley's are so, so blue I want to fall into them. "I prefer a little more realism," I murmur, and something in me can sense the spike of Riley's heartbeat across the narrow gap of the table.

With a rapid blink, the moment is broken. Riley seems to come back to herself. "I'll be honest," she says, rubbing the back of her neck. "I have no idea how this works. Or if 'this' is even anything."

"It's something." What that something is, I'm not ready to say yet, but I'm hopeful, nonetheless.

Riley sets her hand back on the table. "So..."

"So..." I place my hand over hers. "We ride this something until we figure out what it is, and have fun doing it. No rules, no expectations."

Riley grins. "That easy?"

"That easy."

"So, uh..." Her face turns pink again, and she ducks her head, letting her bangs fall over her eyes. "Any interest in going back to mine? After I pay."

"After *I* pay," I insist.

"But I ate all the grits!"

I roll my tongue across my lower lip. "Don't worry about it. I'm sure I'll get plenty to eat."

***

Things stay heated rather than awkward on the ride to Riley's place, but we hit a small road bump when we arrive at her modest building. She holds open the front door, obviously waiting for me to go first, but I can only linger on the doorstep. "Um, Riley," I say, with an apologetic shrug, "I'm a vampire, remember? You need to ask me in."

"Oh!" Riley rubs the back of her neck. "I didn't know it had to be, uh, that official and all. Sorry. Izzy, would you like to come in?"

I give her my biggest smile. "I'd love to."

She takes my hand as we head up the stairs, squeezing it just a little too tight.

Riley's apartment isn't much to speak of. It's a studio, with a kitchenette in one corner, a bed in the other, and a couch and television in the middle of the room. It's clean, though, aside from the rumpled comforter that she hasn't bothered to straighten over the mattress.

When I look closer, I can see little touches of her around the room: framed photos of her family on the shelves, landscape prints on the walls that remind me of something I'd find on the aesthetic blogs I follow, and a potted spider plant hanging from the ceiling above the kitchen table.

"It ain't...it's not much yet," Riley says sheepishly, correcting herself mid-sentence. "Only moved in a couple months ago."

I smile, not at the apartment, but at her. "I think it has potential."

"Huh?"

I turn to face her, wrapping my arms loosely around her neck. The signals from Riley's body are all positive. Her pupils get bigger, and she sucks in a little gasp while smiling. "A few more plants would brighten the place up even more. Maybe a window box? I know you like flowers."

Her face flushes. "Yup."

"Me too."

Riley surprises me by leaning in first. She pauses a centimeter away from my mouth, obviously waiting for permission, and I close the rest of the distance. Our kiss is soft, cautious, but very, very sweet. She tastes warm more than anything, and I slip my fingers beneath the neckline of her sweater vest for something to grip.

As the kiss deepens, Riley's hands find my hips. Her grip starts out light, but it tightens when I suck on her lower lip, and I feel her low groan vibrate against my tongue. She pulls back, and I let her go, just a bit reluctantly.

"What's wrong?" I whisper.

"Nothin'. It's just, did your fangs get longer?"

I run my tongue over them and realize she's right. The tips of my fangs have started to protrude a little more. "Oh. Yes, they do that." I smile, trying to put her at ease. "Don't worry. I don't bite unless I'm asked nicely."

"I don't mind," Riley murmurs. The breathless way she says it, I start to wonder if that's an understatement.

But I can't get ahead of myself. Biting requires trust, and I haven't drunk from a living person in a couple of years. People who go looking for the high the bite gives them leave me uneasy, so I don't go home with them. The others simply don't ask.

"The teeth," Riley says, as if she feels the need to clarify. "I mean, I don't mind your teeth. When we kiss. They don't hurt."

"Good."

I kiss her again, deeper, with less restraint. Riley seems to approve, because she clutches at the material of my dress near the waist. The rasp of fabric shifting lights my skin up, but I know her hands will feel even better.

"Your bed would be more comfortable," I say, stroking the fine hairs at the back of her neck.

I don't have to tell her twice. She backs me toward it, her mouth dipping forward again and again to steal short kisses from mine. I let her guide me until my legs hit the edge of the mattress.

"You sure?" she asks, pulling back to check in one more time.

"Definitely sure." I take Riley's hands in mine, removing them from my waist and turning in her arms. "Unzip me."

Even facing away, I can feel her grin. She pulls down the zipper of my dress, placing a kiss against my shoulder from behind. "You look so pretty in yellow," she mutters, and a shudder races down my spine as her hot breath skates over me.

I know I do, but hearing Riley say it is extra special. My heart flutters, but despite that, I think of something to say: "I'd probably look better in nothing at all."

"You do." She pulls my zipper down to the small of my back, peeling the dress open, and I can't quite stifle a whimper. Her fingertips are so gentle against me, like little licks of flame.

I turn, and the dress falls off completely. Riley swallows—visibly— and I bring one of her hands to my breast, coaxing her to cup it. She takes more than I've offered, cupping both my breasts in her hands and pushing me back down onto the bed. Soon she's on top of me, kissing my neck and swiping her thumbs over the stiff peaks of my nipples. The position brings my face close to her throat, and suddenly, Riley's smell fills my nose—the warm, sweet smell of blood beating beneath skin. There's a pulsing artery right near my lips. My stomach clenches.

To distract myself, but also because I'm desperate, I find the hem of her sweater vest and yank it up over her head. It forces us to separate for a moment, and I'm able to take a deliberate breath of air to clear my lungs.

It doesn't really work. She helps me untuck her shirt and pull that off too before moving on to her pants, and the way her strong fingers work against my stomach as she unbuckles her belt have me trembling. Her hands are shaking too, so I brush them away, guiding her lips back to my chest as I work to unfasten the buckle myself.

The belt gives me wicked thoughts, but I put those away for later. Between the two of us, we just barely manage to pull off her pants and my underwear. We pause for a moment, eyes locked, relishing the knowledge that we're both naked before her thigh slides between mine and our mouths find each other again.

We kiss, and kiss, and kiss some more until my head is spinning and the smell of blood is back in my nose. Riley's body is practically pounding with her heartbeat, and the reverberations cause an ache deep between my legs. I need to taste her—need to taste something. Even though she's taken the lead so far, my impatience gets the better of me. I flip her over, and though she looks surprised as her back hits the mattress and I straddle her hips, she doesn't protest.

Riley's hand settles in my hair as I kiss my way down her body. Her fingers find a home in my springy curls, but she doesn't tug—she merely lifts her hips and spreads her legs, inviting me to travel further down. And down I go, sucking and nipping as gently as I can without breaking skin, enjoying the hisses she makes and the flushed pink patches I leave behind on her breasts and belly.

Her scent is maddening. The closer I draw to her core, the thicker it grows, until my lungs are heavy with it and my mouth is watering. The view doesn't help. The longer I stare at Riley's golden triangle of curls, at her parted pink lips, at the thick red shaft of her clit, the more entranced I become. But I can't taste with my eyes, and I *need* to taste.

I lean in. Riley lets out the softest little sound as my lips make contact. It's sweet and delicious, and *she's* sweet and delicious, and I run my flattened tongue along every inch of soft, shimmering flesh I can reach. The very first taste has my head spinning. She's warm, wet, and salty with just a bit of sugar mixed in, and I can't help but be selfish.

Riley's hips give a jolt and her fingers tighten in my hair. They're good signs, because she moans a moment later and her legs fall further apart. I guide her knees over my shoulders so I can push even deeper. Soon, she's digging her heels into my back and muttering nonsense as she clutches my head. But the fact that Riley's in heaven is only a pleasant side effect. I'm hungry, and since I can't drink from her, this is the closest I can get.

I spend the next several minutes absolutely devouring her. I thrust,

I circle, I flutter. I do everything I can think of to earn more of the slippery heat spilling into my mouth. Her noises give me hints. When I suck her clit, she tenses up and fresh warmth leaks over my chin. When I cover her in slow upward swipes, her limbs lock and start to tremble. When I plunge my tongue into her opening, her head thrashes from side to side and she digs her nails into my scalp. I don't mind. The pain is extra encouragement.

"Izzy..."

I pull away from Riley for the first time since I've started and look up at her. She's panting, and her eyes are flickering with the beginnings of a yellow glow. She's about to change—'going feral', as she calls it— and she's chewing at her bottom lip, waiting for permission.

"You don't need to ask." I drag my tongue along her thigh, enjoying the way she flinches. "It's part of you."

Riley groans, and the change hits a moment later. Fine, ticklish little hairs, a shade darker than the ones on her head, sprout up across her skin. The edges of her nails sharpen to points and the tips of her ears lengthen. I stare up at her for a moment, lost in the lanterns her eyes have become. Then my hunger returns, hollow and greedy, and Riley's all too eager to shove my head back between her legs.

Her taste is stronger this way—a little wilder and even more addictive. I gather all I can from the clasping muscles of her entrance before nosing my way up to her clit and sucking it deep. It's swollen, throbbing with its own little heartbeat, a pulse that twitches on the tip of my tongue. "Izzy," Riley groans again, and the way she says my name is so plaintive, so perfect, that I have to suck her deeper.

She cries out loud and long, tensing up and shuddering so hard that I must grip her hips to keep them still. Her feet flex against my back and her thighs close around my head, but I don't mind the extra pressure. Although we can fake it, vampires don't technically need to breathe. I take full advantage of that fact, tightening the seal of my lips and rolling my tongue over her again and again without stopping.

Riley howls. She comes in hot splashes, and I let my tongue slide down to catch as much as I can without losing her clit completely. I've got my whole mouth wrapped around her, wide enough so my fangs are resting flat against her, but Riley still pulls desperately at my hair, trying to thrust herself deeper.

By the time she's finished squirming and thrashing, Riley is covered in sweat, and the lower half of my face is drenched with her release. I draw back, licking my lips clean and staring up at her heaving chest.

Even without touching her, I can sense the rapid beating of her heart and the blood pulsing through it.

"C'mere," she rasps, cupping the back of my neck and drawing me up to lay on top of her. I let her wrap an arm around me as I rest my head above her breasts. They're the perfect size for a pillow, and I close my eyes, smiling as I listen to her heartbeat. With the satisfying taste of her come on my tongue, I can almost pretend I don't want to drink from her.

"You like usin' your teeth down there, huh?" Riley laughs, stroking down some of my flyaway curls.

"I didn't mean to." I press an apologetic kiss beside her nipple. "I didn't hurt you, did I? I wasn't trying to bite."

"Why?"

I look up at her, confused, but her glowing yellow eyes are full of kindness.

"I don't understand the question."

"Why were you tryin' not to bite me? I hope this doesn't sound stupid, but...you're a vampire. I thought that came with the territory."

My eyebrows lift several inches. That certainly wasn't the response I was expecting. "Well, you haven't asked me. I told you before, I don't bite unless someone asks nicely."

Riley bends down. Before I know it, her lips are on mine, hot and soft. Her tongue sweeps along the seam of my mouth, coaxing it open.

"This is me, askin' nicely," she says when she pulls away. "Okay?"

I smile, teeth and all. "Okay."

"So, uh...how does it...how do y'all...I mean, should we..." Riley is staring straight at my fangs, and to my delight, it seems to be with fascination.

"They're like hypodermic needles. When I bite you, I inject you with a chemical that makes you feel pleasure."

Her eyes widen. "Pleasure?"

"It's not always sexual," I say, although it certainly was for me back when I was dating Natasha as a human. I struggle for the right words to describe it. "It's like...sinking into a warm bath. Nice and tingly."

"Then what?" Riley whispers. I can smell her blood rushing and hear her heart speeding up.

"Then I drink. It won't hurt. You might feel a bit woozy afterwards, but only if I get carried away. Which I won't."

Riley doesn't seem to need the reassurance. Her yellow eyes are still glowing, but the light in them is all anticipation. When she speaks, she's breathless. "So, where're you gonna do it?"

I draw my lower lip between my teeth. Where I'd like to bite Riley and where she'll feel comfortable letting me bite her for the first time are two different things. The fact that I can smell her and hear the quick, excited drumming of her heart makes it even harder to decide. My eyes trail inexorably toward the crook of her throat, where I can see her pulse pounding. It's a cliché, but the neck is the easiest place to find a good artery.

I roll off Riley, straddling her hips instead of lying sprawled across her. "What about here?" I trail my fingertips up from her collarbone to the spot I was staring at. I press in, and Riley shivers beneath me. Her heartbeat gives a little spike, one that sends an answering jolt straight between my legs.

"Yeah?" There's a note of question in her voice at first, but then she clears her throat and says, "Yeah," much more firmly.

"It won't hurt," I remind her as I shift into a more comfortable position. With one of Riley's strong arms curled around my waist and one of my thighs pressed snug between her legs, I feel secure.

"I believe you."

I take her lips in a slow kiss, one that's meant to reassure me as much as her. Then, I begin kissing and sucking my way down the column of her throat. "This is pretty new for me too," I mutter beneath her jaw. "Drinking wasn't on the menu with most of my one-night stands."

"But it is with me? Why?"

I take a moment to inhale the scent that pools at the dip of her collarbone. Smelling Riley makes remembering to breathe worth it. "Because you're sweet." I kiss the spot I've chosen, lightly at first, with closed lips. "Because you talk sweet." I kiss her again, a bit wetter, enjoying the way her body tenses eagerly beneath mine. "Because you smell and taste sweet..." I run my tongue up along her neck, and she whimpers.

"Quit teasin'." Riley's hand stroked soothing circles along my back before sliding down to grip my ass.

"Okay. Just relax..."

That's easy for me to say, I'm anything but relaxed. With my nose and mouth so close to Riley's neck, I'm almost blood-drunk. I can practically feel her on my tongue already, and my fangs have extended to full points.

Riley laughs beneath me. "Kinda hard to relax with you breathin' on my neck like that."

On impulse, I reach up, running my fingers through her soft blonde hair. I kiss the corner of her chin once, tenderly, and then bend back down to suck at the crook of her throat. I don't sink my teeth in right away. I start with deep, rhythmic pulling, rolling my tongue over her skin. Riley squirms beneath me, but I can tell from her panting and the way she's kneading my ass that she's enjoying it.

The sensations are so overwhelming that I have to close my eyes. Riley's smell is even stronger here, and I can taste the light coat of her sweat. My teeth ache, and other places ache even more. I skate the tips of my fangs over Riley's skin, and she goes rigid beneath me as if she's bracing herself. I want to reassure her, want to show her it won't hurt. I sink my teeth into her neck.

Riley relaxes instantly. She lets out a long sigh, melting into the bed, and her grip on my rear loosens. I barely notice. I'm too overwhelmed by the rush of sweetness spilling across my tongue. Every bit of Riley has tasted wonderful so far, but this—this is divine. Her blood is rich and heavy, and the heat alone has my eyes rolling back in my head.

I've forgotten most of how human food tastes in the twenty years since I've turned, but if I had to describe the flavor from memory, the only thing I can come up with is warm cider. She's sweet, but with a pleasant edge of tartness, and she burns a bit going down, in the most wonderful way possible.

I try to pace myself, but she's so delicious that it's almost impossible. I want to pull hard and fast, to drink my fill instead of letting Riley's pounding heart do most of the work. I distract myself by running my hands along her heaving sides, and I realize dimly that she's already exploring mine. Her claws rake along my outer thighs, and she rubs herself above my knee, coating it with fresh wetness.

I'm dripping too. I'm holding Riley's heartbeat in my mouth, and it echoes all the way down to my core. My clit twitches, and even though I'm incredibly comfortable resting on top of her, my hips give a slight jerk.

Riley notices. She wraps her hands around my waist, guiding me into a short grind. This time, I'm the one making a mess of her leg, but I don't care. My head is spinning, and my mouth is sucking to the rhythm of Riley's pulse, and my inner walls are fluttering with need.

"Baby, do you need...?"

Riley's fingertips skate higher along my leg, but her hand hesitates before it cups me. Still latched onto her neck, I look up at her face, and I see the question there. So sweet. She's waiting for permission. I lift off her thigh and spread a little wider, giving her access to where I'm aching.

One of Riley's fingers sinks inside me without any effort. She curls it a little, trying to find the sensitive spot along my front wall, and I pull harder at the artery I've tapped when she does. She groans right along with me. More of her wetness smears across my knee, so I slip my hand lower. I want to touch her, too.

Riley's clit is swollen and slippery and easy to find. As soon as I touch it, she bucks up into me, shaking. She isn't the only one. When she slides another finger inside me next to the first and starts pumping them deep, I cry out against her neck. I can't really ride her, tangled up the way we are, but I do my best to follow her rhythm with my hips.

It only takes a few sloppy thrusts before I'm coming. I clench hard around Riley's fingers, rippling every time she drives into me. The heel of her hand is at the perfect angle for me to rub against, and I pour everything I have into her palm while she keeps spilling into my mouth.

The pleasure is so intense that my vision dims. Blackness closes in around my eyes. All I can feel is Riley's thrusts between my legs and all I can taste is Riley's heartbeat on my tongue. I only break away from the bite as my peak winds down, clutching at her shoulder instead.

As I draw back, still smothering her neck in kisses, I notice that Riley is still trembling. She's a bundle of tightly coiled muscle, shifting desperately beneath me. I suddenly remember I've been neglecting to touch her. My orgasm had completely distracted me. I hurry to make up for the mistake, kissing my way lower—and this time, I don't skimp on the teeth.

"Jesus, Mary, and Joseph," Riley pants, staring down at me with wide, bewildered eyes. If she has more to say, it's lost in a moan when I reach her breast. I sink my teeth in on either side of her nipple, just enough for a quick taste, and more heat runs between my fingers. She tries to keep me there, clutching at my hair, but I kiss my way across to the opposite side.

I drink a little longer there, but not by much—I've still got a ways to go, and I don't want to take more than she can give. I travel down her body as quickly as I can, pausing to suck the sensitive patch of skin beside her navel before settling back between her legs. This time, I don't have to encourage her to put her knees over my shoulders. She does it automatically, murmuring the whole time. "Izzy, please...please..."

I've never been able to say no to a please. Instead of teasing, I latch onto her clit, and this time, I let my fangs prick the plump, swollen flesh on either side of the shaft.

Riley screams to the ceiling. Her entire body goes stiff, and then breaks down in shudders as she falls over the edge—and into my mouth. I didn't know it was possible, but she tastes even better this way, when there's a hint of copper mixed with her natural flavor. She's swearing and shaking up a storm, and it's all I can do to keep up with the frantic bucking of her hips.

By the time her pleasure runs its course, she's limp and sticky with more than sweat. Her heart is still thundering, but her clit merely twitches between my lips. I withdraw my fangs as carefully as I can and place a tender kiss there instead, chuckling at the way she hisses. "Okay, no more," I promise, resting my head on the pillow of her thigh.

"You're insatiable," she says, and something about the heavily accented way she says the word makes me want to laugh.

"Ins*aeshabull*," I repeat, unable to hide my giggles.

"Don't make fun," she says, but her pouting expression cracks into a grin, and she starts laughing too. "S'your own fault, you fucked all the Yankee out of me."

I crawl back up along Riley's body and drape myself over her. I tuck my face back into her neck, but this time, I don't bite. I'm content just to smell her cooling skin. She really does feel like a furnace, and I can't get enough of her warmth.

"So?" I ask, full of hope, "did feeding a vampire meet your expectations?"

"Yup. And then some. It was..." Riley gives a happy sigh, apparently deciding she doesn't want to bother describing it with words. That's okay. She doesn't need to. "But what about you? I only made you come once..."

"Once *so far*." I roll off her and onto the other side of the bed, spreading my legs and giving her a come-hither look. "You can make it up to me. Unless you're tired from losing all that blood."

Riley snorts, looking mildly offended. "Tired? Me? Nah." She flips over, sliding on top of me, and my heart leaps. "Y'all aren't the only ones who can bite, you know," she says, showing off the points of her teeth. "Want me to show ya?"

I know she's trying to be sexy, but I stifle another fit of giggles. She's the picture of adorable with her big, eager smile and her shaggy blonde hair framing her face. She reminds me more of an excited golden retriever than a big bad wolf.

"Show me," I tell her, winding my arms around her.

Riley doesn't stand for that. She grabs my wrist and pins them to the bed, giving them a hard squeeze. Maybe I'm wrong about the golden retriever thing. I'd forgotten werewolves have super strength too. She leans down, her breath hot and wet against my neck, and sinks her teeth in just under my jaw.

I gasp. It's going to be a long and very pleasant night.

Rae D. Magdon

Chapter Three - Riley

IT'S A BEAUTIFUL MONDAY morning, three words I don't usually put together, especially in that order. I skip down the steps to the subway turnstiles with my hands in my pockets, a grin plastered on my face. The usual scent of damp garbage and too many bodies crammed into a small space washes over me, but I'm much too happy to let the stink bother me. The sweet smell of Isabeau's lotion is still lingering in my nose, keeping everything else at bay.

I've just come from her place, the fourth time I've been there in the past eight days. That has to be a record, even counting the girls I messed around with before I moved to New York. I can't get enough of her, and luckily, Isabeau seems just as happy to see me whenever I show up. This has to be the hardest and fastest I've ever fallen in...something.

We've only known each other a week and a half. It's much too soon to use words like love, but I'm definitely lost in a serious case of like, and in danger of much worse if we keep going at this pace. I can't help it. Isabeau is sweet. She makes me laugh. She wears dresses that brighten every room she steps into, or maybe that's just her blinding white smile.

Someone collides with my shoulder—hard.

"Hey, watch it," a deep voice grunts. I jerk back, whirling in surprise. A large troll, at least seven feet tall, is towering over me, his lower jaw jutting out angrily beneath his jagged tusks.

I take a nervous step away, holding up my hands in apology. "'Scuse me, didn't see you there."

He gives me a skeptical look. I shrug sheepishly. A troll that size isn't exactly easy to miss.

"Hmmph," he grunts, and then staggers toward one of the nearby trains, his hairy knuckles dragging over the concrete floor.

Even that near-miss isn't enough to dampen my spirits. By the time I reach my own platform, my grin is back, and I almost feel like howling for joy. I refrain, but only because a mummy waiting nearby is side-eyeing me over her newspaper, as if she's worried my loony smile means I'm crazy.

I don't care. I feel like I could walk on air. I spend the entire train ride, all five stops, in a happy haze. I've got myself a girl—Sort of? Maybe? Hopefully? And nothing can ruin this for me. Nothing, that is, except for the grumpy face of my boss, Mr. Mrglsptz waiting to greet me when I walk in the door. He has a cup of coffee in his hand and his claws drum impatiently against the heat protector.

"Evans. You're late."

"Sorry, sir. I thought I was on time? It's..." I check my watch. Shit. Two minutes late. Not the worst thing in the world, but banks and financial companies live by the clock, and Gragnar, Mrglsptz, & Smith is no exception. "Uh, I thought I was on time."

Mrglsptz sighs, shaking his horned head. "Just get on today's reports as soon as possible." He waves me away. "I've left them on your desk."

"Of course, sir."

I scurry past him, exhaling in relief once I'm out of his field of vision. Not many people make me nervous. I am a werewolf, after all, so it's usually the other way around, but Mrglsptz is one of them. He's a hard ass in addition to being a demon, and the city's given him a tough edge too. He certainly isn't like my old boss back at the feed store in Talbot, where everyone knows everyone else's business. All he cares about is getting a paycheck's worth of work out of his employees.

I reach my cubicle and sink into my chair, spinning around a couple of times before I get settled. My smile returns as I remember exactly why I'm late. Isabeau can be quite the cuddler when she wants, and my mornings are her nights. I yawn, feeling my ears pop. The one downside to seeing a vampire is that it can really mess with your sleep schedule.

"Hey, Riley. Riley? Riiileeey?"

Something pokes me in the back of the head, and I turn in surprise. I'd been so caught up in memories of Isabeau that I hadn't noticed Colin, my selkie coworker and also my best friend, standing behind me. Judging from the pencil sticking out from between his fingers, that's what he prodded me with.

"Did Mrglsptz chew you out for being late?"

I shrug. "Not too bad. He's a softie."

Colin rolls his big blue eyes. "Yeah, sure. But hey, what kept you?" He waggles his eyebrows suggestively. "Was it the French vampire? Did you stay over at her place again?"

"She ain't...she's not French." I correct myself. Sometimes the Southernisms are hard to drop at work. "Her parents are Creole."

"And? Does she speak either language?" From his tone, I know exactly what he's getting at.

"It's a whole unique culture. Not just some kind of bedroom language, you pervert." But I have to admit, I've thought about it. Maybe Ma made me and my sisters watch too many bad romance movies with her while we were growing up. It doesn't matter. The things Isabeau whispers in plain English are more than enough to raise my hair. She could probably recite a recipe and it wouldn't make a lick of difference.

"You still didn't answer my question," Colin drawls. It seems he's determined to tease today. "Did you stay the night again? If it wasn't Monday, I bet I would have seen those same wrinkled clothes yesterday."

I smooth down my vest. "Uh..."

"I'll take that as a yes. You'd better let me meet her soon, okay? I promise to be a perfect gentleman."

"Sorry, Colin," I chuckle, "but that dog won't hunt. Gentleman my ass."

Colin isn't offended. "Speaking of hunting, isn't it your time soon? Shouldn't be more than a couple of days now, right? Are you feeling the itch yet?"

I blink in surprise. Colin is right. I've been so wrapped up in Isabeau that I didn't even remember the full moon. That might explain some of my extra energy, looking back I always get a little squirmy a couple days before my shift, but this time, the buzz is more pleasant than annoying.

"Yeah, guess so."

"And? What does Isabeau think of it?"

In all honesty, I don't have a clue what Isabeau thinks of it. We haven't been together, if that's even what we are, long enough for her to go through one of my monthlies. Now that Colin's mentioned it, my stomach lurches with nervous butterflies. The one time I tried to show a girl my wolf form—not just going feral, but my *actual* wolf form—she ended up jumping from my pick-up and running for the hills not a few seconds after. Literally. Cindy Lou Castle and I never spoke again after that.

I doubt the same thing will happen with Isabeau. She's a vampire, after all, not a seventeen-year-old human. Some of them can even change into animals too, or so I've heard. But even so, the bad memories cast a cloud over my cheerful mood. What if she can't handle it? What if she thinks it's weird?

"If you're worried about it, just talk to her. She's been accepting of your wolf side so far. I bet she won't bat an eye."

I can only hope so. Before I can thank Colin for the bit of comfort, I hear familiar footsteps headed toward my cubicle. "It's Mrglsptz," I hiss, whirling my chair back to face my desk. "Better scram."

Colin takes me on my advice. He leaps—actually *leaps*—over the barrier between our cubicles, and I can hear Ssydra, the dragonborn who works next to me, croak in surprise. Serves her right. She's the nosey type and probably heard our whole conversation.

Still, she doesn't rat us out. By the time Mrglsptz arrives, I'm doing a fair impression of being busy. He snorts a little, but he must buy it, because he only says, "Get those reports finished, Evans," before he continues down the hall.

I sigh in relief. At least that's one problem solved. As for how to talk to Isabeau about the upcoming full moon, I'll have to figure that one out later.

***

"Where are you headed in such a hurry, baby?"

Isabeau loops an arm around my waist before I can slip quietly out of bed, pulling me back onto the mattress and into her embrace. It's only a gentle tug, but I can't resist. The covers are still warm, mostly from me, and her naked body is much too soft to abandon.

"Just need to pee," I whisper, but my bladder can wait. She's sapped my willpower to move.

"Sure, you weren't running out on me?" she murmurs, placing a soft kiss to the back of my shoulder.

I know she doesn't mean it. Isabeau and I have an understanding. It's not rude of me to leave for work in the mornings while she's asleep, but I always make sure to text her later so she can read my messages when she wakes up. Sometimes, though, she rouses herself enough to see me off. My stirring doesn't seem to bother her. In fact, she seems grateful for the chance to say goodbye.

"Never," I say, but then I realize that sounds a little too serious. I try my best to cover it with, "Are y'all awake-awake, or goin' back to sleep?"

"Awake," Isabeau mumbles, but from the way her nose wrinkles and her back arches as she yawns, I doubt that very much. She'll probably drift back off as soon as I leave the bed.

That's what makes me think this might be a good time to bring up my problem. It feels a bit sneaky, slipping it in while she's nice and cozy, but seeing her at ease puts me at ease too. I'm not sure whether I'll get the courage again.

"Uh, Izzy?" I turn around in her arms until we're facing each other, nearly brushing noses.

Isabeau cracks one cat's eye open to look at me. "Mm?"

"Um..." My words dry up. So much for the big bad wolf. I'm mostly a big chicken.

She opens her other eye, her brow wrinkling in concern. "What's wrong?"

"I can't see you the middle of this week. I've got something going on."

I could be reading into things, but I think I catch a hint of hurt on Isabeau's face. It disappears quickly, however. She's the type who always looks for the most positive explanation. "Oh. Do you want to tell me about it?"

I don't. I really don't. But I know I have to. Even someone as optimistic as Isabeau is bound to draw some sour conclusions once in a while. "It's a full moon," I explain, trying to sound casual. "So I've got a date with some Central Park trees and probably a few mud puddles."

Isabeau relaxes. "That's a relief. I thought you might have a date with someone besides me."

My face heats up. Yet again, that's something I hadn't even thought of. "Uh, no..." My mind jumps to the next car on the train. What if Isabeau asked that because *she's* seeing other people? I want to ask, and I think I know the answer, but I'm afraid, just in case I'm wrong.

"It would be okay if you did. Have a date with someone else, I mean. We're not exclusive yet."

I swallow. Isabeau has managed to raise my hopes and also dash them with just four words. 'We're not exclusive' hurts, more than it should since we haven't known each other more than two weeks, but the 'yet' is promising. Does that mean she wants to be, maybe?

My head's all fuzzy, and it's not half as confused as my heart, but Isabeau knows what to do. She rolls on top of me, kissing me softly and sliding her thigh between my legs. The rest of her body is cool, but her mouth is always warm enough for me.

"I'll see you after the full moon, right?" Isabeau asks, gazing down at me hopefully. "Once you get bored of chasing your tail?"

I laugh. Somehow, she knows just how to make me feel better. "Try and stop me."

She laughs too, but her brow furrows with worry after a moment. "I've heard a werewolf's change isn't easy. Not like a vampire's."

"Not like..."

"You know we can change too, right?" I blink in confusion. "Bats, Riley. Some of us can turn into bats."

"Yup. I get it."

I did know that, somewhere in the back of my mind, but I'd forgotten. I never got the chance to see many vampires before my move to the city, and Georgia public schools don't always do the best job of covering this stuff. It's comforting, though. Maybe Isabeau might understand after all.

"So, is there anything I can do to help? If there's any way I can make you more comfortable..."

"There's somethin' you can do for me right now." I slide my hands down her back to grip her ass, squeezing to show what I mean. I've always loved a girl with some decent padding on her, and Isabeau's curves fit just right with every angle I've got.

"Something?" Isabeau kisses me again, sliding her tongue slowly against my bottom lip. "Can you elaborate?"

"Sure can." I roll Isabeau onto her back, bracing myself on my elbows above her. Hopefully this won't make me late for work again, but if it does, I don't care.

***

Works more unbearable than usual the next two days. Even though it's the beginning of October, it's hotter than all hell and half of Georgia. I'm crawling with cold sweat, but my skin won't stop burning. By five o' clock, my sweater vest is gone, there are no buttons left on my shirt to unbutton, and my sleeves are rolled up past my elbows. I'm sure I must look a mess, mopping my brow with my arm to keep strands of damp hair from clinging.

It's not always this bad. My monthlies are, well, monthly, and I'm mostly used to the hot flashes and the jitters. But something about this full moon has me on edge. It just feels different, and I'm pretty sure it has to do with a certain vampire.

Isabeau's been keeping a bit of distance—at my insistence,

probably—but she still texts. A lot. Mostly it's about work, a picture of some pretty outfit she's seen, light stuff. But one question keeps cropping up, a question I'm having more and more trouble deflecting: 'Can I get you anything?'

I know she doesn't mean for right now. She means for tomorrow, when the full moon hits. She wants to help, to be a part of this. It's sweet, but also terrifying. Neither of us is much good at this dating thing, if that's what we're doing. I can't help remembering what she said the other day in bed, *'We're not exclusive yet.'* Isabeau isn't my girlfriend yet. Pretending she is could just set me up for more disappointment.

"Riley?"

I slam my phone down on my desk and swivel my chair around. It's only Colin, but I must look guilty, because his handsome face splits in a grin.

"Texting your vampire again?"

"Shh," I hiss. "Phones ai...aren't allowed at work. Are you tryin' to get me in trouble?"

Colin doesn't seem to be listening as he leans against one wall of my cubicle. "You're not denying it, though."

I sigh. This is what happens when you have friends at work. "Maybe..."

"Still worried about what she'll think when she sees the furrier you?"

It's annoying how Colin always gets right to the heart of things. He's too perceptive for his own good. "I dunno, she's seen a lot of fur so far," I say, but it falls flat. I'm even too nervous for dumb jokes.

"I bet she has." Colin waggles his eyebrows, but his expression quickly turns serious.

Uh-oh. I know that look. He's about to give me dating advice. One thing I don't need from a playboy selkie.

"You're overthinking this. She knew you were a werewolf when she met you. What does she think you turn into every month, a chipmunk?"

"If only..."

"If this wolf thing is bothering you so much, why don't you get it over with? Give her a chance to run for the hills. At least that way, you'll know whether you're wasting your time...and I can say I told you so."

I mumble something noncommittal. It's not as straightforward as Colin says it is. Sometimes girls *do* run for the hills. I've seen it happen before more than once.

"Look," he says, pushing off the wall and putting a hand on my shoulder, "I get it. Opening up to people is scary. I've been there. But if there's one thing I've learned dating while trans, it's that worthwhile people stick around to ask questions, and the trash takes itself out."

"Yeah, but you got a dick when you changed. I get teeth that can rip a person in half."

"Do I detect a bit of jealousy?"

Maybe I am jealous, a bit, but that's a conversation for another day. I've got enough on my plate without thinking about gender issues. The wolf issue is much more pressing. "I get your point. I'll think about it."

"Thatta girl. Thinking's better than worrying." Colin claps my shoulder one more time, then leaves my cubicle.

"Sounds like the same thing to me," I say, but he's already out of earshot, sneaking back to his own desk before Mrglsptz or someone else catches him slacking off.

Once he's gone, I pick up a stray pen from my desk and start gnawing on the cap, which is already riddled with teeth marks. After a few seconds of chewing, the plastic splits, and the sour taste of ink leaks onto my tongue. I swallow and stick my tongue out in disgust, reaching for the gum I keep on the corner of my desk. I've gotta find something better to chew on.

***

Central Park doesn't just look different at night than it does during the day. It smells different too. The scent of stubbed-out cigarettes and fried food has mostly dissolved into the air, leaving behind wet leaves and earth along with the scent of the reservoir. Rain's coming, bringing a heavy sort of dampness in the air, but even that is comforting. It's the closest thing to home I can find in the city.

Normally, the park closes at one, but tonight, it's open 'til five just for us. I see a few other people strolling along the jogging track a couple hundred yards away, heads turned to watch the glowing line of the pink sunset sink behind the silhouette of distant buildings. Most are wolves like me, judging by the smell, but there's a trace of cat nearby. They like to prowl when they change too, although they stick to the trees and leave the ground to the packs.

Technically, I'm not part of a pack up here. In a big city, that kind of thing involves membership dues, meetings, and social events. It's not like back home, where your pack is your parents, grandparents, a few aunts and uncles, and a dozen weird cousins. Down south, everybody knows everybody. Up here, it's more like an exclusive club, one I don't wanna waste my time joining. It's not so bad, though, being a lone wolf. Most of the time, it suits me fine.

As I park myself on a bench facing the reservoir, watching the last rippling reflections of light disappear from the water, my phone buzzes in my pocket. I pull it out a bit too quick. Despite the awkwardness of the past few days, I'm hoping it's Isabeau before I even fumble past the home screen.

It's not. Colin's name is on the screen, along with a dopey looking dog emoji next to a wheel of cheese. I roll my eyes, but I also crack a smile. Instead of putting my phone away, I gaze out over the water once more. It's beautiful here. Even the autumn chill feels nice. I almost wish I'd asked Isabeau to come with me.

She's just doing what you asked. You told her you wouldn't be in touch. You were the one who pulled away. But now, trembling on the edge of my change, I'm starting to regret it. Maybe Colin had been right for once.

I pull up my camera and snap a picture of the reservoir just before the sun sets. Then I pull up Isabeau's text thread and send it to her. She responds almost immediately, like she's been waiting for me to text first. 'It's beautiful there'.

I start to type 'yeah', but after staring at the unsent text for a few seconds, I delete it. I can't stop thinking about what Colin said. Maybe he's right. Maybe I should take a risk and ask Isabeau to stop by after all. What's the worst that could happen?

She could head for the hills screaming, the negative voice in my head says. *It's happened before loads of times.*

But part of me can't help hoping Isabeau is better than that. She's not some human going out with me on a dare to piss off her daddy. She's fifty years old and drinks blood to live. Surely watching me change can't be that strange.

Fine. Do it if you want to. But when your fool heart gets hurt, remember I told you so.

I shut the negative voice down. I don't want to hear what it says anymore. Instead, I text Isabeau. *'Are you free? Can you stop by?'* It takes all the courage I have to hit send.

To my relief, she replies almost immediately. *'Can I bring anything?'*

'Just yourself. I'm by the reservoir, on a bench near the jogging track.'

'Ok.'

Isabeau doesn't reply after that, but I take that as a good sign. It probably means she's on her way. Meanwhile, my stomach is a mess of nervous knots. My hairs raised more than a long-tailed cat's in a rocking chair factory, and I don't even have all of it yet. My skin starts to itch, and I can feel the tips of my fingers and the tops of my ears heat up. It's happening. I don't have a lot of time.

Thankfully, there is a grove of trees not too far behind the bench, and werewolves aren't much for modesty. We can't afford to be. I slip behind a wide trunk for a bit of privacy and strip off my pants. I've made the mistake of waiting too long to take them off before, and it never ends well. Clothes are too expensive to keep on replacing them.

Underwear comes next, then my shirt and binder. The night air should be cold on my naked skin, but I'm burning too hot to notice. It just sort of tingles, and the soft gusts of wind send little nervous zips down my spine. As the last of the light slips away behind the shadowy skyscrapers in the distance, I turn off my phone and hide it under my clothes. Hopefully Isabeau will be able to find me—if she doesn't chicken out.

As soon as the pale glow of the moon peeks through the dark blue clouds, the pain hits. It's not unbearable. I'm used to it after all these years, but it makes me grit my teeth. My muscles cramp up, tensing beneath my skin. Sweat breaks out across my body, but then it melts away as fur sprouts in its place. My limbs lengthen. My knees and elbows crack as they reshape. My bones scream as they stretch, and my teeth jut out past my lips.

When I raise my nose to the sky, it's long and pointed enough for me to see it in front of my face. I can smell everything: the green growth of the trees, the distant smoke of the city, even other wolves close by. I close my eyes. My thoughts slow down, becoming shorter. There are less words. More feelings. Finally, the pain fades. My body feels right. My tongue lolls from my mouth, tasting night. Still early, still fresh. I want to run. Run far and fast. My legs stretch, claws scoring the soft earth. No. Can't run. Have to stay. Waiting for someone. Izzy. My tail wags. Izzy. I hope she comes. Hope...

Rustling echoes above me. I look up. The sky isn't dark anymore. It's all sorts of colors. Blue, purple, black. Other things English has no names for. Stars are shining, except in one small dot. Something is flying. Falling leaves? No. I smell something. Something alive. A small creature swoops down. Bat? Bat! Izzy!

I sing hello.

Izzy swoops down. She's big, maybe the size of my face. Her fur is brown and silver. She sings hello back in her tiny voice. She came. Izzy came. There are so many things I want to show her. The way the water looks at night. The best scratching trees. The best smelling logs. The best grass to roll in. I run, following my nose, while she flies above me. I sprint. She soars. We hit the wind together. The park is all ours.

***

Hours later, we walk the empty track around the reservoir. Izzy has changed back. I haven't yet. She talks, even though I can't talk back. "Thanks for asking me to come. I wanted to. I just didn't want to make you uncomfortable."

I nudge her shoulder with my nose. She's wearing my clothes and I'm happy she smells like me. *It's okay, Izzy.*

"I know your change is different from mine. I can control it, and you're at the whim of the moon. But I hope seeing me in my other form helped."

I whine. Lick the side of her arm. *Yes. It did help.*

"Not all of us are bats, you know. Some turn into cats. Some become mice. A couple can even change into dogs."

I like you as a bat. You can keep up with me in the air.

She smiles, reaching up to scratch between my ears. "You're a good listener, Riley. Not just like this, either. But...I must admit, you look even more like a golden retriever now than you usually do."

I plant my rear on the ground and growl. Izzy turns toward me. Our faces are the same height.

"Oh, don't be like that. I'm sorry, but it's the truth. Look at all this fluffy golden fur." She runs her hands through my coat, scratching behind my ears.

I let her do it. I'm a pushover.

"Who's a happy wolf?" she coos.

I slurp against the side of her face to shut her up.

"Ew," she shrieks, but she giggles as she pulls away. She swipes her arm over her cheek. "No kisses until you turn back, okay?"

Kisses. I could do with some of those. I look past her head, toward the sky. Is it pink yet? Yes. I can feel the sun creeping up. It's faint but warm in the distance, just out of reach.

As the first rays break over the tops of the trees, I begin to change. My limbs shorten, reshaping themselves. My hair recedes. My muzzle shrinks until I've got a normal nose again. I rise on two legs to greet the dawn, stretching out the kinks in my spine. Jesus, Mary, and Joseph, turning into a wolf and back again can leave a body sore.

That's when I notice Isabeau. She's got my shirt pulled up over her head and her arms tucked inside to protect herself. Suddenly, I realize I'm not the only one who's uncomfortable. Isabeau's stayed with me until the sun rose, and I bet she hasn't reapplied her lotion recently.

"C'mon," I say, shepherding her out of the faint sunlight and toward the shadowy grove of trees where I'd first changed. "They've got spare clothes for any wolves that lose theirs during the night. I'll get you some."

"Naked?" Isabeau's voice is slightly muffled with my shirt pulled over her face.

I clear my throat. "I don't mind none. Won't be but a moment."

Leaning into kiss her, then realizing there isn't any bare skin to kiss, I go for an awkward, scratchy hug instead and jog toward the nearest supply tent. I'm not worried over my nakedness, but I wish I had my binder. Running with breasts is a chore.

The werewolf at the tent smirks when he sees me, but thankfully, his eyes stay in polite places. He seems amused more than anything. "Need some spares?" he asks, turning around to dig in a cardboard box behind him.

"For a friend," I say.

"A friend. Sure. What size?"

"Really, for a friend," I insist. "Biggest you got."

He pulls out a damned ugly green and brown sweater, vaguely Christmas-themed, and a pair of grey sweatpants. I take them with a nod of thanks. They aren't fashionable, but I figure Isabeau will be grateful for anything that covers skin.

With a mumbled 'Thanks', I head back to where I left Isabeau, only to find her curled up behind a large tree. She doesn't seem any worse for wear, and she even peeks out at me from over the neckline of my shirt. Her slitted pupils are even narrower than usual. She snorts when she sees what I've brought for her.

"Well...at least it's colorful."

I pass the sweater over. "As long as it covers."

Isabeau is apparently very good at putting on new clothes without taking off her old ones. With some amount of squirming, she manages to trade my shirt for the sweater without showing more than a few strips of skin. She pulls the ugly green fabric up over face too, until only her brown hair poofs out through the top.

"Can you even see with it over your face like that?"

Isabeau chuckles from inside the sweater. "Yes, actually. I can see just fine."

The emphasis of her words has me blushing. I'm still naked as a jaybird, and I just know she's eyeing me through the stretched material of the sweater. I square my shoulders a little and suck in my gut. Might as well give her something nice to ogle.

I put on the sweatpants and let her keep mine. Then I put on my binder and shirt and stick my phone in one of the deep pockets. Not only does Isabeau smell kind of like me, but a bit of her scent has rubbed off on my shirt, so I smell a bit like her coconut suntan lotion too.

Somehow, we manage to leave Central Park without injuring ourselves. I'm bare footed, since Isabeau is wearing my oversized tennies, and I can only see a thin slice of her forehead and the tops of her long lashes, but with me guiding her, we get on all right. We pass a few other folks on the way, weres of various sorts. Most of 'em look tired and happy, like they've run themselves ragged and are ready for a nice long nap. Isabeau attracts a few stares. I can't tell whether it's the awful sweater, or whether they're picking up the faint scent of copper, but my presence seems to steer the nosiest people away. It's pretty obvious she's with me.

"Mind if we go to mine?" I ask as we walk past the uniformed guards watching the entrance. "It's closer."

"Please."

Thankfully it's just a couple blocks. Underneath the shade of the skyscrapers, Isabeau is able to poke her head out at last. She looks a bit like a turtle creeping out of its shell, and I can't help but laugh.

Isabeau rolls her eyes. "Don't look at me like that. How was I supposed to bring extra clothes as a bat?"

"You didn't have to stay 'til sunrise. You coulda flown home."

"Yes, I could have…" We arrive in front of my apartment building, and she slips a hand out of the sweater's oversized sleeve, groping for mine. "But I'm glad I stayed."

I link our fingers together. "Me too."

We take the elevator to my floor together. Isabeau rests her head against my shoulder, yawning slightly. The way her nose wrinkles reminds me a little of how she'd looked as a bat.

"This is bedtime for you, huh? You can grab a few winks in my bed if you want."

"Don't you have work?" Isabeau asks, but her eyelids are already drooping.

"Nope. Legally, I get one day off for 'scheduled transformation purposes'. Just gotta make up the hours here and there."

"So, you're saying we can wallow in bed together for a few hours?" Isabeau gives a dreamy sigh. "That sounds like heaven."

We leave the elevator and head down the hall to my apartment. Isabeau kicks off my shoes near the door and untangles herself from the huge green sweater. Once she's naked, she flops straight onto my bed, burying her face in my pillow. I strip too, cuddling up beside her. She's cool, but I don't mind. Her skin feels soothing against my hot flesh. The two of us fall asleep together, nestled among the blankets without bothering to climb underneath them.

***

I wake up to warm lips on my neck and cold fingers dancing along my side. I squirm, unsure whether I want to press into the ticklish touch or pull away from it. Eventually, I press into it, and I'm glad I do. Isabeau pulls me closer, pressing her breasts into my back.

"Hey."

I turn to look over my shoulder. Isabeau's hair is more flyaway than usual, and her hazel eyes still look sleepy. I kiss the tip of her nose. "Hey yourself."

Her beautiful smile stretches all the way across her face. "About last night..."

I hold my breath. Even though I know Isabeau can't possibly be freaked out now after spending the whole night by my side, my reflex is to cringe. My mind starts racing. It's like Cindy Lou Castle all over again.

"Thank you, Riley. For trusting me."

"Yeah?" I exhale heavily. "Well, thanks for stayin'."

She laughs softly. "I still say you look like a golden retriever."

"You don't have no room to talk. You're a *bat*. At least golden retrievers don't eat bugs."

"Well, mosquitoes and I do have a lot in common."

I roll over beneath Isabeau's arm so I can face her. "Naw. Their bites itch. Your bites..." The bed's still warm from our nap, but I can't help shuddering. "Well, you won't hear me complain."

Isabeau's smirk shows the tips of her fangs. "Really? Because I haven't eaten since yesterday afternoon."

"Say no more."

I wiggle closer, tilting up my chin and scooching so my shoulder is near her mouth.

"Are you sure? I know you must be tired." But there's a flash of hunger in her eyes I can't ignore.

It's my turn to wrap my arm around Isabeau's waist. "It's fine. I don't mind being your midnight...uh..." With the windows closed and my phone who knows where, I can't actually tell what time it is. "Noon snack?"

"It's closer to four. We've been out for almost ten hours."

"That makes it your dinnertime. Close enough."

Isabeau moans with gratitude. Her lips graze my collarbone, just kissing at first, and heat coils in my belly. She's bitten me a couple of times now, but it still makes me nervous. Not the bad kind of nervous, more like the kind when you're about to go down a waterslide head first and you don't have full control.

I moan as Isabeau starts sucking the crook of my throat. She's found a spot; I can feel her running the sharp tips of her teeth over it, but she doesn't sink them in. She's teasing.

"Please?" It's embarrassing to beg, but I'm not too proud either.

Her fangs pierce my neck and my hips give a jolt. My body is suddenly flooded with warmth. The heat starts at the top of my spine, radiating down my arms and legs, finally settling deep in my pelvis. A low throb starts there, pulsing in time with the blood Isabeau is drawing from me.

While she drinks, I pet her hair. It's extra fluffy after our nap, and as I stroke it, she makes a pleased little moan against my skin. The soft vibration shoots right between my thighs. The heat there is starting to get sticky. Isabeau must realize, because I can feel her full lips smiling around the sensitive patch of skin she's sucking.

We stay like that for a couple minutes, her pulling from the artery in my neck, me trying to ignore the growing ache between my legs. It doesn't hurt, but it goes from pleasant to uncomfortable pretty quick. My clit starts twitching as streams of wetness slide down my inner thighs.

Isabeau breaks her seal when she notices my squirming. I can tell from her glassy eyes she isn't quite full, but she seems a little more awake. "Are you okay, Riley?"

"Just sore. Not 'cuz of you. Changing takes a lot out of me."

"Sore, huh?" Isabeau urges me to lie on my stomach. "Maybe I can help..." She straddles the backs of my thighs, running her hands up along either side of my spine to squeeze the tops of my shoulders.

Her cool palms feel like heaven on my overheated skin. "You're an angel," I mumble into the pillow.

Isabeau bends down to kiss the nape of my neck. "Not quite. But I do give pretty good massages."

She kneads my shoulders until I've melted into a puddle on the comforter. All my knots dissolve under her circling thumbs, and I moan quietly whenever her warm lips touch my back. Sometimes her teeth nick my skin, but the little bites never hurt. They just make me shiver.

Isabeau moves lower, until her hands are in the middle of my back and her knees are pressing in on either side of mine. The heat between my legs is near boiling as she presses her thumbs into the dimples at the base of my spine. The muscles there are tender enough to coax a whimper out of me.

"Is this too hard?" Isabeau murmurs against my back.

"Nnn..." I can't form words. I spread my thighs open, hoping she'll get the picture.

She does. One of her hands pauses to cup the swell of my ass, and then she traces two fingers inward, heading between my legs.

Another jolt runs through me as Isabeau's fingertips slide on either side of my clit. She doesn't touch the tip, just strokes the shaft through its hood until I'm slippery and swollen. My stomach does a flip. This is a pretty vulnerable position for me, flat on my stomach with Isabeau sitting on top of my legs. But it's also kind of nice. Sometimes, even the big bad wolf needs a little taking care of.

"This is what you needed, right?" Isabeau purrs. She places another wet kiss to the middle of my back, and I claw at the covers. I'm not just a puddle, I'm a whole ocean, and half of it's dripping from between my legs into Isabeau's hand. She stops rubbing my clit, moving her fingers down to my grasping entrance. "Do you want me inside?"

I bite my lip. My ears have started itching and my skin could sprout hair any second. But for once, I'm not afraid of it. Isabeau's seen me as a wolf. Going feral is nothing compared to that.

"Yeah..."

Isabeau slides inside, slow and deep. Her fingers do things to me that just aren't fair. She doesn't thrust, but she hooks forward, searching for the puffy place that makes me howl. When she hits it, I'm a goner. Pressure shoots through me, and I clutch tight around her curling fingers, trying to hold them in place.

While I hit my peak, Isabeau slides her thumb over my clit. She rubs the tip this time, spreading my wetness around and around. She kisses a sloppy trail back up to my shoulder and takes a few more pulls from the base of my neck, but aside from the extra spike of warmth, I hardly notice. Between her fingers and her thumb, I've plumb forgot how to breathe.

By the time my hips stop quivering, there's a sticky stain under me. I'm trembling all over, but at the same time, I'm totally relaxed. There isn't a bit of tension anywhere in my body. Isabeau has worked it all out. I try to say something, a thank you at least, but all that comes out in a soft groan.

Isabeau releases me with a soft pop. "Better?" she whispers underneath my ear.

I blink to try and clear my head. I'm dizzy, but I don't think it's from blood loss. It's gotta be the orgasm I just had. "Uh-huh..."

"Good." She pulls out and drapes herself over me, almost like a cool blanket. Her springy curls tickle the back of my neck and her nose nuzzles into the crook of my shoulder. It's comfy, but I can feel my strength coming back. Isabeau's done so much for me already. I want to show her how much I appreciate her, too.

I squirm out from underneath her, tipping her onto her back. Isabeau looks surprised, but also pleased as I climb on top of her. "I thought you might go to sleep."

"Naw." I take her wrists, lifting them gently and urging her to wrap her hands around the slats in my headboard. "I'm a service top. We don't leave ladies unsatisfied."

Isabeau chuckles. "Service top? You didn't look like a service top just now."

"I know how to take turns too."

Isabeau just grins up at me. Her smile is so bright, and even without the lights on, my glowing eyes can pick up the golden highlights in her brown skin. Well, if she doesn't believe me, I'll just have to prove it. I kiss her, teasing her lips apart with my tongue and guiding one of her knees around my waist. I start a subtle grind, pumping my hips until I feel her wetness paint my belly. She's already hot and slick, a contrast to the rest of her skin.

I can tell Isabeau wants to wrap her arms around me, but she settles for both her legs instead. We shift and arch together, her clinging to the headboard, me holding her hips and helping her rub against my stomach. It's times like this I wish I had a strap-on or something, so I could thrust inside her.

Isabeau seems to be managing just fine without one, though. She nips at my neck without biting down, making little whimpers every time I push against her. Her lips are spread open and she's wet enough for me to feel the point of her clit as she bucks up into me. I tighten my abdomen. Apparently, the extra muscle that comes with being a werewolf can be useful.

"Riley…" She mumbles my name against my ear with ticklish breaths. "Yes, just like that…"

I keep hold of Isabeau's hips as I kiss down her collarbone toward her chest. Her nipples are thick and dark, drawn into stiff peaks. I take one in my mouth, rolling my tongue around the tip. Isabeau arches, pulling the headboard hard enough to make the whole bed creak. I don't care. This is a piece of shit bedframe anyway. If it breaks, it breaks.

As I kiss across to her other breast, Isabeau's hips take up a faster rhythm. Or, they try to. I hold her steady, forcing her to go at my pace. I don't want this to end too fast. I want to make her feel as good as she made me feel. I want to show her how beautiful she is, how much I appreciate her.

Isabeau's thighs are soft and yielding as I slide my hands down them. I grip her ass, squeezing it in my hands, helping her lift as she rocks against my stomach. She's close. She has to be, the way she's twitching against me, beneath me. Even though I've already come, I'm aching too just watching her. Feeling her shudder and shake beneath me, smelling how ready she is to be taken, brings out more of my wild side than the full moon.

"Riley," she gasps again, louder this time. "Baby, please, make me come."

I groan into her chest. It's hard to choose which part of that sentence I love most. I love the way she says my name, the way she calls me baby, and *especially* the way she's begging me to come. I don't have the heart to deny her. Isabeau's been so good to me already. I bite the tender skin above her breast and speed up for a few more slippery thrusts.

Isabeau seizes up, throwing her head back and shivering all over. A rush of heat spills out of her, smearing my stomach, sliding everywhere. I can feel all her soft parts pulsing against my skin. It's exhilarating. I've never made a girl come just by rubbing against her before. But as hot as it is, it doesn't feel like enough. Isabeau's hips are still giving short little jerks, and even though she's coming, her whines are getting louder.

I let go of my grip on her ass and bring one hand between us, slipping two fingers inside her. There isn't even a bit of resistance. Isabeau stiffens, sighs, and I watch as a huge smile spreads across her face. Her silky walls clamp down tight around me, rippling and pulsing as she finishes coming in my palm.

I start thrusting, pressing the heel of my hand into Isabeau's clit until I'm sure she's finished. It takes a while, but she keeps her hands on the headboard through the whole thing. She's a vision, graceful arms stretched above her head, her whole body open to me. I kiss light circles around her nipples until she stops trembling and the stream of heat running down my wrist subsides.

Isabeau's eyes flutter shut for a moment, but when she opens them, they're full of joy. "Okay," she laughs, "you win. You're a service top. For now."

"I better be." I kiss the point of her chin. "'Cuz you look happy as a Junebug."

She giggles again and rolls her eyes. "Never stop talking the way you do, Riley. It's cute."

Normally, I would bristle at being called 'cute'. But since it's Isabeau, I don't mind. "As cute as a golden retriever?"

"Cuter."

Isabeau lets go of the headboard, winding her arms around me. I'm a little shocked the bed made it, but happier she's holding me. "Hey, Riley..." She runs her fingertips down my back, digging one heel lightly into the back of my leg. "You're still inside me."

I have to swallow down the moisture that rises in my mouth. "Yup." I can still feel her clenching faintly around her fingers.

"So...will you make me come again? Please?"

I catch her lips in a deep kiss and start thrusting. I doubt she'll take long, but I'm gonna try and make it last.

Rae D. Magdon

Chapter Four - Isabeau

"SERIOUSLY, IZZY, WHERE DO you get all this junk? Just this closet could be its own museum! There's some delusional curator out in Portland who'd pay through the nose for vintage neon everything."

I crawl out from the overstuffed bedroom closet I'm half-buried in, brushing stray dust bunnies off my leggings. This is one of the serious downsides of living forever, or in my case, living unchanged for the past twenty years. I've had two decades to collect a bunch of stuff I don't actually need.

"What did you find?" I ask, picking myself up off the floor.

Elyse, my best friend and boss, is currently sitting cross-legged in the middle of a junkpile—old scarves, knitted hats, and even a few stuffed animals. A large cardboard box with bright blue duct tape along one side is sitting in her lap. The corners look thin and frayed, almost like they're going to split apart.

"No idea, but judging from the dust, I'm guessing it hasn't been touched in at least ten years. You really need to clean more often. I already found a middle school yearbook from 1983 and a box full of slap bracelets. Slap bracelets, Izzy."

"I do clean," I protest, but I'm quickly distracted by the sea of treasure around her. "So, where are those slap bracelets?"

"Here." Elyse shoves an old shoebox in my direction. "Knock yourself out. It's not like we have the rest of your apartment to clean..."

I cough in embarrassment. We haven't even gotten to the bathroom yet and I don't want to think about all the empty makeup tubes I'll find that I haven't touched since the turn of the century.

"...just because you're bringing some girl to your place regularly now."

"She's not 'some girl'. Her name is Riley." I slap one of the plastic bracelets around my wrist. Fortunately, it still works. It's a bunch of smiling rainbows with eyes—pride colors, although that's pure coincidence. "Which you already know, because I've seen her contact information in your phone, and I've caught you Googling her at work."

"Until she passes the Best Friend Inspection, which is both arbitrary and specific, because I love you, she's just 'some girl' to me. Look, I believe that you believe she's a mensch, but until I see how great she supposedly is myself, I'm not gonna know for sure." Elyse takes a slap bracelet out of the shoebox and snaps it around her wrist, a blue one with glittery ocean waves. "What?" she says reproachfully when I give her a look. "I lived through the '80s too. I'm a year older than you."

"And yet you still act like you're my mother," I grumble.

"Really? You think this is my overprotective Jewish mother routine? You've met my actual mother, right? You know, the one who thinks I'm dead if I leave the house and don't text her five minutes later to say I got the subway? I'm just showing regular friendly concern."

I roll my eyes, but Elyse has a point. Her mother is a handful, which makes me glad we never dated. "I'll introduce Riley to you, I promise. I just...it's new, okay? And scary. The last time you met someone I was dating—"

"Natasha, I know. But introducing your girlfriend to your best friend isn't a curse. And trust me, I know curses. I've had to undo my fair share of them."

I take another bracelet out of the box and slap it on my other wrist, a pink one this time. "She's not my girlfriend," I protest, but it sounds weak even to my ears. While it's true that Riley and I aren't technically girlfriends, it feels like we're headed in that direction. She'd looked visibly disappointed a few weeks ago during the full moon when I'd reminded her we weren't exclusive. Strangely, her disappointment had actually made me feel hopeful.

"But you want her to be, right?" Elyse asks, leaning forward over the box. She looks eager for details, in only the way a nosey best friend can.

I adjust the patterned pink scarf I've tied over my hair to protect it, shrugging helplessly. "I guess. It's just been a while since I had an actual girlfriend. I'm out of practice."

"Yes, you're extremely rusty with this whole 'I like her, she likes me, we have great sex and are more or less emotionally cognizant of one another' thing. How tragic. Speaking of which..." Elyse nods at the box. "You want me to open it? You know, in case it's from The Dark Beforetimes? The 80s really weren't your worst era, if you think about it."

"I had braces and headgear. They definitely weren't my best."

"All recorded for posterity in that yearbook, and soon to be posted on instagram from my phone."

I glare at her. "You wouldn't dare."

She ignores me. "So? Is that a yes or a no?"

I lean back with a sigh, bracing my weight on my hands. "Yeah, sure, go for it."

Elyse grabs a boxcutter from the nearby desk and slices open one of the sloppily taped seams. The sound of cardboard scratching against cardboard sends a shudder down my spine, and I wince until Elyse manages to pull it open. Her eyes widen in surprise as she peers in, then her lips twitch in a smirk. "Uh, Izzy?" She pulls out a pair of velvet-lined black handcuffs, dangling them from one finger. "You wanna tell me what era this is from?"

My face burns. Of course, I've told her to open a box full of bondage stuff. "I completely forgot about this," I say, half-pleading without really knowing what I'm pleading for. Mercy, I guess. She'll probably tease me about this for the next decade.

"So, is this your Natasha-era, or from before? Or after, even?"

I sit up with a groan, burying my forehead in my hand. The rainbows on my wrist stare back up at me, mocking me. "Yeah, that's Natasha-era. Just get rid of the box, okay? Let's pretend we never found it."

"Uh-huh," Elyse says, but she doesn't make any attempt to close it back up. Instead, she begins sorting through it, drawing out even more embarrassing items. There's a pair of padded black restraints, as well as some soft red rope and lots of silk scarves. "I knew you were a bondage bunny, but this is a lot of stuff. There are doubles of almost everything in here! What, were you worried they'd break from overuse? Pretty sure they don't mean wear and tear quite so literally, Izzy..." She withdraws a slightly bent but well-made riding crop, swishing the hard leather tab through the air so it makes a whistling noise. "If you don't want this, can I have it?"

"No, you cannot." I snatch the crop from her, tucking it under my thighs and sitting on it so she can't get to it.

"Why are you so protective of a bunch of gear you're just going to throw away?" Elyse pulls something out from the bottom of the box: a gleaming steel spreader bar. "You're not emotionally attached to this stuff, are you?"

I chew my lip. It's a complicated question. I'm not emotionally attached to this stuff in particular, but bondage is a part of me. A sorely neglected part of me, since I can't do it with just anyone, but a part of me, nonetheless. There's something freeing about being tied up and vulnerable, completely at someone else's mercy. At least, when that someone isn't a cheating asshole and habitual liar.

Elyse notices my silence. "You wouldn't have boxed it up back then if you wanted to trash it, huh?"

I sigh, then shake my head no.

"Then do you want to keep it?"

I shake my head again. It reminds me of Natasha.

"Well, other than donating this stuff, or at least some of it since you have so very much to spare, to your awesome friend as payment for services rendered, those are your only two options. You need to pick one or the other."

I groan and lean back, lying on the cushion of my hair and staring up at the ceiling. "Ugh, I don't know."

"Do you want my opinion?" The question is a bit of a surprise, since Elyse usually offers opinions without being asked for them.

"Do I have a choice?"

"You always have a choice. Just because I talk doesn't mean you have to listen. But really, I think this one's pretty clear: keep this stuff and use it with Riley."

"Wait, what? No. That's..." I fiddle with the slap bracelet on my wrist. "That's weird, right? How would I even bring it up? 'Hey, Riley. I found a bunch of bondage stuff in my closet that my shitty ex and I used to use. Wanna play with it?'"

"You could work on your delivery a little, but yes. That's basically how you would bring it up. Might want to lead more with the whole 'I want to do this with you' angle, then bring up your ex and unload your tragic backstory in one conversation." Elyse sets the box aside and crawls over to join me by the closet. "Hey," she says, hovering over me with a small, reassuring smile on her face. "This isn't like you, Izzy. You wear the tallest heels and the boldest lipsticks of anyone I know. There's no reason to hide from any of this. These are all good things, remember? And if Riley is the person you so enthusiastically believe that she is, well, she'll probably just want to make you happy. Not like that shemdrick."

I wince. Natasha is a sore spot for me, even twenty years later. Back then, before everything had fallen apart, the two of us had been so happy. Before her face can solidify in my mind, I think about Riley. We haven't known each other long, but Riley is Natasha's opposite in every way. She's a little shy, but brave when it counts, like asking me to come to Central Park with her during the last full moon. She's honest, and she doesn't care too much about impressing other people. She's just herself.

"Okay," I say, scooting back and sitting up. "You win. I'll do it."

"Really? I thought I'd have to wear you down for another fifteen minutes. Then break for lunch, rework the whole spiel, and go at it for another thirty or so. But this is good, too. Great, even." A sly smirk spreads across Elyse's face. "You've got the itch, huh?"

Elyse isn't wrong. I glance at my bed, a shudder racing down my spine. It's not too hard to picture myself spread-eagle on the mattress, tied to the bedposts while Riley stalks across the room toward me. She looks and acts more like a golden retriever than a wolf most of the time, but there has to be a predator buried deep inside her.

"Maybe a little."

Elyse dumps all the stuff she's been rummaging through back into the box and shoves it toward me. "Okay. But I'm taking these." She grabs the shoebox full of slap bracelets.

"Like hell you are." I reach for the other end of the box and tug.

Elyse keeps pulling. "Trust me, they'll ruin your fashion-forward vibe."

"There's a thing called retro. Learn it."

"Retro is for the West Village, and clothing designers when they run out of ideas every twenty years. Which means I'm taking the bracelets."

"You just want them all for yourself."

"To recycle them, hopefully," Elyse insists. "Lord only knows with plastic this old."

"Stop lying." I finally succeed in snatching the box from her. "Here." I grab a few handfuls and toss them onto her lap. "You can have some of them."

Elyse sighs. "Yay," she says, in an absolutely unenthused voice. "Just what I always wanted. I'll be sure to wear one to President Reagan's inauguration, though they might take away attention from my formal parachute pants."

I roll my eyes. "You're hilarious. Keep it up and I won't buy you pizza later."

"You'd better, and God help you if it doesn't have pineapple on it."

I wrinkle my nose in disgust, but don't say anything. I don't want to get into that argument, and since I don't really eat much food anymore, Elyse claims my opinion doesn't count. "Fine. Eat your gross pizza. As long as you help me finish."

Elyse smirks. "I don't think I'll be the one helping you finish…"

I should be annoyed, but the stupid joke sends a lance of heat through my belly. I look at the box sitting beside Elyse's knee. I still don't know how I'm going to bring this up to Riley, but I definitely have the motivation.

***

I hold a scented candle in each hand, leaning in to sniff them one by one. The first is soothing lavender and sandalwood; the other is creamy vanilla with hints of orange. I almost always have some kind of candle burning in my apartment when I'm home, but today, the choice feels extra important. Riley is coming over to spend the night, and I want to set the right mood.

Eventually, I go with the second candle. I put the first candle away and carry the vanilla and orange one into the kitchen to find the lighter. Hopefully, the smell won't be strong enough to bother Riley's sensitive nose.

I've just put the lit candle in the bedroom when my phone buzzes. It's a text from Riley:

I'm waiting outside 🖤

I take a deep breath and adjust the front of my dress. It's a pink wrap that flows off my right hip under the waist tie, but most important of all, it has a slit up one leg. If Riley's eyes don't go there in the first five seconds, she sees me, I'll pull a unicorn's tail. My phone buzzes again:

Am I early?

I hurry over to the door, only slowing down the last couple of steps. I'm more nervous now than I was during our first few dates. Strangely, it feels like there's much more at stake, or maybe my fears are totally logical and I'm being too hard on myself. My previous relationship track record hasn't been great, after all.

There's a soft knock on the other side of the door just before I open it. I turn the knob to see Riley standing in the hallway, holding some steaming cardboard boxes in her hands.

"Heya," she drawls, grinning with one side of her mouth quirked up higher than the other.

My heart melts and I completely forget my nervousness. Soft butches have always been my biggest weakness, and Riley is almost cute enough to make me squeal. She's even got a dapper blue bowtie on, which makes her doubly adorable.

"Hey yourself." I step back, remaining close enough to lean in and give her a peck on the cheek.

She flushes slightly, shifting the weight of the boxes. "I stopped by the Chinese place near my house to bring y'all some food…then I remembered you don't eat much food, so I just bought myself some." She dips her head a bit in embarrassment.

"Don't worry. It was still a sweet thought." I take the boxes, enjoying the warmth that seeps from the cardboard bottoms into my cold hands as I carry them to the kitchen. "Besides, you did bring me a meal."

Riley blinks in confusion as she follows me. "Huh? Oh! Oh…" She clears her throat, rubbing the back of her neck. "I didn't wanna assume."

I set the takeout boxes on the counter. "Baby, you can always say no, but let's just roll with the assumption that I'm pretty much constantly hungry."

Riley's smile spreads wider. "Yeah?"

"Mmhmm."

"For, uh, the sex part? Or for my blood?"

I take another two steps toward her, draping my arms over her shoulders. It's hard not to chuckle at her awkward phrasing. "Both."

If Riley had been in possession of her tail at that moment, I'm sure she would have wagged it. "Good! I mean…great. Great and good. Oh, hell with it." She leans in, pressing her lips to mine. It's soft and gentle at first, but the heat of her mouth sends a jolt through me. I groan and open my lips, and Riley wastes no time teasing them with her tongue. By the time we pull back, we're both breathless.

"What was that for?" I ask her.

"Figured it was about time I stopped babbling and did something smarter with my mouth."

I run my thumb over her lips. They're slightly chapped from the November cold and she's got a smudge of pink lip gloss on them from me. Somehow, this seems like the perfect time to tell her, while we're still tingling from our first kiss of the evening. "By the way, I've got something to show you."

Riley's thick blonde eyebrows arch in surprise. She sniffs and lowers them again. "You smell nervous. Should I be nervous?"

There's no real use hiding it from her. "I'm nervous, but you don't need to be."

"Then what is it?"

"It's easier to just show you." I take Riley's hand, but before I can lead her down the hall, she pulls me back into her arms and kisses the top of my forehead.

"You don't need to be nervous. Not around me. Okay?"

I sigh deliberately. Since I don't technically need to breathe, sometimes I forget. "Thanks. It's not a big deal, really. You'll see."

This time, Riley lets me lead her to the bedroom. When we arrive, the cardboard box is sitting on top of my mattress. "That it?" she asks, letting go of my hand and wandering toward the mattress. She pauses and sniffs again. "Nice candle, by the way. Thought I smelled vanilla out front."

"Thanks. You can open the box. I found it while I was throwing some things out earlier today."

"Wait, you threw stuff out?" Riley looks around the bedroom, which is, I admit, still a bit of a chaotic mess. It's not dirty, because I do take care to dust, but it is pleasantly cluttered. There are knickknacks pretty much everywhere, even without all the stuff Elyse and I got rid of.

"Just a few things. Elyse had to pry them away from me and dump them in the garbage, if I'm being honest."

Riley chuckles. "I still need to meet Elyse. She seems great."

"You will," I promise. "Assuming you don't run for the hills in the next couple of minutes," I add under my breath.

It's a mistake. Riley's ears perk up again. Sometimes I forget how good her hearing is. "I'm not runnin' anywhere," she assures me, looking at me with such sincerity in her big blue eyes that I can't help but believe her.

"Okay."

She pats the edge of the mattress. "You wanna scooch a bit closer?"

I don't, but I'm not sure how to tell her that. Treating the box like it's garlic might make Riley think I'm avoiding her instead. I sit at the foot of the bed, as far from the box as possible. She looks at me, forehead furrowed in confusion, and I scoot a few inches closer.

"Open it," I say, half pleading. "I'm dying here."

"I thought you were already dead." Riley pulls open the box, which Elyse had closed back up by tucking one corner under another. She peers inside, her eyes going comically wide. "Jesus, Mary, and Joseph. I mean...um..." She reaches in, producing a long coil of red rope.

"It's not that much stuff," I say, although the lie is mainly meant for me. "Just some odds and ends from my last relationship."

"Odds and ends. Right." Riley sets the coil of rope aside and dives into the box again. This time, her hand emerges with the padded black restraints. The silver chains on them jingle almost cheerfully. "No real silver in here, right? Gives me a nasty rash."

"Stainless steel, I think. Although that reminds me, I should probably check my jewelry and put all the silver away just in case."

Riley laughs, which I take as a good sign. "I don't think the jewelry you've got on is gonna hurt me."

I notice where she's looking and remember the rainbow slap bracelet. "Elyse and I found those while we were going through my stuff earlier. Living longer means you go through more regrettable fashion trends."

"I thought it was retro," Riley says.

"Right? That's what I told Elyse. I feel so vindicated right now."

"Oh, sweet lord." Riley has reached into the box again, and now she's brandishing a pink jelly dildo with floating beads inside it. She sniffs it, wrinkling her nose in disgust. "This thing can't be safe. Gotta be full of phthalates."

"Full of what?"

"Cheap chemicals. Remember that rash I mentioned? It can give you one in a very...uh, sensitive place."

"It's going in the garbage." I snatch the wobbly dildo from her, trying to remember when I even used it. I can't recall a single instance, but that's probably a good thing. I chuck it in the trash can, running my palms over my dress. "How do you know so much about dildos, anyway? Are you a fan?"

"Well..." It's Riley's turn to look embarrassed. "I've shopped around."

I sit back down, closer to her this time. Since she hasn't freaked out yet, I'm not quite so scared of the box anymore. "Do tell."

"Don't have one of my own yet."

That surprises me. Not to stereotype, but Riley strikes me as the kind of lesbian who would be into strap-ons. "Any reason why not?"

Riley's shoulders slump a little. For a moment, her demeanor changes, and she seems almost sad. "Guess I'm worried it won't...do it for me. You know, like having a real one would. I worry I'd just be disappointed."

I run my hand up her back. "Riley..."

"Hey," she says forced a smile, "it's fine. I've thought a lot about this over the past few years, more since I met Colin. I thought I might be trans for a while, but that didn't feel right either. I'm kinda in between, you know?"

I nod with what I hope is understanding. "Do you still want me to use 'she/her' pronouns, or something else?"

Once more, Riley hesitates. "I...don't know? I'll think about it. You can keep going with 'she' for now."

"If that changes," I say, clasping her hand, "you can let me know."

"I know. I just don't want to be a bother. Because all this doesn't mean I don't like the way things already are, what we already do," she adds hurriedly. "I love it. I don't have any complaints—"

I press the finger of my free hand over Riley's lips. In her face, I can see my own fear from earlier: that asking for something more would make me seem weird, or even inadequate, for not enjoying sex the 'normal' lesbian way—whatever normal even means.

"Hey. I'm into you, Riley. And if that means trying some new things with you, I'm up for it. I mean..." I look toward the box and laugh. "I just shoved a whole box of bondage stuff at you. I'm not exactly closed-minded."

"Yeah." Riley glances at the box too, which is about half-empty without the ropes, scarves, and restraints on top. "So, what about you? Do you have any...complaints?"

"No," I blurt out. "Oh God, no. Things have been great."

"But? I can hear a 'but' in there."

I give her a shy smile. As usual, she's right. "Well...sometimes, I like it a little rough. Especially when I'm tied up and helpless." I can barely get the words out without blushing.

Something dark flickers across Riley's face, and I almost regret what I've said. Then she brightens again. "Yeah?"

"Okay, what was that about?" I'm no wolf, but I'm pretty observant too.

"Oh, just human nonsense."

I can't help snorting at that. Some of the tension is broken. "Tell me about it?"

"The girls I messed around with in high school wanted the rough, tough werewolf, you know? And, yeah, sometimes I wanna be that fantasy. I'm into it. But I want them to like me as a person too, you know? I don't wanna be their fetish...or at least not only their fetish."

"I understand completely." And I do. I've had my fair share of one-night stands that wanted the mysterious, aloof vampire dominatrix and were disappointed when I didn't deliver what they expected.

"You would. You probably get it worse than me."

"It's not a competition, Riley. If it bothers you, it's important to me."

"It doesn't bother me," Riley says, a little too quickly. "Gotta be honest with you, Izzy. I'm interested for my own sake, but I've never done the bondage thing before. Going through all this stuff, I feel confused as a chameleon in a bag of skittles."

I snort with laughter. "You made that one up. That can't be a real Southernism."

"Is so," Riley protests. "My brother told me that one."

"Then he made it up."

Riley shrugs. "Maybe. But I'm telling the truth. I've never done this before, so I'll probably mess up. A lot. I don't wanna disappoint you."

Once more, she's so sincere that my heart throbs hard enough to stick to my ribs. "Riley," I murmur, cupping her warm cheek and stroking it with my thumb, "you could never disappoint me."

She laughs. "I ain't tried yet."

"Doesn't matter." I lean in to kiss her, running my fingers through her hair. She wraps an arm around my waist, shifting so the two of us are cuddled close. Her tongue strokes against mine, but only for a moment, because I pull back before the kiss can get too deep. "I was scared to show you this stuff, but I shouldn't have been. Even if you weren't into it, you would have been sweet about letting me down. You wouldn't have judged me."

"Nope," Riley says, grinning from ear to ear. "Never. So..." Her warm palm runs up along my thigh, following the slit in my dress. "Any chance I can sweet talk you into taking this off for me?"

"What about your food?"

Riley's tongue peeks out to run over her lips. "It'll reheat."

She kisses me again, tipping me back onto the bed, and I lose myself in her lips. It's so easy to kiss her, to relax with her, to welcome her on top of me. Even though we've only known each other a couple of months, she has this way of making me feel comfortable. The taste of her mouth is like coming home even as the brush of her tongue against mine lights a fire in my belly.

I'm so distracted I barely notice her working to remove my dress. It's only when she lets out a soft growl of frustration that I realize she's trying to unfasten the wrap the wrong way. "It's decorative," I chuckle, pulling just far enough away from her to strip the dress off myself. It's not easy to do it gracefully while I'm half lying down, but I don't care. I want it off, so I can feel Riley's hands against my bare skin.

Her blue eyes widen, drinking me in, and my cold skin gets a bit of a flush as my heart twitches into beating. Seeing myself through Riley's eyes, knowing she finds me beautiful, does more for me than any mirror ever could.

"Sweet Jesus, you're gorgeous," Riley mumbles, with an expression that can only be described as awe.

I take her hands in mine, guiding them around my torso so she can unfasten my bra. "And you're a sweet talker."

Riley doesn't have nearly as much trouble with my bra as she did with my dress. After only a little fumbling with the hooks, she manages to pull it open. The first thing she does after throwing it aside is fill her hands with my breasts, and both of us groan at the same time.

Soon, the peaks of my nipples are pressing insistently into Riley's palms. She takes them between her fingertips, giving them a gentle twist, and I almost cut my bottom lip on one of my fangs. They've fully extended, and I can hear and smell the rapid beating of Riley's heart, the rush of her blood beneath her skin.

"So..." Riley gives my nipples another pinch, pulling a whimper out of me. "Wanna show me how to use all this stuff?" She nods at the half-empty box of supplies, and my stomach flips over itself. Kissing her had been so distracting that I'd almost forgotten about everything else.

"Sure." I grab the nearest item, which happens to be a set of black wrist restraints. It's a good choice, because they aren't hard to use, just a little Velcro and a short stainless-steel chain. "How about these for my arms? No knots to worry about."

Riley grins. "I like it." She takes the cuffs from me, unfastening the Velcro on one side. "You want your arms in front or behind?"

I think about it. In front will be more comfortable, but I'm not sure I want to be comfortable. Part of the reason I like bondage is the mild, aching pain that comes when my muscles are trapped in one position. It's a constant reminder of the fact that I can't move. "Behind me."

"Then turn around."

I turn away from her, swinging my feet over the side of the bed and sitting on the edge of the mattress. I can feel Riley moving behind me, but I still shudder when she places a warm kiss on my shoulder. Slowly, she draws my hands behind my back, bringing my forearms together and slipping the cuffs on.

Riley's a quick learner, because it doesn't take her long to fasten the restraints. "This okay?" she asks, her breath hot against the crook of my throat. "Not too tight?"

The tender concern in her voice reassures me that she's exactly the right person to break out this box with. "Just right. Can you slip a finger underneath? If you can't fit it, they need to be looser."

Riley squeezes one of her fingers beneath the cuffs, and I shudder as it grazes my inner wrist. "Feels good to me. What now?"

I look back over my shoulder at her and lick my lips. "Whatever you want to do to me."

It's the right thing to say. Riley lets out a low growl, flipping me onto my back with a surprising amount of force. I squeak in surprise, but she muffles the sound with a kiss, pressing her tongue into my mouth. There's a faint hint of sweetness from my own smeared lip gloss, but most of what I can taste is her—warm and wet and hungry.

We only break apart when Riley decides it's time to strip off her sweater vest. She tears it up and over her head, almost forgetting the bowtie in her haste, and my eyes widen as her stomach and binder come into view. Riley has a thin layer of fat over her abdomen, but her muscles still show through, firm and inviting. She unzips her binder, and her breasts spill free. They're not very large, but they're perky and sit high on her chest.

My mind conjures up what she said before, about wondering if she was trans for a while. "Do they bother you?" I ask, not wanting to ruin the moment, but also feeling it's important to know. I can't really touch them with my arms behind my back, and she's seemed to enjoy having them touched before, but I want to be sure.

"Sometimes, depends on the day."

"If you ever want me to leave them alone, or keep the binder on, you can let me know. I don't mind."

She gives me a grateful smile. "You're the best, Izzy. And if you want me to stop whatever I'm doing, just say so."

Riley takes off her pants and underwear next, shucking them with an awkward little shimmy that doesn't require her to leave the bed. I snort with laughter, but the sound is quickly replaced by a moan as she settles back on top of me. With her naked and me in just my panties, I can feel the heat of her skin bleeding into mine. Her body is like a furnace, and together, we reach just the right temperature.

"God, your skin is so soft," Riley murmurs, running her hands along my sides. Her palms settle on my hips, squeezing slightly, and one of her knees presses up between my legs, putting pressure right where I need it. My inner walls throb in anticipation, and I gasp as more wetness spills out of me, soaking through the material of my underwear.

"Take them off?" I ask, mostly pleading. "Please."

"Please...I like that." Riley's fingers trace fire along my thighs. They start out soft, but then she sinks them in a little further, raking her nails across my skin and sending shudders down my spine. I shift, trying to roll my shoulders, but it's useless. With my arms tied behind me, I can't reach down to grip her or offer direction. I'm all too aware of my own helplessness—the dull ache in my arms, the burn between my legs.

I run the sole of one foot along her side, trying to connect with her, but she catches my ankle in her hand. "Nuh-uh," she says, staring down into my eyes. Suddenly, she doesn't look quite so much like a cheerful golden retriever anymore. She runs her tongue over her sharpened upper teeth, and I shudder as I get a glimpse of the wolf underneath.

To my surprise, Riley brings my foot to her lips. She places a kiss to the top, and I squeal and curl my toes, partly from embarrassment, partly because it tickles. "Don't," I giggle. "My pedicure's all chipped. The top coat's worn off."

"Don't give a damn about your pedicure." Riley slides her other hand up along my opposite thigh, cupping between my legs, massaging me through the clinging material of my panties. "Not when I've got all this to play with."

The contact is indirect, but her possessive squeeze is enough to leave me dripping. I gasp as she finally, finally pulls my underwear down along my thighs, but once they're off, her fingers don't return. My inner walls pulse, but Riley's already reaching for a coil of red rope sticking halfway out of the box.

"Can I use this on your legs?" she asks, holding it up hopefully.

I smile. It's kind of adorable how excited she is about this, especially since I was the one who asked her to do it in the first place. "Yes, please. How about a frog tie?"

Riley's brows lower and her head tilts curiously, ears perking. "What's that?"

"It's one of the easiest ties to do. You just tie my ankle to my thigh, so my legs stay bent." I bend one of my legs to show her.

Riley nods eagerly. "Yup. Pretty sure I can manage that. Time to break out the rodeo skills."

"You're from Georgia," I remind her, stifling a giggle.

"Hush, you."

She brings the rope between us, letting the end trail along my calf. It's a struggle not to squirm, but soon I forget all about being tickled. Riley lifts my foot again, only this time, she ties my ankle to my thigh, winding the rope around them both.

Once she finishes, my first instinct is to test the knot. I try to kick my foot out and straighten my leg again, but she's done a good job. All I can do is let my knee fall to the side. "Not too tight?" Riley asks, running a finger under the cord to check.

It's tight, but not too tight, and the slight cramp in my thigh isn't unbearable. "Just right."

"Good." Riley binds my other ankle to my thigh, winding it around several times before tying it off. This time, I don't need to fight against the knot to see if it holds. Both of my legs are pinned.

Riley places her hands on my knees, spreading them open and pressing them into the mattress. The position puts some strain on my inner thighs, but it's the most wonderful kind of burn. I'm acutely aware of how Riley's palms feel on my skin, flat and smooth, radiating heat.

"Keep these open," Riley says, and I blink in surprise. I appreciate a lover who can give orders, but I hadn't expected Riley to become that lover quite so quickly. There's more to her than I expected, and I'm loving what I'm seeing.

"What are you going to do?" I ask, looking up at her.

Riley grins. It's not Natasha's seductive smirk, but somehow, it's even better in its silliness. "Anything I want," she says, repeating my earlier words. She leans over me, bracing her elbows on either side of my shoulders. I expect her to dip down for a kiss, but instead, her warm lips graze my neck, sucking a sensitive patch of skin.

I gasp. With my arms and legs tied, the sensation of her mouth is more intense. I tilt my chin up, trying to give her more access, but she's already moved on, kissing along my collarbone and down my chest.

When she blows a stream of air across the peak of my breast, my hips jerk up. The involuntary movement puts me in contact with her stomach muscles, and I groan, my head falling to one side. Riley's stomach is wonderfully firm, and I can't help but rub myself against it. Soon, I've painted a line of slickness along her abdomen.

"You're so wet," Riley mutters into the curve of my breast. She sinks her teeth in, then sucks, pulling hard enough to leave a purple-black mark along one side. It hurts for just a moment, but then the pressure of her mouth and the sharp edges of her teeth push me past the pain and into an aching sort of pleasure.

Riley's blue eyes dart up to meet mine, as if she's checking in to make sure this is still okay. I try to reach down and stroke her hair in reassurance, or maybe thread my fingers through it and direct her to my nipple, but then I remember—my arms are trapped. She can do whatever she wants to me, at whatever pace she wants.

There's only one way left to encourage her. "Please," I murmur, arching my spine to try and put my breasts on more prominent display.

Riley takes my nipple between her lips, sucking it into the soft heat of her mouth and rolling her tongue over it. A jolt races through me, straight to my clit. Luckily, Riley's stomach is there, a flat surface to rock into. I try to rub myself against her, but trapped beneath her body, I don't have much room to maneuver.

"Hey," Riley growls around the peak of my breast. She gives my upper arms a gentle, warning press into the mattress, transforming the slight strain in my shoulders into a deeper ache. "Stop squirmin'. You said I could do what I want."

I stop. There's a commanding edge to Riley's voice that she hasn't brought out much before, but I'm discovering that I like it. I shudder, forcing myself to relax into the cuffs and the rope, into Riley's embrace. She returns her mouth to my nipple, and when she starts sucking, I resist the temptation to rock my hips.

It's torture. Riley's abdomen is pressed against me at the perfect angle, slick with my wetness, but I want to show that I have at least a little restraint. I take a deep breath to calm my racing heart. It almost feels like it's beating at human speed, sending warm blood to my cold, tingling limbs.

Blood. I can smell Riley's blood pulsing beneath her skin. My mouth waters and the pit of my stomach simmers with hunger. Riley must be able to scent my need, because she just grins in that infuriating way of hers. "Wait your turn," she mutters before kissing down along my stomach.

It's almost as awful as feeling her tease my breasts. She goes slow, lavishing kisses from my sternum to my navel, taking plenty of time to swirl her tongue around my hipbones. I spread my legs, but it's useless. The pressure of Riley's abdomen is gone and she's deliberately not touching me where I need it most.

I shiver as Riley's teeth sink into my belly, sharper than they had been before. Her ears have gone pointed and fuzzy and her tongue got a rougher, grooved texture, one that makes me tremble. When I look down at her eyes, they're a glowing, gorgeous yellow.

"Riley," I murmur. She's told me to hold still, but she hasn't forbidden me from speaking—yet. "Please..."

Riley snarls, placing two quick kisses to each of my thighs before ducking eagerly between them.

The moment her tongue touches me, I'm a quivering mess. It's hot and rough and slippery, and it can reach almost as far inside me as her fingers. I yelp as it swipes straight for my entrance, forgetting my promise to stay still. I can't, not when Riley's inside me, lapping up each pulse of wetness as fast as my body makes them.

I try to move, but the ropes digging into my skin stop me. My nails bite into my palms and I suck my lower lip between my sharpened teeth. Riley's fingers are bands of steel on my thighs and I can't rock my hips without a fight. All I can do, all I want to do, is let the waves of pleasure wash over me.

Bright polka dots of color flash before my eyes. I'm sure I'm about to come whether Riley wants me to or not, and she seems to sense it too. The only warning I get is a low growl that vibrates through every sensitive lip and fold before she seizes my hips, flipping me onto my stomach with an impressive display of strength.

At first, I'm too surprised to react. In this position, my curly hair is bouncing on either side of my cheeks, and I can't see much. But I don't need to. I can feel Riley behind me, and I cry out as her teeth sink into the cheek of my ass, nipping hard enough to leave an imprint. This is the roughest she's ever been with me, and I want even more.

With another snarl, that wonderful tongue is back, burying itself inside me. Riley's claws rake up and down my thighs, digging in whenever I try to rock back against her face, commanding me to hold still. Her tongue plunges in and out, hitting a white-hot spot inside me, only to stop so she can lick and suck her way down to my clit.

When she draws it into her mouth, I scream into the mattress. I can't help it. Riley's learned all my favorite places and knows the exact amount of pressure to use. She's going a little rough, but that's just what my body needs. I come with a helpless wail, shuddering so hard the mattress shakes along with me.

Riley stays latched onto my clit, lashing me without mercy. It's enough to keep me coming, but my inner walls flutter uselessly, desperate for something to grip. They clutch around nothing, and my moans have turned to sobs by the time Riley figures out what I need and introduces her fingers.

Two of them pump inside me, making a slick noise as my body sucks them in. The moment she rams into the same aching spot her tongue had teased before, my ripples become a riptide. I release a flood around her fingers and onto her face, shouting something that's supposed to be her name. I'm not sure if it is. I can barely form words.

"Ry...lee...mfff—"

That's all I get out before she grasps my hair and shoves me face first into the bed, climbing on top of me and settling her lean hips against my rear. She bucks forward, and I sense a wave of longing coming off her. Instead of withdrawing, she moves her fingers faster, pumping with feverish intensity before I have time to recover.

I've always enjoyed multiple orgasms, but this is ridiculous. I'm so sensitive I can't tell whether my body wants me to squirm away or rock back in search of more, but it doesn't matter. I don't have a choice either way. The stainless-steel chains are cold against my back, clanking with each of Riley's thrusts inside me, but they quickly heat up with her body on top of mine. She's a furnace, radiating warmth.

"Bite me," I beg, my voice muffled by the mattress, but I don't have to.

Riley burrows past my thick hair and bites the back of my neck. Her teeth press in, her burning breaths unfurling in ragged pants against my skin. She's got me pinned beneath her, and she doesn't even need the cuffs and the rope around my aching thighs to keep me in place.

It's that realization, along with the feverish speed of her fingers, that pushes me over the edge again. I don't know whether it's my second orgasm or my third, but I don't care. I clench hard around her fingers, keening into the tangled, soaked sheets beneath me as I spill into her hand.

By the time it's over, I'm a wreck. Every muscle in my body is soft and trembling. She's fucked absolutely everything out of me. I can't even remember to breathe. Gradually, my heartbeat slows down, and I realize that even though Riley's still on top of me, letting me borrow her body heat, I'm actually cold.

Riley notices me shivering. She rolls off, flipping me over onto my back. "You okay, Izzy?" she asks softly. "I wasn't too rough, was I?" Even though her eyes are still yellow, they're full of tender concern. The wolf is gone, and the fluffy golden retriever is back.

I groan softly, blinking the blurriness from my eyes. I can tell from the shiny blue-black smudges at the corners of my vision that my eyeliner is a lost cause and my mascara is probably worse. Still, I can't help but smile. "More than okay. Just...just get me out of these cuffs and give me a minute, and I'll give you a turn."

Riley grins. "That was my turn. And I'll let you out..." She runs one of her hands up along my sticky thigh, which is still bound tightly to my ankle. "If you want me to let you out."

"Riley," I murmur, shaking my head at her. But I don't ask her to let me out. I don't really want her to untie me yet. My limbs are starting to hurt a little, but it's not unbearable. The discomfort is kind of pleasant—a reminder that I'm still totally at Riley's mercy.

"How 'bout I give you a little snack. Recharge your batteries. Then you can make it up to me."

Riley dangles her wrist in front of my face, and I follow it with my eyes, my tongue darting out to run over my lips. I can see her veins beneath her pale skin and smell the arteries running alongside them. My stomach growls.

"Well, I am pretty dehydrated..."

She lowers her wrist to my lips, and I plant a wet kiss on the tender underside without any teeth. Only when I hear her gasp do I sink my fangs in.

Riley's blood is like ambrosia from the gods themselves. It's hot and sweet and syrupy, with just a little tartness in the aftertaste. I take a few quick pulls before I can help myself. I don't want to drain too much or leave Riley dizzy, but I'm really thirsty after having the daylights fucked out of me, and she tastes so good. After a few mouthfuls, I'm able to slow down to a more moderate pace. I suck softer, letting the coppery taste roll around on my tongue so I can savor it a little longer.

Much sooner than I want, Riley pulls her hand away. I whimper, still hungry, but she just smirks at me with that devilish look on her freckled face. "Hey, you'll get more." To my surprise, she slides two of her fingers down her own belly, delving into the sticky pink folds beneath her triangle of soft golden curls. When she withdraws them again, they're covered in clear glaze.

I moan as soon as Riley slips her wet fingers past my lips. I run my tongue around them, licking up all I can get. She thrusts a few times, almost lazily, making my hollowed cheeks expand before pulling out again with a soft pop. I try to chase after her fingers, but the cuffs around my forearms make it difficult to sit up.

"That's not fair," I say, not bothering to hide my pout.

Riley just shrugs and tosses her shaggy blonde head. "Never promised to be fair." She swings one leg over me, scooting up so her knees are on either side of my shoulders. Suddenly I'm treated to a close and personal view between her legs. She's already dripping, and her clit is a rosy red where it peeks out from beneath its hood. "Say please," she mutters, running one hand through my hair.

I swallow. It can't be that easy. "Please?"

"Please what?"

I think for a moment about our earlier conversation, choosing my words carefully. "Please...let me suck you." Riley blinks in surprise. I think she was expecting slightly different wording, but she seems to like what I picked. She lowers herself onto my mouth, and I set to work as soon as my tongue can reach her.

Riley has to be the most delicious person I've ever tasted. She's sweet, heavy chocolate drizzling sticky salted caramel all over my lips, and I can't help but moan. The flavor's a little overwhelming, but in the best way. I can't get enough. I plunge my tongue deeper, forgetting about trying to please her, focusing on drawing out as much of her wetness as I can.

I don't have long to be greedy. Riley rises off my mouth, and I can only whine as she hovers over me. The cuffs behind my back won't let me do much else. "Hold your horses, sunshine," she grins, brushing some loose, springy curls back from my forehead. "Go slow. Do it right."

I have to snicker at 'sunshine', but it's cute, so I let the irony slide. I lick my lips, then rasp, "I'll go slow. Please come back?"

Riley lowers herself again, and this time, I don't go straight for her entrance. I cover her in flat, broad licks, still savoring her flavor, but trying not to be obvious about it. Riley rewards me by pushing harder against my face, letting me feel and taste more of her heat. I can practically feel her heartbeat in my mouth and she's all I can smell as her soft golden hairs tickle my nose.

"Suck me, Izzy," Riley says, and I latch onto her clit, drawing the stiff bud into my mouth. It's already thick and swollen inside its hood, and I run my tongue around and around, feeling it twitch with each circle. "So good," Riley grunts, rocking her hips forward. The pressure puts a bit of a crick in my neck, but I don't care. She's moving with purpose, riding my face, and I suck her almost feverishly, making slurping sounds in my effort to draw her as deep as possible into my mouth.

Suddenly, Riley goes stiff above me. I hadn't noticed how tightly she was wound, or I might have backed off, but by the time I realize, it's too late. Her yellow eyes glow even brighter, and she howls at the ceiling, pulling my hair and shaking to pieces on top of me. Her thighs clamp shut around my cheeks and a river of salt spills down my chin, making an absolute mess of us both.

Riley's flavor is too tempting to resist. I graze the sides of her clit with the very tips of my fangs, drawing in a quick taste. Just a few drops and I'm blood-drunk. More, my mind screams. More, my heart pounds. I moan against Riley's folds, struggling not to tip over the edge right along with her.

She must notice my squirming, because she slides the hand that isn't clutching my hair backwards, slipping her fingers between my legs. It's hard for her to find the right spots at this angle, but I don't care. I'm so close that it doesn't matter. I hit a quick, hard peak, screaming my muffled pleasure between her legs as I drown in her sweetness.

Riley's hips jerk unevenly, and then she slumps over, panting as she braces herself against my headboard. Her shaggy hair is hanging around her face and her cheeks are flushed, but her sharpened teeth are bared in a beaming smile. "You look way too full of yourself," she growls, but I can tell she isn't really mad.

It takes me a moment to respond after she lifts off me, because even though I don't actually need to breathe, I'm still short of air. "You...you have a phrase for this...smug as...smug as a..."

My mind is floating, and I can't find the word.

"Puffed up as a peacock." Riley looks puffed up as a peacock herself, still panting with exertion, grinning almost wildly. She certainly seems very proud of herself as she rolls off me and collapses onto her back, her head lolling back on one of my pillows.

I decide not to argue about which one of us is the peacock. My arms and legs are heavy and tingly with pleasure, but I can't get comfortable while I'm still trussed up like a Thanksgiving turkey. "Uh, Riley..."

Riley stops nuzzling into my shoulder as she realizes what she's forgotten. "Oh, shucks. Sorry, sunshine." Immediately, she's all soft murmurs and tender caresses, untying my legs with surprisingly deft fingers and gently flipping me over so she can unfasten my cuffs as well. The steel chain clinks as she tosses it off to the side, but I don't bother to see where it lands. I stretch my limbs and roll into her arms, sighing heavily.

"How is your language even more old-fashioned than mine?" I tease, pressing a kiss to her sweaty collarbone.

Riley's chuckle vibrates through her chest over the frantic throb of her heartbeat. "'Cause my mama raised me right." I roll my eyes up toward hers, and then flick them toward the coil of rope at the foot of the bed. Riley bursts out laughing. "Okay, fine. So, she might not wanna know exactly what her kid is up to in the big city…"

"I won't tell if you won't."

"That's my girl."

She rolls on top of me, careful not to squish me with her weight, and runs a hand down my arm, kneading the stiff muscles. "You feeling okay? Can I do anything for you? Rub your back? Get you a nice cool washcloth?" She strokes my forearms, where the plastic edges of my slap bracelets have left some imprints with the help of the cuffs. I hadn't even remembered they were still on under there.

I sigh deeply. "That backrub sounds nice."

"Say no more."

Riley lifts herself up on her elbows, and I flip onto my stomach beneath her, resting my cheek against the pillow. It's warm and comforting, and it smells just like her. Her hands are even hotter as they run along the sore muscles of my back, burning pleasantly against the stiff tissue. I'm always, always cold, and Riley's like my own personal space heater.

She takes her time, making sure each and every kink is worked out from the nape of my neck all the way down to my tailbone. By the time Riley's finished with me, I've melted into the mattress like a stick of butter left out on the table. I say so, and Riley laughs.

"Nice one, but that ain't a real Southernism." She's gotten more comfortable letting her accent slip around me, I've noticed.

"It sounds like one though, right?"

Riley places a kiss behind my ear. "Yeah."

In that moment, I realize I really trust her. It's a warm, soothing feeling that just sort of washes over me, but it leaves me shaken. I don't trust easily. I'm friendly. I like people. I believe there's good in everyone and I make it my business to look for it as much as I can. But still, there's this barrier. Whenever I let someone close, they usually let me down. Like Natasha. Like my parents, too, to a certain extent. Elyse is my one success story.

But I think I trust Riley, too. Despite her claims that she knows next to nothing about relationships, she's been so good through all of this, talking it through with me at every step. When I was feeling vulnerable, she made herself vulnerable too, so I wouldn't be so nervous. Something about her kindhearted nature just feeds the optimist in me. It's proof that I haven't been wrong all these years, trying to keep myself soft for the next person who came along, believing there actually would be a next person.

I think...I think Riley might be that Next Person. I think she might be the Right Person.

"Riley..."

"Hmm?" She's moved on to rubbing my calves, which could really use the attention.

"Have you been seeing anyone else?"

Riley's hands pause. She hesitates, and strained silence fills the air between us. "Uh..."

I blurt it out quickly, before I can lose my nerve. "Because I haven't been. And I don't want to. I'd be happy seeing just you."

The quiet continues, growing so thick and unbearable that I have to look over my shoulder. This is it. I've screwed it up. Decades of experience still haven't prepared me for this.

But the moment I see Riley's big, goofy smile, all my tension melts away. "I'd be happy seeing just you, too."

"Really?"

Riley crawls up on the bed next to me, looping an arm around my waist. "Yup. Most definitely. I've, uh...kinda been thinkin' of you as my girlfriend already. Unofficially."

My still heart practically glows. "You have?"

Riley nods sheepishly. "I didn't wanna push..."

"I'm glad you didn't," I say, trying to reassure her. "This was the right time." With a sudden surge of inspiration, I remove one of my slap bracelets, the one with smiling rainbows. I snap it around Riley's wrist instead. "There. It's official!"

She twists the bracelet around a little but doesn't remove it. "Okay," she says, leaning in and kissing my nose.

Just when she's about to go for my lips, my phone buzzes. I roll away from her and grab it from the nightstand, squinting at the glowing screen. It's Elyse, of course:

Did you use the stuff?

I laugh, which makes Riley quirk her brow at me curiously. When I show her the text, she raises the other one too. "So, you actually let Elyse look inside your Secret Sin Box?"

"'Let' isn't the word I'd use. It wasn't by choice." I grab Riley's hand, the one with the bracelet, and link mine with it over my stomach. I snap a quick picture, making extra sure there's no embarrassing naked bits in the frame. Elyse has already seen more than enough (and phone cameras these days can actually capture my image, unlike most mirrors).

I send the picture of our slap bracelets, along with the caption: *we're girlfriends now.*

Elyse immediately texts back: *Is your first date going to be at the Roller Rink? Will you wear leg warmers?? Is she taking you to a Duran concert?*

Shut up. □

I'm just asking the important questions.

"Are y'all always like this?" Riley asks, shaking her head at me in bemusement.

I sigh deeply. "I'm afraid so."

Riley chuckles. "I'm kinda relieved. Colin's a handful, so at least we're on the same page."

"We should probably have them meet one of these days, since we're...girlfriends?"

"Girlfriends," Riley repeats, testing the word out. Her grin spreads wider. "So, girlfriend, how do you feel about a long, hot bath?"

"You just want to use one of my bath bombs."

"Guilty. But do you wanna?"

"In a minute." I snuggle up against her side, kissing the side of her neck. "I just want to hold you for a few more seconds."

Riley slides her arm over my shoulder, so I can cuddle closer. "Sounds perfect."

Chapter Five - Riley

THERE'S NOTHING LIKE THE first full moon of winter. Central Park glitters silvery-white as I sprint across the grass. Frost crunches beneath my paws, and the air smells like crisp, clean snow. Its chilly bite makes my chest tingle. The sun hasn't risen yet, but it's coming soon. There's a pale white strip on the horizon beyond the trees.

I feel like I could run forever. The morning's cold, but my legs are warm. I hear howls nearby, other wolves singing before sunrise. I'm a lone wolf, but the local packs don't bother me none. I've gotten used to them by now.

My nose stops me beneath a black cherry tree. I trot around its trunk, sniffing. Someone's been here. Another loner? No. This wolf smells like pack, but they're running alone. The fur on my spine prickles. Eyes are watching me from somewhere nearby.

Brittle grass crackles behind me. My ears perk up. The stranger? Yes. A black wolf. Wiry hair. Dash of purple on their forehead. Their body's long and lean, with some muscle packed on too. Their tail is level, waving side to side.

I sniff again. Their scent's different. I can't tell their gender, but this wolf looks sociable. I give a soft whuff.

The stranger barks. They lower their chest to the ground, haunches wiggling in the air. *Play?*

Don't see a reason to say no. Only half an hour left before sunrise. I crouch low to the ground, then spring. They leap away. I chase, following their shadow through the naked trees. New Friend is fast. Takes me a while to catch them, but I head them off near one of the jogging paths.

We tumble, mouthing each other without teeth. New Friend and I tussle for a bit, breaking away to run in circles before we go in again. Have to admit, it's nice. I haven't played with another wolf since my brothers back home. New York can be lonely.

At last, the sun shows its face. It warms up my fur and adds a little color to the pale grey tree trunks. New Friend rolls off me and trots a few paces away, hunching over and letting out a low groan.

My own shift doesn't take long. It leaves my muscles sore and a little numb, like I've done too many lifts. I roll my neck and shoulders, wincing at the cracks. Going from four legs to two can really put your joints out of alignment.

"Hey."

I turn to see the stranger smiling at me. Their human form surprises me, although maybe it shouldn't. Like the black wolf, they're thin but muscular, with short, spiky black hair dyed purple at the tips. They've got pale skin and tattoos on their forearms. They're not my type, although I note wryly that Izzy might enjoy the view.

It's a little rude, but my eyes flick down. Well, that answers that question—no traditionally male parts. But the voice is a little lower than I'd expect a woman's to be, and the smell...well, I don't know what to make of the smell. Maybe they're trans but haven't gone to get a potion from a friendly neighborhood witch like Colin did for his transition.

The wolf grins. "Confused?"

My face heats up in embarrassment. "Uh..."

"Don't worry about it. I get that a lot. Name's Li Min. They/them pronouns."

That puts a few more pieces into place. I've spent my share of time on the internet, trying to figure out what's up with me and why I feel the way I do, but I've never met someone in real life who uses different pronouns. My stomach tickles a little. I feel nervous for reasons I can't put into words.

Li Min sticks out their hand, and I shake.

"Riley." I hesitate. "Uh, 'she' I guess?"

Li Min's got a firm handshake. "Nice ta meetcha, Riley." Their voice might be a little low, but it's also fast and excited. They're definitely a talker, no doubt about it. "You live here, or just visiting? Cute accent, by the way."

I cough. "I have a girlfriend."

Li Min snickers. "I'll bet you do. Relax, I said your accent was cute, not that I wanted to go out with you."

I'm kind of relieved. Looks like they're only trying to be friendly. Being out of practice with the whole pack thing has probably made my social skills a bit rusty. "I live here now. Moved from Georgia 'bout half a year back."

"Like it?"

The two of us head toward the edge of the park, where most of the wolves keep their clothes during full moon runs.

"Here, or in Georgia?"

"Either one."

"I like New York fine. Georgia, not so much anymore."

Li Min gives me a knowing look. "Too many humans?"

"Well..."

"Don't get me wrong, they're not all bad. My mom's a werewolf, but my dad's a human who moved here from Korea. But you can only put up with so many weird looks in one day."

I can tell they're speaking from experience, one I'm familiar with. Back home, aside from the local pack, which was mostly extended family, I hadn't fit in well. That's what happens when you put a handful of werewolves in a high school full of humans.

"You grew up outside the city, then?"

"Yeah," Li Min says. "Bumfuck, New York in the middle of the Catskills. Mom's pack was there, so..." They shrug. "Didn't totally suck, but it wasn't great. Most of them weren't sure what to do with a mutt who wasn't a girl or a boy. So, I got the hell out of there and visit for Christmas."

I squirm a little. I'm not used to hearing that word—*mutt*—said so casually, without any venom in it. Had it slung my way a few times, from pickup trucks with crushed beer cans flying out the window, but I imagine Li Min's heard it more. Guess they're the type who got fed up with hearing other people use it like a weapon and decided to use it for themself first. A sort of 'fuck you' to the whole thing. I don't know whether I'd feel comfortable doing the same in their position, reclaiming a slur like that. But it's kind of impressive. Brave, even.

"Don't blame ya," I say to them.

It's almost eerie. Hearing it all, Li Min's story seems pretty damn similar to mine. I probably had it a bit easier, being white, but the sense of not belonging is all too familiar. Only we aren't quite the same. Li Min holds themself like they know who they are. They're comfortable in their body, like most other wolves I've met. Not like me. Nakedness isn't embarrassing for me, exactly, but I know I don't feel the same way about it as most werewolves, or even most humans. Sometimes I feel like my breasts shouldn't be there and I wish my hips were thinner... among other longings that come and go. I never know quite how I'll feel when I look in a mirror.

If some of the same stuff bothers Li Min, they don't show it. They seem happy when we reach the tables where our clothes are, but that's because it's nippy without a coat of fur for protection. "Fuck, it's cold," they grumble as they shove their legs into a pair of khakis and yank a sweater over their head. Their hair pops out even messier than before.

"I like it," I say as I zip up my jeans. "Georgia summers are hotter than Hades. Gets tiring, living right in the Devil's buttcrack."

Li Min chokes on a laugh. "Seriously?"

"You're a New Yorker. Shouldn't you be used to a bit of snow?"

"Just 'cuz I'm used to it doesn't mean I like it."

Li Min ties a dark green smock around their waist, one with a nametag and a pin clipped on. The pin is a little purple button that says 'They/Them', presumably for customers.

"Headed in for a shift? Sorry 'bout it."

"Yeah. Being a barista is fun, for like the first two weeks. Then the crazy schedule messes up your sleep, and you realize you don't get health insurance or days off during the full moon unless you're full-time. 'Oh, you work thirty-six hours instead of forty? Suck my dick, you can't take off.'"

I make a face. My job ain't anything to brag about—it's boring and the pay's kind of crap—but I'm guaranteed 40 hours a week, and I do get the odd day of paid leave for full moons. "You at least get free coffee, right?"

"Only perk of the job. That, and all the weirdos who come in. I get a lot of good material."

"Material?"

"Writer," Li Min says. "Poetry and the odd short story. My goal for this year is to get something published."

"Yeah?"

"Yeah." Li Min grabs their bag and slings it over their shoulder. After digging around in it for a second, they pull out their phone. "So, trade numbers? Nothing sketchy. Bring your girlfriend by the Scream Bean and I'll sneak her a free cup of coffee."

I pull out my phone too. "Sure. Don't you start flirting with my girl, though. It's a miracle she's into me at all, and I don't need her reconsiderin'." *My girl.* It still feels damn good to say that. Izzy and I have only been exclusive for all of two weeks, but the buzz hasn't worn off.

Li Min's eyebrows arch. "Picture?"

I pull one up. It's Izzy, trying to decide on an outfit. She's got on a flowy purple top and bright yellow leggings that would look strange on most folks but are just too cute on her. Her thick curly hair is pulled back under a scarf, and she's gone heavy on the lip liner. I took the picture, though, because the shirt's low cut. I try not to be a hound about it, but I can get lost in her cleavage if I'm not careful.

"Sexy," Li Min chuckles, nodding in approval. "Vampire?"

I'm surprised. "How'd you know?"

"Sunglasses indoors, blackout curtains in the background. How'd you snag a girl like that after only six months in New York?"

"I surely don't know," I say, shaking my head. "But I'm not gonna ask, in case she doesn't know either."

Li Min closes out of my photos without snooping and starts typing their number into my contacts. "Here's my number. You haven't signed up with anyone, right? Don't worry, I'm not a recruiter. I'm trying things out with the Ramblers, but I'm not sure if I'll stay yet."

I nod. The Ramblers are one of the bigger packs in Central Park, mostly in the mid-south by the lake. I've seen them run a few times when I head down from the reservoir. "Let me know how it is. It's not so bad though, being a loner."

Li Min nods. "Nope. Not bad. I gotta head in, but shoot me a text later?"

"For sure."

We shake hands and wave goodbye, heading off in our separate directions. For some reason, their smell stays with me long after they've left. Something about it feels nice. Not in a sexual way. It's more like...I wish I smelled like that. I wish I could walk with that kind of confidence. Looking at Li Min made me feel both really good and a little bad: good because they seem nice, but bad because I'm—jealousy isn't the right word, but it's a weaker version of that. I've caught a case of jealousy's little cousin or something.

I take my phone out again and pull up the picture of Izzy. That puts a big smile back on my face. We have a date planned for tonight, so at least I've got something to look forward to.

***

Work crawls by slower than sap from a sycamore tree. I can't get comfy at my desk, and I take more coffee and pee breaks than I probably should. My eyes keep flicking toward my phone, itching with the urge to text Isabeau and Li Min. It feels like my brain's working out a puzzle, clicking pieces together into a picture that seems clearer the longer I tinker with it. By lunchtime, my absentmindedness attracts attention.

"What's up with you?" Colin asks as the two of us head to the elevator. Most of our coworkers are filing toward the break room where the fridge is, or heading down to the cafeteria to buy something, but we have different plans today.

"Nothin'," I say, not too convincingly.

Colin gives me a skeptical look but doesn't call me out 'til we're in the elevator and the doors are shut. "Seriously, though. You look like someone kicked your puppy."

"Do not," I grumble, popping the tab of my tupperware lid on and off without actually opening it. "And if that's your best dog joke today, you've gotta up your game."

"Fine. Then you look like you got stumped by the *Times* crossword. You've got cartoon question marks floating over your head."

I sigh. He's right. And really, Colin's probably not a bad person to talk to about this. It's not like we don't have precedent—he's the one who told me where to get my binder. "Well..."

The elevator stops and opens onto the top floor. Colin and I head over to the maintenance staircase that leads up to the roof. We step outside once we get to the top, and the sky showers us in pale sunlight through a thin layer of clouds. Working here isn't perfect, but this is one of the perks: the building is tall enough to make the loud traffic noises below us sound far away, but not so tall that the wind is a problem most days. We sit down with our backs against the large metal AC unit, where we're the most sheltered.

"Well?" Colin pops open his lunch, and I salivate at the smell of shrimp. It's raw, of course, but for a werewolf, that ain't exactly a deterrent.

"Can I have some of that? I'll trade ya."

"Depends. What'd you bring?"

I pop open the tupperware. "Beef."

"Just a couple pieces. I'm not gonna let you scarf down my whole lunch."

I know beef isn't Colin's favorite—seals aren't exactly known for eating cows—but I decide to let him be nice to me, because I'm really jonesing for a bite of his shrimp. I scoop up the pieces he offers me and pass over my container, so he can grab himself a chunk of my lunch.

"Stof distahctin meh," he mumbles through a partially full mouth. He swallows, then says, "What's going on, huh?"

"Met someone at the park this morning."

Colin's blond eyebrows shoot up. "Someone? I thought things were going great with you and Isabeau."

"They are," I insist, a little sulkily. At least, they are on my end, and Izzy hasn't had any complaints so far. I shake off the lack of confidence. "It's not that. It's...they were really cool."

"They?"

"Li Min. They're a Rambler."

"So, nonbinary 'they'?"

I shrug. "Guess so."

"Ah." Colin gives me a smug look, like he knows something. I roll my eyes and take my beef back from him so I can pick at it. Suddenly, I'm not as hungry as I thought I was. "Why is that bothering you, though? I thought you'd be happy to meet another nonbinary person."

"I mean, I don't know if I am. At least, not compared to Li Min. They were really proud of it. Had a they/them pin and everything. They even smelled different, kinda like they were on a low dose of hormones?"

"You don't have to compare yourself to Li Min," Colin says. "You don't have to use gender neutral pronouns or take a low dose of T. And you don't have to come out to everyone if you don't want to, either. If you do all those things, that's great, but there isn't a list you have to check off to qualify."

"But—"

"There is no but. I won't claim to know what it's like being nonbinary, but I do know for sure there isn't just one way to do it. You have to figure out Riley's way."

It sounds so easy when he says it but hearing it and feeling it deep in my gut are two different things. I can't even tell whether the churning there is hope or fear of failure.

"I think the hardest part is...I'm not ready to give up everything about being a girl. I mean, I like being a lesbian. I'm proud of it."

"So? Be a lesbian too."

"But if I'm nonbinary, I'm not a girl, so can I even call myself that?"

"Who says you can't? Gender's a grab bag, Riley. Grab what you want from all the bags."

"I dunno. Sometimes it feels weird, like I'm betraying women by saying I don't wanna be one of them. I love women—"

"Trust me, I know," Colin laughs. When he notices I'm still frowning, he lowers his voice. "Hey, I'm not trying to be flippant or anything. It was hard for me too. This shit is complicated to figure out.

Have you talked about it with Izzy?"

Izzy. That's a whole other kettle of fish. "Yeah, kinda. She knows I, uh...have feelings about some of my parts. One time she said she would use different pronouns if I wanted."

"Hey, that's great. Your girlfriend's supportive."

"Yeah." I crack a small smile. "But what would I be if I'm not her girlfriend?"

"Besides incredibly depressed?"

I growl at him. "For serious."

"Fine, fine. What about her werefriend?"

"Werefriend?" It sounds kind of dumb the first time I say it, but when I toss the word around in my head, it starts to feel less weird. "Hm. Maybe."

"Try it if you want," Colin says. "If you don't like it, stop."

I flop my head back against the AC unit with a low metallic thud. "It's really that easy?"

Colin finishes his shrimp and leans his head on my shoulder. "Easy? No. Simple? Yeah. You won't know which parts of the grab bag you wanna keep and which to toss back unless you go fishing."

"Easy for you to say. You can actually fish."

Colin smirks. "Well, I can hold my breath for an impressively long time. So, if Izzy has any hot friends..."

I roll my eyes. "Shut up."

Both of us are quiet for a while. Then I lean my head closer to his and say, "Thanks, Col."

"You're welcome, Riley. For the record, I think you're awesome."

***

It takes me another week to work up the guts to talk to Izzy. Telling her should be easy, since she already kind of knows, but it isn't. Not even a little. When I show up on the front steps of her building on Thursday, my knees are wobbling like jello and my hands are sweating in my pockets despite the nippy autumn wind. When she opens the door, all I can offer is a sheepish grin and a weak, "Hey there, beautiful."

Luckily, that seems to be enough to charm her. "Hey yourself, handsome," Izzy drawls, looking me up and down. I fidget with my collar. I've left the sweater vests at home for once and I'm wearing one of my only blazers over a slightly wrinkled blue shirt. I was in too much of a tizzy to iron it before I left home—not that I usually remember to iron anything anyway.

I gulp, all too aware how long each of my stares lasts. I want to drink Isabeau in, but I don't want to be all awkward about it. From bottom to top, Izzy's got on fuzzy boots, thick grey stockings, a powder-blue poodle skirt (complete with an actual poodle appliquéd onto it), a button-up white top, and a striped blue-and-white knitted cap with her curly hair spilling out the sides. She looks adorable, but then again, I can't remember a time when she hasn't looked adorable.

"So..." Izzy tilts onto her toes and places a soft kiss in the middle of my mouth. It's brief, but I get to kiss her back for a moment before she pulls away. "You ready to see where I'm taking you?"

The kiss gives me a jolt of heat and confidence. Colin's probably right—maybe this won't be so bad. And I don't have to talk about it tonight if I don't want to. "You bet. Subway?"

"Cab," Izzy says.

I rub the back of my neck. "You don't have to spend that much on my account."

Izzy just laughs. "Maybe it's because I want to make out with you on the way, *mon chou.*"

My face burns, but not in an unpleasant way. It's a cute nickname, even though it is a little embarrassing to be compared to a creampuff—which Izzy insists I look like as a wolf. "If you're sure."

"Come on. Let's go on an adventure. You can redeem your makeout points in the cab, or when we get home later."

I take Izzy's chilly hand in mine, hoping she won't mind the sweat. At the very least, the heat radiating from my palm should keep hers warmer. "Lead the way."

We walk hand in hand down the steps and over to the street. Izzy doesn't live on a heavily trafficked road, by New York City standards, but a cab comes along before we've strolled more than a minute. She hails, rolling her eyes as the first one passes by. I throw up my hand for the next one to save her the trouble.

"Taking bets. Do you think that first was one a race thing, a species thing, or because he didn't see me?" Izzy asks with a long-suffering sort of amusement.

"Dunno, but I'll take a bet on whether the cabbie gives me a dirty look once he gets a load of my ears and teeth."

To my relief, Izzy laughs. "I'm not made of money, and I'm already buying you dinner."

It turns out we're both wrong, because our cabbie happens to be a troll. His bright shock of braided orange hair is a blinding contrast to his blue skin. "Where to, ladies?"

I feel a strange pang when he says 'ladies', but I push it down and look at Izzy.

"The Botanical Gardens, please." She slides in, and I scooch next to her, closing the door behind me.

"Can do."

Our cab pulls back into traffic, and I take Izzy's hand again. "So, why the Gardens?"

"You've never been there, right?"

"Nope. Not exactly a safe spot for wolves to run."

Izzy aims a sly smile in my direction. "Then it's a good thing we're not running, isn't it?"

My mouth goes dry at the heated look she's giving me, but I'm saved from answering by a buzz in my pocket. I fish out my phone and glance at the screen. It's Li Min. We've been texting the past few days, mostly me texting them with annoying questions in the middle of the night. That's when my brain has too much time to wander...and worry.

Li Min: *'Have you talked to Izzy?'*

I squirm with guilt. Even though I'm not lying, it feels weird to be sitting on this not-so-secret information when Izzy is right next to me. I put the phone to sleep and shove it back in my pants.

"Everything all right, *mon chou?*"

It takes deliberate control not to wince. Izzy's looking at me with such soft worry in her eyes, but her concern only makes my stomach churn. Usually, just being in her presence is relaxing, and dates with her are fun and exciting. I hope she doesn't feel as off tonight as I do, because this is all my fault anyway.

"Yup," I tell her, struggling to sell the lie. "A new friend I made at the park."

Izzy's outlined eyebrows lift with interest. "New friend?" Her voice isn't accusatory, but I know her history. Her last serious girlfriend really did a number on her trust. Now that we're exclusive, it makes sense she'd be a little skittish.

"Not my type."

"I wasn't saying—"

"I know, just heading it off at the pass. Li Min's...well, have you ever been drawn to someone, only it's not romantic? More like you admire them, or...I dunno, want to be like them?"

Izzy relaxes. "You mean hero worship?"

I pull a face. "That's a little extreme. They're just someone I ran into last week."

"They?"

Dammit. Girl cuts to the chase quicker than a knife through hot butter. I give playing it cool one more try. "Yup."

Izzy remains thoughtful for the next two minutes, but her hand creeps over to rest above my knee. Even though I'm nervous going on terrified, I don't move it. Part of me wants the contact.

Don't be stupid, I try and tell myself. *You know she* won't *care. She came right out and said so before.* But the voice in my head doesn't do much to calm my racing heart. It feels like a hundred horses galloping at once.

We pull up to the curb, and the cabbie parks. While Izzy thanks him and pays our fare. It doesn't feel right, letting my lady pay, but I did promise to let her treat me. I hop out of the cab and stretch my legs. They're full of restless energy. I wish I could shift and take off running. Not away from Izzy, exactly, just...somewhere.

"Riley?" Izzy's waiting on the curb, one arm extended. "You sure you're all right?"

I take a deep breath and take her hand. "Yeah. I bet it'll be real pretty."

"It will," Izzy says, sounding a bit smug.

"Hmm?"

"You'll see."

The two of us stroll in under a big white sign set atop a pair of stone pillars. Izzy flashes a smile and a pair of tickets at the attendant, and he opens the chained gate for us. Beyond, I see something I'm not expecting. I was prepared for some beautiful rows of flowers, probably some trees and water features, but I'm looking at something else instead—a bunch of beautiful glass sculptures that glow from within. They're like sea anemones captured in freeze-frame, curling tendrils stuck in place, but giving the illusion of movement.

The more I look, the more sculptures I see. There aren't only two or three of these things, they're all over the place, lining the sidewalks and illuminating the flowers. It's like I stepped into an early rainbow Christmas.

"Whoa," I say, looking around more than a little slack-jawed. "I got a Southernism for this, but it's kinda stupid."

Izzy sidles up closer to me. "Let me hear it."

"Back home, we'd call something like this 'prettier 'n a new set of mud tires.'"

Izzy cracks up, and my heart grows wings. Things feel good again.

"Prettier than a new set of mud tires. Elyse will love that one."

"Wait, you've been telling your best friend all my dumb similes?"

"Yes." Izzy flutters her lashes. "Is it silly that your knowing the difference between a simile and a metaphor turns me on?"

I exhale a cloud of breath. "Naw. But don't tell her how goofy I am right away. You gotta ease her into it. Otherwise, she'll think I'm an idiot when she meets me."

"She won't," Izzy insists. "I didn't."

"Heaven knows why. I, well...uh, words. I jumble 'em."

"It's cute." She gives my hand a squeeze, and we start walking down one of the paths. The sculptures are perfect, because they cast the flowers in beautiful glowing lights without making Izzy wince or take out her sunglasses. Dark and light don't matter much to a wolf's eyes, but I'm happy she's comfortable.

"Riley?"

"Yeah?"

"Not to poke a sleeping bear...don't look at me like that."

I grin anyway. "Not exactly Southern, but you're gettin' the hang of it."

"Anyway, you don't have to answer if you don't want to, but what about Li Min made you want to be their friend right off the bat?"

She knows. I know she knows, but the words are still lodged stubbornly in my throat. *Come on, Riley,* I growl in my own head. *Stop being such a chicken. She asked about your pronouns. She knows you wear a binder. Colin's right, she's not gonna judge you.*

But I'm still judging myself. I let go of Izzy's hand, shuffling over to a bench a few feet away and slumping down onto it. She sits next to me, and though she starts to reach out, she doesn't touch me right away.

"Riley" she says, in a low and soothing voice, "you know I'm queer, right?"

I blink in surprise. "What?"

"I mean, I usually round up to lesbian because it's simpler, but my sexuality has a little more nuance than that. If someone I cared about didn't fit into a neat box, I'd understand."

Shit. At this point, she's basically coming out *for* me. It's getting a little ridiculous. "I don't know what the hell box I'm in," I tell her, almost desperately. "One day I think I'm okay with being a girl, and I like it fine, and the next day I'm all squirmy in my own skin and it feels wrong when people call me ma'am and I just...I don't get it. I don't get myself."

"Okay."

I blink at her. My brain was expecting the best and the anxious pit in my stomach was holding out for the worst, but Izzy seems...nonplussed? I know my gender issues aren't new information, but I was hoping for more of a response.

"That's it? 'Okay?'"

She takes my hand at last. "I'm sorry all those feelings frustrate you so much, Riley, but it doesn't change this. It doesn't change you and me. I'm here for whatever you need."

The knot of fear in my chest unravels. I almost collapse into Izzy's arms, which wrap around my torso to stroke my back. I'm not crying yet, but my heart is beating loud in my ears and my whole body is shaking. I don't know what else to say except for, "Thank you," in a raspy, choked-off voice.

"Çé bon, mon chou. Don't cry."

Of course, that makes me want to cry more. I sniff and blink back tears, but my eyes still sting. "Sorry. I dunno know why I—"

"Hey. This is important stuff. It's okay to have feelings about it."

I bury my face in Izzy's shoulder and take a few deep breaths. Bit by bit, the scent of suntan lotion and her shampoo calms me down. I relax and squeeze her hand to let her know I'm getting there. She squeezes back, and I finally lift my head.

"That wasn't really about you. I mean...I really want to figure out who I am, but I'm scared of leaving who I was behind. Does that make sense? It's not stupid, right?"

Izzy gives me a sharp-toothed smile that still manages to be warm and gentle. "No, not stupid. But you don't have to leave everything behind. Not me."

"Yeah." I swallow and say it with more conviction. "Yeah, I don't."

"Do you want to keep walking around the gardens, or sit a little longer?"

"Sit," I say. Another delicious smell besides Izzy catches my nose, and my stomach rumbles. I'm pretty sure there's a hot dog stand further along the path. "But can we grab something to eat after? Think I smell a food cart."

Izzy laughs. "You never stop thinking about food for long, do you?"

I laugh too. "Nope. Sorry."

"Riley." She cups my cheek and kisses me, soft and sweet. "You've got nothing to be sorry for, baby."

***

The rest of the evening passes in a happy blur. I feel feather-light as I stroll around the gardens with Izzy, holding her hand in one of mine and a hot dog with all the fixings in the other. We talk, sometimes about the feelings I'm working through, sometimes about other things. The conversation ebbs and flows, but even the silences are comfortable. Things feel right again.

"Is it weird that I didn't always know?" I ask as we pause beneath a group of silvery trees. "Colin talks about how he felt 'different' as a kid, but I didn't feel that way...at least, not about gender. The werewolf part, yeah."

"It's not weird." Izzy's arm is linked with mine, and she huddles close, trying to steal some of my body heat. "I didn't know I was interested in women until after high school. Then again, that was several decades ago. People didn't talk about being gay in the eighties, and they *definitely* didn't talk about vampires." She sighs. "Sometimes I wonder if I'd have made the Choice, if it was offered to me back then. If I'm being honest, probably not."

"I'm not sorry you did."

"Oh, really? So, you wouldn't have wanted to go out with me if I was a fifty-year-old human?"

"Hold up, I never said that. There are some fine older women out there. Just to look at, I mean."

"Looking is fine." Izzy stops us along the side of the path, wrapping her arms around my neck. "We've all got eyes...well, except Mole People. But you better save all your touching for me."

"What kind of touching?"

Izzy scoots closer. "The kind we shouldn't do in public, unless you're feeling extra frisky."

My mouth goes dry. All the moisture in my body has headed south. I'm definitely interested, but part of me is also wary. Izzy and I have grown comfortable with each other over the past couple of months, but tonight is different. My head is crowded with all kinds of doubts screaming for attention. *What if sex changes now? What if Izzy isn't as into me as she usually is? What if I feel weird about something, I've already let her do before and have to ask her to stop?*

108

"Riley?"

I squirm in my shoes. "Yup?"

"It's okay to say no."

"I know. But I wanna, um...with you, I...what if it's different?"

Izzy strokes a lock of my shaggy hair away from my eyes. "Then it's different. What, does sex always stay the same for you?"

"Dunno." I shuffle nervously. "I haven't usually done it with the same girl more than a couple times. Wait, I phrased that wrong—"

"I know what you meant. But if you want some incentive..." She gives me a seductive smirk, running the tip of her tongue over her teeth. "I actually have another surprise planned for you tonight."

"A surprise?" I perk up.

"Yes, but it's back at my place."

Butterflies tickle the inside of my stomach. I can smell Izzy's excitement beneath her perfume and coconut sunscreen, and it's making my mouth water. "Well, I got something to eat, but your belly's probably sticking to your spine. I guess I could be dinner?"

Izzy stands on tiptoe to give me another kiss, deep and wet and slow. "If you're on the menu, I'm happy to order."

My tension melts away. We've come this far, the two of us, and Izzy's always made me feel safe. I feel a stirring inside me, a tingle of energy and anticipation. As soon as I get Izzy back to her place, I'm gonna show her how grateful I am.

***

We don't make out on the cab ride home, but we do hold hands the whole way. Izzy's thumb strokes the side of my hand, drawing ticklish patterns meant to tease me. Her smell is stronger, much too faint for anyone without a werewolf's nose to notice, but painfully obvious to me. I'm carrying an ache in my stomach and my heart is beating fast—and for the first time tonight, it's not 'cause I'm scared.

Izzy pays the cabbie, and we hurry into her building. We rush up the stairs so fast it might be embarrassing, except the two of us want the same thing—each other. Once we get to her apartment, I can't wait anymore. I back her into the door and kiss her, bracing both arms beside her head.

As soon as our lips meet, Izzy moans into my mouth. Heaven almighty, she tastes even better than she smells. Even though I've had her lips before, it still blows me away every time. It's a flavor I'll never tire of, and it leaves me craving more.

"Inside," Izzy pants against my mouth. "We should—"

I groan. The last thing I wanna do is stop kissing her but doing it horizontal is probably a good idea. I give Izzy enough space to pull out her keys and fumble with the lock. It clicks open, and the two of us stumble into her apartment, kicking off our shoes as we go. I steer Izzy toward the couch, since it's the closest piece of furniture that'll hold the two of us, but she takes control, pulling me back into her bedroom by the collar of my shirt.

Once we stagger into the room, Izzy falls backwards onto the mattress and drags me down too. My body settles over hers, and she wraps her leg around my hip to keep me close. We kiss again and again, until I'm so lightheaded I can barely remember my own name, let alone how worried I was about this. Like the rest of our date in the Gardens, this feels right.

Izzy sucks my lower lip, digging in gently with the needles of her teeth. A surge of warmth shoots through me, throbbing between my legs. Izzy's fangs never hurt, but the tingly sensation I feel every time she drinks is overwhelming. It makes me squirm on top of her, searching for something to rub against.

Our clothes are in the way. I yank off my blazer and start on my shirt, but Izzy takes over, unfastening the buttons with shaking fingers. I know I should let her take it off, but I can't stop kissing her. Her lips taste so sweet. The short sucks she takes from my mouth have me shaking with need.

I feel pressure building within me, a drumming pulse in my head that means I'm close to losing control. With anyone but Izzy, it'd be embarrassing, but she doesn't spook when I go feral. She seems to sense it coming, because she finishes unbuttoning my shirt and mutters, "Go ahead, baby."

Red heat overtakes me. My hair gets a little thicker, and my ears and teeth go pointy, but the biggest change is inside. There's a wildfire raging within me, and I can't contain it. I grab Izzy's wrists and pin them to the mattress, sinking my teeth into her shoulder. Her skin is almost as delicious as her mouth. I groan, running my tongue through the salt at the crook of her neck. Izzy's taste drives me wild, and my hips move on instinct.

Each push ends in frustration. I want her—so, so bad—but she's still got on her shirt and skirt and stockings, and I'm wearing my binder, pants, and a sticky pair of boxers. As much as I want to strip, I need

Izzy's skin more. I let go of her wrists and rip her shirt off, sending scraps fluttering, so I can kiss my way down her chest. I'm too impatient to pull off her bra, so I yank the left cup down and wrap my lips around her nipple.

Izzy wails. Her hands shoot down to my head, twining into my hair. The scratch of her nails on my scalp makes me shiver like crazy. I kiss across to her other breast, but she only lets me suck for a moment before pulling my head up. Immediately, I'm lost in her eyes. They're such a beautiful hazel-brown that I forget to breathe, and I can see the lanterns of my own reflected in them.

"Riley," she pants, her chest rising and falling with each rapid breath. Her fangs are all the way out, and there's a slight trace of blood on her lip. "Let me up for a second. I need to get your surprise."

I rumble in protest. I don't want her to leave. Letting her body move even a few inches away from mine seems like it'll be unbearable. But she looks so excited, so hopeful, that I can't say no. I roll off her and use the time to strip off my pants and boxers.

Izzy leans over to open the drawer of her nightstand. She pulls out a baggie made of velvety material, and I can see there's something heavy-looking inside. "Sorry I didn't have time to wrap it."

She offers the baggie and I take it from her. "Thanks, Izzy, but you didn't have to." In my mind, I'm already back on top of her, kissing my way down her body. No matter what the present is, it can't compare.

"I wanted to. Open it. Just remember, if you don't like it, you don't need to use it."

I open the drawstring. Inside the bag is...something. Something long. Something long and thick and flesh-colored, with a familiar shape. I pull it out, but I already know what it is.

My face burns, and my eyes water without me fully understanding why. I've wanted a strap-on for ages, but I've always been too afraid to buy one. It's not embarrassment so much as fear of disappointment. Sometimes I feel awkward about my lower parts, and I always worried a fake cock wouldn't be close enough to the real thing for me. And that's what I longed for on those sad nights: something like the real thing.

I look at it, blinking away tears. There are two parts: a sculpted shaft with a set of balls at the bottom, and what looks like a funny-shaped suction cup. The coloring is pretty detailed. There's redness at the tip, sculpted folds of skin under the head, and what looks like the outline of a vein.

"It's enchanted," Izzy says. "A transmutation spell. If you put it on, you'll be able to feel when I touch it."

"Wait, really?"

Izzy must hear the hope in my voice, because she smiles wide. "Yes, really. I have my sources."

My heart swells with hope, and a big helping of gratitude besides. I put the strap-on aside and pull Izzy in for a tight hug, forgetting all about how turned on I am for a moment. I don't know what I did to deserve this—not just the gift, but this woman—but I'm so, so lucky. All I can think to say is, "Thank you," but it doesn't seem like enough.

Izzy doesn't ask for more. She holds me tight, letting me hug my feelings out until I calm down enough to pull away. That's when I remember how close our bodies are and how much I want to touch her. Izzy's skin is normally cool, but some of my warmth has seeped into it, and once in a great while, I can feel the slow beat of her heart. For a vampire, its tempo is pretty fast.

"I wanna try it." I'd be fibbing if I said I wasn't nervous, but there's more to it than that. Maybe it's because I finally came out to Izzy officially, or maybe it's finally the right time, but I want to use the strap-on. I reach for it.

"Are you sure?" Izzy asks.

There's no hesitation on my end. "I'm sure."

"Do you want to put it on, or me?"

I chew on my cheek. Having her put it on is kind of hot, plus I don't know if I'll do it right. But part of me wants to do it on my own. Maybe I'll be clumsy, but I feel like I need to do this. "Me. Is that okay?"

Izzy just laughs. "That's sort of the reason I bought it, *mon chou*."

I stick my tongue out at her. She sticks her tongue out back at me. I lean up so I can pretend to bite it, and then we're kissing again, only this time, I'm hyper aware of the shaft in my hand. Imagining that I might feel Izzy's heat wrapped around me makes the ache inside me worse.

This time, the two of us aren't so urgent. Izzy pulls down her stockings and skirt, and I groan at the sight of her bare stomach. She's so soft, so curvy, so gorgeous and squeezable that I want to gather all of her up in my hands at once. My eyes dart between her plush thighs to steal a look at the bare lips in between. She's wet. Really wet. I can see it as well as smell it, because there's a glistening sheen on her skin.

"Riley?"

I blink. I was so wrapped up in the vision of her that I forgot what I was doing. The urge to touch her is back, even stronger than before. But first, I need to put this thing on. I have a suspicion that once we get going, I'm not gonna want to stop again any time soon.

With a deep breath, I bring the toy between my legs. It doesn't look very stable. The shaft itself is pretty firm, but I don't see how it's going to stick. I put the cup over myself anyway, and gasp in surprise. It kind of suctions onto me, molding to the shape of my lips and clinging between them. The sensation isn't uncomfortable, though. After a few seconds, I don't really feel it.

What I do feel is pressure between my legs. I'm stunned at first. The sight of a shaft pointing up toward my belly is strange and unfamiliar, but also...right, somehow. My insides are still churning, and I can't stop staring. I run my fingers along its length, and it gives a slight twitch. I can feel the graze of my own fingertips, light and ticklish.

"Is it just supposed to stay on like this, or...?"

Izzy's staring between my legs too, but she smiles when she meets my eyes. "I told you, I got it enchanted. The deluxe package."

I can't help it. "Heh. Package."

Izzy rolls her eyes. "Riley..." She leans in, resting her hand on my thigh a few inches short of the cock.

My cock? Yeah. Guess so.

"Riley," Izzy says again, bringing her face close to mine. "Do you want me to touch you?"

You. Not it. I swallow nervously. All I can croak out is, "Yup."

Izzy's fingers are gentle as they curl around me. I'm surprised how much I can feel pressure, texture, temperature. The coolness of her palm leaves me tingly. She squeezes, and I feel the shaft start to warm up. A small pulse shoots along it, and my muscles tense.

I look down. The sight of Izzy's hand on me is incredible all by itself, but there's more. A pool of something is shining on the rosy head of the—of *my* cock. When Izzy spreads it around with her thumb, rubbing the slickness over the tip, my hips jerk on instinct.

"Fuck." The word slips right out, mostly because I'm astonished. If I'd known that enchanted strap-ons felt this good, I would've shelled out for one a long time ago. I watch in awe as a few more clear drops well up, only for Izzy to gather them on her thumb and offer me a taste.

I hesitate. I wasn't expecting her to do that. But I'm curious, so I take her thumb between my lips. The flavor on my tongue is familiar. This is me. I feel full and content inside, almost...proud?

Izzy offers me two more of her fingers to suck, but only for a moment. Then her hand gets back to work between my thighs. She strokes me from bottom to top with a twist of her wrist along the way.

Thanks to my spit and the fluid I'm leaking, every motion feels smooth and silky. Soon I'm clenching the muscles of my backside, fighting the impulse to thrust up into her fist.

"How's this?" Her eyes shift between my face and what she's doing. "Too slow, or just right?"

My mouth hangs open like I'm trying to catch flies. I couldn't have answered even if I knew what to say. It all feels so good that I can't think straight. All I can do is pant and moan and let her jerk me off however she wants.

Izzy takes my noises as her cue to move faster. She keeps an eye on me the whole time, waiting for some sign she should stop, but the last thing I want her to do is stop. I'm hard and throbbing in her hand, like my heart's hammering in her palm.

I do have enough sense left to reach out and brush her springy curls. I draw her in, guiding her mouth to my shoulder. If she's going to keep doing this, it's only fair I give her a meal to keep her energy up. Izzy takes the hint. She latches onto the crook of my neck, and I feel a hot wave of need crash over me as her fangs pierce my skin.

It's too much. I'm so sensitive, and there's so much pressure building in the base of my new shaft, and Izzy's mouth feels so good on my throat. I come with a strangled shout, long before I planned, spilling all over Izzy's fingers in time with the steady pull of her mouth.

Once I've started, I can't stop. My cock pounds harder each time Izzy pumps her fist. When she moves her hand down to cup my balls, I send another spurt splashing onto my stomach. She stays there, squeezing softly until I'm a shuddering mess with nothing else to give.

When it's over, most of my body is still sticky and trembling. "Holy shit," I mutter, slumping forward to rest my forehead on Izzy's shoulder. She unlatches her mouth and laughs, kissing my burning cheek.

"That good, huh?"

I groan. "Any better, and you might've pulled the soul outta me."

Izzy's lips move up to my temple and linger there. "Does that mean you need a rest?" She gives me another squeeze, and I feel a sharp tug in my shaft. Maybe this thing is taking directions from my clit, because underneath, I'm still wet and ready to go, even if my limbs are shaking and my lungs are still screaming for air.

"No, just gimme a minute."

I tilt my head to catch Izzy's lips, and we kiss for a while, exploring each other's mouths. Kissing turns to touching, and touching turns into me stretched out on top of her. Sooner than I think, I've got my energy back. I'm still a little dizzy, but that's not a bad thing. Plus, I'm still happy and lightheaded from Izzy's feeding. She feels warmer with some of my blood in her, and downright fiery when I slide my hand between her legs.

My fingers find wetness right away. Izzy's a dripping mess, and there's no resistance when I push my fingers in. Her muscles clench, and I shudder with want. Soon, I'll get to feel her tightness wrapped around me.

The thought grips my guts and gives a sharp tug. I growl, nosing at Izzy's neck, and rock my hips forward. The tip of my cock skims her soft belly, but it isn't what I need. I want to find out how she feels inside. I've thought about it, dreamed about it more than I'm comfortable admitting.

"Riley," Izzy murmurs. She spreads her legs wide, staring up at me with those beautiful brown eyes. "Fuck me."

Her plea only makes me hungrier. I line my pelvis up with hers and take my shaft in hand. Touching myself isn't as good as when Izzy does it, but I don't care. I'm about to feel something even better.

I use the last of the patience I have to trace the head between her slippery lips, making sure I skim over all her sensitive bits and nudge her clit. Izzy sighs and wraps her arms around me. Her nails rake down my back and I can't wait anymore. I find her opening and push.

The warmth is overwhelming. Most of Izzy's body is a heatsink, but she's a furnace between her legs when she's turned on—and she's definitely turned on, dripping all over me. She's a pool of liquid fire I'm desperate to enter.

I do a few slow strokes first. The thrusting motion is new to me, and kind of awkward too. It pulls my thighs and lower back in strange places, but soon I get the hang of it. Izzy gasps as I work the head inside her, and then she says two words that almost make me come again right then and there: "Riley, more."

More. Izzy wants more of me. My chest nearly bursts with pride. I brace myself on my elbows and try to get deeper. Another inch of my shaft sinks inside, and Izzy's tightness pulls a groan straight out of me. I can feel her walls clenching around me even as they stretch to let me in. It feels so damn good my vision blurs and I have to stop for a second.

Before I can recover, Izzy gets greedy. She drags her right foot up along the back of my thigh and digs her heel into my ass, tightening the hook of her knee around my waist. I slip forward nice and easy. She's tighter than a first-gear hairpin and hotter than all hell, but so slick there's hardly any resistance. After a couple more thrusts, I'm buried balls deep and not sure I can breathe.

Izzy starts moving first. She lifts her hips beneath mine, pressing her clit into me. The motion sends a jolt straight through me. My first thrust is on instinct, but the second one's on purpose—and then I can't stop. I pump in and out of her, not caring that I'm sloppy and awkward. It feels too incredible to stop.

Izzy's like satin shivering around me and it feels amazing, but the sounds. Heavens above, the sounds my girl makes. They're the sweetest things my ears have ever heard, a string of broken moans and high-pitched whimpers. I speed up. I'm of a mind to fuck her 'til she screams my name, and I won't give up, even though pressure's already building in me again.

I try to shut my mind off, to slow down the rush of sensation. *Think about something else. Anything else. Not about how tight she is, or how soft she feels inside, or how warm and wet and—shit.* I bury my face in the pillow beside her head, but my hips have a mind of their own. They keep plowing forward, unsteady and desperate.

Izzy doesn't mind. She wraps her arms around me and holds me close, kissing behind my ear. "You feel so good, baby. Filling me so good..."

My rhythm falters. It's not my name, but I lap up the praise like a lost soul in the desert. I want to fill her good. To make her feel as amazing as I feel. To thank her for being so warm and kind and caring, and for the incredible gift she's given me. After how wonderful she's been to me tonight, she deserves it. I shift my angle a bit, trying to grind the base of my shaft into her clit. She's so wet that I can rub right over it with each thrust, again and again.

That's how I finally make her come. Izzy stiffens beneath me, shuddering from head to toe. The next time I push in, she yelps my name to the ceiling, ending on a sob.

"*Rileeeey!*"

Her nails hook into my back, struggling to find a grip. The sharp little crescents drive me crazy, but not as crazy as the rippling of her inner muscles. They've started pulsing, squeezing me so hard I see spots flash in front of my eyes.

I can't hold up against that. I hit my peak right after Izzy does, jerking hard as all that fullness bursts out of me. I bury my face in her shoulder, flooding her core with each uneven stroke. I can't stop moving, but I've forgotten how to move. My limbs are quivering, and my chest is burning and my cock keeps twitching as I ride out my release—and hers.

I'm not sure how long it lasts. It can only have been a couple seconds, but I feel like I'm suspended in time. There's just Izzy wrapped tight around me, and me spilling all I've got. When it's over, I collapse on top of her in a heap. I'm covered in sweat, a little embarrassed by how exhausted I am. I can't have been fucking Izzy for more than a few minutes, but I'm so done she could stick a fork in me.

"Jeez," I mumble, mostly to myself. "I think I might've left my body for a moment there."

Izzy laughs beneath me, and I grunt as she ripples with a few more aftershocks. "Please don't," she says, petting my spine. "I love your body the way it is. With or without your present."

"Yeah?" I ask, after a few more gulps of air. "Really?"

"Yeah, really." Izzy lowers her legs but makes no other move to push me off or wiggle out from under me. She seems content to lie right where she is, with me still inside her. "I thought you were cute the first time I saw you. That hasn't changed."

"M'not cute," I grumble, a little put out.

"Of course not. You're a very fierce and intimidating wolf." But she can't hide her giggles, so I sigh and chuckle along with her.

We relax after that, cuddling close. It's so quiet I can hear her rare breaths and the slow beat of her heart. I nuzzle her shoulder, inhaling her scent. It smells like home, especially overlaid with mine.

"Hey, Izzy?"

"Mm?"

I swallow a lump in my throat. For some reason, I'm getting all emotional again. In the circle of her arms, I feel completely safe, but also tender and open in a way that leaves me vulnerable. "Thank you. For this. For sticking by me. I would've understood if it was too much."

Izzy brings a hand up to caress my cheek. "I'm finding out there's an awful lot I'm willing to do for you, *mon chou*. But this isn't a problem. I think it's beautiful. I had a sense about you on our first date."

"Really?" I sigh. "Wish you would've told me."

"You needed to be ready. Now you are, and I'm proud of you."

I kiss her. Her mouth is warm and welcoming, and her tongue tastes as sweet as ever. When I break away, I say, "So, we can do this again? With my cock? Not all the time. Just sometimes."

"Whenever you want to. And maybe sometimes when *I* want to."

"And..." My heart starts beating faster. "Could you try calling me 'they' sometimes? I just wanna try it out. See how it feels."

"Of course. Just tell me what pronouns you want me to use that day, and I will."

I smile. "Izzy, I..." I swallow down the words I'm close to saying and go with, "I'm so lucky to have you. You're amazing."

She just laughs and says, "I know. So are you."

That's when my phone flashes from somewhere beside the bed. I squint over and see it sticking out of my pants pocket, flashing with a text. Without getting up to look, I can guess who it's from. Li Min probably wants to know how my date went and whether I talked to Izzy or not.

I sigh and settle back on top of her. I'll fill them in later. Right now, I just wanna live in the moment and think about how lucky I am.

Chapter Six - Isabeau

MY ARMS ACHE AS I struggle against the cuffs around my wrists, burying my face in the sheets to muffle my screams. Riley is behind me, shoving my head into the mattress with one hand, plunging in and out of me with the other. Their rapid strokes rock my entire body forward, but I roll my hips back for more after each one. I want Riley to take me *harder-faster-deeper,* until I can't stand it anymore.

The strain in my shoulders has become a scream. It didn't hurt when Riley first wrenched my elbows behind my back to bind my forearms, but now my joints are burning. It would be all I could think about if Riley wasn't driving into me at such a relentless pace. Their fingers hit my front wall every time they plunge inside, and I can't swallow down my yelps. "Riley," I slur into the covers. They're pounding me so hard I'm drooling, and not only from my mouth.

Riley makes good use of my slickness. They slam all the way in and curl their fingers, applying enough pressure to make me sob. "That's right," they mutter, their voice a low, guttural growl. "You want it rough, huh?" Their hand leaves my hair, but I barely have time to recover before it cracks across my backside, leaving a stinging handprint behind. The sensation morphs into a tingle, then melts into throbbing heat that spreads throughout my core.

I turn my head sideways and try to speak, but all that comes out in a long, needy whine. Riley seems pleased with the sound, because they stop curling their fingers and pick up their rhythm again, using their thigh to add extra force. "You're close. I can feel you clenching."

It's true. I'm not just clenching Riley's fingers, but rippling greedily around them. They've got me riding the razor's edge of release. It will barely take anything at all to push me over.

Riley leans over my back, pressing their breasts into my shoulders. Their hot breath skims the nape of my neck as they rumble possessive words into my prickling flesh. "Tell me who owns you, baby. Tell me who you belong to."

I freeze.

My throat closes up. I can't breathe—and for once, it feels like I need to. My slow-beating heart pumps frantically, and a chill runs through me, making me forget all about the warmth bleeding from Riley's body into mine. Riley's words echo in my head, growing higher and sharper, laced with a familiar edge of derision—*Tell me who owns you, baby.* I try to drown it out with my own voice, but nothing will come out of my stupid mouth. *No make it stop, no make it stop, no make it st—*

"Stop!"

Riley stops. They keep their fingers in me but lift their body off mine to give me more freedom. "What's wrong? Do you need out of the cuffs? I didn't hurt you, did I?"

I don't know how to answer. Riley hasn't *hurt me* hurt me, but I'm still shivering with sick, clammy fear. Cold sweat beads on my skin as I struggle against the cuffs, trying to get loose. Can't stay like this. Need to move. All I want to do is free myself so I can dive under the covers.

I'm strong enough to rip through the Velcro padded cuffs, or even the steel links between them, but I don't need to. Riley pulls out and unfastens them for me. I feel worry and hesitancy in their touch. Their fingers are light as bird feathers, and just as delicate and uncertain.

Once my arms are free, I calm down. I roll onto my side and draw my knees up to my chest, ignoring the sticky wetness clinging to my thighs. *What was that? What happened to me?* My thoughts sound small and distant in my own head. *Did I just...have a panic attack or something?*

"Izzy?" Riley sounds heartbroken as they lie down behind me, settling into a spooning position without actually touching me. "I'm gonna touch your back now, okay?" They wait, giving me a chance to say no. I don't say anything at all. Riley's warm palm presses between my shoulder blades, and it's enough to loosen the knot in my chest.

"Sorry," I croak, confused tears running down my cheeks. "I don't know...I'm not sure what..."

Riley wraps their arm around my waist, pulling me closer. "Hey, sunshine. It's okay. You don't have a damn thing to be sorry for, you hear? I'll just hold you 'til you feel better." Their sweet words make me cry harder. I shake in Riley's arms, letting them hold me while I sob it out. My mind is a jumble of anxiety and confusion, but having their body pressed into mine helps. I clutch their hand, squeezing their fingers until I stop quaking.

When my breathing evens out, Riley kisses the back of my

shoulder. "Hey."

"Hey." My throat still hurts, but otherwise, I feel utterly numb and exhausted. If I didn't know better, I'd think I was about to float away into the air.

"Anything I can get you? Somethin' to drink? Heating pad? A fluffy blanket?"

"Thank you." It's all I can think of to say. Riley's kindness hurts, but almost in a good way. It's not something I'm used to getting from people, except on really bad days when I can't hide behind a smile.

"Nothing to thank me for." Riley pauses, seeming uncertain, perhaps even guilty. "Do you wanna talk about it? You don't have to."

I flip onto my other side so Riley and I can look at each other. "It wasn't your fault. It's just...you remember my ex?"

I don't have to explain further. Riley gets it—that Natasha used to say the same thing. I can tell from the look in their eyes—all guilt. "I'm sorry," they say, and my heart breaks a little more.

"Don't be. How could you know?"

Riley's face scrunches up, but they can't come up with an answer. They hold me for a while, calming me with their warm breath and the steady beat of their heart.

Eventually, I say, "Thanks."

The word sounds loud in the silence. Riley's brow furrows. "What for?"

"For being you."

Riley cracks a small smile. "For showing my girl some basic human kindness?"

It's supposed to be a joke, but I don't laugh. I nod yes. A shadow crosses Riley's face as it clicks for them. I wasn't always shown that kindness. I didn't always think I was good enough for it.

"Baby..."

"We don't have to talk about it," I murmur, then correct it to, "I don't want to talk about it right now."

Riley seems okay with that. "What should I do?"

That simple question reassures me that I made the right choice in picking Riley. I can tell they're worried and hurt, but they're putting my needs first. Like a lover is supposed to.

"Just hold me. That's all I need."

Riley wraps their arms tighter around me. We lie like that for a long time, and the silence isn't uncomfortable.

***

I pull my cardigan tighter around my shoulders as I walk through the frozen section at the local Whole Foods. I usually head for Stop & Go, since it's closer to my apartment, but their selection is less than ideal. I've been craving goat blood rather than the usual cow or pig (or werewolf) lately, and the smaller grocery stores always seem to be out of stock.

It seems today's my lucky day. At the end of the aisle, near a rather pretentious sign, I spot a five-gallon jug of the stuff: the very last one. I push my cart over, but stop short when another cart turns the corner, converging on the same spot. The woman behind the cart looks at me, offering a tight smile.

Shit!

"Natasha."

"Isabeau. How are you?"

I try not to stare too hard, but I can't help it. I haven't seen Natasha in years, but she still looks the same, aside from a more modern hairstyle. Tall, thin, blue eyes. A dancer's body. Despite her slenderness, she has an aura of power around her, an invisible projection of strength that's difficult to describe. Maybe it's the way she moves, confident and graceful, like she knows exactly where she's going and how to get there. Years ago, I wanted nothing more than to be with her, be like her. Now...

I eventually manage a forced, "Fine. How long have you been back in the city?"

"Oh, only a year," Natasha says, in her usual breezy way. "It's hard to keep track, you know."

I do know. I know because I took the gift of immortality under the assumption that we'd spend our eternal lives together. Despite what most people with average human lifespans think, there are some serious downsides to the Choice. That's why the government makes you fill out so many forms before they let you do it—and why so many people do the bite illegally and pay the fine afterward. With eternal life, even the poor ones have plenty of time to pay it off if they aren't screwed on interest rates.

"I got tired of being on tour," Natasha says, "so I accepted a position here. I needed something more permanent."

It takes everything I have to not roll my eyes. Natasha definitely doesn't do permanent. Never has.

"That's...nice."

"What about you?" Natasha asks. "Are you still working at the computer store?

My jaw clenches despite my best efforts. "Learning center. I enjoy it."

"And what about Elyse?"

"She's great."

"Tell her hello."

I have no intention of doing that, and both of us know it. My phone buzzes in my purse, and I pull it out, grateful for the interruption. It's Riley, calling instead of texting. That's unusual, so I pick up out of habit. I'm not going to turn down a conversation with my favorite werewolf to make forced small talk with my ex.

"Sorry," I say to Natasha, turning away and hitting the talk button. *"Bonjou, mon chou."*

Riley laughs on the other end of the line. *"Hey. That kinda rhymes."*

Their voice makes me smile. "Still not over that?"

"Nope. What're your plans for dinner? I would've texted, but I wanted to hear your voice."

I know the real reason—because Riley's still worried about last night. They're checking in on me while still trying to give me a little space. I don't know what I've done to deserve them.

"Sure, I can do dinner. Your place or mine?"

Natasha gives me a curious look, like she's paying attention for the first time.

"Is mine okay? I've got a steak I've been meaning to thaw out and a quart of blood in my fridge."

"I don't know." I shift my weight to one hip, murmuring in a husky voice. "Werewolf sounds pretty delicious right about now."

"Oh?" Riley sounds surprised, but hopeful.

"I can head over now if you want."

"Sure. I just gotta throw a load of laundry in. Text me when you get here."

"All right. Bye, baby."

I end the call and turn to Natasha. Her smile is a little icier than before. "New girlfriend?"

"New werefriend. It's going really well." I nod at the jug of goat blood. "You go ahead and take that. I have dinner plans anyway."

"Thanks," Natasha says, still looking vaguely unsettled. Good. At least that makes two of us. I don't know what she was expecting. Was I supposed to pine after her forever? Probably, now that I think about it. She's always had a high opinion of herself.

"Bye. See you around." I push my cart away, taking the short route to the checkout counter. I don't want to stay here any longer than I have to.

***

By the time I get to Riley's, my hands are shaking. A storm of emotions churns in my stomach—fear, anger, guilt. It embarrasses me to admit I'm afraid, even after all these years, not because Natasha would ever raise a hand to me, but because of the pain she put me through. It was more than lying. It was more than cheating. Honestly, those were the least of her sins. I could have forgiven those if she'd showed sincere regret. It was that she'd made those things feel like my fault, like I was obligated to forgive her.

My anger toward her isn't a new emotion, but it's one I thought I was mostly done with. It's frustrating to feel the burn in my chest, the tension in the corners of my jaw. I've been so happy these past few months with Riley that I've hardly thought about Natasha at all, and I'm pissed she's popped my happy bubble, even for a moment.

But the guilt is the worst. I know it's stupid, but even after two decades, I still feel guilty for the way things ended. There's always that stupid voice in the back of my head whispering, *"You should have given her another chance."*

I'm not going to. Logically, I know she doesn't deserve it. But even though the last thing I want is to get back together with her, part of me feels bad for ending things. Maybe it's habit. I forgave her mistakes for so long, made excuses for them, blamed myself for them. I've spent a long time traveling out of the fog, but it only took one chance encounter for me to get lost in it all over again.

I stare down at the welcome mat in front of Riley's door, a pretty blue one that says, 'Please Come In' so I can enter their home whenever I want. If there's two things I know about Riley, it's that they're not like Natasha, and more importantly, they care about me. I need to be around someone who cares about me right now. I open the door, which is already unlocked for me.

Riley is waiting for me on the living room couch. They smile, and I manage a small smile in return. "C'mon in, sunshine," they say, even though the mat is all the invitation I need.

I step over the threshold, and when I do, Riley gets up from the couch and goes in for a hug. They hesitate a little, like they're not sure they're allowed. I put a stop to that line of thinking. "You can touch me like normal, Riley. I want you to. What happened last night doesn't have much to do with you at all."

Riley embraces me and relaxes. "Sorry. It's just, you smell upset."

I sigh. That's one of the downsides of dating a werewolf. Riley always seems hyper-attuned to my emotions. "A little. I'll tell you about it if you want."

We head over to the couch. The inside of Riley's apartment looks a lot prettier than the first time I saw it. The sheer yellow curtains do a lot to brighten up the living room, and the spider plants hanging from the ceiling in the adjoined kitchen are doing well. Riley was afraid they'd fail at basic plant ownership, so I'm glad to see they've proven themself wrong.

Riley looks at me nervously. "So, what's going on?"

I summon my courage. I don't really want to talk about this, but I owe Riley a cursory explanation instead of just sulking silently over dinner. That's not the type of person I want to be. "Had a not-so-great moment at the grocery store. I ran into Natasha in the frozen food aisle."

"Natasha, your ex?" Riley's nose wrinkles like a wolf's might when they're about to growl, and I can practically see their hair bristle.

"Mmhmm."

Riley pushes aside their initial reaction and seems to calm down. Instead of getting angry on my behalf, they look concerned. "I'd call that a shitty day instead of a not-so-great moment."

"I try not to generalize days. It helps me to remember things can still turn around."

"Fair 'nough. I know I just did, but can I hug you again?"

It's such a sweet request that I open my arms. "My hugs are always free for you."

We embrace again. Riley doesn't let go for a long time, and neither do I. It feels good to hold them, to remember the way our bodies fit together, to savor the physical proof that I've built something for myself that has nothing to do with my old life.

After a little while, they dip their head to kiss me, asking permission first with a brief hesitation. I kiss back, sighing as their warm lips slide against mine. Riley tastes like Riley, and a little more of my pain ebbs away. The ache isn't gone, but that's okay for now, because it isn't the only thing I feel anymore. I break away from Riley's mouth, but not before sharing one more softer kiss to end the first one.

"Can we cuddle for a while? Watch a movie?"

Riley smiles. "Sounds good to me. *Miss Congeniality* or *Legally Blonde?*"

I chuckle. *"Legally Blonde.* You know me so well."

We snuggle up under Riley's afghan, them with both arms draped over the back of the couch, me on my side with my head in their lap. They start the movie, then settle in to stroke my hair.

The next hour or so is nice. I'm able to force a few laughs, and Riley cracks a couple jokes. In the middle of the movie, they silently offer me their wrist, and after checking to make sure it's okay, I bite down and tap an artery for a few small sips of blood. Not enough to make Riley dizzy or horny, but enough so they won't worry about me being hungry or cold. They've probably noticed I haven't asked for anything to eat yet and don't have much of an appetite.

"That's it?" They ask when I break away and lick my lips.

"You sound disappointed."

"Well, it does feel good for me," Riley says. "But really, I wanna make sure you're okay."

"I'm not too hungry, but thanks. Sometimes you just need to eat even when you don't feel like it."

We settle back into silence, and Riley resumes stroking my hair.

I try to keep watching the movie, but my mind is floating elsewhere, drifting backwards through memories. Maybe my feelings about Natasha wouldn't be so confusing if they were all bad, but they aren't. I still remember our first trip together. She took me to Paris, on her dime. We spent our days at museums and old churches, peering up through stained glass windows. We spent our nights under satin sheets, making love until our trembling bodies were bathed in sweat. We rode on a ferry boat together as the sun was setting and the streetlights came on, and Natasha held my hand and told me she loved me.

At the time, I hadn't been sure I loved her yet. Our relationship was still so new, but it was exciting and full of wonderful possibilities. So, I'd said I loved her back, and she'd kissed me as the stars came out. Even now, as deep as Natasha has scarred me, and as much as I've come to care for Riley, remembering Paris makes me smile. The memory is beautiful, but bittersweet. Thinking about it makes me want to cling tighter, and also let go faster, because holding on hurts.

"Izzy?" Riley must have noticed me drifting off into my own world, because they stop stroking my hair. "You okay?"

I flip over onto my back, so I can stare up at them. "Yes…no. Not really."

Riley tilts their head. "Why not?"

I sigh, struggling to put it into words. "Have you ever been in a relationship that seemed perfect? Like some kind of dream? But when you looked closer, every little thing that went wrong ended up being your fault somehow?"

Riley's brow furrows. "No. But you know I haven't had many relationships to speak of."

I do know. Riley's told me some about growing up in Georgia, in a majority-human school. The girls who had dated them had done it for the novelty, mostly, taking advantage of their sincerity and sweetness. I can relate to that. My relationship with Natasha was different, but I remember how it feels to have my good intentions used against me.

"A friendship, then. Or a family relationship. Someone who you loved being around, but the more time you spent together, the more you felt like you were constantly making mistakes?"

"Not really. Sorry. But it sounds awful."

"Don't be sorry," I say. "I'm glad you haven't known someone like that. But that's what it was like for me, all the time. It was just little things at first. If she was late for work, it was because I didn't wake her up soon enough, even though she didn't ask me to. And she had this really beautiful car, right? A Bugatti from the continent. It got sideswiped once, because she was going too fast through a construction zone and didn't realize the lanes were merging. She said it was my fault for 'distracting' her while she was driving."

Riley continues listening, shaking their head slowly. "She sounds…well, like she's got her nose so high in the air she'd drown if it was rainin'."

I chuckle. "Sometimes. But it wasn't all bad, or it would be easier to hate her. Or I never would have fallen for her in the first place. She could be really sweet. She gave me flowers, bought me presents. Took me on nice dates. Told me I was beautiful and that she never wanted to let me go." I pause, draping my forearm over my forehead. I need just a little protection, a little bit of distance, even though Riley's eyes are full of nothing but empathy. "But it was a pattern. She'd do that after she blew up at me."

Riley doesn't say anything. They nod for me to keep going.

"Want to know what happened when I caught her cheating on me?

She broke down crying. She had a total meltdown, I'm talking mentally unstable. She said she was sorry, but it was my fault for not having sex with her whenever she wanted, however she wanted. She swore she'd never do it again, but she'd looked elsewhere because I wasn't emotionally present enough for her. She loved me, but she needed to feel loved and appreciated, because I wasn't giving her enough."

"Sounds like she had enough 'buts' to fill an ashtray."

"That sounds about right."

"I'm sorry, I know those words probably don't mean much—"

"They do," I insist.

"Good. But I wish someone you loved hadn't blamed you for everything they did wrong. You don't deserve that."

I give Riley a faint smile. "I know that now. It was harder to see in the middle of it all. The thing about emotionally abusive relationships is you constantly question yourself. I'd lie awake nights thinking, 'What if I really did neglect her? What if I'm a horrible person? How does she even put up with me?'"

"You're not a horrible person. You're a beautiful person."

I turn my head to the side on Riley's lap and face their stomach. "So are you." I place a kiss on Riley's belly through their shirt, and they stroke my hair again.

"How did it end?"

"Exhaustion, and Elyse. She and Natasha never liked each other, so I had to walk a tightrope to split my time. It was Elyse's birthday, and we have this tradition. Every year we go out and do some kind of community service, then after we finish for the day, we get drunk and stay awake all night." I smile as I talk about it. The combination of wine and sleep deprivation during those early morning hours has made for some pretty entertaining memories.

Riley grins. "Not a bad way to spend a birthday."

"And there are donuts. Always lots and lots of donuts. So many donuts, Riley."

"Is Elyse havin' a birthday any time soon? Because I don't wanna intrude, but that sounds like a tradition I'd like to be part of."

"I'll ask. Anyway, Natasha asked me not to go. She kept changing the reason, but eventually, she came right out and said it. 'If you go, it means you don't love me.' And I thought about it and said, 'You know what? Elyse isn't the one asking me to choose.' I wasn't going to be with someone who thought me loving my friends meant I didn't love her. If she loved me, she wouldn't punish me for having other relationships."

Riley's quiet for a long time. "You were right to leave, Izzy. You deserve to have friends."

"I know," I whisper.

"Can I ask a question?"

"Shoot."

"Is that why I haven't met Elyse yet? And why you haven't gotten around to meeting Colin?"

I feel a stab of guilt. Riley's tried to get us together a few times, but I've been flaky on the subject instead of taking their offers. "Sort of. It's irrational, but part of me is afraid you'll ask me to choose too. I know you're not like that...I guess I'm still carrying around some baggage."

"It's okay. I...I...care about you, baggage and all."

Although Riley tries to hide it, I can't help but notice them stammer. It's obvious what they were going to say, and it should scare me, but it doesn't. Maybe it's how safe they make me feel, or maybe I'm starting to feel it too. The fact that Riley's biting their tongue and letting me have this moment means something. Natasha would have made it all about her.

I smile up at Riley from their lap. "I know you do. Kiss me?"

When I crook my finger, Riley bends down. Their lips are warm and soft against mine, and unusually tender. Riley seems to be worried about pushing me into intimacy while I'm emotional, but I thread my fingers through their hair and around the back of their neck, urging them to kiss me harder.

We kiss that way for a while, slow and deep. It's calm, unhurried, and the fire in my belly is a steadily growing simmer. Pulling Riley down toward my mouth starts to get uncomfortable, so we adjust. They hesitate, but I guide them on top of me, sighing as their body stretches out over mine. I've gotten used to Riley's weight, to the way we fit together.

"You don't have to worry," I whisper near Riley's lips. "I'm a little raw right now, but I'm not going to have another anxiety attack."

Riley doesn't look convinced. Their brow gets an adorable little furrow, and they frown with worry. "You didn't know you would last time either."

"True." I run my palm down Riley's back, stroking their spine through the fabric of their shirt. "But I don't want to put sex on hold because of one bad experience. I want you." A thought occurs to me. "Unless you don't want to?"

Riley rocks their pelvis forward into mine. Their tongue swipes along my lower lip, then presses gently into my mouth. Apparently, they do want to. Stripping out of our clothes is a gradual process. I peel Riley's shirt off slowly, savoring their bare skin beneath my fingertips. They start kissing my neck and need to be coaxed away so I can get their arms out of the sleeves. As soon as the shirt's gone, Riley's right back on me, hot mouth latched onto my collarbone. Usually Riley's a bit of a biter—vampires aren't the only ones—but tonight, they seem content just to taste my flesh.

I return the favor. I'm still not that hungry, but it doesn't stop me from nibbling the lobe of Riley's ear and kissing the sensitive spot behind it. Riley shudders, and their blue eyes go slightly yellow. They unzip their binder, which surprises me a little, but when they bring one of my hands to their breast, I give it a tentative squeeze. Apparently, that's okay today. I sigh into Riley's mouth, rolling their nipple lightly between two fingers.

That earns me a groan of approval. While I'm occupied, Riley wiggles one hand under me, searching for the zipper on my dress. There isn't one, so I regretfully let Riley go, giving them a slight push. I stand, then pull the dress off from the bottom up before letting it fall onto the floor by my feet.

The look of wonder in Riley's eyes makes losing their warm body to the cold caress of the air worth it. They simply stare at me for a moment, lips slightly parted, the corners of their mouth twitched up in a smile. "You're beautiful," they breathe, with just a bit of a growl in their voice.

I know Riley doesn't just mean my body. While I'm up, I pull off my leggings and underwear. Riley keeps staring while I do, but then they get the hint and start kicking off their pants. By the time I saunter back to them in just my bra, they're completely naked. I'm more subtle about it, but I'm in awe of Riley too. Their broad shoulders, their firm stomach, the patch of golden hair between their legs with a hint of pink wetness underneath—the sight of it all leaves me breathless more than I already am.

When I reach the couch, I swing one knee over Riley's lap, straddling those lean, powerful hips I love so much. Riley wraps their arms around me, and they unfasten the hooks of my bra, peeling it off so they can guide one of my nipples into their mouth. The swirl of their tongue makes me tremble, and I clutch the back of their head with one hand, their shoulder with the other.

Riley spends a long time on my breasts, not just sucking the peaks, but kissing around their curves, leaving soft indents in my flesh with their teeth. Soon, my nipples are slick and straining against the air, and the ache between my legs has become a serious distraction. I'm dripping already, spilling slickness onto my inner thighs.

"I'm gonna touch you. Okay, sunshine?" Riley murmurs into my sternum, sliding one of their hands down my back to squeeze my rear. The other runs up my leg, gathering up a little of my wetness on the way.

I place a kiss on top of their head. "Okay."

Riley cups their hand between my thighs. They press in gently at first, massaging my outer lips without dipping between them. I gasp anyway. The pressure feels good, even if it's indirect. A groan slips out of me when Riley draws my nipple back into their mouth. They start to suck, and I twitch hard beneath their fingers.

Despite my urgent noises, Riley takes their time. It feels like forever before they slide deeper, gliding from my entrance to my clit. The touch is feather light, and I squirm and rock my hips in search of more. Riley kneads my backside, digging the edges of their nails in. They won't demand it, but they don't want me to move.

I manage to hold still as Riley strokes me, but it's a struggle. Their fingers feel so good that I can't help but want them inside me. I whimper and spread my thighs wider, hoping that might speed things along. Instead, Riley focuses on my clit, massaging the shaft through its hood with their second and fourth finger. Their middle finger flicks the tip, spreading my wetness all over it.

My body quivers. I'm suspended between sensations, lost to the warm pull of Riley's mouth and the steady stroke of their fingers. The push and pull is gentle, but in the way waves on the beach are gentle, with a whole ocean of power rocking behind them. Need courses through me, but I'm content to float. In Riley's arms, I know I'll be borne safely to paradise.

Only when I'm desperate does Riley slide inside me. They sink in with one finger at first, stirring slowly, stroking in search of familiar pleasure spots. When I whine and rock forward, one finger becomes two. Riley hooks them forward, drawing cries from deep within my chest. They feel so good inside me. Almost too good. My vision blurs with tears and my heart, which hardly beats at all these days, pounds like a drum.

Riley releases my nipple with a pop, gazing up at me with their bright yellow eyes. "Izzy, I..." There is a look of helplessness on their face that hooks right into me. I know what they want to say. I can feel the words swelling inside me, too. But Riley swallows it down, because they love me enough not to tell me they love me while I'm so vulnerable.

Maybe that's what convinces me to speak. Yet again, Riley has put my feelings before theirs. They're aware of my comfort in a way no other lover has ever been—in a way that leaves me utterly defenseless. It doesn't feel like a choice, more of an inevitability when I open my mouth and say, "Riley...I love you."

The lanterns of Riley's eyes grow wide. They gasp, as if they can't quite believe it, but then a wide smile of wonder spreads across their face. Even with the pointy teeth, there's no way that smile could be anything but gentle. It's overflowing with love, and it has me close to overflowing too as I clench around their fingers.

Riley takes that as a sign to resume moving inside me. They take me with gentle thrusts, adding a third finger and positioning their thumb on my clit. "I love you too, Izzy," they mutter into my shoulder, placing soft, wet kisses there. Riley had struggled to speak before, but now, the words come pouring out: "I didn't wanna say it before you were ready, but I love you. I've loved you for a while now. I'm not sure I'm ever gonna stop."

The truth of that love shines up from Riley's face, and I can't help but bend down and kiss them. Our lips meet, and it feels like the sealing of a promise: not one that scares me, but one that offers security and reassurance. Riley makes me feel safe. I kiss Riley as tenderly as I can, trying to show them without words.

Once our lips meet, Riley puts their all into making me come. They still take their time, but there's passion behind every touch, a determination that makes me tremble. Their fingers pump in and out, stretching me, hitting my deepest places. When their tongue swipes against my lips, asking for entrance, I open so Riley can press into my mouth. My hunger has returned, so I nick their tongue as gently as possible with my fangs, sucking softly for a taste of blood.

Riley shudders beneath me. They hold their mouth still, allowing me to drink as they speed up their strokes inside me. Their fingers curl at just the right angle, with the perfect amount of pressure, and I begin to clench. At first, I consider holding back. This moment is so beautiful, so precious, that I want to make it last as long as possible before it becomes a memory. But my wistfulness doesn't last, because I realize I've got time. Lots of it. Plenty of time to make as many memories as I want with Riley, some of which might be so wonderful that I can't even imagine them yet.

I come with the next stroke of Riley's fingers. Their thumb rubs slippery circles over my clit, and I unravel at my very seams. I squeeze tight around them, giving myself over to the churning deep within my core. The ocean inside me overflows, streaming down into Riley's cupped hand and running in gleaming ribbons down my thighs. Riley groans into my mouth, but lets me keep sucking their tongue, allowing me to have my fill of them.

In that moment, I know with calming certainty that I will never have enough of them, in any sense of the word.

Riley strokes me through my peak, trying to time their movements with the rippling of my muscles. Our first time together was beautiful, all those months ago, but now it's beautiful in a different way. Because Riley knows me. Because Riley loves me. Riley loves me, and I love Riley.

Since my mouth is locked with theirs, I say I love you as best I can with my body. I come until I'm a puddle of myself, slumped over in Riley's lap, still twitching with aftershocks. Our lips finally part, and Riley wraps their free arm around my waist, letting me huddle against them. They kiss my head, and I hear them inhale my scent deeply.

"I love you, Izzy." Riley still sounds enamored of the words, as if they can't believe how wondrous it is to speak them.

I can't believe it either. "I love you too, Riley. I do."

Riley chuckles softly. "Then I'm the luckiest person in the whole world."

I smirk into Riley's neck. "If you aren't now, you're about to be."

I take my time kissing my way down Riley's body. There's so much skin to savor, so many places for my mouth to linger. Riley tastes like sweat and passion as I drag my tongue along their collarbone, and their sighs tell me they're eager for me to go lower. After checking in to make sure I'm allowed, I move on to their breasts, dusting kisses until their tight pink nipples are red at the tips. Riley grasps my hair, tugging lightly. Their glowing eyes are full of need, and I can't say no. I lick my way down Riley's stomach and slip off the couch, kneeling at their feet.

My mouth waters when Riley's scent hits my nose. It's strong, but not overpowering—and I want more. I run my hands up Riley's calves, urging them to hook their knees over my shoulders. When they do, I have an even better view between their thighs. Riley's gleaming pink lips are already parted, and their clit is slick and swollen.

I decide not to tease. Riley's already given me so much tonight, and I want to give back. I draw them between my lips, and I'm rewarded with a fresh stream of wetness.

Riley inhales, tipping their head back. "Izzy..."

I move my tongue in deliberate circles, searching for the right amount of pressure. I know I've found it when Riley's backside lifts an inch off the couch, like they're about to float away. "Just relax," I murmur, kissing their outer folds. "Relax and feel loved."

Riley melts into the couch. Their hand relaxes on top of my head, and they spread their legs wider. I take that as my invitation to drink my fill.

There's no rush as I slide my tongue through Riley's sweetness. The urge to taste every bit of Riley at once is almost overpowering, but my desire to make this last is stronger. I've got all the time I could need or want to relearn Riley's landscape with my mouth, to seek out the spots that make them shiver. Sometimes I use my lips, dragging wet kisses where I know they'll make Riley moan the loudest. Other times, I use my fangs. Riley never tenses, not even when I pierce their tender flesh and drink. They tilt their hips up, rocking forward each time I draw.

Something about Riley's flavor is different. They've always tasted wonderful, right from the first night I fed from them—hot and sweet and tingly, like fresh apple cider in fall. Tonight, though, the rush of their blood leaves me dizzy. Maybe I'm being sentimental, or overly present in the moment, but if I could drink nothing else for the rest of my immortal life, I wouldn't be disappointed. Riley isn't just feeding me. They're sustaining me.

Soon my belly is full of warmth and Riley is jogging desperately against my mouth. Their movements aren't rough, but they are needful—and they're so wet that the lower half of my face is drenched. "Izzy. Please, love..."

My heart swells at the sound of my name on Riley's lips. I stop thrusting my tongue against their entrance and return to their clit, sucking the stiff bud as deep as I can. Riley groans, pulling my hair just enough tilt my head up. As I gaze into their eyes, they finally come.

Riley's orgasm isn't merely a physical release. It's a profound moment of connection that stretches between the two of us. There are new depths within Riley's golden eyes I've never reached before, and neither of us blink as a pulsing river spills over my chin. Riley's shivers are mine, and so is their pleasure. I can taste it, even feel its echoes in my own body.

Most of all, I feel love. It should scare me, but it doesn't. It's a feeling of intense warmth, like being held by a pair of strong arms after standing alone in the cold.

Eventually, Riley stops bucking. Their ripples grow softer, and their grip on my hair loosens. I pull back, running my tongue over my lips. The warmth inside me hasn't faded. It only grows brighter as Riley smiles at me. "Hey," they murmur, stroking my full lower lip with the pad of their thumb. "C'mon up here and gimme some sugar."

I climb back into Riley's lap, framing their face in my hands and leaning in to kiss them. I stroke my tongue along theirs, letting Riley taste themself before resting our foreheads together. "I probably shouldn't ask and ruin the moment, but what does this mean to you? What does 'I love you' mean?"

Riley wraps an arm around my waist, tracing patterns on the small of my back with their fingertips. "For me, it means my heart's extra full when I'm around you. It means the moments I'm with you are my favorites. And it means I don't know what my future'll be like, but I'm damn sure I want you in it with me." Their forehead crinkles with concern, like they're worried they may have overstepped. "Is that okay?"

I kiss Riley again. "I couldn't have put it better."

***

"Hey, don't be nervous, sunshine," Riley says, placing their hand over mine on the table. "It'll be okay. Promise."

"I'm not nervous," I insist. We're at Crossbones, tucked away in a cozy booth at the back of the restaurant. I'd hoped familiar surroundings might bolster my courage, but so far, it isn't working. I'm stupidly and irrationally terrified.

"Honey, you're sweating like a whore in church."

"Am not. Vampires don't sweat."

"Maybe not as much as humans or werewolves, but your hand's awful warm."

I scowl because Riley's right. My fingers do feel sticky under theirs, and my heart's beating much faster and more frequently than it's supposed to, especially considering I haven't had much blood today. That probably explains my overheated skin, although the dizziness is definitely nerves.

I pull my hand away. "It's not a big deal."

Riley puts their palm on my thigh under the table. "Yup. You'll be back to your pleasant perky self in no time."

"You know that isn't really me, right?"

Riley frowns. "Whatcha mean?"

"The energy and optimism. It's something I do, not who I am. My mind likes to tell me everything's horrible all the time, so...I've developed this persona." I sigh. "Sometimes if I keep telling myself everything is wonderful, I can trick myself into believing it."

"Wouldn't call it a trick." Riley steals another squeeze of my leg. "I'd call it being balanced. And just because you work harder to feel happy than most folks doesn't mean it's all fake, either. You wouldn't try so hard if you didn't think happiness was important."

It seems simple when Riley says it. Sharing the struggle with someone else makes it feel less overwhelming. I lean over and rest my cheek on their shoulder. "I really do love you. You know that, right, *mon chou?*"

Riley grins. "Yup. I know. I love you back."

The tinkling sound of the bell above the door makes me lift my head. I've been listening for it above the ambient noise of the restaurant, but until now, I've only seen strangers enter. This time, I catch a glimpse of Elyse approaching the hostess desk to ask for us.

"You heard that all the way across the room?" Riley asks.

"Ears of a bat. Literally. When I am one, I can hear a moth's wings a mile away."

"Damn, woman," Riley chuckles. "And I thought my hearing was good."

"What's good?" Elyse asks as she approaches our table. "The appetizers you already ordered, I hope."

"Yes, I got your fried pickles," I grumble, rolling my eyes. Elyse never changes.

Elyse plops down at the table across from us, and her purse hits the seat beside her with a thump. "You know, Riley, when this one first told me fried pickles were A Thing in the south..." Elyse nods her head at me with raised eyebrows. "I thought she was nuts. Who looked at a pickle one day and thought, 'I know! I'm going to dip this in a greasy frying vat and see what happens.'"

Riley seems slightly taken aback at first, like they weren't expecting Elyse to treat them in such a familiar way within seconds of meeting. But, true to form, Riley rolls with it like a champ. "Some guy in Arkansas, far as I know." They stick their hand out across the table. "Riley Evans."

"Sorry, I'm an ass." Elyse takes Riley's hand and shakes. "Elyse, the one who's been snooping on your Facebook."

Riley looks sheepish. "Oh, uh...yeah. I'm not on that too much."

"It's okay," Elyse says. "I won't judge a werewolf for liking cat videos."

"Speaking of, Leecy, did you ever figure out the deal with Mrs. Grimmaldis' laptop?"

Elyse leans in toward both of us with a conspiratorial look. "Online poker. Big time. Guess she's gotta keep all those cats in the kibble somehow."

Riley's brow furrows in confusion. "Wait, is this Mrs. Grimmaldis a werecat, or does she just have a lot of cats?"

"Both," Elyse and I say together. Then Elyse says, "Jinx!" before I can get it out.

While I press my lips together, stewing in silence, Elyse fixes her attention on Riley. "Some free advice...don't play jinx with an actual sorceress. So, interview time. What are your intentions toward my best friend, Riley Evans?"

Riley sputters, looking adorably confused and helpless. "Like, sexually?"

"That depends. Is that how you want to answer the question?"

Even though I can't speak because of the jinx, I use my eyes to maximum effect, glaring daggers into the side of Elyse's head. She pretends not to notice.

As it turns out, Riley doesn't need my help. They shrug. "My moments with Izzy are my favorite moments. Can't get enough of being around her. And I wanna make all her moments with me happy, too. Don't know how to put it simpler than that."

Elyse seems surprised by Riley's eloquence, but I'm not. I've had months to soak it in, to get to know the eloquent soul under the cute, awkward exterior. At last, Elyse sighs and snaps her fingers, returning the use of my voice. "Okay, Izzy, you can give me your speech about what an overprotective best friend I am now. It's for your own good, you know."

I wiggle my jaw to loosen it. "I don't think you're overprotective. Considering the train wreck, I dated last time, I think it's warranted."

"Well, this one definitely isn't like Natasha. That's a point in anyone's favor."

Riley grins. "Gotta start somewhere, I guess."

Our basket of fried pickles arrives shortly after. Elyse immediately chows down, and Riley munches on a few while eyeing the steak two tables away from ours. "Really?" Elyse mumbles, her mouth full of pickle, "No one wants more?"

"Blood only, Elyse."

"Meat," Riley says. "Preferably raw."

"Where were you guys when I needed college roommates? I could've used one who didn't eat everything but the ice in my refrigerator."

"Sounds like you had more fun at college than me," Riley says.

Elyse raises her eyebrows. "How come?"

"Did my undergrad online. Easier to work ahead and prepare for my monthlies." They smile. "That's why I came to New York. I wanted to get out of Georgia—"

"Who wouldn't?"

"and maybe meet girls who were fine with the werewolf thing and weren't also my cousins."

Elyse looks at me. "Guess Izzy checks both your boxes then."

Riley pats my knee under the table again. "Oh, I've got a long list...but I took one look at her on that subway and I was a goner. I swear, I was useless as a pogo stick in quicksand."

Elyse glances at Riley, then stares intently at me, waiting expectantly. She's not even bothering to hide the grin on her face.

I sigh. "Just get it over with."

She cracks up. Absolutely loses it until she's almost crying into the pickles. I laugh too, and Riley joins in. Eventually, I forget why we're giggling, but it doesn't matter, because it feels good. Comfortable.

"Hope you were laughing with me instead of at me," Riley says after we've recovered.

"With you," Elyse snorts around her lingering giggles. "It's adorable. Don't ever change the way you talk, *please*."

Riley flushes. "If you say so. I've got plenty more dumb similes if you want 'em."

"Tell me," Elyse says, without any hesitation.

I settle back in my seat to nurse my drink. Introducing Riley and Elyse was definitely the right decision—although I have a feeling I might come to regret it sometime in the next couple of minutes. For now, though, I allow myself to relax. I have two people who love me in the same room, laughing and joking with each other. That's all I can really ask for.

Chapter Seven - Riley

I CLENCH MY TOES in my sneakers and squeeze my seat's armrests, focusing on the music blasting through my earbuds. It doesn't do much to drown out the plane's engine, but every little bit helps. I've never been a fan of flying, but today, I'm more nervous than usual. I'm headed back south for the first time since moving to New York, and I've got company with me.

"Riley?"

Izzy pops out one of my earbuds, stroking back a stray lock of my hair. Her lips move, but the noise of the engine swells louder and covers it up.

"What?"

Izzy rolls her eyes, although her frustration isn't aimed at me. "I said, are you okay?"

I clear my throat, reaching for my plastic cup of water before remembering the steward has already taken it away. I've had a lot to drink on the flight, mostly to calm my stomach, but now it's coming back to bite me. I need to pee something awful, and the turbulence beneath the plane's wings isn't helping.

"Yeah..."

Izzy isn't convinced. She puts my earbud back in for me, takes my hand in hers, and rests her cheek against my shoulder. I can tell from the way she's gripping my fingers that she's trying to convince me everything will be okay. Logically, I know it will. Physically, I'm not sure. Maybe vampires enjoy flying, but wolves like me just aren't meant to go thousands of feet off the ground.

Lucky for me, the flight's almost finished. I wince and clutch the hell out of Izzy's hand as the plane touches down, but after an awful squeal, the worst is over. The engine quiets and the plane slows down to a crawl.

Izzy lifts off my shoulder and opens the window shade, which I'd politely asked her to keep shut. We're on the runway, and I'm relieved to see the maintenance machines and suitcase trolleys, yet more proof that we're back on terra firma.

"Doing all right, *mon chou*?" Izzy asks.

I pull my headphones out and turn my music off. "Yup. I'm alive." My bladder starts to clench in protest. "And I hope we get off soon, because I really gotta go."

"Well..." Izzy gives a sly flash of her fangs. "I can't do anything about a bathroom for you yet, but I can get you off if you really can't wait." She pinches my thigh through my jeans, and I push her hand playfully away.

"Stoppit. And don't do that in front of my folks."

Izzy raises her eyebrows. "Why not? I wouldn't have thought they were prudes, judging by how you turned out."

"Har. Nah, they ai...aren't. I just don't want you to encourage 'em when they tease me. They're bad enough on their own without your influence."

"I just hope I can keep them all straight," Izzy says. "Seven siblings. How did you even survive?"

I grin at her. "By gettin' good at wrasslin'."

Izzy looks me up and down. "Well, you have the muscles for it."

My face heats up. Suddenly, needing to pee isn't the only reason I'm uncomfortable. To my relief, it doesn't take long for the rows in front of us to empty. I slip out first and grab our backpacks from the luggage compartment over the seats. Izzy tries to take hers, but I sling one over each shoulder. She aims a disapproving look in my direction. "You do know I can deadlift about a thousand pounds, right?"

I do know. When Izzy's had enough blood to drink, her strength is pretty incredible. I saw her lift the front of a small car once when its tire popped in a pothole. I helped but seeing her do that did make me wonder about getting a gym membership to keep up.

"It's the principle of the thing."

I huff but pass her backpack over. We head off the plane and through the covered ramp before finally stepping out into the airport. Immediately, I sprint for the nearest bathroom sign. My eyeballs are pretty much floating.

As usual, there's some discomfort when I step into the ladies' restroom. Part of me feels like I shouldn't be there, but I wouldn't be any more comfortable in the mens. I glance down at my shirt. It's good I haven't cut my hair in a bit, because my chest is pretty flat with my binder on. Less likely some nosy old hen will ask me why I'm in here.

There's enough stalls that I don't have to wait. I dart into one of them and go as fast as I can. Before too long, I hear the soft swish of ballet flats against the tile floor. "Riley? You okay?"

It's Izzy. Some of the tension melts from my shoulders. "Yeah. Just be a sec."

Knowing she followed me makes me feel better as I come out to wash my hands. Izzy's waiting there, arms folded, one hip propped against a dry and clean part of the sink counter. She didn't have to go at all. She just came to keep me company.

"Thanks," I say.

"No thanks needed. How am I supposed to know where to go without you?"

I laugh as I switch on the blow-dryer. "Oh, you'd recognize my folks."

"Family resemblance?"

"Yup. Big time."

We head out of the restroom and follow the signs for arrivals. No sooner have we passed through security than I notice three tall, broad-shouldered, towheaded figures loitering near the baggage claim. I see them and I smell them a moment later, even through all the distracting airport scents.

"Papa, Mama, Monty!" I hurry over, dragging Izzy along behind me.

My parents spot me. "Riley," Mama says, opening her arms for a hug. I pick her up off the floor, spinning her around. She's tall, but not as tall as me, and thin too, and she still smells like a fresh baked peach pie.

"Hey, mama. How you been?"

"Glad to have my baby home."

I grin. "Thought Monty was the baby."

Mama chuckles. "You're all my babies, no matter how old you get."

"Don't encourage her," Monty says. He's my only little brother, four years younger than me—a happy surprise, Mama always said. In the past year, though, he's grown from little to not-so-little. His shoulders have filled out, and he's not as much of a beanpole anymore.

"Heya, bud." I hug him too. We've always stuck together, me and Monty. I'm the second-youngest, so I never minded him hanging around me. We were both outsiders at school, the ones who didn't fit in. I got into more than a couple scrapes for his sake in elementary and middle school.

"Heya, sis. Missed you." I can tell he means it, and I feel a little guilty for waiting this long to come home.

"Missed you too."

"My turn." Papa nudges Monty aside and pulls me into a bear hug. My spine cracks, and the wind rushes right out of me

"Down," I wheeze, tapping his shoulder. He sets me down, and I kiss his stubbly cheek.

"C'mon, girl," he says, clicking his tongue. "Don't tell me being all citified has made you soft now."

I feel a slight twinge when he says 'girl', but I push it down. "Not a chance in heck." I turn to Izzy, who's waiting a couple feet back. "Papa, Mama, Monty, this is Izzy. Please be nice and don't scare her off."

"Scare her?" Papa says. "Where'd you get the fool idea we're gonna scare her?" He approaches Izzy and sticks out his hand. "It's a pleasure, Izzy. That short for somethin'?"

Izzy isn't put off by his friendliness. New Yorkers aren't known for warm introductions, but she uses her best Southern manners and smiles wide. "The pleasure's mine, sir. My name's Isabeau. Isabeau LaCour. But Izzy is just fine."

"Sir?" Papa chuckles and looks at me. "Her, I like. She's polite for a Yankee."

I roll my eyes. "Stop it, Pa. First of all, we Southerners ain't always that great. Too many white folks 'round here believe revisionist history, even some of the nonhumans who should know better." Monty snorts in agreement, which I file away for later. Sounds like he's been hanging around a liberal crowd. "And second, Izzy ain't a Yankee. She's from Louisiana."

Papa grins. "Really? The gator tail there as good as they say?"

Izzy laughs. "Sho is," she says, in a Louisiana drawl I've rarely heard from her before. Not like my family's, but certainly not 'citified', as Papa would say. "But you won't see me turning down no frog legs neither."

Mama goes next. She clasps Izzy's hand, but also goes in for a big old hug. I shift nervously. I'm not sure how much of a huggy person Izzy is with strangers, since we had sex on the first date and hugs between us were kind of just assumed after that. But Izzy takes it in stride. "Nice to meet you too, ma'am. I see where Riley gets her looks."

"There you go, buttering me up," Mama says. "Welcome to Georgia, sugar."

"Happy to be here. Wish it could be for more than a couple days."

"No, you don't," Monty says. He clasps her hand to say hello. "I'd trade places with you in a hot minute."

"Not 'til you finish college you won't," Papa says. "I know I can't keep you in the nest forever, but them's the rules. Once you get your diploma, you can run away up north with your sister."

"Quit pickin'," Monty grumbles, sulking a bit. If he'd had his tail, it would've been drooping.

"Y'all got your bags yet?" Mama asks. "Plenty of room in the truck."

"Just the one suitcase." I check the scrolling sign above the luggage carousel, and our flight number's up. A moment later, I spot a flash of powder blue, Izzy's suitcase. I head over to grab it before Izzy can. I know Papa will chew me out for it otherwise.

Before I can turn around, I feel a hand on my hip. Izzy's standing beside me. Sometimes, I forget how fast she can be. "Let me guess," I say. "You wanna take this?"

Izzy smirks. "I do."

"To prove a point, or...?"

"No point. But it doesn't feel right to make you do all the work."

I sigh. "You're gonna wound my nonbinary butch pride and make my daddy scold me."

"Just give it here." Izzy's still smiling and sweet, but I know she's serious. I pass the handle over, and she rewards me with a peck. I get the feeling the kiss might've been longer if my folks hadn't come up to meet us.

"Truck's outside," Papa says. "Y'all can hop in. We've got supper on at home already."

I glance at Izzy, then rub the back of my neck. "Uh, about that—"

"We picked up some blood at the store," Mama says. "I hope cow's all right?"

"Cow is just fine, thank you."

"C'mon, girls," Papa says, clapping me on the shoulder. "Don't let the grass grow. Riley, why ain't you bringing this nice young lady's bag?"

Once more, I flinch at the word girl. I don't hide it well this time, and Izzy notices. She holds my hand with the one that isn't pulling her suitcase. "I've got it," she says. "And I don't know if someone on the unfortunate side of forty is really all that 'young'...present company excluded, ma'am."

"Seeing an older woman," Mama laughs. "You always were trouble, child."

"Now, if you were pushing five hundred, I might've had some concerns about the age gap," Papa says. "As it is, we've both got a good twenty years on you, I expect."

Izzy seems surprised. "Really?"

"Werewolf genes," I tell her. "Most of us reach a hundred and fifty at least, even two hundred."

"Well, color me surprised."

While Izzy and my folks chat, I glance at Monty. It's true he's not the most talkative kid, but this is awfully quiet, even for him. Usually, he would've chimed into the conversation. Instead, he looks at me with a worried wrinkle in his brow. I'll need to check in with him later.

***

It's a long drive out to my family's house. We've lived on the property for the past three hundred years, and it's a fair distance from the airport, or from any civilization, really. That suits the wolf in me fine, since it means there's plenty of pack land to run on. The rest of me, not so much. My humanoid form enjoys easy access to drug stores and restaurants, as well as the relatively short commute New York City offers.

I start feeling all nostalgic as Papa turns the truck onto the access road. I know it like the back of my hand, every bump and turn. Dust churns beneath the tires, puffing up on either side of us and spraying the windows with a light cloud of brown.

"You weren't kidding," Izzy says, peering through the small dust storm to the landscape beyond. "There isn't much around. Just fields, fields, and more fields."

"And cows," Monty says. He's sitting next to us in the back, since there are three seats.

"Cheaper for the pack to raise our own food," I explain, for Izzy's benefit. "Be self-sufficient and all."

"Why Riley Evans, you didn't tell me your folks were farmers."

"It's a group effort," Mama says from the passenger's seat. "Pa and I handle the business side of things for the pack. Finances and all. Most of our sons help in that area, like Monty here. But a few of our boys take care of the animals with the other families instead. The ones who like to get outdoors most."

"Riley was supposed to join the family business," Papa adds. "She's the one with the head for numbers. But the pull of the big city was too strong, I guess."

I sigh. As much as I miss my family, being around them can start to wear on me. Apparently, it's starting early this time.

"You can't blame Riley," Izzy says, coming heroically to my defense. "I expect it's hard to make friends and meet girls out in the middle of nowhere."

"True," Papa says. "A young wolf needs to run around, meet new people, experience new things. There's plenty of space here, but not many folks except family and pack."

"Sure," I grumble, only a little sulkily. "You listen when she says it."

"Well, the woman speaks sense."

"Quit, you two," Mama says, in a soft but commanding voice. "Riley, mind your father. James, you were awful critical of her decision to leave. Don't rewrite history."

"I was just—"

"We're here," Mama says before he can keep complaining.

Papa pulls the truck to a stop on the grass outside our house. It's a big, sprawling ranch-style affair, and despite its asymmetry, there's a lot of love in it. My heart swells when I see it sitting there in the glow of the sunset, as if it's been waiting for me.

I grasp Izzy's hand, and she threads her fingers through mine. "Beautiful," she whispers, and I know she's not just talking about the house.

We open the doors and step out into the warm, muggy air. Cicadas buzz from the trees, and nighttime frogs in the pond nearby add to the chorus. Those are the sounds I fell asleep to as a kid, the music I remember while running through the fields on full moon nights.

I keep Izzy's hand close. "Well, this is it." It feels like an important moment, sharing something this intimate with her.

She rests her head against my shoulder. "I'm glad to be here with you, Riley."

"'Course. Come on in." I lead her up the steps to the front porch and open the door. It's already unlocked, and as soon as I open it, the smell of supper wafts out to greet my nose. I breathe it in with a grin, but the moment's ruined when a bunch of people stampede from the kitchen to greet us. It's my other six brothers, all blue-eyed and blond-haired, in various states of dishevelment.

"Riley!"

They surround me for hugs, jostling each other in the process. Poor Izzy gets caught up in it, and I shove them away, laughing as I fight a path toward freedom. "Piss off, you animals. You're scarin' my lady."

Izzy is the opposite of scared. She smirks with amusement as my brothers pile onto me. When I look at her, though, they stop fussing over me. They cluster around her instead, although they make an effort to be a bit gentler with their one-armed hugs and handshakes.

"Izzy, right?"

"Nice to meet you!"

"Welcome to Georgia."

Izzy takes it in stride. "Glad to be here. So, I'm going to try my best with names." She lowers her sunglasses and squints, trying to memorize faces. I don't envy her the task. Sometimes even I get them mixed up when they're wolves and running downwind of me.

My brothers introduce themselves:

"Austin."

"Macon."

"Harris."

"Butler."

"Dallas."

"Jackson."

Izzy is clearly a bit bewildered. I just shrug. "If you mix 'em up, don't feel bad. They're used to it."

"At least you won't get Riley confused," Dallas says.

"No, because Riley's the cute one."

There are a bunch of 'oohs', and Dallas laughs along with the others. I give Izzy a grateful look. Not only did she expertly deflect a comment about my gender, but I've noticed she's avoided pronouns for me since we got here. It's a little thing, and 'she' doesn't always bother me at places like work, but the silent gesture of support in a place where my identity is 'the daughter' and 'the sister' really does help.

"What's for supper?" Izzy asks. "I probably can't eat more than a few bites, but I bet it tastes amazing."

"Slow-cooked brisket and beans," Jackson says, practically bouncing with excitement. "Fresh out of the crockpot."

My mouth waters. Like most werewolves, I enjoy my meat raw sometimes, but part of that is because it's hard to cook it as good as Mama does. Her brisket is like biting into heaven.

That's when Mama, Papa, and Monty come in through the door behind us, with Monty carrying Izzy's suitcase. "What are y'all doing out here?" Mama says when she notices the gathered crowd. "Get your tails in the kitchen and help Janie and Mel set the table. I won't have them doing all the work for you boys. And you're on cleanup afterwards."

My brothers scurry back to the kitchen while Izzy looks at me. "Janie and Mel?"

"Sisters-in-law. Austin and Macon are married." I take Izzy's suitcase from Monty before she can snatch it for herself. "C'mon, sunshine. Let's get set up in my room. Then we can come back for dinner and meet them."

"Your parents seem pretty egalitarian," Izzy says, obviously approving.

"Yeah. My brothers and I got the same chores as kids." I lead Izzy out of the living room, heading down the hall to my old bedroom. Once the din from the kitchen fades, I exhale with relief. It's not that I don't love my family. I know I'm lucky to have them. I'm just more of an introvert than they are, and sometimes they can be overwhelming.

When I open the door to my room, I'm not surprised to see it hasn't changed. I can tell from the smell of detergent that the sheets have been freshly laundered, and the nightstands and dresser have ben dusted, but otherwise, it doesn't seem like anyone's touched it since I left. It has the same furniture, the same pictures on the walls, even the same smell.

Izzy takes everything in. "This is where teenage Riley lived?"

"Not just teenage Riley."

Izzy's smile shows her fangs as she glances at a superhero poster. "Oh?"

"Knew coming here would be embarrassing," I grumble.

I set Izzy's suitcase at the foot of the bed, and she's there to hug me when I turn around. "Seriously, though, how are you holding up?" she asks. "I know family can be stressful."

I bend down to rest my forehead against hers, sighing deeply. "S'not their fault. My folks are great. I'm just different now than I was back then. I've learned more about myself. I met you."

"I'm glad you did," Izzy murmurs. "It's okay, Riley. You've changed, and this place hasn't."

"That's it. Guess I shouldn't be surprised a vampire understands."

"I'm only a new vampire. But yes, I understand. The longing to move forward, the yearning to go back. And family obligations."

I kiss her adorably puffy hair, then take a seat on the edge of my bed. Izzy sits next to me, burrowing under my arm to cuddle against my side. "You've never told me much about your family," I say after a while. "Just that your Mama's still in Louisiana."

"Other than her, I don't have much family left to speak of. I'm not sure I would have been so eager to become a vampire otherwise. For a long time, Natasha and Elyse were my family. And sorceresses live for hundreds of years anyway."

"You don't regret it, do you? Making the Choice?"

Izzy sighs against my neck. "Not anymore. The state-mandated counseling helped. It's supposed to weed out people who can't handle the mental strain of immortality, but it also gives you strategies for coping. I went back after Natasha and I split. Ever heard of the hundred-year blues?"

"Can't say I have."

"New vampires usually hit a rough patch somewhere around their hundredth birthday. If they were human before and not a hybrid, most of their same-aged relatives and human friends have died off. Things are different, too. Technology changes, culture changes. The world you're in isn't *your* world anymore."

"Which is why you do the work you do."

"Mmhmm." Izzy presses a kiss to my pulse point. It's tender, not meant to turn me on, but I shudder a little anyway. "I had the fifty-year blues instead. That's when the breakup happened. My Mama had a fall and moved into assisted living, which was a wake-up call for me. I realized time was going to pass me by, and I didn't want to be left behind. I convinced Elyse to let me teach some classes."

My heart swells up with all sorts of confusing feelings. There's happiness, because despite Izzy's bubbly, extroverted attitude, she takes a while to trust people with stuff this heavy. There's bittersweetness as I think about what it would be like, staying the same as the world transforms around me. And there's sadness as I realize— not for the first time logically, but the first time emotionally—that unless something changes, Izzy is going to outlive me by hundreds of years. I was just too damn glad to be around Izzy before to think about it for more than a few seconds at a time.

Of course, there is a way, if you decide you really want it, a voice in my mind says. *Humans aren't the only ones who can make the Choice.*

"Izzy, can I ask a question without you freaking out?"

Izzy looks at me with a furrow in her brow. "Of course, Riley. You can ask me anything."

"I'm not sayin' now, because I know it's way too soon, but what would you think if I—"

Before I can finish, there's a knock on my door. Izzy lifts her head off my shoulder, and I flinch even though we aren't doing anything embarrassing. "C'mon in."

Monty peeks his head into the room. "Supper's on," he says, glancing between Izzy and me. It still feels like something's off about him. Monty's never been the most outgoing person, but I know my little brother. He's worried, I can tell.

"Thanks, Monty," I say out loud. Then I lean in, whispering beside Izzy's ear. "Will you be okay with my family in the kitchen for a few minutes? I wanna talk to Monty."

"Sure. I'm a big girl. I can handle a rowdy pack of wolves."

"Then go on to supper. I'll be there soon."

With a kiss to my cheek, Izzy leaves the bedroom, giving Monty a friendly smile as she passes. As I expect, he slips into my room once she's gone. His posture is slumped, nervous, the humanoid equivalent of a droopy tail and flattened ears.

I pat the space where Izzy was sitting on the bed. "C'mon, bud."

He shuffles over and sits, his knee barely touching mine. "Riley, how'd you know you were gay?"

"Er, well…" Unfortunately, I don't have much advice for the poor kid. I always knew I was drawn to girls, even if I didn't understand the sexual attraction part of it 'til after puberty. But Monty's looking at me with big eyes, like he's hoping I have all the answers. "I had a sense of it when I was a kid, I guess. Everyone at school was already calling me a lesbian anyway, so figuring out wasn't too hard. Why?"

"I think I might be," Monty mumbles. "I don't know. It hit all of a sudden and…"

I try not to panic. *Come on, Riley. What would Colin say? He's good at this stuff.*

"People realize at different times, bud. Just 'cuz I figured it out early doesn't mean it's the same for everyone."

"I feel stupid, like I should've figured this out by now. I'm twenty, for fuck's sake."

I stifle a laugh. "You realize how young twenty is, right? Not to sound condescending or nothin', but that's still pretty early. Some people don't realize 'til they're Mama and Papa's age or older."

Monty sighs. "I don't even know if I am, though."

"Straight people usually don't struggle too hard with the 'am I gay' question. Some might wonder a bit, especially if other kids at school are teasin' 'em, but they don't pay it as much mind." I grin and nudge his arm with my elbow. "Do you wanna kiss boys?"

He sputters, looking embarrassed. "Uh…"

"Then you're probably not straight. Maybe you're gay, maybe you're bi, maybe something else. Doesn't much matter. Either way, there's a family out there for you. I know things are sparse 'round here, but it's different in the city. You meet all kinds of folks there."

Monty relaxes a little. "That's why I wanna go to New York City like you. Or even just Atlanta. Somewhere bigger."

"Yup. It was right for me." I pause, considering my options. "Hell, I'm still figuring things out about myself. I met a werewolf at the park a month back who's nonbinary." I wait for a look of recognition or understanding on Monty's face, and when there isn't one, I explain. "Some parts of being a girl feel right to me. Other parts, not so much. If you took some girl and a little bit of boy and a handful of something else and shook it all up in a Coke can, I guess that's me. I'm just...me."

He blinks, then nods. "So, you're just figuring this out?"

"Well, some things from when I was a kid make a hell of a lot more sense, but yup. Just figuring it out."

Monty gives me a nervous smile, but I can see a bit of hope in it. "So, if I wanna find out more about you being, uh, nonbinary..."

"I can send you some stuff online," I tell him. "You don't gotta treat me any different right now. It's enough to know you know. And I'm glad you talked to me, bud. I don't have all the answers for you, but I know you'll find 'em. And if you need a bunk in New York City, my apartment's open."

"You sure your girl won't mind?" Monty says, a smirk playing 'round his mouth.

I feel like I've gotten through to him. That's the Monty I know. "Nah. Izzy's a sweetheart and she's got her own place. You won't bother us none."

"Thanks, Riley."

Monty leans in, and I hug him, rubbing his back through his shirt. "Anytime, bud. Supper?"

"Yup. The smell's callin' me." He takes a sniff of the air, and I do too, feeling the strong urge to lick my chops.

We hop off the bed and head down the hall, following our noses to the kitchen.

***

"Mama, that was delicious." I lean back in my chair, folding my hands over my stomach. My belly's so full I'd need to loosen my belt if I had one. I settle for unbuttoning my pants, giving Mama my best post-dinner smile.

"Don't you be napping now," Mama says, clicking her tongue. "Just 'cause you don't live here anymore doesn't mean you get out of doin' the dishes with your brothers."

"M'not napping," I mumble, although I do feel a mite sleepy if I'm being honest. "Just resting my eyes."

Izzy gives my shoulder a soft squeeze. She's sitting beside me, looking as content as I feel. "I've heard that song before. Get up and start moving before you doze off." Then, as an aside to my Mama, "Thank you, ma'am. The bites I had and the juice from the crockpot tasted so delicious they made me regret my dietary choices."

"Aw. You're welcome, sugar. You sure you got enough to eat? There's more bags of blood in the freezer we can warm up."

"More than enough." Izzy's hand curls around the back of my neck, playing with a few wisps of my hair. "Besides, I've got a mobile juice box right here if I need a snack."

My brothers snicker at me from around the table, and I blush. "Izzy..."

"What? Your blood tastes better than store-bought and saves me on grocery bills."

"Not really, 'cause then you've gotta feed me real food to keep making blood."

"You two are way too stinkin' cute," Austin says, his blue eyes dancing.

"Yeah, I know," I say. "We're hard to compete with."

That gets a chuckle at Austin's expense from his wife Janie, who's sitting to his left. "She's got you there, hon."

"Just wait 'til the kid's born," Austin says. "Then we'll see who wins the cute competition in this family."

I laugh. Janie's pregnant with her and Austin's first child, and it's still a little bewildering to me that I'm gonna be an...Oh. Will I be an aunt? I'm not sure how I feel about that. It's a pretty gendered term, but sometimes I don't mind those all that much. It's frustratingly inconsistent depending on the day. It might be something I need to figure out over time.

As always, Izzy's there to take my mind off the confusing stuff. "Don't make that face, *mon chou*. I'll always think you're the cutest."

"*Mon chou?*" Dallas repeats, jeering from across the table. "What's that mean?"

"Nothin'," I mumble, but I know it's too late.

"What's it mean, Izzy?" Butler asks, obviously full of hope.

"It's difficult to translate. The Parisian French term is longer and fancier, but in Louisiana French, it means something like..." Izzy takes a deep breath.

"Don't you dare," I warn her.

"...creampuff. Sometimes cabbage, even."

The boys start cackling, and I hang my head in shame. I'm not really that upset, just a little embarrassed, which I'm sure Izzy can tell. She wouldn't have said it otherwise. "Fine, have your laugh," I grumble. "But you're all creampuffs too when you have your monthlies."

"That sounds adorable," Izzy says. "I'm picturing a whole pack of fluffy golden retrievers running around, startling all the cows."

"Takes a lot to startle these cows," Papa says. "They're around wolves all the time. They don't scare easy."

"Dumb as posts," Macon agrees. "You can bark right in their face and they don't bat an eye."

"Macon and Mel have started working at the Richards' farm," Mama says. "You remember the Richards, right Riley?"

"Yes, Mama. How could I forget? There's only five or six families 'round these parts. Plus, the Castles."

"The Castles?" Izzy asks, mildly confused.

There's an assortment of growls from around the table.

"Castles. Hmph."

"Good for nothing felines."

"Now I've told you boys this a hundred times, but I'll say it again," Papa declares, "I don't wanna see you taking up with no Castle girls."

"Or boys," I can't resist adding, although I don't look in Monty's direction.

Papa looks a bit startled. "Or no Castle boys, I suppose. Y'all can do better, like your brothers and sister."

Izzy leans over and whisper to me. "Castles?"

"Werecat family down the road," I whisper back. "We're kinda like the Hatfields and McCoys with less violence and more tail-chasing."

"Riley Evans," Izzy says, "are you telling me your family goes out and chases poor kitties every month?"

"Poor kitties my ass," Papa grumbles. "They're Florida panthers. They can take care of themselves."

"James," Mama says, a warning note in her voice, "don't you start now."

"Why don't we get the dishes, Mama?" Jackson says, trying to make peace. There's a bit more grumbling, but everyone stands up from the table and starts to carry their plates to the kitchen. I take Izzy's before she can get it, and she only puts up a minor fuss before letting me go.

In the kitchen, Papa corners me next to the counter. "Izzy seems like a mighty fine girl, Riley," he says, giving me a gentle slug on the shoulder.

I grin. "Glad you think so, 'cause she is."

"Why don't you take her for a drive around town? Show her the sights."

"Sure, I guess? Not much to see other than the drug store and the McDonalds..."

Papa reaches into his pocket, tossing me the keys to his truck. "C'mon. Taking your lady for a drive in the country is a Southern tradition." He glances over at my brothers, who have managed to splash more water than necessary out of the sink while rinsing their plates. "And I'm sure she could use a small break from this rabble before settling in."

He has a point. Plus, I'm pretty touched by the gesture. I remember him giving the keys to my older brothers all the time for their dates when they were in high school. It was a rite of passage I never really got to participate in, aside from one or two not-so-great attempts with human girls before I learned to guard myself better. When I look into Papa's eyes, I sense he knows what he's offering. He's being sweet, trying to help me make up a bit for lost opportunities.

I put the keys in my pocket. "Thanks, Pa."

He pats my back. "Don't be out all night. I know Izzy's a vampire, but I'm sure the girl needs her sleep too."

I doubt it, but I don't say so. The thought of spending part of the night with Izzy under the stars is too appealing.

***

"I can't decide whether this is creepy or beautiful," Izzy says as we drive along the dirt road. It's dark, but there's not much of a view to speak of, just cow pastures and a few distant farmhouses. Even so, it puts me at peace. I've got the truck windows rolled down, and nighttime sounds carry above the noise of the engine and the tires churning in the dust.

"What do you mean, creepy? You're a vampire. Not much can touch you."

Izzy finds my hand on top of the gear shift. "I used to be human, though. A human who saw the original *Texas Chainsaw Massacre* when

I was way too young."

"None of that here." I spread my fingers, and Izzy's slide between them. "It's boring out in the country."

"I'll take boring over *Deliverance.*"

After that, we're quiet for a while. I'd gotten into the truck without a destination in mind, but now I know where I'm going. A few minutes later, we cross over the train tracks and into town. It's not much—a single paved road with businesses on either side. There's the library, closed of course. The barbershop. The Publix. Freddie's Diner and Luanne's BBQ Shack. They always have the best milkshakes.

"It's totally abandoned," Izzy says, peering out the passenger's side window. She's right. There are no headlights on the road. No pedestrians. In New York, there are people out at all hours. Here, we're all alone.

"I like to think of it as peaceful."

Izzy gives me a sidelong look. "Where are you taking me, anyway?"

"You'll see. We're only a minute away."

I drive out the other end of town, where a faint golden-white glow is waiting. We've arrived at the high school and its empty football field. The floodlights have been left on their lowest setting, offering enough illumination for safety. I pull off the road and into the parking lot, but don't stop in one of the spaces. I drive onto the grass and put the truck in park next to the chain link fence behind the bleachers.

"This is it?" Izzy asks.

I turn off the engine. "Yup. This is it."

"Riley Evans, are you suggesting we park?" Izzy asks with a smirk.

"We are parked."

"You know what I mean."

"It was too late to take you for a milkshake," I say, gently teasing. "And I dunno if Luanne's has blood on the menu as one of their flavors."

Izzy strokes my forearm. "I'll have you know I'm a good girl, not the type who climbs into the back of pickup trucks with big bad wolves."

I unbuckle my seatbelt and lean closer. "I dunno if I believe you. You're here with me, aren't you?"

Izzy tugs playfully at her own lower lip with the tips of her fangs. "I guess I am."

"So..." I steal a short, closed-mouthed kiss, then nod toward the truck bed. "I've got a couple blankets in the back."

Izzy kisses me again, longer and deeper. Heat rushes from my pounding heart to the tips of my toes, but most of it settles low in my belly. I don't know what it is about her kisses that drive me crazy, but I'm not complaining. I could spend an eternity kissing her. *An eternity. Am I sure about that?*

I push the thought from my mind. It's too soon. Our relationship is sweet, the best I've had by far, but also really new. We might be right for each other now, but I can't guarantee we'll be right for each other for the next hundred years, and especially not the next thousand.

Izzy doesn't let me dwell on it for long. She hops out the passenger's side, and I do the same on my side, hurrying around to meet her at the truck bed. "Allow me," I say, lowering the back and hopping up to spread out the blankets. Soon I've made a cozy nest for the two of us. I offer Izzy my hand, and she accepts, allowing me to help her up.

"Hey," she murmurs, snuggling against me.

I wrap my arm around her shoulders. "Hey yourself."

Despite the earlier smooching, we don't keep kissing right away. Izzy rests her head on my chest, and the two of us lie back, looking up at the night sky. Despite the faint floodlights illuminating the football field, it's still dark enough to see the stars overhead.

"See that one?" Izzy says, pointing upward. "Pisces."

"Yeah?" I follow her finger, connecting the dots in a 'v' shape. "Looks like a uterus to me."

"Seriously?" Izzy sighs with mock exasperation. "You're too much." Nevertheless, she lowers her hand to my thigh and lets it rest there.

I search the sky, finding Orion's belt and moving right. "There's Canis Major. And Sirius."

"Favorite constellation?" Izzy asks wryly.

"Pretty much the only one besides Orion and the Big Dipper I know how to find."

"That surprises me," Izzy says. "You spend a lot of time out at night."

"Well, yeah. Running around as a wolf, chasing deer—"

"Chasing werecats."

I give Izzy my silliest grin. "And sometimes beautiful girls."

Izzy laughs and rolls on top of me, dipping down for more kisses. We stay like that for a while, resting chest to chest. Our kisses are slow and exploratory. Neither of us are in any kind of rush. She tastes like lip gloss and melted sugar, or a sweet tea in summer. Her eyes have the only stars I want to see.

Before I know it, I've slid the straps of Izzy's pink sundress down her shoulders. The soft light on her smooth brown skin gives the edges of her shoulders a bronze glow, and her heart-shaped face is all smiles. She shifts a little, peeling away the top of her dress, and my breath hitches as her breasts spill out. I love all of Izzy's curves, her plush softness, but these really are something else.

"You're lucky," Izzy says, stroking the back of my head to draw me close. "I don't let just anyone get to second base."

I kiss my way down Izzy's chest. The taste of her skin is addictive, and I flatten my tongue against her sternum for a broad lick. "Mm. Does that mean I'm special?"

"Very. Ohhh..." Izzy shudders on top of me as I draw her nipple into my mouth. It's hard and swollen, easy to suck. I circle the tip, enjoying her soft whimpers.

I want to stay nuzzled between Izzy's breasts forever, kissing back and forth between them. The sounds she makes are delicious, especially when I use the edges of my teeth. She pleads with me to switch often, guiding me from one nipple to the other so neither of them is left lonely for long against the air.

Only when Izzy's hips have started trembling over my lap do I reach around to pull down her zipper. Her sundress comes right off, leaving her bare before me except for her panties. They're pink too, with a large dark patch in the middle. "Is all this for me?" I mumble, cupping between her thighs.

Izzy gasps as I squeeze her, and more wetness seeps through the cotton of her underwear. "No. It's for the other handsome werewolf I'm making out with."

I bite the top of her breast, thrilled by the adorable squeak she makes. "S'that so? Can I touch anyway?"

"Please," Izzy moans, rocking her hips forward.

I dip my fingers into her panties. She's all slippery, and so swollen that her pouting lips puff out, as if she's trying to suck my fingers in. Her clit is full too, pounding hard. When I pull the peak of Izzy's breast back between my lips, she twitches under my touch.

For the next several minutes, I'm in heaven. With my fingers sliding slowly through Izzy's warmth and her nipples in my mouth, I have everything I could ever want. Well, almost everything. I can smell Izzy's rising need, and I know she needs more. I release her from my mouth and make my offer: "In the mood for a midnight snack?"

Izzy sighs deeply. "You read my mind."

I don't want to leave those gorgeous breasts of hers unattended. I raise my arm, offering Izzy my left wrist so I don't have to take my mouth away. She takes my hand in hers and latches on, tapping an artery to suckle. It's completely painless, and after a few pulls, I feel a sudden spike of pleasure. No matter where Izzy bites me, the sensation always travels right between my legs. My own underwear is as wet as her panties are.

More of Izzy's heat drizzles over my fingers, coating them until they're nice and silky. Once they're slick enough, I probe her entrance. She's tight, but so wet and open that I sink right in. I go inside with one finger first, then add another, massaging her inner walls.

Izzy quivers around me, muscles clenching. She whines against my wrist but doesn't stop drinking. My head spins as more of my blood pulses into her mouth, but it's nothing compared to the pulsing in the palm of my hand. Izzy's close, I can tell. Her throbbing picks up speed until it's almost constant and her walls squeeze down without stopping.

I tug her nipple between my teeth, then whisper into the cushion of my breast. "Love you, sunshine. Glad you're here with me." I don't just mean in the back of my Papa's pickup truck, either. I'm glad she's here to see my family. Hell, I'm just glad she's on this Earth with me, because her presence makes it even more beautiful. Most of all, though, I'm glad she's mine.

Izzy lets go of my wrist and cries out to the stars. Her hot walls ripple, and she smears more wetness into the heel of my hand. Even without the physical signs, I'd know she was coming. It's in her eyes as she gazes down at me, along with a whole lot of love and tenderness.

"Riley!" Izzy cries. Her orgasm continues to swell, but she sags over to mouth at my neck. She alternates between kissing and nipping, stealing a few sips of blood here and there. It makes my core ache and my skin chafe under my clothes. There's a familiar tingle along my spine. She's got me close to feral, and I'm too relaxed and happy to hold back.

I remember the first time me and Izzy slept together. It wasn't making love yet, not quite. We didn't know each other that well. But it was sweet and affectionate in a way my other fumbling high school experiences by the bleachers never were. Back then, I spent most of the time in a sweaty panic. There were always fears in the back of my mind. *What if I go feral? What if she thinks I'm weird? What if she's afraid I'll hurt her?*

Now, Izzy and I are on another level entirely. Not only is fear utterly absent, but I'm brimming with warm, happy feelings. I don't care about going feral—haven't in several months. Izzy's already seen me as a wolf, so a little extra hair and yellow eyes are nothing. I let my instincts take over, giving into the pull.

Izzy kisses along my jaw, fondling the pointed tips of my ears. "Can I taste you?" she asks, a hopeful note in her voice.

I withdraw my hand and spread my legs. I can't say no to an offer like that. "You go right on ahead."

Izzy peels off her ruined panties, tossing them to the side. Then, she makes quick work of my clothes. My t-shirt comes off first, leaving my hair ruffled. Next comes my binder, a front-zip for the hot weather. She looks at me, waiting for permission, and I guide her to my breasts, letting her plant a few kisses there. It feels good enough, and I'm feeling close enough to her, that it doesn't put me off.

She doesn't stay for long. Her hot mouth continues down my belly until she reaches the fly of my cargo shorts. After placing a kiss on the button, she pops it open and pulls down the zipper. I lift my hips, sighing with relief as Izzy tugs off my boxers. The air feels good against my bare skin.

Once I'm naked, Izzy picks up where she left off. She dusts kisses around my navel, sliding my legs over her shoulders. I shake as she nuzzles my inner thighs, still a few inches away from where I need her, but I try to be patient. Waiting will only make the payoff better.

At last, Izzy sweeps her tongue through my wetness, fastening onto my clit. She sucks me deep, fangs nicking the tender flesh on either side of the shaft. If having her feed from my wrist made me warm and wobbly, the way she's drinking now sends licks of fire through my bones. It's a hundred times more intense.

Izzy's mouth is amazing. It takes all the willpower I've got to keep my hips from bucking. I'm already so close, but I don't want it to end. I don't want any of this to end. Not making love under the stars, not our first trip as a couple, not any of it. I want a hundred trips together, a thousand nights under the stars, a million kisses, all with Izzy.

*Maybe in the future, I could...we could...*I can't focus on the thought. Izzy swirls her tongue in slow circles, and my peak hits like a freight train. I stiffen up and shudder, catching my claws in her fluffy hair as I come. I hold her mouth close, knowing she won't pull away, but needing something to hang onto.

My orgasm shreds me to ribbons. I'm a mewling mess by the time it's over, covered in a layer of sweat as the stars swirl above me. As aftershocks twitch through my muscles, Izzy laps up my juices, making sure to lick me clean. I'm pretty sure I've left a wet spot on the blanket too. Her tongue thrusts inside me a few times, extending my pleasure just a little longer, before she shifts from under my calves, flopping down next to me.

"Hey," she says, brushing my bangs away from my face.

"Heya." I hesitate, not because I'm scared, but because looking at Izzy takes my breath away. "You're the most beautiful woman I've ever seen, and I love you."

"Flatterer. I love you too." She leans in for a kiss, but I stop her, cupping her sticky cheek.

"No, I'm serious. Izzy, I..." My courage falters, but I press on. "I don't wanna pressure you. I know your last relationship wasn't great, and we've only been seeing each other a little while and just got to I love yous, but—"

Izzy presses her finger to my mouth. From the expression on her face, I know she knows what I want to say. "Not yet, *mon chou*," she whispers, caressing my bottom lip with the pad of her thumb. "This night has been perfect. I don't want it to slip away."

My chest churns with bittersweet feelings. There are a hundred things I want to tell her, but I can sense she isn't ready. She's been so trusting of me, and I don't want to cross her boundaries. *But she didn't say no. She said, 'not yet.' Maybe, someday...*someday is enough for me. I don't want to sign up for forever yet. I'm not ready for a step that big. But letting Izzy know it's on my mind is a start. I'm going to take that 'not yet' at face value.

"Riley?" Izzy asks, her forehead wrinkled with worry. She seems upset, or maybe she's worried that she upset me.

I roll on top of Izzy and kiss her, pouring all my feelings into it. Izzy kisses me back, and I know we're going to be all right. Nothing bad can touch us here under the stars. This moment is just for us. Whether I make the Choice in the future or not, there will be many, many more like it. Who knows? Maybe some will be even better, although I can't imagine anything better than this.

***

Morning dawns warm and sunny. I move my arm from over my eyes, yawning as I take in my surroundings. I must've fallen asleep in the truck bed, because I'm still sprawled naked amidst a pile of blankets. I guess I passed out in Izzy's arms after our last round of lovemaking. Thankfully, she had the sense to cover me in case any passersby decided to visit the high school on a weekend.

I look around, but Izzy isn't cuddled next to me. Her smell is strong, though, so I sit up and check the inside of the truck. She's in the passenger's seat, slathering sunscreen on her skin. She must hear me, because she turns around and smiles through the back window. A moment later, the passenger door pops open. "Morning, sleepyhead. Get dressed and come help me get my back?"

I scramble back into my discarded clothes from the night before. They smell kind of like sex, but they're better than nothing. Once I'm dressed, I hop out of the truck bed and circle around the passenger's side. Izzy passes me the tube of sunscreen she always carries in her purse, but I don't take it until I've kissed her square on the lips. When I pull away, she follows me, stealing a second smooch before turning around and lifting the puff of her hair.

"You're gorgeous," I sigh as I squirt some of the lotion into my palm. I spread it across her shoulders, making sure to get well under the back of her sundress. Don't want my baby to burn because I wasn't thorough.

"And you're sweet for noticing. Your parents aren't going to be upset we stayed the night out here, are they?"

"No, but I'm starting to regret it." My legs are obnoxiously itchy, most likely from mosquito bites. I balance on one foot, scratching my calf with the other.

Izzy looks over her shoulder and laughs. "Should've brought bug spray."

"Ha fucking ha. Why didn't you get bit?"

"Vampires barely breathe. Mosquitos are attracted to the carbon dioxide in your breath."

I heave a sigh. "Of course."

"You should be happy I didn't get eaten alive," Izzy says, pretending to pout a bit. "It's not like I have much blood to spare."

"True." I finish slathering her up, working the lotion over her shoulders for good measure before placing a kiss on the back of her neck. It tastes like sunscreen, but I don't care. Izzy smells good, and I'll never turn down an opportunity to show her affection. "Ready to go home for some breakfast?"

"I want to go home for some sleep," Izzy says. She takes the lotion back and caps it, slipping it into her purse. "I didn't get much last night."

I raise my eyebrows. "Oh? So, you just watched me sleep?"

She gives me a smirk that I can tell is supposed to be evil but ends up just being adorable. "Yes. I am nocturnal, you know. A frightening creature of the night."

I roll my eyes. "Keep tellin' yourself that, sunshine. C'mon. I'll drive us home and get you tucked into bed for a nap."

Once I hop in the driver's seat, we're off. There are a couple cars on the road this time, and a few tractors too. Some people honk and wave, probably because they recognize Papa's truck. I wave back, and I catch a few glances of surprised recognition. Guess people aren't expecting to see me back in town. In a place this small, people notice who comes and goes.

"Friendly atmosphere," Izzy says as we churn down the dirt road.

"Sometimes a mite too friendly. Someone's always got their nose in your business 'round here."

We make it home without incident. I park the truck on the lawn outside the house and walk around to open Izzy's door for her. She sighs, but lets me, and we walk into the house hand in hand.

Inside, there isn't too much of a crowd waiting for us. It's still early, and my brothers are all apparently snoozing away in their rooms. The only folks I see are Mama and Papa, who are busy making breakfast in the kitchen. The smell of sizzling bacon hits my nose, and my mouth begins to water.

"Sure you don't want breakfast?" I ask Izzy, resisting the temptation to lick my lips.

Izzy shakes her head. "No. I had plenty to eat last night, remember?"

My face heats up. I do remember.

"C'mon, then. I said I'd tuck you in."

"It's fine, *mon chou*. Go get yourself some breakfast. I can hear your stomach growling."

"What?" At that moment, my stomach lets out a mighty rumble. "Fine, at least lemme give you a goodnight kiss."

"A good morning kiss," Izzy says, but she wraps her hand around the back of my neck and pulls me down. Our lips meet soft and sweet, and I don't want it to end when Izzy pulls back. With a squeeze of my hand, she's gone, heading off down the hall to my room.

I sigh and head into the kitchen. Hopefully Papa won't be too mad at me for staying out all night with his truck. I might be an adult now, but it's still kind of rude while I'm staying under their roof. Luckily, my folks are all smiles when I sit at the table.

"Morning, baby girl," Mama says, with a knowing look that makes me blush even hotter than before. I'm even too embarrassed to mind the 'baby girl.'

Papa turns away from the stove where he's frying up the bacon and scrambling some eggs. "You got my keys for me?"

"Yessir." I slide them across the table for Mama to pick up on her way to get some plates. She slips them in Papa's pocket, and I groan in mock disgust when I catch her grabbing his butt.

"Ma!"

She turns with her hand on her hip. "Stop fussing, Riley. If I didn't like your papa's behind, you and your brothers would've never been born."

Mama has a point, and I can't complain much since I spent all night out with my girlfriend getting up too much more intimate things.

"Thanks, Papa. You too, Mama. For, y'know, lending me the truck."

Papa scrapes the bacon out of the pan and onto the plate Mama is holding out for him. "Not a problem. Next time, though, try and be in before sunrise." He scoops some eggs on the plate too and sets it in front of me while I mumble a thank you.

"Where's Izzy, by the way?" Mama asks. "Sleeping?"

"She's nocturnal. She'll be up in a few hours. Vampires don't need much sleep."

"I'll admit I had my reservations about you seeing a vampire, but she seems like a real nice girl," Papa says.

"I like her," Mama agrees. "And her job sounds really interesting."

"Yeah, she's..." I hesitate, scraping my plate with my fork. How can I explain all my feelings with something as simple as words? They don't seem sufficient. Being with Izzy has made me feel special, boosted my confidence, even taught me more about who I am.

My stomach churns a little when I think about that. The food in front of me isn't as appetizing all of a sudden. I still haven't told Mama and Papa about all my gender stuff. I know it won't be too bad—they were confused but supportive when I came out as a lesbian—but it still makes me nervous.

Not too nervous, though. After coming out to Izzy and Colin and Monty, the prospect doesn't make me feel like I swallowed a whole bunch of snakes. I'm only an acceptable amount of jittery. *I don't have to tell them now,* I think to myself. *I can take my time if I want.* But at this point, not telling them has me more antsy than just spitting it out. Hopefully, it won't be a big deal.

"Mama, Papa? Izzy's been great for me for a whole lot of reasons.

But one of 'em is, well...being with her has helped me figure out some stuff."

They turn toward me. "What do you mean?" Mama asks. Papa seems worried. Maybe he can see how jumpy I am or smell it instead.

"S'not a big deal," I say, then shake my head and take it back. "No. It is a big deal. I'm, uh..." It's a struggle to put what I want to say into words. I doubt my parents know much of the language about genders other than 'boy' and 'girl'. I have to keep it simple enough for them to understand. "I don't always feel like a girl. Inside."

Mama's eyes widen. She and Papa exchange a glance, and then Papa says, "Riley, are you trying to tell us you're transgendered?"

This is going to be harder than I thought. "No, I'm not. Not like you're thinking. First of all, I know y'all are accepting, and I don't wanna be rude by questioning my elders, but...it's transgender, not transgendered. You wouldn't call yourselves 'werewolved'. It's a noun."

They nod and keep looking at me, waiting.

"But I'm not transgender. I'm...I guess the best way to explain it is kinda with colors. You know. Pink for girl. Blue for boy. I'm purple. Some parts of me are like a girl and some parts of me are like a boy, and they're all mixed up together. Some parts of me are neither one. They're a new color all its own."

Mama leaves Papa and walks over to me, putting her hand on my shoulder. "Sweetie, just because you're a lesbian, wear more masculine clothes, and like some things that aren't traditionally feminine doesn't mean you can't be a girl."

I know she's trying to help, but I have to contain a wince. "I know, Mama. Some girls are still girls even if they have short hair and wear overalls and chase other girls in pickup trucks. It's not about what I do or who I'm attracted to. It's about how I feel inside."

Papa gives me a soft smile. "You know we love you, Riley. I'll be honest. I don't quite get what you're saying. But if Izzy has helped you figure out this thing about yourself that makes you happy, I'm happy."

My eyes start to sting. "Thanks, Papa. I guess...lemme try another way. You know how you see someone on TV or read about a character in a book? And they seem so familiar that you think, 'Wow, they're like me?' Or 'I wanna be like them.' Sometimes I look at girls and feel that way. Sometimes I look at boys and feel that way. And I met someone in Central Park who's nonbinary like me, and when I looked at them, I felt that way. They reminded me of me."

"Nonbinary?" Mama asks.

"That's what I am. Nonbinary. It's like there's a line with a point on either end. You know, man and woman. Binary, with two points. But I don't sit on the ends of the line. I'm in-between, and sometimes I go back and forth like a slider from one end to the other."

I see a bit more recognition on Mama's face. Apparently, my confusing mix of three completely different metaphors is starting to sink in. "So, what does this change about you? Being nonbinary?"

"Not that much, to be honest. Sometimes I wear binders to make my chest look smaller because I, uh, don't always want to have boobs."

Mama laughs. "I think everyone who has 'em wishes they'd go away some days. Maybe not for the same reasons as you, but they can be annoying."

I laugh too. "Yup. Ain't that the truth."

"Oh, thank goodness," Papa says, heaving a sigh of relief. "I thought I was goin' plumb crazy. Not that I spend much time staring at your chest, but I knew you had some when you left for New York and I was wondering where they went!"

We all laugh. It feels good, like a reminder that things will be okay.

"Yeah, they're still here," I tell him. "Just strapped down for now. And, uh...you don't have to start right now, because this is all new to me too, but sometimes nonbinary people like to use 'they' and 'them' instead of 'she' and 'her'."

"What, like two people?" Papa asks. "Sounds a bit odd."

"Not as odd as you think. What would you say if you were talking to someone at work, and found out you had a new coworker? And you didn't know the new person's name or gender? You'd ask, 'What's their name', right?"

"I guess," Papa says. "'What's his or her name' sounds kinda silly now that I'm thinking about it."

"Okay," Mama says. "Any more bombshells while we're talking about this?"

"Nope. That's pretty much it. Uh, how are you two doing with this?"

"Confused," Mama admits. "But I'll always support you, baby. I'll need to do some research on the internet, I guess. This stuff is on there, right?"

"Everything's on the internet," I tell her. "Including a lot of stuff that shouldn't see the light of day."

"What's this about the internet?" a voice says from the doorway.

I turn to see Dallas, as well as six other blonde heads poking into the kitchen. Apparently, my brothers have been summoned by the smell of bacon. That reminds me of my own plate. Suddenly, I'm ravenous.

"Nuffin'," I mumble as I shovel some eggs into my mouth. They've started to get cold, but they still taste delicious.

"Have you been browsing naughty websites, Riley?" Macon asks. He heads to the stove to grab himself a plate, and the others form a line behind him.

"Shuddup." I swallow my eggs and start on my bacon. If I don't hurry, I'm sure some of the boys will come sniffing around my plate once they wolf down their share.

"She hasn't been looking at internet porn," Butler says. "She was out all night with her giiirlfriiiend."

That gets a bunch of laughter, and I roll my eyes. "I'm twenty-five, dummies. Not twelve. Plenty old enough for a girlfriend."

"Don't listen to them," Jackson says, plopping down in the seat beside me with a steaming plate. "Izzy seems like a sweetheart. Where is she? Sleeping?"

I sense the opportunity for a little bragging. "You bet she is," I drawl, giving my brothers a sly look. That gets some more hoots as they come to the table to join me. Monty takes the other seat beside me, and I give him a wink. He looks confused for a moment, but when I glance at Mama and Papa, he seems to get it. He grins and nudges my shoulder in congratulations.

"I didn't wanna ask last night," Harris says, interrupting us, "but what is it like dating a vampire? You know, with the whole drinking blood thing."

I squirm in my seat. "It's actually not that big a deal." That isn't quite the truth, but it's all I'm willing to share. "It doesn't hurt. Just makes you feel all warm and tingly. And you gotta drink some juice or eat a cookie afterward. Keep those sugars up."

"An excuse to snack," Harris says. "Lucky you."

I look around the table. My older brothers are tearing into their food. Monty's eating a bit neater, but he seems more confident than yesterday after our talk. Then there are my parents, who reacted about as well as I could've hoped to my coming out, considering this is all new to them. And even though Izzy isn't here at the moment, just knowing she's down the hall makes me feel at peace. I can feel her presence still, and it makes me warm and happy.

"Yeah," I say, spearing another bit of bacon with my fork. "I sure am lucky."

Rae D. Magdon

Chapter Eight - Isabeau

I PEEK OVER THE top of my book in time to catch Riley glancing away from me. They're nervous, drumming their fingers on the armrests of the waiting room chair, scooching the soles of their shoes against the linoleum floor. Part of me feels guilty for bringing them here, to the nursing home where my mother lives, but I remind myself that I have a very good reason. If we're going to be together long term in any way, shape or form, Riley needs to understand some important things.

The ticking of the clock on the wall marks the seconds as they slip by. Riley twitches, biting their lower lip, looking here and there. Their gaze falls on an old white man with a walker before flicking over to the bored-looking receptionist at the intake desk. She's a fae, wings glittering beneath the garish fluorescent lighting, her red hair braided in a crown on top of her head.

I shoot Riley a smirk. "Enjoying the scenery?"

"What?" Riley's cheeks turn pink, and they reach behind their head to rub their neck. "Uh, nope, not at all—"

I slide my hand over to squeeze their thigh. "Relax. I was trying to lighten the mood. Besides, I wouldn't hold just looking against you."

That gets a quiet chuckle out of Riley. "Oh. Yup." They drift into silence again, obviously lost in thought.

I listen to the clock tick a few more times. "Riley, you don't have to go in with me if you don't want to."

"I want to," Riley says, much too quickly. They seem to realize it, because they clear their throat and try again. "I do, Izzy. I'm just a bit antsy, I guess."

I can relate to that. I was nervous when I first met Riley's family, although they proved to be a warm and welcoming bunch. Unfortunately, this visit won't be nearly so happy. My mother and I weren't always close, not even when I was younger and human. These days, I'm lucky if she remembers who I am.

"It'll be okay," I whisper, looking into Riley's worried blue eyes. "This will be a short visit. Then we can get some dinner in the French

Quarter. Maybe go for a carriage ride."

Riley brightens. "That'd be real nice...assuming the horses don't spook when they smell me."

"They won't. I guarantee they've carried all kinds of mythical beings before. One werewolf won't even register."

Riley sighs, relaxing into their chair. The silence loses some of its tension, at least until someone else approaches, a smiling human nurse in a pale green uniform. "Sorry about the wait," she says in a chipper voice. "You came at an awkward time. We just finished her bath, and we had to dispense her afternoon meds. Your mother's ready to see you now."

I rise from my chair, and beside me, Riley does the same. "Thanks for letting us know."

"Do the two of you need directions or the room number?"

"Thank you, but we'll be fine. I know the way."

The nurse looks surprised, probably since she hasn't seen me drop by for a visit before, but her smile doesn't fade. "Of course. Let me know if you need anything."

I nod, and Riley dips their head politely. We walk down the main hallway, past several doors with golden plastic numbers hanging on them. The rooms start at 101 and climb, odds on one side, evens on the other. At 124, I stop, and Riley comes to stand beside me.

"This one, Izzy?"

"Yeah." I sigh, patting down my hair. It's still fine under my pink and yellow headscarf, but it's a worry habit I can't help.

Riley pulls my hand away, giving it a squeeze. "Hey, sunshine. Everything's gonna be okay."

I look at Riley looking at me, and part of me can't help but believe them. Despite their own wariness, I can see sincerity in Riley's soft blue eyes. "I know."

The door is automatic, and when I touch the handle, it opens on its own. Gradually, the room comes into view: a small white square with handlebars placed at strategic points on the walls. The lone window has safety locks installed, and the only items of furniture are a dresser, a media stand with a tiny television set, and a bed. The bed is currently occupied. My mother is propped up against the pillows, blinking at me from behind the thick lenses of her glasses.

That reminds me to remove my sunglasses, so she can see my face better. *"Bonjou, Moman."*

She studies me closely, and I can tell she's trying to place me. Her brown eyes, so dark they're almost black, suck me in for a moment before a spark of recognition lights up her face. *"Mô fiy. Isabeau."*

I steal a look at Riley. They're waiting patiently by my side, although they perk up when my mother says my name.

"Mérikin ojordi?" I ask her. *English today?* My mother was fluent in four different languages while I was growing up, five including Parisian French, but I know it's harder for her to switch around these days. Some of the words get mixed up in her head.

"Sho." She nods, licking her lips in a rasping, reflexive gesture. "You been gone a few months now. Who this with you?"

It's been almost a year, actually, but I don't bring that up. I make regular phone calls, some more successful than others. Frequent visits are difficult for the both of us. *"Moman,* this is Riley."

My mother's face pinches up, and she shifts under the covers, her way of attempting to lean forward. With a shaking hand, she adjusts her glasses again. "Riley." She smiles briefly, showing that she's taken her dentures out.

I'm relieved. That's a better reaction than I was expecting.

"Hi," Riley says, returning the smile along with a small wave.

That's a mistake. My mother's eyes get big as she notices Riley's sharpened teeth, and she gasps, making a gurgling noise in her throat somewhere between fear and anger. *"Rougarou!"*

I'd warned Riley in advance that something like this might happen, but the wounded look that flashes across their face still makes me feel guilty. I step forward, positioning myself in front of them. "It's okay, *Moman.* Riley's okay."

My mother looks at me and shakes her head, choosing not to speak.

"Do you remember about me? How I became a vampire?"

From the unhappy smacking of her lips, I can tell she does. She avoids my gaze for a moment, refusing to maintain eye contact, but eventually seems to come to some kind of decision. *"Mô fiy."* She knows who I am, and she's acknowledging me as her daughter. That's about the best I can hope for when she's in a paranoid mood.

Riley shuffles closer to me, brushing my hand with theirs to let me know everything's okay. I take it and squeeze, then head over to the television stand. Beside it is a small chair, which I bring beside the bed. My mother doesn't object when I sit down. She keeps looking at me, waiting.

"I'm still in New York City." Sometimes, our visits are mostly me talking to my mother instead of with her. "I'm happy there."

My mother takes a moment to digest that. Then, she says something that impresses me. "You been working with them computers?"

"That's right, mom. I'm still working with the computers. Teaching older folks how to use them."

"The emails." From the light in her eyes, I can see she has a follow-up statement, but she loses it. Her lips move soundlessly, and her gaze dulls, drifting toward the window.

I touch her hand, coaxing her to look back at me. "Do you mean my emails that your aide reads to you?" I have an arrangement with one of her caretakers. Since phone calls are tricky, thanks to my mother's inconsistent memory and erratic moods, he prints out the emails I send and reads them to her. Sometimes, he helps her write back.

My mother makes a low moan of frustration. She reaches out with a shaking finger, pointing beyond me at Riley.

"*Moman*, are you asking if Riley is from the emails?"

She mutters something under her breath that I don't quite catch, even with my boosted hearing.

Riley gives me an awkward shrug and smile. I can tell it hasn't sunk in for them yet—that if they don't make The Choice, this will be them in a century or two, and if they do make The Choice on my account, this will be all of their family and most of their friends. Werewolves live longer than humans, but eventually, even they grow old and die.

"*Rougarou*," my mother snaps again, lisping without the help of her teeth.

"Yes, Riley is a werewolf," I say in my most patient voice. "But Riley is also really nice. They grew up on a farm, and now they work at a bank in the city."

"Where?"

"Where does Riley work, or where did they grow up?"

"Grow."

Riley clears their throat, tugging nervously at their shirt. "In Georgia, ma'am."

My mother seems to like that. Rural Georgia doesn't have the unique melting-pot culture of New Orleans, but in her eyes, it's better than New York, the fast-paced, faraway city that took her daughter away and turned her into a vampire. "Good."

"I like it fine," Riley says. "Not many places to go, but you can't beat the view of the stars."

For a moment, my mother understands. Her mistrustful body language softens, and she gives Riley a toothless smile. Then she turns away, either distracted, tired, or suspicious once again. It's impossible to say, really. It's always like this when I visit my mother—she's there one moment, gone the next.

*   *   *

After an hour, my mother reaches her limit. Her pauses become longer, and when she does vocalize, it's the same two things over and over: pointing out that Riley is a werewolf—as if anyone could miss it—and asking about my emails. Once in a while, she just stares at me and mumbles my name. That's when I decide to call it.

"We're going to leave and get some dinner, *Moman.* We'll be back tomorrow, okay?"

At first, she doesn't acknowledge me, but eventually, her drooping brown eyes meet mine. My heart clenches, because I don't recognize her in them. *How long has it been since we had a real conversation? Ten years? Fifteen? Damn it. I'm only in my fifties and I'm already losing track of time.*

"Tomorrow," I repeat as she continues to stare. "We'll be back."

She nods, and I think she gets it. I leave my chair and give her a hug, placing a kiss on her dry and wrinkled cheek. She smells different, sterile like this room instead of the perfume she wore while I was a child. "Bye," she says in English, which is something of a surprise. I could be reading into things, but I choose to take it as a small victory. Maybe she remembered me asking her to speak in English for Riley's sake.

I check on Riley as I return the chair to its proper place. Riley looks a little awkward, but they're still wearing a sweet and well-intentioned smile.

"You ready to go, baby?"

Riley shifts from foot to foot, as if trying to wake up their tingling toes. "Sure, sunshine. Bye," they say to my mother, offering another wave. My mother doesn't wave back, but she does dip her head in what seems to be a shaky nod.

Once we leave the room, we run into the same human nurse right outside the door. "Sorry, I was just coming to check up on things. It's almost mealtime again."

"It's okay." I put on a big smile. "We were just heading out."

The nurse does a double take. *Oops.* Suddenly, I'm in Riley's position. I forgot that fangs aren't a common sight in this human-majority nursing home. Fortunately, the nurse gets over it quickly and wishes us a pleasant evening before slipping past us into my mother's room.

"Seems like a pretty good place," Riley muses as the two of us leave the building, passing by the bored looking fae at the front desk. She barely spares us a glance as we sign out in the guest log. "I mean, since your mama seems like she needs a little help."

It's more than a little. *Come on, Izzy. Be positive. Look at the glass half full.* "It's lonely, living in a different city than her, but it's best for both of us. If she sees too much of me, she gets cranky." *Great.* That's *your version of positive today?* "You might not believe this, with the way she kept shouting about how you're a werewolf, but I think she likes you."

Riley blinks, and then grins. "You think?"

"Mmhmm. You should've seen her with Natasha. My mother barely had a kind word to say to her, and she definitely didn't ask questions like she tried to do with you."

"I'll take it."

I pause to touch up my sunscreen with the travel-sized bottle in my purse, and then leave the building with Riley, stepping out onto the sidewalk. It runs alongside a narrow road, one that's a little out of the way, but still close enough to some of the larger thoroughfares to have some foot traffic. I spot a harpy flapping overhead, and there's a goblin waiting at a nearby bus stop.

"Guess New Orleans ain't so different from New York," Riley says. "Not sure why your mama was so surprised to see me."

"Depends on which part of the city we're talking about. This area's mostly human, but you get a couple of non-human passers-by sometimes." I nod at the retreating harpy and take Riley's hand in mine. "How would you like to see one of the more diverse parts?"

***

"Well, sunshine, you were right about the carriage ride," Riley says as we jostle down the cobblestone street, the fringe on our cheerful red carriage swaying in the breeze. "Just didn't expect our horse to be a centaur instead."

"Dat de truth?" Our carriage driver, a palomino with a glossy golden coat and off-white mane, whickers in amusement. "Don' dey got centaurs up in de Big Apple?"

I scoot a little closer to Riley on the carriage bench. It's not cold out by most people's standards, but their temperature runs hot, and my blood flow is far from what it used to be. "Sure," I tell the driver. "Lots of them. But the carriages in Central Park generally use unicorns."

The driver snorts. "Unicorns. *Coo-yon.* Sho, dey pretty, but you try trainin' dem for to carry a werewoof like your boo dere."

"He's got a point," Riley concedes. "Never met a unicorn who didn't get flighty 'round me and mine. I heard they gotta clean the whole park of scent-marks after every full moon before they start up the carriage rides again."

"Yeah, you rite. I done tol' you awready, get you some centaurs," the driver says, clicking his tongue. He comes to a stop, pausing beside the entrance to Jackson Square. "You gettin' down here, ladies?"

Riley's nose wrinkles at the word 'ladies', so I give their hand a squeeze before rummaging in my purse for my wallet, producing a generous fold of bills and passing them to the driver. "*Merci.*"

He tips his hat in gratitude and offers a toothy smile. "Dere ya go! Y'all take care."

Riley hops out of the carriage, extending their arm back for me. I take it and step down to join them, and the driver swishes his cream-colored tail before clip-clopping off down the sidewalk.

"Do you know how perfect you are?" I tell Riley. They don't seem to have a storm cloud over their head from being misgendered, but a little reassurance can't hurt.

Riley shrugs, pulling a smile that seems genuine to me. "You've told me a time or two." They tilt up their chin, sniffing the evening air. "Smells like green."

"Probably all the trees."

Jackson Park is cradled within a circle of stately oaks. As we walk through the gates, they open to reveal a red brick pathway cutting across a short-clipped lawn.

"...And manure," Riley adds.

"Well, we can't expect regular horses to be as refined as centaurs—"

"And strawberries?"

A dreamy look crosses Riley's face. They lick their lips and, like a bloodhound on a scent, make a beeline for one of the street vendors alongside the path. I laugh and follow them, leaving a bit of my own sad shadow behind. Not that vampires have shadows, and not that I'm great with metaphors, but that's what it feels like. Something dark and dreary has been following me around all day, no matter how I try to shake it off.

By the time I catch up to Riley, they've already got a small plastic container of strawberries in one hand and their credit card in the other. I push their arm down, digging in my purse for the rest of my cash. "Don't worry about it, *mon chou*. My treat."

"You sure?" Riley asks, but I'm surprised they aren't drooling onto their shirt already. If they had their tail, it definitely would have been wagging.

"Of course." I pay the vendor, a bushy-bearded gnome perched on a three-legged stool. He has a felt strawberry sewn onto his pointy green cap, which I can't help but admire. "Nice hat," I tell him, and his thick grey eyebrows wiggle with happiness.

With our purchase made, Riley and I stroll along the sidewalk, heading toward the shadowy steeples of St. Louis Cathedral. Sunset has come at last, but there's still a sizeable crowd wandering the park, humans and non-humans alike. A brass quartet bugles some 1920s jazz from a nearby corner, and further down the street, a wizard has turned his fingers into fire-sparklers, painting pictures in the air and collecting tips.

"St'awberreh?" Riley asks, offering me the container. Both of their cheeks are stuffed full of fruit, and a thin trickle of juice runs from the corner of their mouth down their chin.

Although I can't enjoy human food the same way I used to, I pluck a strawberry from the bushel and nibble on it as we stroll past the bronze statue of Andrew Jackson on his rearing horse. My mood takes another dive, and I flick the leftover green strawberry stem at the horse's hooves. Other monuments of slaveholders hailed as heroes have finally been taken down—I made it a point to go and gloat at some empty pedestals during my last visit—but this one's still up, for now.

I don't get it. I don't think I ever will. I'll never be able to reconcile those two words, 'slaveholder' and 'hero', in my brain. Sometimes, I wonder if I would have survived as a Black vampire in that era, or any era before I was born. On good days, I tell myself I might have been resourceful enough to thrive. Maybe I would have even left my mark on history. On bad days, I doubt it. *And there's no guarantee the future will always be bright or just, either. No guarantee you won't be alone for most of it, either.*

I glance over at Riley. They've stopped stuffing their face with strawberries, and a wrinkle of concern forms in their brow when they notice me staring at them. "Hmm?"

"It's nothing." I loop my elbow through Riley's, leading them away from the statue and toward the church. "Just wondering how a wolf like you got such a sweet tooth."

"Well, excuse us werewolves for not bein' obligate carnivores like y'all." Riley peeks back over their shoulder at the statue, rolling their eyes. "I can chuck some strawberries at him, if that'd cheer you up."

I heave a sigh. "Don't waste your strawberries on that stupid statue. It's not even what's bothering me. I just..."

"Your mama?" Riley's voice softens with sympathy. "That visit must've been rough on you, with her not bein' fully aware."

"Sort of."

"Then what else?"

I chew my lip. It's difficult to figure out how much I should say. After some hesitation, I lead Riley over to one of the benches by the cathedral. Its curlicue iron armrests cut through the middle of the bench as well, to prevent anyone from lying down sideways. (Sadly, some of the touristy parts of New Orleans are hostile to homeless people as well as nonwhite and nonhuman people.)

Riley tosses the empty strawberry container in a nearby trash can, and then we both sit. Instead of leaning back, they rest their elbows on their knees. "So, what's got you down in the dumps?"

"I guess staring down eternity in my mid-fifties is getting to me. When I first looked into becoming a vampire, I felt really positive about it. I had Natasha, or at least I thought I did, so I assumed that even if my future had some speed bumps, things would never be that bad. At the very least, I wouldn't be lonely."

A worried shadow crosses Riley's face. "Izzy, if this is about that night in the truck, I shouldn't've—"

"No. At least, it's not *only* that." With the sun all but gone, I untie my headscarf so I can enjoy the night air a little more, but just end up twisting it around in my lap. "I'm not afraid of the idea of...maybe someday, if things go well, making a...well, a *very* long-term commitment to you."

Riley reaches over the armrest to still my hands. "You sure about that? 'Cuz I wouldn't blame you if you were afraid. I know you got burned bad last time."

"Fair enough. I feel like I'm staring down a sharp wooden stake." I look at Riley's fingers where they're twined with mine, resting on top of my scarf. "It's got nothing to do with who you are. You're sweet and funny and kind, and I know you aren't anything like Natasha. It's just...how do you see this ending for us? Because even if we stay together for your lifetime, that's what, maybe two hundred years tops? Then you'll be the one in assisted living, not sure who I am."

"Maybe not," Riley says.

"Or," I continue, speaking faster as anxiety bubbles up in my stomach, "you make The Choice to be with me, and realize after a decade or so that we aren't right for each other. Or maybe you realize that we *are* right for each other, but immortality isn't as great as you thought. You'll have to watch your parents die, and your brothers, and the other members of your family. The world will change around you until you barely recognize it anymore, like some of my students. And when it happens...how do I know you'll be able to look at me and see somebody you love, instead of somebody you resent for putting you through all that?"

Riley brings my hands to their lips, kissing the tops of my knuckles one at a time. It takes a few of my very slow heartbeats before their eyes meet mine, but I don't see any negative emotions only a tender expanse of blue.

"I can't promise I'll never regret it," they murmur, running their thumbs over the kiss spots, which are still tingling and warm. "But when I look inside my heart, I don't think I will. I think what I'll gain is more important than what I might lose."

I open my mouth, but no words come out. I don't know what to say.

"S'okay," Riley says, leaning over the armrest to place their forehead against mine. "I didn't ask a question, and you don't gotta answer. I just wanna let you know that I don't regret us, and I ain't expecting my feelings to change."

When I kiss them, they still taste like strawberries. Their mouth is addictively hot, and I press my tongue forward without meaning to, sweeping it over their bottom lip. Riley makes a quiet sound of pleasure, with a hint of a low whimper wrapped up inside.

Part of me is scared, but a larger part of me is hopeful, and this time, I'm not forcing it. The feeling swells up inside me, growing too big for me to overlook even if I wanted to. I don't want to.

The only reason I eventually pull back is so Riley can catch their breath. Their short, fluffy golden hair catches some of the sunset's fading light, and I run my nails through it, teasing the soft strands. I don't know what the future holds, but tonight, I feel like having an adventure. I want to do something a bit risky, maybe even stupid. And I know exactly which stupid, risky thing I'm in the mood for.

"Do you trust me, Riley?"

Riley's smile is as loving and open as their eyes. "'Course I do."

"There isn't really a delicate way to put it, but...how do you feel about public sex?"

***

It takes the two of us about an hour to pop back to our hotel room, grab what we need, and arrive at our destination—St. Louis Cemetery #1, eight blocks away from Jackson Square.

"Your idea of public sex is, uh, kinda different than I pictured, sunshine," Riley mumbles as we approach the entrance.

The maze of eighteenth and nineteenth century mausoleums isn't exactly public, not for the past four years, since the Catholic Archdiocese closed it to foot traffic, and certainly not at this time of night. The moon has had enough time to rise in the sky, a mere sliver of Cheshire-cat smile that smirks down at us as if it knows.

"Outdoor sex, then."

I take Riley's sweaty hand in mine and pull them toward the flaking iron gate. It's enclosed on either side by a thick white wall, with uneven cracks along its stuccoed surface. From the outside, the wall looks normal, but inside are the cemetery's famous wall vaults, housing hundreds of the dead stacked on top of each other. To the left is a tiny guard station. A faint light shines within the window, a head and shoulders sized square cut out from what appears to be the only door.

"I'm just sayin'..." Riley pauses, glancing nervously over their shoulder as if someone might have followed us. "A cemetery? You gotta admit, it's strange. And a little creepy."

"I promise I'll explain, but let's get inside first."

"That's what she said," Riley says, and I know for sure that, although they might be a little nervous, they aren't unhappy about this. Cautious, maybe. Curious, definitely. Their inquisitive head-tilt and bright eyes give them away.

I let go of Riley's hand, but before I leave, I reach between our bodies, palming the bulge at the front of their jeans. They're wearing the toy I gave them, the one that transmits sensation and lets them come inside me. That was part of my request. What I have in mind won't be gentle. Although I appreciate Riley's tenderness more than I can say, it's not what I need right now. It's not what I need to continue feeling alive in my undeath.

Riley stiffens as soon as I squeeze them. They choke a little, making a strangled noise of surprise, but I feel an approving throb through their pants. I'm even more convinced that they're okay with this when their embarrassed squeak becomes a growl. Riley grips my ass in both hands, kneading firmly and causing the hem of my skirt to ride up along the backs of my thighs. Suddenly, they're the needy and impatient one.

"Give me a second." I kiss Riley's chin in apology as I remove their hands from my rear. "I'll be quick—that's what she said," I add before they get the chance twice in a row.

Riley snorts and lets me go. Before they can change their mind, I walk over to the guard house and rap lightly on the window. At first nothing happens, but then the window creaks open, and the light gets brighter. I squint, wishing I'd kept on my sunglasses.

"What you want?" a rough voice asks. It's a gargoyle, his stony face set in a frown. One of his protruding fangs is chipped, and his eyes glow yellow.

"Excuse me," I say in my sweetest voice, "I'm a resident pass holder." I open my purse and pull out a laminated white ID card, which I've already removed from the back of my wallet for convenience.

The gargoyle gatekeeper doesn't take the card. "We're closed," he grunts, preparing to shut the window again.

"I understand, but I'm a vampire." The guard and I both know that all public institutions, and most privately-owned ones too, are supposed to make accommodations for nocturnal beings. I do all right in the daytime with sunglasses, consistent sunscreen application, and proper clothes coverage, but some other vampires aren't as hardy as me. It all comes down to chance, really, after making The Choice.

I wonder how Riley would react? Werewolves don't always take to vampirism well...No, a more sensible voice in my head says. *Don't think about that. This isn't a decision either of you have to make right away.*

The gargoyle grumbles, but he finally takes my ID and scans it, the light from his eyes bouncing off the card's plastic laminate. "Fine." He hands my card back and disappears inside the guard house. A moment later, the gate swings open. Although it looks old fashioned, it's also electronic.

"Thank you very much," I call out, hoping the guard can still hear me. I don't receive a response, so I return to Riley, who's snickering under their breath and staring at the top of the gate.

"Heh. Lookit." They point up at the large metal cross that looms overtop the entryway. Its spearlike tip resembles a shaft thrusting upward into the starry sky, and the curling, decorative vines that fill the space between the middle of the cross and the bottom look like two giant balls.

I can't help but chuckle as I remember my first time visiting St. Louis Cemetery #1, many years ago. Seeing the stupid design above the gate was one of the few things that had made me smile on that gloomy grey day. "Appropriate, isn't it?" I murmur as I take Riley's hand, leading them under the phallic cross and into the cemetery.

Beyond the gate, tombs line both sides of the path. They look like mismatched miniature houses, and no two are the same size, shape, or color. While Riley takes it all in, craning their head in every direction to see as much as possible, I watch their face. Their nervousness has been replaced by a look of fascination, and it's pretty adorable to witness.

"This is incredible," they whisper, grinning with excitement.

"It is. There's a reason Mark Twain called it the City of the Dead."

I squeeze Riley's hand tighter as I lead them off the path, into one of the narrow 'alleyways' that runs between the tombs. "There are some amazing people buried here. Plessy, the plaintiff in *Plessy v. Ferguson*. Dutch Morial, the first Black mayor of New Orleans. And...Queen Marie Laveau."

Riley's forehead puckers. "That name sounds familiar, but I can't place it."

"She's probably one of the most famous voodoo priestesses in American history. Some people still try to break into the cemetery and make wishes. That's why all the security. The legend says if you draw three x's on the wall of her tomb, she *might* grant your request."

"That's not where we're goin', is it? Because I can be adventurous when I wanna be but fooling around at a voodoo priestess's tomb is a line my superstitious side ain't gonna cross."

I laugh and shake my head. "No, baby. I guarantee the owner of the tomb we're visiting won't mind us stopping by." We turn another corner, and then we're there, in front of a modest two-story tomb of white marble. It's newer-looking than most of the other tombs nearby, and the embedded nameplate is recent enough to gleam. There are no dates yet, but the name reads: *Isabeau LaCour.*

"You?" Riley asks, looking at me with wide eyes.

"Me." I drop Riley's hand, resting my palm on the tomb's cool marble face as I drift back in time within my own mind. "For as long as I can remember, I've had a bit of a fascination with death. You can call it depression, I guess, for simplicity's sake, but it's more than that. I thought about death often. Feared it. Spent a lot of time wondering what comes after." I try to look at Riley, but I know I'll just see worry on their face, and I can't bear that right now.

"As I got older, I learned to take a strange sort of comfort in the fact that, no matter how bad things might get for me, there was a way out. Of course, 'escaping' might've sent me somewhere worse than here. Honestly, I don't know what I believe about the afterlife or any of that."

With a sigh, I remove my hand from the marble, allowing my shoulders to slump. "When I met Natasha and considered making The Choice, I bought a tomb here. Before, when I was mortal, if I got really depressed I could think to myself, 'Maybe a bus will hit me tomorrow. Maybe I'll get cancer or some fatal disease.' It sounds stupid, but..." My eyes start to sting, and I blink back tears. "Knowing I *might* die randomly at any time kept me from taking matters into my own hands more than once."

"Izzy..." Riley reaches out, grasping my shoulder. The warm weight of their hand is comforting, and I turn to face them at last. "It ain't stupid at all. Death is scary but living can be scary too."

"I know," I say in a shaking voice. "That's why I bought this tomb. To remind me that even though I'm essentially immortal, I don't *have* to live forever unless I've got something to live for. Undeath is difficult, Riley. These are questions you'll have to think about if you want to...before you decide to..." I exhale in frustration. "Sorry. It feels strange for me to talk about this. Natasha never wanted to."

"Well, ain't she a peach," Riley mutters.

I have to laugh at that. "Couldn't have said it better. She considered undeath a never-ending party, but for us—for people who aren't self-centered narcissists—it's harder."

Riley moves their hand on my shoulder to my face, cupping my cheek and wiping their thumb through one of my tear-tracks. "Just 'cuz something's hard don't mean it ain't worth holding onto." Their other arm wraps around my waist, and they pull me close, encouraging me to rest my head beneath their chin.

I sigh, feeling more relief than I expected. The future doesn't seem quite so scary when Riley's holding me. "You right, *mon chou*. You right."

We stay like that for a while, hugging each other and letting the nighttime darkness wrap around us like a warm, heavy blanket. Riley sways me back and forth, gently at first, then with a noticeable rocking motion. It's almost like we're slow dancing to music no one else can hear.

At last, I raise my eyes to look at Riley's face. It's pale in the moonlight, but absolutely overflowing with love. "So, uh," they stammer, with something of a silly smile, "feel free to slap me if I'm outta line, but...I know something else that's hard." They squeeze my ass and give their hips a little push, making sure I feel the shaft of their cock pressed into my lower belly.

A fresh wave of tears comes, but they're from laughter. I bury my face in Riley's shoulder and absolutely lose it, clutching their arms and giggling into the material of their shirt. "Hey now," Riley huffs, sounding a little hurt, "I was just tryin' to lighten the mood. You're the one who wanted to come here and—"

I manage to suppress my giggles into softer gasps, and I start kissing the column of Riley's throat instead. The warmth radiating from their skin increases, and I feel them tense as I nip a tender spot underneath their right ear. "Don't apologize. You're perfect. Ridiculous, but perfect." And that's the truth. Today has been messy and confusing as hell, but Riley has been my anchor through it all.

Riley claims my lips with theirs, growling possessively as they slide their tongue into my mouth. I open for them, and before I know it, my shoulders hit hard marble. Anywhere else in this cemetery, I would've felt guilty about desecrating somebody's final resting place. But I've bought this tomb, and it feels strangely right to affirm my choice to live up against the reminder that I still have the choice to die.

Living, even in undeath, is sweeter for having chosen life deliberately. Living is sweeter for having chosen Riley, too, and extra sweet for being chosen by Riley in return. Sweet like a fresh strawberry, or maybe like the pulse of Riley's blood, which I can smell and *almost* taste while I suck on their tongue.

When I bloody the kiss, Riley doesn't mind. They're used to my teeth, I guess, because they shudder as my fangs nick their bottom lip. I've been too anxious to realize how hungry I am, and once I get a taste of Riley, I have to remind myself to keep it slow. I don't want to take so much blood that they start to feel woozy.

"You're so pretty," Riley rumbles into the string of kisses, and I almost start snickering again. Their voice is low and rough and possessive, and juxtaposed with the sweetness of their words, I can't help but see humor in the contrast. I think that's why I love Riley. They make me laugh without even trying. Despite the happy face I put on for the world, I don't laugh genuinely very often...except when I'm with them.

"You're amazing," I say. Riley preens a bit under my attention as I run my hands up and down their strong arms. I lick another drop of blood away from the small puncture mark I've left in their lip, and then move my fingers lower, unfastening their fly.

Riley's cock is warm and heavy in my hand. Thanks to the enchantment, it feels incredibly lifelike as I wrap my fist around it, so much so that I can hardly tell where the toy joins their body. I start stroking, delighted by the pool of wetness welling at the tip. It's proof that Riley wants me, that I am desired. It isn't the only proof, either. Riley's eyes glow a beautiful yellow as they look down at me, and I can see their sharpened teeth lengthening further.

Desire tugs sharply within my core. There are lots of misconceptions about werewolves and their different forms, but I've seen the truth plenty of times—and I've learned to appreciate Riley's wild side, although going feral is no guarantee that they'll forego their usual gentleness. But I *want* them to forego it, because for me, tonight's about feeling. It's about filling myself up with good emotions, so I can remember why I'm still here on this earth. Why I want to stay.

I give Riley's cock another teasing stroke, and that seems to be their breaking point. With a growl, they pull my hand away and pin me more firmly to the side of the tomb. I clutch Riley to me tightly as their sharpened nails run up my legs, bunching my skirt against my belly. Their fingers graze me through my panties at first, stroking the soaked fabric, and I tremble as they pull the elastic to one side for full contact. Damn, their hands are magic. They rub my clit in swift circles that feel oh-so-good, and my eyes roll back in my head.

Soon I've got one leg wrapped around Riley's waist and my teeth set against the throbbing pulse point in their throat. "Go 'head," they growl, and I bite down, letting their rich taste wash over my tongue. At the same moment, their fingers slip inside me, first one, then two, hooking forward to hit a swollen spot against my front wall. I feel like I could come right here and now. Riley's only been inside me for a few seconds, but they're hitting all the perfect places.

Riley seems to sense that I don't want gentle this time. They take me hard and fast, muttering things in my ear. Sweet things. Things that are completely disparate from the rough plunge of their fingers and the flexing of their forearm. "Love you, Izzy. So soft and warm. So beautiful."

I *feel* beautiful as the heel of Riley's hand grinds into my clit, making my entire body quiver. Heat is rising within me, a heat my cold flesh doesn't often feel. As their fingers curl and their life stains my lips, a sense of peace washes over me. Moments like this are the reason the burden of eternal life seems worth it.

My first peak crests gently at first. The tingling sensation breaks over my body in a gentle wave, and the tight knot in my chest unravels. Instead of staring down the future, I'm living in the present, a present where Riley, the person I love, is kissing me, tasting me, taking me.

As they realize I'm coming, Riley doubles their efforts, speeding up the motion of their hand and applying more pressure. The waves grow tumultuous, crashing more violently, stripping away my fears in their undertow. I could exist for an eternity in this ocean, in this fragile time and place where everything is right.

Eventually, I relax, enjoying the aftershocks rolling through me. I release Riley's neck and gaze up into their eyes. The look on their face is pure lust, undiluted, and I realize they haven't come yet. I fondle the pointed tips of their ears, scratching their scalp beneath their shaggy blonde hair, and repeat the same words they said to me earlier. "Go ahead."

That's all the permission Riley needs. They withdraw their fingers, and my inner walls clench in protest until the head of their cock settles against my entrance. Despite how thick Riley's shaft is, they slide inside me easily. I'm dripping wet, and even though I've just come, I want the joining of our bodies so badly I think I might cry. The stretch makes me gasp, but with pleasure instead of pain. All of the hurt is *good* hurt, the cleansing kind.

"Slow down?" Riley asks, their brow knitted worriedly above the glowing lanterns of their eyes.

That's the last thing I want. I press my heel into Riley's lower back, urging them to sink forward another inch. I crave them with every fiber of my being, and I want them to know it. "Harder," I beg, clutching their shoulders to let them know I mean business.

"Anything for you, sunshine."

Riley slides both hands under my ass and lifts me off the ground, bearing my weight completely as they thrust the rest of the way inside me. The stars in the sky above us aren't half as bright as the ones that float before my eyes. For all I claim not to know what I believe about any sort of afterlife, I'm pretty sure I catch a glimpse of heaven as Riley moves within me.

So big. That's the only coherent thought in my head. Riley's girth is splitting me open just how I love it, and each movement reminds me exactly why I wanted this. I'm full at last, and there's no room for anything else in me but Riley, physically or emotionally.

Then, they start moving. Riley's rhythm carries me higher than when I'm actually flying. My heart stirs within my breast, fluttering faster than usual, almost as though I'm alive again. It jolts as Riley takes their turn at biting, sinking their teeth into my neck and growling around the mouthful of flesh they've claimed for their own. Their hips pump faster, and the length of their cock throbs within me.

Two more thoughts battle within my mind, trying to drown each other out: *too much* and *need more.* The harsh slap of Riley's pelvis against mine, the way they plunge in and out, the low grunts they make around my aching shoulder, all of it causes an explosion of sensation that I can barely contain. But it leaves me addicted, too. Each time Riley withdraws even a few inches, I'm left empty. There is a hollow pit deep within my core that wants nothing more than to hold them forever.

Forever. The taste of that word isn't so scary anymore. A dam breaks, and all my feelings flow out of me as I mumble beside Riley's ear, kissing and nipping it desperately. *"Yes.* I want you. Want you always. Please, more?"

I whimper as Riley withdraws from me, leaving me empty, but it's only so they can set me on my feet, turn me around, and press me face-forward into the front of the tomb. I barely have time to find a hand-hold along its smooth marble sides before they tear my panties down completely and slot their hips against mine, pushing eagerly back inside.

The new angle is perfect. Positioned behind me, pinning me between their arms, Riley can hit places that leave me panting and pleading for more. My breath, much faster than a vampire's should be, leaves a watery patch of condensation on the marble in front of me. I don't care. I want everything they have to give me, and I know I won't ever get enough.

"Love you," Riley snarls again, running their tongue along the side of my neck. It's raspier when they're like this, and it sends delicious tingles zipping up and down my spine. Their strength is awe-inspiring, and even though being a vampire gives me extra strength too, they've got just enough to keep me pinned and squirming.

The only thing that comes out of my mouth is a needy cry. Watery tears leak from the corners of my eyes, and I can't stop smiling. Even when I'm completely at Riley's mercy, I always feel so safe. The crack of their palm against the fullest part of my ass does nothing to lessen that feeling of security. Riley slows down their thrusts and keeps their hand cupped protectively over my rear, waiting for my reaction. Although I'm facing the other direction, I can practically see their eyes light up when I moan and arch back for more.

"You ain't gotta worry about all the heavy stuff right now," they huff beside my ear, hitting my cheek with puffs of hot breath. "Just worry about feelin' good. And makin' me feel good."

My heart swells with love. Riley understands. They *get* me. With them, I'm able to let go in a way I never could with Natasha, or anyone else. We just fit, and for the first time, I believe—really believe—that the two of us might have a chance. That we might be more than a doomed romance.

Riley pulls me back to the present with another smack to my ass. It's not a hard spanking, but it's hard enough to leave my backside warm and throbbing. I spread my thighs wider, trying to give Riley more depth, but there isn't any extra room for them anyway. Their cock bottoms out on every thrust, and I can feel the soft, trimmed thatch of their pubic hair tickle my swollen outer lips.

Instead of slapping my ass again, Riley's hand curls around my hip, delving between my legs to tease my clit. "Gonna come," they mumble, rubbing swift and strong. "Come with me?"

"Oui. Jouis en moi, mon chou. Donne-moi tout ce que t'as." Come in me. Enjoy me. Give me everything you have...and I'll give you everything I have.

Maybe it's the French, or maybe they just can't hold back any longer, but Riley digs their teeth in and pulls me down onto their shaft with the strength of desperation. Their rippling abdominal muscles clench, and their claws leave stinging pinpricks in the cheeks of my ass as they come, flooding my core with powerful pulses of warmth.

Feeling Riley come is enough to bring me with them. With each spurt of heat that spills inside me, my walls twitch greedily around Riley's length, pleading for more. I'm undoubtedly going to feel this in the morning, but right now, I don't care. I want to drain everything I can from this moment, because I can already tell its sweetness will sustain me for a very, very long time.

Riley keeps fucking me through our shared orgasm, barely even slowing down. Their animalistic side has gripped both of us, and it's a while before our bodies reach anything like satisfaction. Only when they're drenched in sweat, enough of it to make my skin sticky as well, does Riley finally release my shoulder. They groan, slumping forward to rest their forehead on the tomb.

I can relate to their exhaustion. My body feels as spread and sluggish as the Mississippi. Still, there's enough of a tingle remaining inside my belly that I suspect we'll pick things up once we get back to our hotel.

"This wasn't supposed to be so hot." Riley tries to sound sulky, but their wide grin gives them away immediately. "I was just goin' along with it for your sake."

"Riley Evans," I sigh, reaching back to caress their ears, "you're a terrible liar."

"Am not." Riley can't contain their chuckles for long. They nuzzle my neck, planting butterfly kisses around the bruise they've left. "I'm just glad you didn't wanna do it in the church. Then we definitely woulda been caught."

"Next time."

"Nuh-uh. At least here, we won't piss anyone off...except maybe that voodoo priestess."

"I have a feeling Marie Laveau doesn't care all that much."

"Hm." Riley pauses, thinking. They lean past my cheek, placing three kisses on the marble wall of the tomb next to my nameplate. "Three X's," they explain when I give them a curious look. "For a wish."

"I don't think she grants wishes on other people's tombs, *mon chou.*"

"Fine. Then I'm askin' the universe or whatever."

After a while, I can't contain my curiosity. "What did you wish for?"

Riley smiles at me. "That the two of us'll be happy together for a real long time."

A long time.

Neither of us can be sure how long that will be, but it sounds like a perfect wish to me. I offer the universe my own three kisses, turning my head sideways and craning my neck to peck Riley's cheek, chin, and lips. The last kiss deepens quickly, and I gasp as Riley adjusts our positions, causing them to stir inside me. Looks like we'll be continuing before we get back to the hotel after all. We've got all night if we want it, and as many other nights as the two of us feel like sharing.

Chapter Nine - Riley

ELYSE BANGS HER MUG of tea on the table, causing the dregs to slosh around inside. "As the host of this little gathering, I'd like to officially bring this meeting to order."

There isn't enough left in the cup to overflow, but a worried look crosses Li Min's face. "Careful. I'm the one who has to wipe these tables, y'know."

"I don't have a gavel," Elyse says, as if that explains everything.

Li Min raises an eyebrow. They shift their weight, folding their arms over their brown work smock. "Also, technically I'm the host? I'm the one who works here."

"And I'm Izzy's best friend. If our goal is to plan the perfect surprise party, I should be in charge."

I share a look with Colin, who's sitting to my right. He seems amused, judging from his grin. "When you told me we were meeting Elyse for coffee, you didn't mention the free show."

I elbow him lightly in the ribs, but it's too late. Elyse and Li Min both glare at him.

"And what's *that* supposed to mean, funny boy?" Elyse leans forward over the table, staring directly into Colin's eyes.

He puts on his most disarming smile. "You think I'm funny? Good. Because I think *you're* pretty."

Elyse's mouth falls open, and her eyes go wide behind her glasses. She seems lost for words, so I clear my throat. "Izzy. Surprise party. What's the plan?"

Elyse blinks rapidly, shifting her gaze from Colin to me. "See? Riley recognizes what a valuable resource I am. And to prove my value..." She reaches into her purse and pulls out a crisply folded piece of paper, spreading it open on the table. It's an idea web, complete with pictures printed on it. "Here are all of Izzy's favorite things."

Li Min bends over for a look. "Reese Witherspoon? I can get behind that."

Legally Blonde," Elyse says. "It's her favorite movie."

Rae D. Magdon

"Okay," I say, to forestall another argument. "You think we should watch that?"

A smirk spreads across Elyse's face. "Actually, I'm envisioning a rooftop viewing. We've got big screens and projectors at work for PowerPoint presentations."

"You think the super of your building would allow that?" Colin asks.

Elyse's smirk grows wider. "My super's an asshole, but Izzy buys her super a bottle of wine every year for his birthday. He loves her."

"Everyone loves her," I can't help adding, because it's absolutely true. Just thinking about Izzy makes my hands all tingly and sends my pulse into overdrive. We've been dating almost a year now, but she still makes my heart flip-flop like the first time I saw her on the subway.

"She's a sweetheart," Colin says.

I elbow him again. "Hey. Don't you be putting the moves on my girl."

Colin leans away, offering up his best innocent look. "I'd never steal my best friend's Georgia Peach. Besides, there are plenty of other pretty ladies in New York."

"Yeah," Li Min chuckles. "And you've slept with half of them."

Colin shrugs. "I can't help it. Selkies like getting wet."

He and Li Min high-five while Elyse rolls her eyes.

"If the children are done speaking, one of the adults in the room has more ideas. We need snacks, so I'm going to use my donut contact—"

"You have a donut contact?" Colin says. "I didn't think you could get more perfect."

Elyse scowls, but a blush creeps onto her cheeks. "The point is, we're having donuts."

"If you have this party planned already, why do you need us?" Li Min asks.

"Because A, I need your help setting up, and B, I need to make sure you know what presents to bring."

Colin sighs. "Set-up? So, you're using me for my body. I see how it is, Elyse."

"I'm inviting you because, for reasons beyond my understanding, Izzy likes you. And I'm inviting Li Min because they're my donut connection. Plus, Riley needs someone to hang out with during my time with Izzy."

That comment digs a little, but I get why Elyse is possessive. She and Izzy have been friends longer than Izzy and I have been lovers, plus

188

Izzy's ex Natasha never wanted her to have friends. Still, I have to speak my mind. "You know I respect your friendship with Izzy, but I'm her S.O. If you're gonna block out a whole schedule for this shindig, you'd better pencil me in for a generous portion of time."

Elyse waves me off. "Relax, Riley. You'll get plenty of time with her."

"Did the two of you just completely gloss over the fact that *I'm* the supposed donut connection for this party?" Li Min says. "No one told me I changed careers to back-alley snack distributor. Besides, can Izzy even eat donuts if she's a vampire?"

"She can," I say, "although I'm sure she'd like 'em blood-filled."

Li Min pulls a face. "Ew. I mean, I guess I could ask the morning baker? He owes me a favor."

"I'll pay if you ask him," Elyse says. "Now let's talk presents. Li Min, the donuts will count for you. Colin, what are you getting her?"

Colin strokes his chin in thought. "You mean besides my radiant presence? I was thinking perfume. I've got a pretty discerning nose."

Elyse nods her approval. "She'd love that. What about you, Riley?"

Internally, I panic. Elyse has voiced the same question I've been turning over in my mind for days. I get Izzy little gifts all the time, but this is her birthday. I need to go big.

"Actually, I was hopin' for some advice on that front, if you don't mind. I really wanna impress her."

"You've come to the right girl." Elyse whips out another piece of paper, sliding it across the table toward me. "Here's a list of ideas."

"You didn't think I'd be able to come up with somethin' on my own?"

"You just told me you haven't," Elyse points out. "But it's more that. I thought you'd want to do a really good job."

That flattens my fur a bit. Elyse can be bossy, but her heart's in the right place. We both love Izzy to bits, albeit in different ways. "Thanks. I'll take a look at the list later." I give it another fold to make it smaller and tuck it in my pocket. "What time's the party?"

"Eight in the evening, on the day of. None of this 'we'll celebrate on the weekend' bullshit. Show up at Izzy's place around six to help me set up the roof. I have her scheduled to get off work at seven thirty, and it takes her a while to get home."

"I'll ask for the evening off," Li Min says. "My boss is a gremlin, so he likes doing the night shift himself anyway."

Elyse shoots Li Min a disapproving look. "Gremlin?"

"I mean he's *literally* a gremlin," Li Min says. "I wasn't using it as a pejorative. He self-identifies as a gremlin."

"What about you?" Elyse asks Colin.

"I end every day at five. You can count on these..." He flexes his arms, toned but not bulky, and gives Elyse a wink, "to be at your service."

Elyse rolls her eyes, but I catch the hint of a smile on her face. "Riley? Izzy would never forgive me if you had a scheduling conflict."

I shrug. "I'll be there like shareware."

"Good wolf." She lets out a long, loud breath. "Okay, let's talk about the playlist."

***

"You don't have to do those, *mon chou.*"

I lean away from the dirty dishes in the sink, looking over my shoulder as Izzy sways into the kitchen. She's wearing her sunglasses, and her shiny pink purse is looped over one shoulder. My heart melts faster than butter in summer. My girl is absolutely adorable.

"Well hey there, sunshine. Work go okay?"

Izzy places her purse on the counter, then takes off her sunglasses, scrunching up her face and pinching her forehead. "Fine, except Mrs. Morris still doesn't understand the difference between right click and left click, and Mr. Patil almost fell for his third Nigerian scam today."

"Well, he *is* a genie. It's not surprising he wants to grant people's requests."

"You know how genie wishes work. If you wish for a room full of gold, it'll fall right on top of you and kill you before you can spend a cent."

"I got a feelin' that's how Scrooge McDuck died."

"I pity the scammer more than Mr. Patil," Izzy says. "But seriously, Riley, you don't have to do my dishes for me."

I shut off the water and set the last plate on the drying rack, wiping my hands on a nearby towel. "It don't bother me none. Besides, I'm the one who makes most of 'em. You usually drink from me or one of those blood bags of yours in the fridge."

"And you've saved me a lot on grocery bills, so it evens out." Izzy sidles up to me, and I pull her into my arms, bending down to steal a kiss. It's juicy and sweet, tasting like the remnants of her lipgloss.

"Welcome home, babygirl."

Izzy makes a growling noise, tugging my lower lip playfully between her sharpened teeth. "I kind of like having you here to wait on me. Is that wrong?"

"Not at all." My hands, as they so often do, find themselves wandering to Izzy's rear. Her breath hitches as I squeeze, and she rests her head on my shoulder. "So, have you thought about what you want for your birthday?"

"You mean besides the surprise party Elyse is planning?"

"How'd you find out about that?"

Izzy stops nuzzling my neck and looks up at me. "Sometimes I forget we've only been dating ten months. It feels like so much longer."

I have to agree. It's hard for me to remember what life was like before Izzy. Usually, I don't want to. In a short period of time, she's become a mainstay in my life. Being around her makes me feel more at home than my actual apartment does, which is probably why I spend so much time in hers.

"Elyse does this for me every year. The theme and the activities change, but..."

"I get it. She goes all out."

"And I'm grateful."

I pick up on what Izzy isn't saying. Although my girl is super friendly to every single person she meets, she doesn't have many friends to speak of. Part of that is the introverted nature she conceals as best she can, but it's also thanks to Natasha, her shitty ex-girlfriend. She poached most of Izzy's former friends during their break-up, with Elyse being the major exception.

"Will you be okay with Colin and Li Min coming this year? 'Cuz I know Elyse invited them."

"Of course. I like your friends."

"They're becoming your friends too, I hope." It's true that Colin and Li Min are more my friends than Izzy's, but over the past few months, we've had a lot of fun spending time together. It feels like the start of our own New York City multi-species pack.

"They are."

Izzy inhales deeply at the crook of my shoulder, and a shudder shoots down my spine. She isn't only thinking about Colin and Li Min and the surprise party, that's for sure. I feel the pull of her hunger crawling along my skin, and I can't really blame her. She just got home from a long day at work, and I know the 'juice' boxes she keeps in her office mini-fridge only go so far.

"You hungry, sunshine?"

"Always." Izzy runs her tongue over her teeth, fangs already extended. "Just smelling you makes me ache."

I can relate to that. Smelling her makes me ache too, although the sensation's more likely to live between my legs than in my belly. I untangle myself from her and sit down in one of the kitchen chairs, leaning back and patting my lap. "You c'n grab a bite if you want. I had a big lunch, so I can afford to share."

"If you're offering." Izzy saunters over, rolling up her skirt a bit to straddle my thighs. My hands return to her backside while she drags her tongue along my throat, searching for a good spot. Her nostrils flare when she finds my carotid, and she latches on, not biting down, but sucking the flesh hard enough to leave a hickey.

"Hey now. Colin's never gonna let me hear the end of it if you mark me up like a teenager."

"You *like* it," Izzy mumbles. She drapes both arms over my shoulders, and I groan as her fangs sink into my neck. It never hurts, although it leaves me feeling like I've been sucked into a spiraling tornado. Izzy always makes me dizzy in the most wonderful way, and I'm pretty sure it ain't just from blood loss.

Her feeding has another side effect. The blood I still have makes the decision to pool between my legs, throbbing there with its own heartbeat. I should be used to it by now, but it takes me by surprise every time, how turned on I get when Izzy drinks from me. The pressure leaves me whimpering. I buck without meaning to, squeezing the soft, full cheeks of her ass through her skirt.

Izzy gets the message. She removes one of her hands from my shoulder and slides it down my belly, flipping open the button of my fly and peeling down my zipper. Those magic fingers of hers have no trouble finding their way inside my pants. My boxers are already soaked, a discovery that makes Izzy moan around her mouthful of my neck. She draws harder, and pleasure-spots flash before my eyes.

All I can manage is a mumbled, "Please?"

Izzy swirls her fingers over my clit, causing me to twitch in time with the pulls of her mouth. The rhythm leaves me helpless. I spread my legs as best I can with her thighs resting on either side of mine, trying to give her more room to work, but she doesn't need the help. She knows exactly where and how to touch me.

I scatter kisses on the side of her face, along her rounded jawline and her cool cheek. When I reach her ear, I nip the very edge, careful not to disturb the golden hoop in her lobe. "Make me come, baby? I need it."

My begging must make Izzy happy, because she slides her middle finger inside me, curling into the spot I love most. The extra bit of pressure has me howling. I peak with heavy pulses, grinding my clit into the heel of her hand. I'm not spinning anymore, but floating, grounded only by the weight of Izzy's body on mine.

Izzy suckles my neck for a few more seconds, but let's go eventually, placing a gentle kiss over the bitemark she's left. "Thanks for dinner. I didn't drink too much, did I?"

I blink stupidly, struggling for words. It's hard to tell how much of my wooziness is from her feeding, and how much is from my orgasm. It was a quick one, but it hit me like a Mack truck. "M'fine," I mumble, which seems to put Izzy at ease. She pulls her hand out of my pants, licking a trail up her wrist, and I clench with aftershocks when I realize she's gathering up what's left of my wetness.

"Just in case, stay in that chair for a while."

Izzy lifts off my lap, heading over to the fridge with a cheerful bounce in her step, plus a matching one in the springy curls of her afro. She pulls out a jug of apple juice and pours me a cup, offering it with a kiss on top of my head. "Drink up, *mon chou*. I don't want you passing out."

I down the juice in a few gulps. The rush of sugar gives me back some energy, and soon I feel strong enough to sit upright instead of slumping like a sack of potatoes. "Izzy, what d'you want for your birthday?"

Izzy sits in the chair next to mine, reaching over to take my hand. "What brought that on?"

I shrug. "Nothin'. You just make me happy, and I wanna make you happy. So..."

"Elyse gave you a list, didn't she?"

"Yup."

"Thought so." Izzy rubs her thumb across my knuckles, a tender gesture that makes my stomach fizz and pop like a fresh root beer. "Tell you what. Just ignore the list. I'm sure I'd love any of the things Elyse suggested, but I want something from *you.*"

"Somethin' from the heart?"

"Exactly." Izzy pauses, her brow furrowing adorably. "Do you know what I really want, Riley?"

"What?"

"More of you. More of this. Every day."

My grin stretches wider than the distance between stars. "Yeah?"

Izzy gazes at me from beneath her lashes, eyes half-lidded. "Yeah. Think you can manage that?"

I stand up, pleased to see that some of my strength has returned. "Hell yeah, I can manage that." I pull Izzy up with me and draw her into a hug, swaying her back and forth. "I love you, sunshine. And on your birthday, I'll give you all the Riley Evans you can handle."

Izzy nips at my ear. "Is that a promise?"

"A double promise. You won't know what hit ya."

***

Next morning at the office, the words on my computer screen smear together before my eyes. I can't keep my mind on work. It's all *Izzy*, and I feel like a lovestruck fool. It's true that we're still new, coming up on our first anniversary, but since our trip down to Georgia and New Orleans, things have been different between us. More serious.

I give my head a good shake, trying to refocus. Sylvan Solutions is one of our biggest clients and making a mistake on an account owned by the fairy folk is *not* a mistake I'm prepared to make. They've got keen memories, and they can hold grudges for a long, long time.

What about you? Would you be willing to live that long, for Izzy's sake?

Her words from yesterday evening float back to me. *"Do you know what I really want, Riley? More of this. More of you. Every day."* Did Izzy mean every day of my lifespan, or every day for the indefinite future? And if she meant the second one, how can I tell her I want to give that to her without spooking her?

I chew my lip as I remember our talks. Izzy's cautious about the subject, but she hasn't said no either. Part of me knows she wants me. I believe that with a confidence the old Riley might not have been capable of before I met her and came out as nonbinary. Izzy's changed me for the better. If I did spend forever with her, I can only imagine we'd keep growing together.

That plants the seed of an idea in my brain-soil. I ponder for a second, then glance over my shoulder, checking to make sure Mrglsptz isn't lurking nearby before pulling out my phone. I switch to data instead of wifi and open up a browser, typing in my search term: *Vampire Immortality Counseling.*

Several options pop up, some quite close to work. I click on the first one and scroll through their website, pleased to see they've got a tab for hybrids. If I'm gonna do this, I need to find a place that's non-human inclusive.

"Evans!"

I shove my phone between my legs and swivel my chair around. Mrglsptz is standing behind me, arms folded across his chest, tapping one of his shiny shoes on the carpet.

"Yessir?"

"Did you finish making the corrections to the Sylvan Solutions account?"

I swallow the lump in my throat. "Just about done, sir."

Mrglsptz narrows his eyes at me, clearly suspicious. "Send it to me when you finish." He pauses, then lowers his arms to a slightly less threatening position. "Also, I received a message from employee resources. They've made a note in your file that you prefer gender neutral pronouns and titles. All future communications from the company should reflect the change, including your pay stubs and insurance paperwork."

My heart does a full-on backflip. "Really, sir?"

Mrglsptz smiles ever so slightly, one of the only times I've ever seen a pleased expression on his craggy face. "It's taken care of, Evans. Now, get back to work. I want that account finished before your lunch break."

He turns and walks away, his spiky tail swishing behind him. I pick up where I left off on my computer, typing with renewed enthusiasm. This may not be the job I want for all eternity, but it's nice to know I'm working in a place that respects me. Mrglsptz might be a hardass, but I have to admit, he's been supportive in his own way.

I bet the company would be supportive if I did decide to become a hybrid, too.

I lean forward in my seat, trying to focus on my work. The faster I get this done, the sooner I can take lunch and research more counseling options.

***

"Be careful with that," Elyse calls to Colin and Li Min, who are doing their best to set up the projection screen.

Colin casts a sultry look over his shoulder, batting his eyelashes.

"Aw. Don't tell me you're worried for little ol' me?"

"Don't flatter yourself," Elyse grumbles. "I'm worried for my equipment. I need it back in the classroom tomorrow."

Colin pouts, his lower lip wobbling as though he's been deeply wounded. "So, you wouldn't be the *least* bit worried if the screen fell on me?"

"Don't test that theory, seal boy," Li Min says. "If it goes down on me, I blame you."

"Heh. Goes down."

"That's what she said."

Elyse rolls her eyes and turns to me. Fortunately, I've been given the less complicated task of setting out the refreshments on the long, rectangular table Elyse somehow got ahold of before we arrived to help set up. There are two punch bowls—one with blood for Izzy, one with sangria for the rest of us—and four fresh pizzas with various fixings. At the end of the table are the donuts Li Min scored for us.

"Remember to tell Izzy that the ones with pink icing have blood filling inside," Elyse says. "The ones with white icing are blood-free."

It's the fifth time she's told me, but I let it go. I can't blame her for wanting Izzy to have the perfect party. After all, I've been stressing over getting Izzy the perfect present, although I think I made the right choice. At least, I hope I did.

Elyse clears her throat. "Riley?"

"Sorry, I'm a mite distracted."

Elyse's annoyed look softens, and a smirk curls her lips. "Oh?"

My face heats up. It's true that just thinking about Izzy is enough to distract me, and I *did* double promise my girl the best birthday sex of her life. Somehow, it feels like Elyse knows that. "It's nothin'."

"By the way, what present did you end up getting?"

"Um…"

I'm saved by a triumphant sound from Colin and Li Min. They've succeeded in setting up the tripod and projection screen, and it's only ever so slightly crooked. "How's this, Elyse?" Li Min's a bit breathless, but I can't tell whether it's from exertion, or because of Elyse's low-cut top. Considering where their eyes have landed, it could be either one.

I guess Colin isn't the only one with a bit of a crush, I think. *Let's hope they're more mature about Elyse than they are about everything else.*

"That's good," Elyse says. Li Min and Colin both smile.

I pull my phone out and check the time. "We've got ten minutes. Is the projector ready?"

Elyse nods. "It's all set up. Let me test it."

She goes over to the wheeled cart with the projector sitting on top and switches it on, making adjustments until the title screen of *Legally Blonde* is centered in the right place.

I swallow, straightening my bow tie. The folded brochure I picked up from the counseling center on the way home from work feel heavy in my pocket. I'm not sure when I'll give it to her, but hopefully the right moment will come along. Sweat sprouts along my skin, rolling down my back as the seconds tick by.

Before I know it, the door to the roof opens, and Izzy glides through like she's walking the runway. My jaw drops. Those legs are made for strutting, and she's squeezed into the tightest yellow dress I've ever seen in my life. It must be new, because I don't remember her wearing it on any of our dates. Her boobs are practically popping out, and the bottom hem rides high enough to reveal a *lot* of thigh.

"Wipe the drool off your chin," Elyse drawls beside me.

I shake my head but remain dazed as Izzy claps her hands over her mouth and makes a delighted noise. "Oh my god, you guys! This is amazing!" She bounces over to us, giving me and Elyse a front-facing double hug with one arm around each of our necks.

"Anything for you, birthday girl," I say.

Izzy plants a loud, smacking kiss on my cheek, then bonks her head gently against Elyse's. She lets us both go, but I'm still entranced by the sweet scent of her perfume mixed with her coconut sunscreen.

"I went simple this year," Elyse explains while I recover. "Pizza, donuts, and your favorite movie."

Izzy's eyes are shining. "You're the best, Elyse. You too, Riley. I'm sure you helped with this...as much as Elyse actually let you."

"We all helped," Colin says from behind us. "Li Min and I were the muscle."

Izzy side-steps me to give him a hug too. "I'm sure you were. Thanks, Colin. And Li Min, thanks for being here. It's nice to have a bigger party!"

"Five is the perfect number of guests," Li Min says. "Small enough that shit doesn't get crazy, but big enough to drink a lot of alcohol without feeling weird."

"Well-put," Izzy says, giving Li Min a hug as well. She peeks back at me, offering a sly smile. "Speaking of alcohol, who's gonna get me a drink?"

I hurry to comply. Anything for my sunshine on her birthday.

***

The evening flies by in a blur of laughter. Li Min's donuts are a huge hit, and we down a few drinks before starting the movie. We've all seen it before, so there's plenty of time for the five of us to talk. Colin's his usual charming self, and he manages to make Elyse blush and stammer more than once, a hilarious reaction considering her usual take-charge demeanor.

To my relief, Li Min doesn't mind. They actually seem to encourage Colin's flirting, but that doesn't stop them from getting in a few lines of their own. It's like a competition, but without any rivalry, since they seem to be on the same team—the Make Elyse Flustered team.

"What d'you think about those three?" I whisper to Izzy.

"I think they should go on a triple-date," Izzy whispers back.

The idea's a bit much for my old-fashioned Southern heart, but it's also kind of adorable, in its own odd way. "Really? Would Elyse say yes?"

"Maybe. She's never been the monogamous type anyway."

"Neither has Colin. What about Li Min?"

Li Min is currently leaning into Elyse's personal space, grinning widely. Elyse doesn't seem to mind.

I shrug, then stretch my arms above my head, wrapping one of them around Izzy's shoulders. She seems chilly, so I cuddle up as best I can while we're in separate chairs, offering some of my body heat. "They're all adults. Maybe somethin' good'll come of it. If not, Colin's a trans man, Li Min's nonbinary, and Elyse is bisexual. Queer folks stay friends even when romantic stuff doesn't work out...unless there's a good reason, of course."

Izzy doesn't respond right away, and I worry I might've done something wrong by bringing up Natasha, even indirectly. To my relief, Izzy leans her head on my shoulder and sighs. "I'm so lucky, Riley. You make me feel safe. Even if we split up, I know you'd always be my friend."

I kiss the top of Izzy's head. "Nope. Not a chance. Although I can't see myself fallin' out of love with you, to be honest."

We relax in silence for a while, but soon Izzy starts shifting, like she's struggling to get comfortable. When I give her a curious look, she stands up from her lawn chair and scoots over, plopping herself in my lap.

"Gross," Li Min says.

"Yeah," Colin agrees. "Gross."

"I'm *cold,*" Izzy protests. "Besides, you two are the ones making the moves on my best friend. I think *that's* gross."

Colin and Li Min look appropriately embarrassed, while Elyse cackles. "They should be so lucky. Here, Izzy, you want a blanket? I brought some up." She tosses one over, nearly beaning Colin in the face. Fortunately, Izzy catches it, draping it over both of us. I have to admit, it's nice. The two of us, all warm and cozy under a blanket.

We watch the movie for another couple of minutes, but the vibe has changed. Holding Izzy in my arms reminds me of the other birthday gift I promised besides the pamphlet. I try to be patient, but it's hard. Izzy's so soft and warm, and she smells so good.

My resolve weakens when Izzy guides my hand to her thigh. I hold still at first, afraid to move, but she encourages me to start petting. It's not quite as fun as playing with certain other parts of her body, but she does have great legs, and since she's wearing a dress, I get to enjoy feeling her bare skin. She's running a little warmer than usual, which I take as a good sign.

It's easy to sneak my hand beneath Izzy's dress under the cover of the blanket. She shifts in my lap, spreading her thighs wider. Compared to the rest of her body, there's a fire between her legs. Heat radiates outward, warming my palm through her panties. I give a gentle squeeze, and wetness seeps through the thin fabric.

Izzy bites her lip, swallowing a moan. "Riley?"

"Just watch the movie, sunshine." I massage her swollen lips through the clinging lace, keeping my motions slow and circular. I can tell from the way Izzy's stomach muscles twitch against my forearm that she wants to buck, but that would give us away. She holds still, shaking with the effort.

We stay like that a while, her trembling, me teasing. I can't help but smile into her neck. Izzy's scent is so delicious that I could just eat her up, but I settle for a kiss behind her ear. I've gotten used to the taste of sunscreen on her skin, and the smell of her shampoo is enough to stir my desire all by itself.

Another smell blends with the others, growing stronger as I spread Izzy's wetness around through her panties. It's the scent of her need, demanding and mouth-wateringly delicious. Having a werewolf's nose in a crowded place like New York is usually a pain in the ass, but moments like this almost make my keen sense of smell seem worth it.

"You're ready," I whisper.

Izzy shudders in my arms. She's more than ready, eager enough to risk arching for a better angle. I splay my other hand over her stomach to keep her still. I can't get over how soft she is, how silky and smooth her skin feels. The slippery heat between her legs is even softer, though. We both gasp as I slide my fingers beneath her panties, stroking without barriers.

"Is this my birthday present?" she asks, barely moving her lips.

I steal a glance at our friends. They're watching the movie, and if they can tell I'm feeling Izzy up under our blanket, they're polite enough not to look in our direction. I doubt they have any idea what's going on. "No, baby." I position my index and middle finger on either side of Izzy's clit, forming a 'v' over the shaft. "That comes later. I'm gonna take you to bed. Fill you up."

Izzy's breath hitches, and she curls her fingers tight around my knee. "Fill me?"

"Count on it." I stroke light and slow, enjoying the way Izzy squirms. It could get us caught, but her reactions are so beautiful. I rub a little harder, whispering in her ear: "You'd like that, huh, birthday girl? Being stretched nice and wide?"

More of Izzy's wetness spills around my fingers. Even though I'm not inside her yet, I can feel her pulsing. She wants it bad, maybe even worse than me—and that's saying something. My core is pounding, and if I was wearing my cock, it'd be pressing right into Izzy's perfect ass.

"Riley, please?" Izzy licks her lips, aiming an imploring look at me.

I check the movie. To my surprise, it's almost over. Elle Woods is driving past the White House, and when she winks at the camera, it's like Reese Witherspoon herself is telling me to go and get me some. *Besides, it's Izzy's birthday. You can't say no to your girl on her birthday.*

I pull my fingers out of Izzy's panties and slip them in my mouth while no one's looking. She tastes tangy-sweet, as always, and I forget myself for a moment as I suck them clean.

"Riley?" Izzy shifts in my lap, looking extra needy.

"Don't tell me you already forgot all the other words besides my name. I ain't even made you come yet."

"Just take me downstairs for a minute," she grumbles. "You've got me all hot and bothered, so it's your job to fix this."

"You got it." I scoop Izzy into my arms and stand up, holding her bridal style. The blanket falls, pooling around my feet. "Sorry, folks.

Bathroom break."

Colin gives a thumbs up.

Li Min smirks.

Elyse rolls her eyes. "Bathroom. *Riiight.*"

"I drank a lot of that punch," Izzy mumbles, but no one buys it.

"And yet, you're still so thirsty." Elyse dismisses us with a wave of her hand, and I carry Izzy over to the stairwell, blushing as Colin and Li Min's laughter follows us.

Izzy sighs. "I'll never live this down, will I?"

"Nothing to be done about that now. But I can fuck you so good that their ribbing'll seem worth it."

Izzy kisses me. I know it's partly imagination, but her mouth makes the lingering taste on my tongue seem stronger. Despite the distraction of her lips, and it's a mighty overwhelming distraction, I take the stairs two at a time. It's like Elyse said. We're both thirsty as hell for each other, and I won't wait a moment longer than I have to.

I just about break down the door to Izzy's apartment in my hurry to get us inside. Even though the couch is tempting, I walk us to the bedroom before Izzy finishes untucking my shirt. My hair ends up mussed, and I almost get my head stuck in my sweater vest.

"Off," Izzy says, tugging impatiently at my clothes.

I have to pause to undo my bowtie, but eventually I manage to get it off, along with my vest and shirt. After some hesitation, I decide to keep my binder on. Izzy doesn't seem to mind. She licks her lips with approval, and it seems to me that the current view is more than enough for her.

Stripping by myself is no fun, though. I wanna see the skin I could only feel before. I toss Izzy on the bed and drop to my knees, hitching up her dress and taking her panties down with me. A wave of her scent hits my nose, and it's utterly divine. I'm drawn forward like a moth to a porch light. Before I know it, my mouth is on her pussy and my hands are kneading her rear.

Damn, that ass. I've always appreciated curvy girls, but Izzy's thicker than a snicker, with hips and thighs to spare. My only regret is that while I'm eating her out with my hands on her backside, I can't touch her tits too. *Later,* I promise myself. *I'll play with them as much as I want, but only after I've made her come so hard, she really does forget everything but my name.*

Soon Izzy's yelping and pulling my hair, both heels digging into my back. The first rush of sweetness hits my tongue, dripping down my chin, but stopping is the last thing on my mind. I suck as much of her quivering flesh as I can fit in my mouth, swirling my tongue everywhere. There isn't much technique in it, but Izzy doesn't care. I must've really worked her up on the rooftop, because she comes hard, spilling everything she's got and staining my cheeks.

I keep going as long as possible. Her pulses are rhythmic and deep, so when they start to fade, I fuck her with my tongue, sliding in and out until my jaw aches. She squeals and clenches around me, but I keep groping her ass, holding her firm against my face. The extra bit of pressure makes her clit twitch, and more of her juices smear around my mouth.

Only a mumbled, "Stop," and a gentle push on top of my head convinces me to pull away. Izzy flops on the mattress, completely overstimulated. Her pupils are dilated, and if she wasn't a vampire, I know she'd be sweating up a storm. She smiles at me, fangs fully extended.

"Too much for ya?" I tease, raking my nails up her legs.

She hisses and narrows her eyes. "Get your cock."

I hop to my feet and hurry over to my bag, only a little unsteady on my legs. Devouring Izzy has left me dizzy, too. I throw aside a few pairs of boxers until I find what I'm looking for—my strap-on, sitting on top of the plastic baggie with my toiletries. I shuck my pants and underwear, losing a sock in the process. Izzy laughs while I toe out of the other, and I glare at her. "I said I'd fuck you silly, not put on a strip show for ya."

Izzy winks. "I'll have to make a more specific birthday wish next year."

"Oh, you were plenty specific."

While I position the cup-shaped end of the toy over my privates, Izzy removes her dress. I'm a little jealous I didn't get the chance to do it myself, but I forgive her when she finishes peeling it off and smirks at me, looking more wolfish than I do on the full moon. "Was I?"

"Yep. You sure were."

I grunt as the cock merges with my flesh. The enchanted shaft acts like an extension of my clit, and even though I should be used to it, I still feel a sense of wonder as I pump my hand. It's the best gift anyone's ever gotten me, and I'll take Izzy with it as many times as she wants, however she wants, as my way of saying thank you.

Izzy crooks her finger, beckoning me. "Come here."

With a growl, I leap onto the bed, straddling her stomach and pinning her wrists with my hands. Even though I've seen her deadlift a two-ton SUV, Izzy doesn't fight me. Her attempts at resistance are token at best, a slight flexing of her arms. She looks up at me, and the trusting sort of helplessness written on her face sets my heart aflutter.

"Love you," I say, bending down to kiss her nose.

She giggles. "Love you, too."

That's when I realize the tip of my cock is resting just beneath Izzy's breasts. It throbs as I straighten up to admire the visual. Izzy's tits are big and soft, with thick brown nipples and wide, dark areolas. My hands are drawn to them like magnets, and soon I'm massaging them just like I did her ass. Honestly, I don't know how I manage to keep from fondling them all the time, even while we're in public. Lucky for me, no one's here, so I can touch as much as I want.

"Riley, baby? Are you going to fuck them, or just play with them?"

Fuck them? There are plenty of things I want to do to and for Izzy's beautiful body, but for some reason, that thought hasn't crossed my mind before. Once she says it, though, the idea sets me on fire. Suddenly, I want nothing more than to watch my shaft slide between her breasts. I squeeze them together and scoot forward, nudging my cock through the channel I've created.

The visual is so stunning that I just about swallow my tongue. Izzy's tits overflow from my hands, with my length resting between them. They're warm and smooth around me, and I twitch with need. It doesn't feel as good as being inside her, because there isn't any wetness, but seeing the tip of my cock poke out from between the tops of her breasts almost makes up for that.

Izzy's staring too, and the smile on her face tells me she appreciates the view as well. "There's sunscreen on the nightstand," she says, and I gasp with delight when I realize what she's suggesting. I let go of her breasts—a monumental sacrifice—long enough to lean toward the large pump bottle sitting on the nightstand. Thank goodness my girl's a vampire, or we might not've been so prepared.

Once I've filled my hands with a generous portion of sunscreen, I go straight back to her breasts, slathering them in the lotion with special attention to her nipples. Izzy squeaks when I twist them, so I do it again and again, until she starts chewing her lip and wiggling beneath me. I've always been curious whether I could make her come just from playing with her tits. Maybe tonight's a good time to test that theory.

Izzy isn't the only one enjoying herself. Massaging her breasts has me even more hot and bothered than before. Once they're nice and slippery, I slide between them again. The difference is incredible. It's more like gliding than grinding, and the slickness makes her tits feel even softer. I squeeze them together and start thrusting, gritting my teeth against a groan.

When Izzy bends forward to flick her tongue against the tip of my cock, I almost lose it. She smirks up at me, all innocent and sweet, and if my hands weren't glued to those fantastic tits of hers, I'd grab her hair, push right past those plump, juicy lips, and ruin her makeup. But I can't bear to let her breasts go. They're so full and round and pliable, and before I know it, I'm fucking them faster.

I have to loosen my grip a little as my nails sharpen into claws, because I don't want to scratch Izzy too deep, but giving myself permission to go feral is a relief. I exhale a shaky sigh, but it becomes a grunt as Izzy catches my cockhead again and starts sucking. She pulls an unpleasant face, and I immediately stop what I'm doing until she lets my shaft fall out and laughs.

"Sunscreen," she explains, smacking her lips around her tongue. She starts up again anyway, swirling over my slit as though searching for my flavor.

I'm more than willing to let her have it. My cock leaks as I slide between her breasts, and my breathing gets heavier each time she teases the head with her little kitten licks. It's hard to choose what's better—the slippery swells of her tits pressing around my shaft, or the heat of her tongue darting against me.

As much as I'm enjoying myself, I can't last long. I try to distract myself by tweaking her nipples, savoring the needy noises she makes. I even push her breasts up and in so my cock brushes against them when I thrust through her cleavage. But her tits and mouth are too much for me, and Izzy makes it even more unfair by untangling one of her hands from the sheets, sliding it between my legs to give my balls a gentle squeeze.

I'm a goner. I come with a strangled shout, shooting everything I've got. Izzy gives the tip of my cock a few firm sucks, swallowing greedily, then lets it fall out, so I'll keep coming on her tits. Watching myself spill all over her chest drives me wild. I've got the crazy feeling she *planned* this. Somehow, she figured out that coming on her breasts would push my buttons before I had the slightest clue. Being the simple country werewolf I am, I hadn't even thought of asking permission to do something that dirty.

What did I do to deserve someone with a body straight from heaven and such a wicked mind? I empty with a few final spurts, making sure to cover the straining buds of Izzy's nipples. A few pearly droplets cling to them, and without thinking about it, I scoop one up with my thumb and slide it into her mouth. To my shock, Izzy goes rigid beneath me, arching off the mattress with a muffled moan. Her fangs pierce the tender flesh between my thumb and forefinger, and as she starts to draw, I realize she's coming. Apparently, she *can* have an orgasm if I mess with her tits for long enough.

She doesn't drink or come for long, but there's no mistaking what happened. When she unlatches from my hand and gives me a sheepish smile, I can't help puffing up with pride. "You might've enjoyed that more than I did," I say, bopping her nose with my thumb.

"Stop bragging and fuck me." She gives my balls another squeeze, and my shaft, which has finally gone soft, starts to stir again. Although my inconsistent bouts of dysphoria can be uncomfortable—to put it mildly—I have to admit, having an enchanted, not-so-permanent dick comes with some advantages. One of them is that I'm always up for round two.

I scoot down, lining my body up with Izzy's. Her breasts are absolutely beautiful, and I wanna kiss them all over—so I do for a little bit, sucking her nipples until they're even slicker and puffier than before—but it's not enough. I've been neglecting her ass, and it's just as gorgeous and deserving of attention.

"Get ready for it," I growl, taking hold of Izzy's hips and flipping her over. "I'm gonna give you the best birthday sex you've ever had."

Izzy lifts her rear and spreads her thighs, giving me an enticing target. Her pussy is dark and swollen, even wetter than before. There are strings of arousal dripping all the way down to her knees. When I position my cock against her opening, her muscles practically pull me inside. In spite of how ready she is, she's still unbelievably tight. My eyes roll back in my head, and my hips stutter as her velvet walls clamp down, pulsing hot around me.

I fuck her fast and sloppy, desperate to get deep inside. Even when my cock hits the end of her channel and my pelvis can't push any further into the perfect round cushion of her ass, I keep trying. My heart hammers in my chest, sending blood rushing through my ears. It sounds like *Izzy. Izzy. Izzy. Mine. Mine. Mine.*

"Riley, yes!" Izzy shoves her fingers between her thighs, rubbing frantically over her clit.

I seize her wrist and yank her hand away. "Nuh-uh. My job." I take over stroking her, but that means I can't hold onto her hips with both hands or give any attention to her beautiful backside. Soon I'm back to kneading Izzy's rear, and she reaches for her clit again, rushing toward orgasm way too fast. If she comes early, I know I will too.

It takes my fuzzy brain a while to figure out a solution, but when I scan the room, I catch sight of my belt. It's still threaded through my pants, which are in a crumpled heap next to the bed. Pulling out of Izzy is practically torture, but I manage to withdraw for the split second it takes to bend over and grab the belt.

Before Izzy can whine in complaint, I double the belt over and drag it straight through her pussy. She hisses at the texture of leather, and when she arches up for more, I give the back of her thigh a light tap. It's not hard enough to sting, let alone leave any sort of mark, but from the blissed-out noises Izzy makes, I could've been fucking her again.

Even though her body is signaling yes, and we've done this before, I check in just to be sure. "You ready for your birthday spanking, sunshine?"

She nods, wiggling her rear in anticipation.

"Don't touch your clit, or this goes around your arms," I warn her. "You hear me?"

"Yesss," Izzy hisses, casting a pleading look over her shoulder. Her adorable pout is too much for me to resist, so I shove back in, picking up right where I left off. I need one hand to hold the belt, which means one less hand to stroke her backside, but I do get the pleasure of watching her ass jump when I snap the belt against it. My strikes are gentle, barely blows at all. Only enough, I hope, to give her cheeks a pleasant glow.

I regret my creative choices when Izzy starts clenching. Each time I give her one of my love taps, she squeezes, milking me so hard that I can barely move. I bend over her back, leaving bite marks up and down her spine, just because I need to hold some of her sweet flesh in my mouth. She mewls while I pant for breath, struggling to fight off my peak. As much as I'm enjoying this, it's supposed to be for her.

"You like that, huh, babygirl? Getting fucked silly while I take my belt to this fine ass of yours?"

Izzy's right-hand creeps toward her clit again, a deliberate motion I'm sure. She's barely even trying to be sneaky about it. Just like I promised, I snatch her wrist and haul both her arms behind her back, winding the belt around them.

It's not a tight method of restraint. Izzy could tear through the leather like tissue paper, or even just wiggle free. But she doesn't. She falls forward without her hands to support her, releasing a muffled scream into the mattress. A spike of desire stabs through me. "Warned you not to touch, didn't I? That's my job."

"P...puh..."

I resist my instincts, which are shouting for me to thrust, and stay still. "What's that, sunshine?"

"Please!"

I could make Izzy wait for being disobedient, but I don't have the patience, and I can tell she doesn't either. With her arms bound, she's already close to coming. The promise of her warm, tight walls pulsing around me is more than enough to get my hips churning again, especially when Izzy moans, coaxing me to settle into a fast, selfish pace.

Since I don't need to hold the belt anymore, I grab her ass with both hands, massaging her cheeks. They're hot to the touch, much hotter than her cool skin usually feels. For some reason, that makes me proud. I'm tickled pink that Izzy trusts me enough to make herself vulnerable like this. Her trust has been abused in the past, so I'm honored she chose me. Honored and lucky.

"Lucky," I mumble, without really thinking about it.

Izzy makes a confused noise. "Huh?"

"Nothin'." I stop groping her rear long enough to give it a reassuring pat. I don't have the words to explain now. The pressure pounding along my length is unbearable, and Izzy's insides are already twitching with the start of an orgasm. I keep my word, rubbing three fingers directly over her clit until she tosses her head and lets out a sharp cry.

Izzy comes first, just like I planned. Her wails could rival a banshee's, and they're so loud I'm pretty sure the whole building can hear. It's embarrassing, but that thought, combined with Izzy's clenching muscles, pulls me over the edge. I can't help it. It ain't polite or proper, but I *like* the thought of other folks, even a bunch of strangers, knowing that Izzy's mine—and very well-satisfied, too. She's told me more than once that no one else makes her feel as good as I do. When she comes this hard, I gotta believe it.

It's hard to concentrate in the middle of my climax, but I do my best to commit the moment to memory. I stare at Izzy's graceful arms, straining helplessly against my belt—helpless by *choice*, which somehow makes it hotter. I stare at her ass, which flexes in my hands each time she squeezes down. I stare at her pussy lips, stretched and pouting open to hold me. With all that beauty sitting right in front of me, laid out for me to enjoy, I can't help but pump everything I have inside her.

I could do this forever. Come inside her forever. Make her come a hundred thousand times and never get bored.

That word, *forever,* is something folks use frivolously. Most of the time, they don't mean nothing by it. But I mean it. I believe in it, and not just in a sex way. I could also talk with Izzy forever. I could look into her eyes forever. I could walk in the park with her forever and watch movies with her forever. Even future movies from 2246 or some ridiculous year like that.

I could have that with her, if I wanted. We could have forever.

Exhaustion sneaks up on me, and I finish with a few shallow thrusts, relieved to see that Izzy seems ready for a break too. She twitches weakly around my shaft, but her contractions have become ripples. She sighs in satisfaction, and I know my job is done, at least for the next couple minutes. "You okay there?" I ask as I unfasten my belt. My voice comes out hoarse, and I realize my throat is sore. "Damn, was I hollering too?"

"What do you mean, 'too'?" Izzy asks, glancing back at me. "Was I that loud?"

I wink. "Like a werecougar in heat."

Izzy clears her throat, embarrassed. "I'm fine, by the way," she grumbles, wiggling her shoulders before planting herself face-first on the mattress like a plank. I settle on top of her, not bothering to pull out. I can tell she doesn't want me to, and I'm content to stay inside her.

It takes a while, but eventually, we summon enough strength to move. There are a few long kisses after I withdraw and Izzy flips over, but we're both smiling as we roll out of bed and put our clothes on.

"We have to do a walk of shame up to the roof, don't we?" Izzy says as she shimmies into a clean pair of underwear from her drawer. "It's not like I can just text them and tell them to go home without saying goodbye."

"It ain't so bad." I pause before I put my shirt back on, wrapping Izzy in a gentle hug. "I won't let 'em tease ya too much."

"My hero." Izzy nuzzles my shoulder, and suddenly I know this is the right moment. It's time to give Izzy her real present. I reach into my pocket, pulling out the brochure before I lose my courage.

A wrinkle appears on Izzy's forehead. "Riley?"

"Aw, it's nothin'," I stammer. "Just, um, your birthday present."

I offer the brochure, and Izzy takes it. Her eyes go wide as she reads, and for a second, I think I've screwed the pooch. Then she smiles, showing all her teeth, and relief melts over me faster than butter in a frying pan.

"Riley?" Izzy says again, only this time she's hopeful, not apprehensive.

"I wanna sign up for some private sessions here. Maybe go to a group meeting or two. Just, y'know, to see if it's somethin' I might be interested in down the line."

Izzy squeals and throws her arms around my neck, squeezing the air right out of me. I cough but return the hug as best I can. She's vibrating with excitement, and I know I've made the right choice. "I shouldn't be so happy about this," she mumbles into my neck, planting short, eager kisses against it. "I should tell you it's too soon."

"Not too soon. I'll take my time decidin'. But this way, you know I'm takin' it seriously. Makin' sure each step is right for both of us."

She lets me go, framing my face in her hands and drawing me down for a real kiss. It's deep, but also tender, and I can't help but moan into her mouth. When we pull apart, I notice her lipstick is smudged. I do my best to fix it with my thumb, but it's a lost cause.

"How 'bout I go up and tell the others you'll be a minute? That way I can take the brunt of the teasin' while you fix your makeup."

Izzy shakes her head. "No. I'm spending the rest of the night right by your side, Riley Evans. They can wait another five minutes."

I know it'll be more like ten, but I nod in agreement. "We were already rude party guests, slippin' out like we did. Guess it don't matter now."

"But I'm not a guest. I'm the birthday girl, so I make the rules. Now put your shirt back on. That bowtie of yours is cute."

I groan, rolling my eyes toward the ceiling. "Dammit! I coulda used the *bowtie* for your arms! Didn't have to fuss with that stupid belt."

"Next time," Izzy says.

A grin spreads across my face. There'll definitely be a next time, probably later tonight once the party's over for real, but for now I'm content. This turned out better than I could've hoped. Even though I don't have a crystal ball, some deep part of me knows that the future— our future, mine and Izzy's—is gonna turn out better than expected, too.

Chapter Ten - Isabeau

I FIDGET ON MY therapist's waiting room couch, failing to get comfortable. The cushions sag beneath me, and the back support leaves a lot to be desired. If I sit here much longer, the sofa might swallow me whole. To distract myself, I flip through some of the pictures on my phone. It's about time for a new background, but I'm not sure what to pick.

Choose one of Riley. You certainly won't mind seeing their face several times a day.

It's true. A year into our relationship, I still get butterflies whenever I see Riley's smile. But using a picture of us as a background, or even just a picture of them, feels kind of cheesy. Maybe it's because part of me always wished Natasha would have kept a picture of me on her phone...

I wrinkle my nose. I've been doing a good job not thinking about Natasha lately, but she still pops into my head from time to time, especially on therapy days. *Well, I won't let her make my mood worse today.*

I scroll through my photos until I find one of me and Riley together, sitting in a booth at Crossbones. They've got their arm around me, and their cheek is smushed on top of my head. I add the picture to my background and lockscreen. Sometimes, being happy just takes a bit of effort...or a lot of effort.

"Isabeau?"

I spot my therapist wheeling out to greet me in her chair. Janine is a mermaid, although she keeps most of her tail covered under a comfy-looking crochet blanket. Her upper half is humanoid, but glittery blue scales peek out above the collar of her blouse, and her long green hair cascades over her shoulders like strands of seaweed. She reminds me of a beautiful Disney princess, if a beautiful Disney princess looked about sixty by human standards.

"How are you doing today?"

I put my phone in my purse. "All right, thanks. What about you? Any luck reasoning with your neighbor?"

Janine chuckles. "No. She keeps asking if her kids can use the 'pool' in my backyard, no matter how many times I explain that it's a therapeutic saltwater habitat."

I roll my eyes. "Humans, right?"

"Enough about my problems. Let's get started, and you can tell me what's going on with you."

I pull myself free from the sunken divot in the couch and follow Janine to her office. It's warm and cozy, although the air is damp thanks to the humidifier pumping out steam in one corner.

"How has your week been?"

I sigh. "Work stress. Bill stress. Just stress. My landlord wants to raise my rent again."

"Again?"

"Well, I guess it's been a few years...five, or maybe seven...ten?" My forehead wrinkles as I try to remember. "Oh no. I'm becoming one of *those* vampires, aren't I? The kind who forgets what shorter lifespan schedules are like."

"It doesn't surprise me that your frame of reference for time is changing. We all deal with it as we get older, some species more than others."

"I guess."

"If your landlord does raise your rent, what will you do?"

I chew my lip. I have a few thoughts on the subject but bringing them up makes me feel oddly guilty. "It'd be really nice if Riley moved in with me, but I don't want to pressure them. And what if they think it's just because I want help with my rent?"

Janine adjusts the frames of her glasses. "Would letting Riley help be so bad? They're your partner. Helping you should make them happy."

It makes sense. Dividing our financial burdens in half and contributing to one household would make things easier for both of us. "I guess I always thought moving in with a new partner was supposed to be more romantic."

"Who says it can't be romantic, too? Stuff can be two things."

"Stuff can be two things," I repeat, snickering to myself. "Wise words."

Janine shrugs. "It might not be a quote for the ages, but it's true. Just because asking Riley to move in with you is practical doesn't mean it can't be romantic as well."

That gets the gears in my head turning. "Maybe if I frame it in a romantic way, I can get them to understand how I feel."

"Sounds like a good plan," Janine says. "Now, I have to ask, are you sure you're prepared to take this step?"

It's a good question, but I struggle to articulate an answer. My feelings are all jumbled up, and it's hard to sort through them. "I think so? Well, my heart thinks so, but my brain has a bunch of alarm bells going off."

"Because it didn't work out last time. Have you considered asking your friends what they think?"

"I'm sure Elyse will have an opinion. Plus, if I get her involved from the start, she's less likely to be jealous."

Janine's ridged brow arches above her ocean-blue eyes. "Why would Elyse be jealous of your happiness? Does she worry you'll choose Riley over her?"

"I'll choose whichever one of them doesn't ask me to choose. But right now, neither of them is asking, which means I made a good decision. And that means moving in with Riley is probably the right choice."

"It seems like you've figured it out for yourself already."

More of my tension melts away. "Guess so."

"Don't be afraid to mull this over for a while. You have time to think about it."

Deep down, part of me already knows what decision I'll make. *It's less about what I want to say, but how to say it. I want Riley to be excited about moving in with me. But how do I ask? And what if they say no?*

My face falls, and Janine notices. "Where did your brain go just now?"

I stare into my lap, twisting my hands. "What if Riley doesn't want to move in with me? I know they're serious about us, but it might be too soon." Even as I say that, my mind wanders back to the week before my birthday, when I came home and found Riley doing my dishes. They don't hesitate to make themselves at home in my apartment, and I'm always happy to see them. In fact, they're one of the only people whose presence gives me energy instead of draining it away.

"If Riley says no, I'm sure they'll have a good reason," Janine says. "You'll process that reason together and decide what to do as a couple."

I let out a long breath. Together. As a couple. Riley and I are a team. We'll make this decision as a team.

***

"Yes, absolutely!" Elyse says, in a voice that's far too loud for the Scream Bean. Both her palms are flat on the table, and she's practically vibrating with excitement. "Do it. Do it soon. Next month? I'll give you time off to help Riley pack their stuff if you want."

I laugh, leaning back in my chair. My mug of tea warms my chilly hands, and the sweet smell brings with it a sense of peace and relief. Not many people go in for a mixture of blood and cinnamon, but I like it, almost as much as I like the fact that Elyse has taken my news so well.

"I didn't expect you to be so enthusiastic."

Elyse huffs. "Can't your best friend be happy for you?"

"Of course." I stall by taking a sip of my tea, trying to figure out the best way to word my concerns. "But you didn't react this way when I moved in with Natasha."

"That's because Natasha's a stone-cold bitch," Elyse says with a roll her eyes. "Riley's a sweetheart. They're good for you."

I arch an eyebrow, setting my mug back down. "I agree, but aren't you a bit..."

"Jealous of all the time Riley gets to spend with you?" Elyse finishes for me. "Maybe once in a while. But that's the beauty of this arrangement. If you move in with them, you'll spend more time together at home. That means you'll get your Riley fix there, and you can go out with me more."

"I'm not sure that's quite how it works."

Elyse gives me a knowing smirk. "Oh no? Couples who live together go on less time-consuming dates, because they already see a lot of each other. Your home-alone time is about to merge with your Riley time, which leaves more time for me overall. Plus, Riley can cook, so you don't need to order a bunch of food whenever I come over."

"It's certainly an...interesting theory, but you'll have to ask Riley nicely if you expect them to cook for you."

"They will. I'm irresistible."

My smile fades a little. "Don't get too far ahead of yourself. I haven't asked yet. Riley could say no."

Elyse snorts. "Like Riley would ever say no to you. You've got that wolf wrapped around your little finger."

I rest my elbows on the table, looking thoughtfully at Elyse. "How should I ask them?"

"Riley's a pretty straightforward person. Just spit it out. 'Hey, we already see a lot of each other. I never get tired of being around you. Would you like to move in with me?'"

It sounds simple, but my stomach churns with uncertainty. "I feel like it should be more than that. Asking them means a lot to me. I never expected to..." My voice trails off, and I stare into my mug, avoiding Elyse's eyes. The truth is, I never thought I would move in with someone again after Natasha, at least not for a very long time.

"Where's this fear coming from, huh?" Elyse reaches out, putting her hand over mine. "You were the one who asked Riley out in the first place."

I chuckle at the memory. That particular day has imprinted itself on my heart. I'll be able to revisit it hundreds of years in the future, no matter what happens. "I couldn't help myself. They were so cute, and I could tell they were checking me out. I knew they wouldn't make the first move, so..."

"You were brave. You can do it again."

I squeeze Elyse's hand. I really hope she's right but asking Riley back to my place for one night isn't the same as asking them to move in with me. Making our relationship official, opening up about my past, meeting Riley's family and introducing them to my mother, their sessions at the immortality counseling center? All those events are stepping stones on a very specific path. The destination at the end of that path could be eternal happiness, or a whole lot of pain.

Probably both. Life is like that. Never just one or the other. My chest constricts, and I drop Elyse's hand, searching for some semblance of calm within myself. It isn't easy. My doubts and worries swell from faint whispers into a shouting storm. At first, they're all I can hear. *Riley will say no. They don't really love you. Why do you think this relationship will turn out better than your last one?*

I take a deep breath, calling up an image of Riley. I think about their light dusting of freckles. About the way their cheeks dimple. About the sound of their voice, their laugh. How fluffy their fur is when they transform, and how their gentle blue eyes look exactly the same no matter what shape they've taken. I think about how good they smell, and how warm their hugs are. I even think about how they taste—rich and delicious, but also like coming home.

Maybe it's strange, but Riley's become something like comfort food for me. I want all those things, for as long as Riley wants to give them to me. *And aren't they worth the risk?*

"Yes," I whisper. Elyse stares at me from across the table, concern written on her face. She smiles when I meet her gaze, and I smile back. "I can do it again."

***

I wrap my arms around myself, staring up at the pale grey face of the full moon. Its shape becomes fuzzy and less distinct as the first rays of sunshine break over Central Park, but it doesn't disappear from the sky. Sometimes it hangs around longer in winter, which means Riley gets a few extra minutes to run around in wolf form.

Elyse is generous about giving me time off during Riley's monthlies, but even when I have to work nights, I make an effort to meet them after their runs. I like tucking them in the morning after, bringing them breakfast in bed, bundling them up safe and warm in covers that carry their scent. They usually fall asleep in a matter of minutes.

Maybe someday soon, it'll be our bed they snuggle into after their runs. It's a nice thought, and I smile while I wait with the small crowd by the volunteer tables. Some of the people there are working, while others watch for their werewolf loved ones to come in. Several faces are familiar to me, and I exchange a few polite nods.

After a while, the moon melts into the sky, becoming indistinguishable from the hazy dawn. My grin widens when I catch sight of a fluffy golden form loping toward me. I'm always able to recognize Riley, even from a distance. As I watch, they transform, switching their gait from four legs to two. Their fur recedes, their muzzle shortens into a nose, and their wagging tail disappears. It's a surprisingly smooth shift, and they finish right before coming to a stop in front of me.

"Hey there, sunshine," Riley says, standing naked in the early dawn light. I've never known anyone with the ability to balance adorable and sexy quite like they do. Their shaggy mop of straw-colored hair is endearing, and so is the faint dusting of freckles on the bridge of their nose, but their tall, lean form is packed with a surprising amount of strength. They've got just the right mix of hard muscle and soft padding, and it's an intoxicating combination.

I hug them. "Morning, *mon chou*. How was your run?"

"Just fine." Riley kisses my temple, withdrawing from my arms. I hand them their boxers, then their binder, helping them dress quickly so they won't be cold. Their temperature runs hot—a major benefit for snuggling—but that doesn't mean they don't find the nippy winter air uncomfortable at this time of year. After pulling Riley's sweater over their head, I plant a kiss on their lips, which are pleasantly warm.

"How was work?" they ask.

I wince. "Well…"

"That bad, huh?" Riley ambles over to the sign-in sheet and scribbles their name on a clipboard. Once they set the pen down, I take their hand in mine, and we stroll out of Central Park together.

"Not bad, just embarrassing."

"More internet porn?"

"*Why* do these people think they can get away with searching for porn at the center when they know literally nothing about computers?"

"What was it this time?"

"Ugh. SeXXXy single selkies or something. I know the sealfolk have the whole mystical attraction thing going on, but seriously. Can't people wait until they're using their own computers?" It's a useless complaint. Lots of my students don't actually have their own computers, which is one reason they come to the center and use ours. Unfortunately, lack of access, combined with lack of experience, leads to lots of awkward situations.

"Could be worse," Riley says.

"I try not to think about how. At least the FBI didn't get involved this time."

Riley chuckles. "Poor Mr. Kendrick. How's he doin'?"

"Cleared. He finally managed to convince them he was only googling 'how to make a bomb' for book research. I shudder to think what else comes up in authors' Google searches."

"Doubt you'll be gettin' a signed copy of the novel, then."

We walk in silence for a while, simply enjoying each other's company. Riley's apartment isn't far, and despite early morning traffic on the sidewalks, people of all kinds hurrying to work, we get arrive at our destination quickly. "C'mon in," Riley says, even though they don't really need to. The downstairs welcome mat with the smiling bats is invitation enough.

We decide to be lazy and take the elevator. I keep hold of Riley's hand as the numbers tick upward, trapped within my own thoughts. *What if Riley actually likes living here? It's closer to the park than my place, and to their work. I could always move in with them.*

I'm not enthusiastic about the idea, but I won't rule it out, either. Riley's apartment is only a little cramped, and they've added a lot more personality to it over the past year. There are plenty of bright posters on the walls, and their beloved spider plant is decorated with Christmas lights.

"What's up, buttercup?"

I notice Riley staring at me. "Just thinking. How about I tuck you in? You can doze while I make breakfast."

"I might fall asleep."

"Then I'll feed you when you wake up."

"Thanks, sunshine."

We walk down the short hallway to Riley's room. They collapse into bed right away, and I shake my head, laughing softly. "You could've taken off your shoes and socks."

Riley turns their big, pleading blue eyes straight on me and pouts. "Help?"

I remove their tennis shoes—Riley calls them sneakers, of course, thanks to their Georgian upbringing—one at a time, setting them carefully beside the bed. Next come their socks, and they groan as I help them sit up so I can pull off their sweater and binder. They wriggle out of their sweatpants awkwardly, mostly without help, but I'm the one who tosses them in the hamper. I enjoy taking care of Riley this way, mostly because of how grateful they are.

"Thanks," Riley says, rewarding me with a sleepy smile.

I drop a kiss on top of their hair, which smells like the trees outside. "You're welcome."

I start to leave, but Riley wraps an arm around my waist, pulling me back for another kiss on the lips. It's soft, but long, and I forget my worries until they break away, nuzzling their nose against mine. "You're off today, right? Stay here?"

"I'd love to."

This time, there are no objections as I head for the kitchen. I whip up some scrambled eggs and bacon on Riley's stove, even though they'll probably be too tired to eat. By the time the eggs are done, I hear quiet snoring. Hopefully, Riley's nose will wake them up long enough for a few bites.

My hunch proves right. When I enter the bedroom, they crack their eyes open and sniff the air. "Breakfast?"

"Right here."

I slide an extra pillow under Riley's back, then set the plate in their lap. They shovel the eggs into their mouth with a blissed-out look on their face, and then start crunching on the bacon, moaning with happiness. "S'good. Fank oo."

"Á rien, mon chou."

"S'not nothin'," Riley says through a mouthful of food, only pausing to swallow. "You take good care of me. I appreciate it."

"I know." I look down and notice Riley's plate is empty except for a few crumbs. Apparently, their hunger won out over exhaustion. I take the plate away, and Riley shimmies back under the covers, sprawling out with all four limbs stretched to the edges of the mattress. If I want to nap with them later, I'll have a bit of trouble finding room to curl up. "Sleep sweet, baby. I'll be back soon."

Riley yawns, snuggling into their pillow. "Okay." I leave the bedroom, but before I slip into the hallway, their voice stops me. It's soft and sleepy, but clearly audible: "Wish you were always here."

I freeze, the plate shaking in my hands. It's a sweet sentiment, so I don't know why it's got me so nervous, but it does. The cold sensation of fear coiling in the pit of my stomach is impossible to ignore.

Once I regain the ability to move, I hurry from the room and into the kitchen. I put Riley's plate and fork in the dishwasher, then pace, staring at my feet as they carry me back and forth across the tiled floor.

What's wrong with me? Why am I panicking? I'm the one who wants to move in with them. I grab a seat at the table and close my eyes, letting my chin drop forward. My hands clench on my thighs a few times, and it takes some effort to relax them.

Only by reminding myself that Riley is fast asleep, incapable of making any decisions, do I manage to bring myself down. I pull out my phone, staring at the background picture of me and Riley. We look happy together, so happy I have to believe we'll stay that way for a long time.

Isn't that what Riley says they want? For me to always be here with them? I lower my cheek to the table, letting my hand and the phone rest limp beside my smushed face. Nothing, good or bad, is going to happen right this second. I have time.

It takes almost an hour before I gather enough courage to return to Riley's bedroom. They're just the way I left them, snoring peacefully and drooling on one of their pillows. They don't seem to notice me slipping into the bedroom, and they barely stir as I strip out of my clothes, pull back the covers, and climb into bed beside them.

Riley's bed is warm and cozy, and it smells like them. The scent puts me at ease as I squeeze into the largest open patch of bedding, wriggling underneath one of their heavy arms to make a spot for myself. They groan and hook their elbow around my waist, pulling me back against their chest.

I tense as Riley's lips graze the back of my neck, but they remain asleep. After nuzzling affectionately at the soft spot behind my ear, their hot breaths even out, and their snoring resumes. I release a long sigh. Relaxing is a process, requiring me to concentrate on each individual muscle, but Riley's presence is helpful. Being near them puts me at ease.

That's the instinct I choose to trust most of all. How Riley makes me feel. Our relationship might make my brain nervous, but Riley always makes my heart feel at home.

***

I awakened to a hot, wet mouth on my neck and soft fingertips stroking my inner thigh. My mouth twitches at the ticklish touch before falling open in a moan. Riley's body is pressed against mine from behind, wrapped around me like a warm blanket.

"Was wonderin' how long it'd take you to wake up." They tug my earlobe gently between their teeth, cupping a hand between my legs. "This okay?"

It's more than okay. Riley must have teased me while I slept, because the indirect pressure of their palm makes me realize how needy and sensitive I already am. My clit throbs against the heel of their hand, and wetness spills out of me to greet their fingers. I'm glad I took off my clothes earlier, because now there are no barriers between us.

I roll onto my back and spread my legs, welcoming Riley on top of me. Their weight keeps me in a sleepy, relaxed state even while the slow-burning fire inside me swells into a hungry blaze. I coil my limbs around them, and they hitch my knees up to their waist, rocking forward to apply pressure between us.

Riley's stomach offers me a firm surface to grind against. My first stroke paints a trail of wetness along their abdominal muscles, which makes the next thrust smooth and slippery. Riley cups my rear, urging me to rock faster. Their lips catch mine, and we kiss until they're breathless and my heart is beating much faster than usual.

"What d'you want?" Riley asks, gazing down into my eyes.

"Anything," I answer honestly. I'll take anything Riley is willing to give. Fast or slow, rough or gentle. As long as it's them.

Riley nibbles my neck, finding a place to suck above my collarbone. They grasp my hips in urgent hands, guiding me, helping me to grind. I want to look at their face, but the feelings are too intense. I close my eyes, chewing my lower lip. Something in me needs this to last. If I watch Riley watching me, I won't be able to hold out.

"Izzy…" Riley's thumb swipes along my lip. I force my eyes open. "What is it, babygirl?"

I thread my fingers through Riley's hair and quiet them with a kiss. Their concern is sweet, but I don't want to talk. I want this, just this, more than anything. Riley seems to get the message. They kiss their way down my body, taking their time, lingering in all the places they know I love and lavishing them with attention. They place feather-light kisses along my jawline, drag their tongue along my shoulder, even suck a spot on the underside of my right breast long enough to leave a bruise.

Only after I've squirmed for several minutes does Riley roll their tongue over one of my nipples. Forcing me to wait has left me so sensitive, I almost can't handle it. They stay at my breasts for a long time, sucking the peaks to stiff, straining points. Even the soft whisper of their breath is enough to make the wet buds throb. My hips jerk in answer, and I drag my clit against Riley's stomach, smearing more wetness on their skin.

"Easy," Riley mutters against my sternum. "I got you."

I got you. I don't know how Riley knew I needed this, but they did, just like always. It's an emotional release as well as a physical one, and I relax as they kiss down my belly, still murmuring endearments. "So beautiful. Perfect. Can't get enough of you."

It's almost embarrassing how much I crave Riley's praise and approval. By the time they reach the join of my legs, I'm begging, sobbing with need. "Riley. Riley, baby, please…" That's all I can say, *Riley* and *please,* until their mouth closes over me, and I forget how to speak.

The fire of their tongue is gentle, but persistent. It has me clutching their hair and arching off the mattress in an instant. My very foundation quakes, and I'm afraid I'll come before I get to fully enjoy their talents. Luckily, Riley knows me. They back off, nuzzling my inner thigh until I calm down enough for them to resume.

"That's it, sunshine," they mumble between open-mouthed kisses. "Relax for me." They work their way around my clit, teasing the root, until I'm so swollen the air itself hurts. My whole body is one quivering heartbeat, hammering harder each time Riley takes me in their mouth.

They start with my tip, sucking lightly. Before it becomes too much, they widen their area of attention, fluttering the flat of their tongue between my lips and lavishing attention on each one. When my hips buck too hard, they pause, biting down on the softest part of my leg until I fall still.

Riley's gentle demands are unlike anything other partners have given me. They can command me and my body without being harsh, and every touch, no matter how firm, is full of so much love and tenderness that my heart overflows. I feel it in the way they cradle my hips and the steady strokes of their tongue.

Eventually, Riley finds my entrance. It's enough to make me whine and grip their hair, but when I do, they draw back. They don't have to tell me that I'm on their time. If I want my turn, I'll have to wait. Only after I melt back into the mattress do they slide inside me. Hot, silky pressure spreads me open, and spots flash in front of my eyes.

I'm hungry, so hungry, and soon the burning pit in my belly is all I can think about. I toss my head from side to side, but Riley's scent has drifted up into my nose. They've got my heart pounding twice as fast as usual, and my body needs blood almost as badly as it needs release. I need both. I need Riley.

"Please," I rasp, the only word I can manage.

Luckily, Riley knows what I need. They realize that I can't bear to lose their mouth, but they also know if I can't taste them soon, I might very well pass out. Before my brain can come up with a solution, Riley turns around on top of me. I sigh with relief as they swing their leg over my face, positioning their knees above my shoulders.

They don't need to ask. As soon as Riley lowers themself over me, I'm off, licking and sucking every bit of slick, sweet pink flesh I can reach. They're wet, salty, and the smell of their need fills my lungs. I could breathe them in forever, and I want to drink everything they have to offer.

I spend a blissfully long time between Riley's legs. Sometimes I graze my fangs over their flesh, which they seem to enjoy, judging by their moans. Their right thigh tenses as I nose their femoral artery, and they suck my clit harder, causing my hips jerk. That's about the clearest 'yes' I can expect while both our mouths are busy.

There's no resistance as I sink my fangs into Riley's flesh. They exhale deeply against me, and their body relaxes on top of mine. All the tension seeps out of their legs, and a flood of sweetness fills my mouth. Their blood gives me a high I've never felt drinking from anyone else, and I'll never tire of its taste.

Riley's hips start rocking, seeking attention, so I press my fingers between their legs. I toy with their clit first, rubbing through the hood, but they shift slightly until I'm lined up with their entrance. Riley isn't always up for penetration, but it seems like they're in the mood today. I slip inside with two fingers, savoring the way their warm muscles clench around me.

It doesn't take much searching to find Riley's sensitive spots. I have all of them memorized. Soon they're whining between my legs, tickling me with needy vibrations. Their licking has become less intense, more sporadic, but I don't mind. I'm focused on making them come and keeping my hunger in check. This lovemaking session might have started sweet and lazy, but I'm waking up thanks to the free meal.

"Izzy," Riley mutters against my thigh. "Fuck, Izzy, make me come."

I can't help but give Riley what they want. They've been so good to me already and making them happy is my favorite thing to do. I detach from their leg, licking gently to make sure my fangs' puncture-marks are sealed up, and fasten my lips around their clit, rolling my tongue over its tip.

Riley comes right away. They stiffen, then sigh, quivering with a surprising amount of force. Their soft blonde curls tickle my nose, but I resist the temptation to laugh, holding on as long as I can. I can bear a little discomfort if it means sustaining their moment.

As their contractions speed up around my fingers, Riley pushes inside of me as well, seemingly determined to return the favor. The sudden stretch sets me trembling too, and before I know it, I'm coming right along with them, letting the waves carry me. The climaxes Riley provides always make me feel like I'm at the mercy of something incredibly big and powerful, like a storm or an ocean. I'm hopelessly addicted to the vulnerability as well as the physical sensations.

We find a rhythm together, riding the waves until Riley's sweaty form collapses on top of mine, squishing me against the mattress. I let go of their clit and withdraw my fingers, placing a tender kiss on the thigh I didn't bite. "You all right, baby?"

Riley laughs breathlessly. "M'good. So good." They rake their blunt claws down my legs, and I squirm, shaking with giggles.

"Stop. Tickles."

"Mm."

Riley rolls off me with an adorable huff, flips over, and scoots up to join me at the head of the bed. They snuggle against my side, draping an arm over my waist. "Love you, sunshine."

As I gaze into their shining blue eyes, something inside me knows this is the right moment. "Move in with me? I've been thinking about it, and...just, move in with me."

Riley's bold blonde brows lift in surprise. Their lips twitch, as though they're about to smile, but then their forehead furrows. "What?"

"Move in with me," I repeat, before I lose my nerve. "Or I'll move in with you. I don't care which."

Riley gapes like a goldfish, looking adorably confused or, at least, it's adorable at first. It becomes much less cute and much more frightening when they remain silent, as if they don't know how to answer. *How can they not know the right answer? No...oh no. They don't want to move in with me. This was a mistake. A huge mistake—*

"C'n I think about it?"

It's my turn to say, "What?" and stare stupidly at Riley's face, like I'm not really seeing it at all.

"I, uh...I asked if I could think about it. It sounds nice..."

Riley doesn't have the heart to add a 'but' to the end of the sentence, but I can hear it in the silence.

A hard lump forms in my throat. "Oh. Of course."

"Izzy..."

Riley leans closer, cupping my cheek in their hand. "I love you. No, listen. I *love* you."

It still feels like my heart has a hole in it, but those words are my lifeline. As disappointed and embarrassed as I am by Riley's non-answer, I can't help but cling to them. "I love you, too."

"I'll think about it," Riley says, in a tone that promises the truth.

"Okay."

***

"What do you mean, they said *no?*"

Elyse's indignance should make me feel better, but it's still hard to meet her eyes. We're sitting in her office, grabbing lunch between classes, with her sitting on the desk and me in her usual chair. She offered it to me. Elyse is always good at reading my moods, and she knew I was upset the minute I walked into work today.

"They didn't say no," I mumble, letting the straw of my juice box slide from my lips. The end is all chewed up, visible proof of my anxiety. "Riley said they'd think about it."

Elyse isn't the least bit mollified. "What is there to think about?" She gestures with her sandwich, which she's only taken two bites from, because her mouth has barely stopped moving except when I'm talking. "Riley loves you. You love them. You should live together."

"Not everyone likes living with people," I say, even though it pains me. "Riley grew up with seven siblings. Maybe they just want a little more time alone before they commit to sharing a space with someone else again...possibly forever."

Elyse glares. "Stop being so reasonable. You should be pissed."

I want to be, but Riley has been so sweet and reasonable about the whole thing. They've been extra attentive, bringing me flowers, making sure to get my favorite blood at the store, texting throughout the evening on the days when I'm busy. On the other hand, they haven't offered a concrete explanation, and I've been too chickenshit to ask.

"I think you're pissed enough for both of us," I say to Elyse.

"How could they say no to you? Don't they know how much courage it took for you to ask?"

My mind takes that statement and runs in the obvious direction: *Since last time ended so badly.* It had ended badly. Not with physical violence—Natasha was never that kind of abusive—but with crying fits, guilt trips, and gaslighting. That's the tricky thing about emotional abuse. I can always say to myself, *It's not so bad. At least she doesn't hit me. Maybe I'm overreacting.*

That's when the lightbulb goes off. This situation with Riley is nothing like my old issues with Natasha, but my reaction is exactly the same. I'm doing what I used to do then. Minimizing my feelings, making excuses for something my partner's done to upset me. I grind my teeth behind my lips. *Damn it, Izzy. You should know better.*

I look Elyse in the eye. "I need to ask them why. I just...don't know if I'm brave enough."

Elyse slides off her desk and stands in front of me, bending down to place her hands on my shoulders. "You *are* brave enough. You asked Riley out in the first place. You've been working so hard to have a different kind of relationship with them than you had with...her."

I crack a smile. For some reason, Elyse's reluctance to even say Natasha's name cheers me up, like she's not even worth mentioning.

"Seriously. You *are* brave enough."

"Fine. I'm brave enough."

She squeezes my shoulders, then let's go. "That's my girl. Want to practice what you're going to say? Might make it easier."

The knot in my chest loosens a little. "Sounds good."

***

I drum my fingers on the couch armrest, waiting for Riley to arrive. The temptation to check my phone is strong, but I'm too embarrassed. I've looked several times in the last half-hour, and I don't want to seem desperate, even to myself.

Eventually, impatience gets the best of me. I pull my phone out of my skirt pocket—more skirts should have pockets—and check my texts. The last one from Riley is thirty minutes old, saying they've left work and caught the subway. They should be arriving any second.

A buzz from my phone makes my heart leap and my stomach sink. No, not Riley. The text is from Elyse, asking: *'Did you two talk yet?'* I don't respond. I need to save the ebbing courage I have for my conversation with Riley.

What feels like years later, there's a knock on the door. I flinch but restrain myself before leaping to my feet. Instead, I take a deep breath, stand up, and smooth the front of my skirt. *This is Riley. You know them. They would never do anything to hurt you.*

I repeat that mantra until I reach the door. Riley stands awkwardly on the other side, short blonde hair disheveled by the wind. They're holding a bouquet of flowers, which they thrust forward at me a little too vigorously. "Sorry for takin' so long. I went and picked these up."

A lump forms in my throat. I cradle the bouquet in my arms, thin tissue paper crinkling, and lift it to my nose. They're sunflowers. Big, bold sunflowers whose brightness reaches right inside me. "Don't apologize. They're perfect."

Riley's grin hangs wide like the moon. "Almost." They finesse a single sunflower stem apart from its fellows and snap the blossom off, tucking it behind my ear. "Now you're perfect."

I sniff, wiping my mascara before it can run too far. "This is stupid. I love you. Why won't you move in with me."

Concerned wrinkles form in Riley's brow. "Is that what you've been in a tizzy over?"

"Was I that bad?"

"You want my honest answer?"

I nod.

"You were actin' 'bout as lonely as a pine tree in a parking lot."

I can't help but chuckle. Riley's Southernisms always have that effect on me. "I should have said something sooner. Can we talk about it? I don't want to pressure you—"

Riley's blue eyes open wide. "Pressure me? Darlin', I've been worryin' all this time about pressurin' *you.*"

Well. That certainly isn't the answer I'm expecting. I suppose I'd braced myself for something harsh: like that I'm 'too much' to live with. Too loud, too needy, too demanding. Thinking of it like that makes it seem silly. Riley never sees me that way.

"Why did you think you were pressuring me? I was the one who brought up moving in together."

Riley rubs the back of their neck. "I've just been takin' a lot of steps forward lately. Goin' to immortality counseling. Tellin' you how I feel all the time. I didn't want it to be too much, 'cuz I couldn't bear it if I scared you off."

I clasp a hand over my mouth, stifling a quiet sob. All this time, Riley's been thinking about me. My feelings, my reactions. It's a world of difference from the relationships I'm used to, and it's thrown me for a loop.

"So, you were hedging to give me space to back out."

"And you were sulkin' 'cause you thought I didn't wanna live with you."

We stare at each other, sighing through sad smiles. "Making this work might be hard if this is how we keep doing things."

Riley cups my cheek. "Then let's do things different. Stop makin' assumptions for each other. 'Cuz you know what they say about those."

"Yes, I know."

I let my head fall forward onto Riley's chest. The smell of their cologne puts me at ease, and my eyes drift shut. "Should we move into your apartment, or mine?"

Riley scoffs. "Yours. Mine's, uh, cramped."

I take the opportunity to wind my arms around their waist. "But I *like* being close to you."

"How close?"

That's an invitation if I ever heard one. "Well, we aren't technically moving into a new place." I give Riley's backside a firm squeeze. "But it couldn't hurt to make sure you're *really* comfortable in *every* room of the apartment. If you think you're up for it."

"If I think I'm up for it, huh?" Riley stands tall, as if their pride has been questioned. "That some kind of challenge, sunshine?"

I lick my lips. "Maybe."

Riley pounces, every bit the wolf as they pin me against the kitchen counter. The bouquet of sunflowers goes sliding across the granite, and the one behind my ear flutters, knocked loose by Riley's enthusiastic kissing of my neck. I don't bother reaching for it. Riley and I have made love on my countertop before, but now we're about to make love on *our* countertop. The distinction feels important.

Riley's already got one hand half-way up my blouse when I feel a buzz in my pocket. They perk up, giving me a curious look. "Your phone?"

"Elyse. She's probably wondering if I had the guts to talk to you."

"She c'n wait." Riley takes the phone out and switches it to silent, setting it aside. "Right now, Isabeau LaCour, you're all mine."

I've got no problem with that. Elyse and my therapist will be thrilled, but they'll hear the news in good time. Right now, Riley has my full attention, and that's exactly how it should be. This is exactly how a *relationship* should be. It's healthy, and whole, and I want to watch it grow for centuries

About Rae D. Magdon

Rae D. Magdon is a writer and author specializing in sapphic romance and speculative fiction. When she felt the current selection of stories about queer women were too white, too strictly gendered, and far too few in number, she decided to start writing her own. From 2012 to 2016, she has written and published ten novels with Desert Palm Press, won a Rainbow Award in the 2016 Science Fiction category, and was runner up in 2015 for the Golden Crown Literary Award in the Fantasy category. She wholeheartedly believes that all queer women deserve their own adventures, and especially their own happy endings.

Connect with Rae online

Website raedmagdon.com
Facebook raedmagdon
Tumblr raedmagdontumblr.com
Email raedmagdon@gmail.com

Note to Readers:

Thank you for reading a book from Desert Palm Press. We have made every effort to edit this book. However, typos do slip in. If you find an error in the text, please email lee@desertpalmpress.com so the issue can be corrected.

We appreciate you as a reader and want to ensure you enjoy the reading process. We would like you to consider posting a review on your preferred media sites and/or your blog or website.

For more information on upcoming releases, author interviews, contest, giveaways and more, please sign up for our newsletter and visit us as at Desert Palm Press: www.desertpalmpress.com and "Like" us on Facebook: Desert Palm Press.

Bright Blessings

54077013R00134

Made in the USA
Columbia, SC
25 March 2019